Praise for Warren C. Easley

MOVING TARGETS
The Sixth Cal Claxton Oregon Mystery

"With *Moving Targets*, Warren Easley delivers another humdinger of a tale featuring the City of Roses. But there's so much more to like about this story than just its evocative Portland setting. Cal Claxton is a guy worth rooting for, and the gang who aid him in solving the complex and dangerous mystery involved are a fun bunch to follow. If you're not familiar with these gems out of Oregon, now's the perfect time to give Warren Easley and Cal Claxton a try. You won't be disappointed."

—William Kent Krueger, award-winning, bestselling author of *Ordinary Grace* and the Cork O'Connor series

"Intelligent dialogue, evocative descriptions of the Oregon landscape, and sly pokes at the current cultural climate make this a winner."

—*Publishers Weekly*

"Easley continues in every installment of this series to get a better handle on his characters and the vital balance between principal and supporting plots."

—*Kirkus Reviews*

"It's a familiar trail of crime syndicates, money laundering, and contract killers, but what's most interesting is Claxton himself—good-natured, superficially dull as dishwater, not at all deft with the ladies. He's generally slow to anger, too, but when the greedheads, on top of their internatio[...] quarry outside Claxton's home, [...] known better."

BLOOD FOR WINE
The Fifth Cal Claxton Oregon Mystery

A Nero Wolfe Award Finalist for 2018

"I've been a fan of Warren Easley's Cal Claxton series since I read his first book, and they've gotten better with age, like the fine wine at the center of this complex novel of suspense. If you enjoy wine and a really good mystery, *Blood for Wine* is a must read."

—Phillip Margolin, *New York Times* bestselling author

"Warren C. Easley blends my favorite subjects—wine, food, a really cool dog and, of course, murder—into a tasty thriller set in Oregon wine country. With more twists and turns than a rain-swept coastal road, *Blood for Wine* is the fifth in this series with a tantalizing backlist just waiting for me to get my hands on. It promises to be a mystery maven's haven."

—*Bookreporter.com*

"Oenophiles and aspiring vintners will enjoy the wine lore in this well-wrought tale of love and betrayal."

—*Publishers Weekly*

NOT DEAD ENOUGH
The Fourth Cal Claxton Oregon Mystery

"Masterfully crafted, this tale of greed, deception, and revenge has an added benefit—the stunningly beautiful descriptions of the lush landscapes of Oregon's Columbia River country. Easley's characters bring enough complex complications to keep you reading long after regular bedtime."

—Anne Hillerman, *New York Times* bestselling author

"The narrative spends much time absorbing sights and smells of the glorious outdoors and detailing the political fights they engender....fans of Tony Hillerman and C. J. Box won't mind... Advise readers not to jump to that last page. Easley deserves his surprises."

—*Booklist*

"With a very likable sleuth, *Not Dead Enough* is sure to appeal not only to mystery lovers, but also to those interested in Native American history, Oregonian culture, and environmental issues like salmon migration. Although *Not Dead Enough* is the fourth in the series, it can easily read as a standalone, allowing fans of Tony Hillerman or Dana Stabenow to dive right into Cal Claxton's life."

—*Shelf Awareness*

NEVER LOOK DOWN
The Third Cal Claxton Oregon Mystery

"*Never Look Down* is an impeccably crafted novel that hits every note. Memorable characters, a unique plot, and a wonderful sense of place. By all means, get this book and settle in for a great read."

—Philip Donlay, bestselling author of
the Donovan Nash thrillers

"Easley exquisitely captures Portland's flavor, and his portrayal of street life is spot-on. Readers of John Hart and Kate Wilhelm will delight in trying a new author."

—*Library Journal*

"From four stories up the side of a building, a young graffiti artist, 'a runaway teenager,' witnesses a murder, and then finds herself in the killer's sights. Oregon attorney Cal Claxton teams up with the young artist to identify the killer and uncover a smuggling racket, along the way working with Portland's homeless and helping members of the Cuban-American community whose lives were affected by the murder. The Portland cityscape is as much a character as are the colorful graffiti artist and the lawyer who walks Portland's streets with his dog, Archie."

—*Ellery Queen Mystery Magazine*

"The killer, who leaves a bloody trail in his wake, and Cal race to find her, but Kelly avoids them both, not knowing whom she can trust. When Cal and Kelly do connect, they make a formidable and unlikely team as they try to find justice for the killer's victims. Cal's name is on the title page, but plucky and resourceful Kelly steals this tense adventure."

—*Publishers Weekly*

DEAD FLOAT
The Second Cal Claxton Oregon Mystery

"A fast-paced, tightly woven who-dunnit that kept me guessing to the end. Easley's vivid landscapes and well-drawn characters evoke comparisons to James Lee Burke, and Cal Claxton is as determined and resourceful as Burke's Dave Robicheaux."

—Robert Dugoni, *New York Times* bestselling author

"*Dead Float* starts with a man's throat cut ear to ear and Claxton's fishing knife found nearby, and gathers momentum like the midnight freight trains nearby. As a Deschutes [River] aficionado myself, I'll never listen to those lonesome whistles again without thinking of this story, and thanking the stars it was only fiction."

—Keith McCafferty, bestselling author
of the Sean Stranahan thrillers

"When someone tries to drown Cal, he uses his fishing skills to good advantage. What a showdown finish! Easley's folksy style belies an intense drama revolving around corporate greed and espionage. The second outing for this action-packed Oregon-based series succeeds in quickly bringing readers up to speed. Pairs nicely with other boomer thrillers such as those by H. Terrell Griffin and also with fly-fishing mysteries by Keith McCafferty and Victoria Houston."

—*Library Journal*

MATTERS OF DOUBT
The First Cal Claxton Oregon Mystery

"Warren Easley has created a character you can root for—a man who has experienced loss but still believes in a better future, a lawyer who vigorously pursues justice for the most vulnerable clients. *Matters of Doubt* proves that legal thrillers can indeed be thrilling."

—Alafair Burke, *New York Times* bestselling author

"A fast, fun read with a fascinating defendant and our hero, Cal Claxton, a small-town lawyer who risks his life to solve a big-time cold case."

—Philip Margolin, *New York Times* bestselling author

"Easley brings alive the world of street kids and the alternative social groups they form…"

—*Publishers Weekly*

Also by Warren C. Easley

The Cal Claxton Oregon Mysteries
Matters of Doubt
Dead Float
Never Look Down
Not Dead Enough
Blood for Wine
Moving Targets

NO
WAY
TO DIE

NO WAY TO DIE

A CAL CLAXTON OREGON MYSTERY

WARREN C. EASLEY

Poisoned Pen
PRESS

Published by Poisoned Pen Press, an imprint of Sourcebooks
P.O. Box 4410, Naperville, Illinois 60567-4410
(630) 961-3900
sourcebooks.com

Library of Congress Cataloging-in-Publication Data

Names: Easley, Warren C., author.
Title: No way to die / Warren Easley.
Description: Naperville, IL : Poisoned Pen Press, [2019]
Identifiers: LCCN 2019021353 | ISBN 9781492699231 (hardcover: acid-free
 paper)
Subjects: | GSAFD: Mystery fiction.
Classification: LCC PS3605.A777 N6 2019 | DDC 813/.6--dc23 LC record available
at https://lccn.loc.gov/2019021353

Printed and bound in the United States of America.

SB 10 9 8 7 6 5 4 3 2 1

For Marge, who makes it all happen

"There are no coincidences in the universe, only convergences of will, intent, and experience."

—Neale Donald Walsch

Prologue

Waiting was the worst thing. A teenager with a man's body and a baby face, Kenny Sanders sat at a table in a small windowless room with his mother, Krysta, and his attorney, Arnold Pierce. A security guard dozed on a chair in the corner as he had for the last hour. "It looks pretty good," Arnold said, aiming the comment at Krysta, whose fear-tinged, red rimmed eyes betrayed the lack of confidence she was struggling to conceal. "Remember, they can only convict with a unanimous vote."

Krysta's eyes flashed at him. "You mean we shouldn't expect a not guilty verdict?"

Creases furrowed Arnold's forehead, and he pursed his lips. "No, Krysta. I'm just saying a guilty verdict's a high bar. I'd settle for a hung jury. That would be a good thing."

Her glaring eyes never left him. "Well, Arnold, you haven't done—"

"That woman, juror number seven," Kenny interjected, "kept watching me the whole time. I think she believes I'm innocent."

"She's Dave Bradford's cousin," Krysta answered, hope rising in her face. "She has two teenagers. She should be appalled they're trying you as an adult."

"It only takes one holdout," Arnold said nodding with his lips pursed again, in what Kenny months earlier started calling "the trout look." Kenny told himself he wouldn't have to look at that stupid expression much longer.

Time dragged by, sandwiches were ordered in, and when the jury finally adjourned for the night, Kenny was manacled and taken back to a holding cell. The look on his mother's face as they led him away stayed with him. Not that he hadn't seen that mixture of fear, sadness, and shame before. God knew she was suffering even more than he was. For Kenny, the whole ordeal had a kind of unreal, almost dreamlike, quality to it. *This can't be happening to me*, he kept telling himself. *Surely, they'll realize I'm innocent, that I didn't kill anybody. No way that jury would vote to convict me. No way I'm spending the rest of my life in prison. No fucking way.*

He lay back on his bunk and stared up at the chipped and cracked ceiling, knowing that sleep, if it came at all, would be filled with dark, threatening images. He couldn't make any sense of his dreams, but they always left him feeling anxious in the morning. The events of that night sixteen months earlier drifted back like scenes in a movie, scenes he replayed in his head over and over again. If he'd just gone out with Stefanie, none of this would have happened. Stefanie. The thought of her still stirred him, her face below him, her ocean-blue eyes locked on his, her hot breath in his ear, urging him on. God, it had been a long time. But the minute he was arrested, she dropped him like he had the plague.

So much for true love.

He'd had no choice but to cancel his date with Stefanie that night. What could he do? He was offered a job and needed the money. Deliver the package, collect the payment, drop off the cash. The usual routine, he was told. Okay, he knew his supplier was bad news, but shit, times were tough on the coast, and everybody needed a hustle, didn't they? How else was he going to have money for community college? It sure as hell wasn't going to come from his stepdad, that tightwad son of a bitch. Anyway, the buyer never showed, and when the deputy sheriffs came by the next afternoon to say they wanted to talk to him at the station, he wasn't particularly worried. He didn't know what was in those packages, after all.

But he'd been in trouble before, and his mom sounded worried. "You haven't done something stupid again, have you?" she asked.

"No. Don't worry, Mom. I'll be back soon enough."

It seemed like the right thing to say at the time. If he'd only known what was coming...

———

On the morning of the verdict, Kenny jerked awake when he heard a key grate in the lock of the holding cell. A guard handed him a bowl of grayish looking oatmeal and a cup of brown water they called coffee. By the time he joined his mom and Arnold in the secure room adjoining the courtroom, he actually felt revived and full of hope—that is, until he looked more closely at his mom. She wore her best dress and bravest face, but as always her eyes betrayed her. Arnold smelled of booze and looked hungover. They waited, mostly in silence. There just wasn't anything left to say.

Two and a half hours later the bailiff stuck his head in the room and said, "The jury's back. They have a verdict."

The courtroom was jammed with the friends and relatives of both Kenny and the victim, the latter outnumbering the former by at least four to one. The room fell silent when Kenny was led in and allowed to take his seat next to Arnold Pierce. Kenny's mother and grandmother sat directly behind him. The tag team of prosecutors marched in next, a skinny-legged old veteran with a grizzled face, who Kenny called the Coyote, and his deadpan female counterpart, Dracula's mother. After the jury was seated, the judge came in through a side door and mounted his perch. The judge had sagging jowls and tired, hound dog eyes. Deputy Dawg. It occurred to Kenny that the judge hadn't said much through the whole trial, except to grouchily slap down some objection made by Arnold, who would sit back down looking like a whipped puppy.

Today, however, the judge looked invigorated, and all eyes were on him as he asked the foreman if the jury had reached a verdict. "We have, Your Honor," he answered. Kenny looked intently at the woman—juror number seven. She sensed his stare, and it was when she looked away and dropped her chin that fear gripped his young heart for the first time.

The foreman stood, cleared his throat, and looked down at a sheet of paper, his hand trembling slightly. "We find the defendant, Kendrick Dennison Sanders, guilty of aggravated murder."

Chapter One

FOUR YEARS LATER
THE EAST FORK OF THE MILLICOMA RIVER, OREGON

The Oregon Coast Range started as a string of volcanic, offshore islands sixty million years ago. The congealed lava hopped an eastbound tectonic plate that eventually collided with the continent, pushing up a respectable mountain range that ran the length of the state and spawned twenty-two of the prettiest rivers on the planet. It was early spring, and I was hip-deep in one of my favorites, the East Fork of the Millicoma, which lay fifteen miles northwest of Coos Bay, the largest bay on the Oregon Coast. Oceangoing rainbow trout, or steelhead as they're commonly called, were returning to the river to spawn after a two-year jaunt in the Pacific.

As my Australian shepherd, Archie, watched from the bank, I was trying to provoke a steelhead or two into hitting the fly I offered up. Ichthyologists claim that migrating steelhead don't strike the fly—in this case a gaudy chartreuse, red, and gold number called a Miss Molly—out of hunger but more from anger at having their space encroached upon by another aquatic creature. After strafing the water for a couple of hours with no luck, I was beginning to suspect that these particular steelies were the more even-tempered and inclusive types.

I was fishing downriver from a moss-encrusted chunk of pillow lava that bordered a long, deep pool—the kind that attracted steelhead taking a breather. A light breeze riffled the emerald-green water and stirred the Douglas firs that had marched down through the rugged terrain to the river's edge. "I know you're in there," I said, as much to Arch and me as to the fish. "Last chance." When Miss Molly swung across the pool without being molested, I reeled her in and worked my way back to the bank. I'd just poured myself a cup of coffee from my thermos when I heard a high-pitched *whoop* followed by "Fish on!"

It was my daughter, Claire, and she had apparently tied into her first steelhead of the season. It was no mean feat. Like the fabled North Umpqua that lay a watershed further south, the Millicoma was a river for those who seriously practiced the art of catching a steelhead on a fly. I set my coffee down, and Archie led me upstream to watch the fun.

"Whoa, it's huge," Claire screamed again as I reached her. Her eight-weight graphite was seriously flexed, and I saw the surface stir with a glint of silver as the fish started to run downstream. She brought the rod tip up hard, and line screamed off her reel. The lunker finally got the message, stopped, and turned to face her. She started taking line back, a grudging fight that lasted several minutes. When she finally got the fish up close to her, it took off again and came out of the water like it was trying to take flight—once, twice, and with the third leap, threw the barbless hook.

"Aw, damn!" Claire cried out.

Archie stood at the edge of the bank and yelped with crazed excitement. He'd never gone in after an escaping fish, but I feared he might this time.

Claire spun around, her eyes wide, her mouth agape. "Did you see that? Wasn't it beautiful?"

"Yep. Big, too, maybe twenty pounds, and his adipose fin wasn't clipped."

"A *native*. How cool is that? How did you do, Dad?"

I laughed. "Skunked. But seeing that beautiful steelhead just made my day. And he did you a favor by getting off. Releasing that monster would have been harder than landing him."

It was moments like this that made me grateful I had a daughter who insisted I take some time off. My law practice and workaholic tendencies left me little time for leisure. Fortuitously, things slowed down after a busy winter, and I was able to clear the decks without too much hassle. Claire had flown in from Boston, where she held a postdoctoral position at Harvard in environmental science. Over dinner at the Aerie, my farmhouse retreat in the Red Hills of Dundee, we settled on a two-week getaway on the southern coast of Oregon with thoughts of fly-fishing, hiking, and long walks on the beach. This early morning outing from our beach house to the Millicoma was the first item on our agenda.

We fed Archie some kibbles and enjoyed our coffee break after the great fish escape. The morning was still young, and the sun had yet to pierce the low cloud cover, which boded well for fishing. Steelhead are famously skittish and less likely to bite in sun-drenched water. We separated again, and I worked my way around a sweeping oxbow downriver until I came to a gentle eddy on the opposite bank that looked promising. I clipped off Miss Molly and tied on a big, purple fur ball called a woolly bugger, an impressionistic rendition of the caterpillar of the same name. "This oughta get 'em," I told Archie.

I was on my fourth cast when I heard Claire cry out again, faint but distinct over the river clatter. No declaration of a fish on this time, it was a full-throated scream, and the sound of it nearly stopped my heart.

I slipped and slid back to the bank on mossy boulders, dropped my rod, and took off upstream. Archie had already disappeared around the oxbow, barking all the way. I saw Claire just as Archie came up to her. She dropped to one knee and hugged him like she hadn't seen him in a year.

"What is it?" I said a bit breathlessly as I ran up to them.

She stood, pointed upriver, and grimaced. "There's a man in the water. He's dead." I followed her to a big, bleached-out snag that lay in the current at an angle to the bank. She pointed again. "He's on the other side of that log. It's horrible, Dad."

Not a big fan of dead bodies, I sucked a short breath when I saw him. Caught on a broken branch and buffeted by the current, the body gyrated in a macabre dance as if trying to free itself. He was faceup with glazed, wide-open eyes and blue lips that traced a circle. The image in Munch's *The Scream* flashed in my head. Wearing a well-used fishing vest and patched-up waders, the body was a white male, maybe thirtysomething, showing some bloating and discoloration, indicating he'd been in the water for a while. His arms were pulled behind his back, and his legs were folded at the knees. As he bobbed in the current, I could see his hands and feet were not only tightly bound but fastened together. It looked like he'd been surprised while he was fishing, and I shuddered at the thought of him being tossed hog-tied into this cold river.

I looked up at Claire, who was watching me from the other side of the snag. "Looks like he drowned, and it was no accident."

She made a face. "I didn't think so."

"I'm worried he might pop loose." I extracted my phone from a sealed case in my vest. "No bars here. We should—"

She cut me off. "I'll go upriver and call 911. You can watch him." I hesitated for a moment, suddenly uneasy about her traipsing off alone. She gave me a look, the one that always brought back her mother. "I'll be okay, Dad."

"Be careful, then. Take Archie with you."

Claire and Archie started off, and I inched out on the snag to where I could grab the body if it came loose. I felt sadness at seeing a young life snuffed out, and anger and revulsion at what was obviously a cold-blooded execution. As he bobbed and twisted in the current, I saw a piece of blue plastic protruding from the left top pocket of his fishing vest. I hadn't noticed it earlier and figured it might be working its way loose. I reached down and plucked it away before it could swirl downriver. A plastic sleeve, it contained a sodden but readable fishing license belonging to a Howard Coleman, thirty-six years of age, resident of Coos Bay, Oregon, and a business card that was almost illegible. I glimpsed something else while out on the snag—the victim's hands and feet were bound with small diameter, multifilament steel cable. An unusual choice of material to hog-tie someone.

I laid the license out on the snag to dry and then examined the remaining ink on the washed-out business card. I could just discern the faintest remnants of the letters "Mi i Yo da" written across it and the numbers "541 0 9" in the right-hand corner. The numbers had to be what was left of a phone number, since 541 was the area code for most of Oregon. I played scrabble with the letters for a while but didn't come up with anything. I laid the card next to the fishing license and shook my head. Here I was, playing detective out of habit. Okay, I told myself, all you did was discover the body. This is not your problem. Remember, you're on vacation.

It was good advice, and I had every intention of heeding it.

Chapter Two

A deputy sheriff finally arrived with Claire and took charge of the situation. We were detained for about forty minutes until a crime scene tech and two paramedics arrived. The last thing the deputy said was, "Thanks again, Mr. Claxton. Recovering that fishing license saves us valuable time." He glanced at Claire, then back at me. "I'd appreciate both of you not disclosing the name until we confirm the victim's identity and notify next of kin."

"Of course."

The sky remained overcast, but Claire and I had lost our desire to fish. After retrieving our fishing gear and backpacks, we hiked back to the car, loaded Arch, and headed back to the beach house. We'd been up since the crack of dawn, and I was relieved when Claire quickly dozed off in the car. I wasn't looking forward to discussing the ugliness we'd just witnessed. I had a lingering sense of unease I couldn't quite put my finger on—perhaps shame mingled with helplessness. I felt as though the curtain had been pulled back, revealing the evil and depravity humans were capable of, and I wanted to shield my only child from this reality. But, of course, I couldn't.

I glanced over at her—the delicate nose, sculpted cheeks, and mouth with turned-up corners were all her mother's. The firm line of her jaw, even in sleep, had more to do with me. I had vowed to be the best possible parent I could be after Nancy's death. Of course, Claire was a grown woman now and knew the realities of the world only too well. She'd been through the suicide of her mother, and later, a harrowing hostage situation that added an extra helping of salt to my salt-and-pepper hair. But still...

Whoever said you never ceased being a parent was right.

The beach house we were staying in was just south of Coos Bay, near Yoakam Point, a rocky finger of land jutting into the Pacific. The bleached-out structure stood on a lot dotted with stunted, wind-sculpted conifers. The interior was tastefully furnished and featured lots of interesting art on the walls, including a large Jackson Pollock print in the living room that I joked to Claire looked like a paintball fight gone bad.

A plank deck spanned most of the back of the house, affording a commanding view of the Pacific, and a steep, wooden staircase led down to a long stretch of sand known as Lighthouse Beach, owing to a decommissioned lighthouse looming at its southern boundary. A client offered the house to me out of appreciation for a favorable settlement I'd won for him. "We never use it in the spring, Cal. Stay as long as you want," he told me.

Needless to say, I wouldn't have been able to afford such a choice spot otherwise.

On arrival we unloaded our gear and immediately leashed up Archie for a walk—needed by all of us. The sun had broken through and a brisk, offshore breeze blew the tops off the head-high breakers rolling in from the northwest. There were no other dogs in sight, so I unclipped Archie, who dashed off down the beach, scattering a tight cluster of shorebirds. The short-legged critters took flight, swept out in a broad semicircle, and regrouped at the waterline farther south.

Claire looked at me like I'd just murdered a puppy. "Dad, those are *snowy plovers*. They're endangered. Dogs upset them."

"Oops, my bad." I made a mental note to brush up on my

shorebirds and their ecological status as I whistled at Archie to heel.

We walked a long time just breathing in the delicious sea air. Finally, Claire broke the silence. "Are you okay, Dad?"

It was just like her to be worried about me. "Yeah, I'm fine. I'm sorry you had to see that up on the river."

She shot me a look that said I shouldn't worry about her. "That poor man. Why would someone do something like that?"

I shrugged. "Hard to say. Avarice, wrath, lechery, one or a combination of your basic, deadly sins, most likely. Whatever drove the killing, it was a strong statement, probably designed to put others on notice."

Claire shuddered visibly. "In that setting, on that gorgeous river, it just seems so incongruous, so…inhuman. How could anyone be thinking of murder there?"

"Just remember the beautiful steelhead you caught. Not many fly-fishermen can say they hooked a native on that river. Think of that when you think of the Millicoma."

She laughed with a tinge of bitterness. "Sure. What about you? Don't let this conjure up bad memories, Dad."

She was referring to a brush I had with the FBI, a Russian oligarch, and his hired assassin. It was a wrenching, violent experience, but even worse was that during that same period, a woman I deeply cared about broke off our relationship. Claire insisted I take the time to decompress from it all. "No problem," I answered with more conviction than I actually felt. "Nothing's getting in the way of this vacation."

The plovers finally circled around behind us, and after another quarter mile I got permission to free my dog again. He immediately launched himself down the beach, this time in pursuit of a couple of low-flying gulls who were definitely not on the Endangered Species List. They veered off over the surf, and he followed suit. A wave smacked him head on, and he came up sputtering with a shocked look on his face.

Claire and I howled with laughter, and it occurred to me that my daughter might be onto something, dead bodies notwithstanding.

———

A squall blew in the next morning, thrashing the Pacific into a white lather and pinging rain against the big bay window in the living room. It was spring in Oregon, after all. While Claire sat curled around a book—Tartt's *The Goldfinch*, if memory serves—I was busy putting breakfast together, an omelet made with spinach and mushrooms, some fried Yukon Golds, and fresh-squeezed orange juice. There's nothing like a front row seat to a Pacific storm to give you an appetite. The squall left a sodden, drizzly sky in its wake, so we grabbed our raincoats and headed for Coos Bay, leaving a pouting Australian shepherd behind.

As we crossed the South Slough on the Cape Arago Highway Bridge, the pleasure boats and commercial fishing fleet at the little harbor town of Charleston came into view to the west near the narrow entrance to the Bay. It looked like most of the boats stayed home that day, which seemed a wise decision. After taking a sharp bend to the north, the bay stretched out—some twenty square miles of it—in a lopsided, inverted U with the cities of Coos Bay and North Bend nestled neatly in the crook. Clinging stubbornly to the remnants of the logging and fishing industries, the contiguous cities had decidedly blue-collar vibes. We picked up some groceries to augment what we'd brought with us, got Claire a new pair of Tevas for beach-walking, and then the caffeine bell went off.

We stopped at a little, flat-roofed shop on the Coast Highway just below the Coos Bay/North Bend dividing line. Called Coffee and Subversion, it was an indie bookstore that promised "The Best Espresso in Town," according to a sidewalk sign. A chime on the door announced our entry. Claire inhaled a lungful of air. "I love the smell of books."

"Me, too, especially when it's mingled with the smell of strong coffee."

One side of the place was filled with books, new and used, and the other housed a coffee shop with threadbare but comfortable-looking chairs and low tables. Most of the seats were taken by people in deep communion with their little screens. "Good morning," a woman behind a counter on the book side called out. She was tall and broad with a raging shock of silver hair streaked with magenta highlights. "Make yourselves at home." We nodded, and I went for the coffee and Claire for the books. As Claire browsed, I sipped a double cappuccino and perused the items on a community bulletin board, an exuberant hodgepodge announcing everything from yoga and Pilates classes to theater auditions and community protests.

The item, "Wanted: female drummer for ecofeminist folk metal band," made me chuckle. Another one printed in bold, red letters caught my eye: "Stop the LNG Terminal. Sign the petition at the desk. Get involved." Like most Oregonians, I knew about the controversial proposal to site a liquid natural gas terminal in Coos Bay for foreign export, pitting environmental activists against a Canadian multinational energy company that promised jobs in a region that badly needed them. This bookstore looked like ground zero for the activists.

I had moved to the book side of the shop and was looking through the mystery section when I overheard a name that stopped me dead, "…Howard Coleman…" I closed the book in my hand and began listening intently to the conversation, which drifted over the tall bookrack from the sales counter. "Yeah, no kidding," a male voice said. "They found him over on the Millicoma. Somebody tied him up and threw him in the river."

"Oh, God, no. He was *murdered?*" It was the woman with the magenta hair. Her tone was fraught with emotion. "Do they know who did it?"

"I don't think so. But, you know, when he wasn't fishing, he ran with a rough crowd. Must've gotten sideways with somebody."

The woman sighed deeply. "I'll have to tell my grandson."

A long pause. "Yeah, I guess you will. How's he doing, anyway?"

"Not well, not well at all."

The bearer of news left the shop. I didn't see the book I was looking for, so I went to the counter. "Looks like you don't have Nesbø's *Macbeth*."

She swept a length of variegated hair off her shoulder and looked at me with intelligent eyes. "Wouldn't you know it? Sold the last one two days ago. I can order a copy and have it here by noon tomorrow."

I told her to do it, and we left after I signed the anti-LNG petition. I felt torn, because I knew the region needed jobs, but I'd had it with the global-warming deniers and felt it was time to move away from burning fossil fuels of any kind. Besides, if I'd balked, my daughter would have disowned me. As we walked to the car, I said, "The woman at the counter knew the man you found in the river."

She stopped and looked at me, startled. "*Really?* How do you know that?"

"I heard her talking to that tall, bearded guy who left ahead of us. He was filling her in. I think her grandson must have been close to the victim."

"Did you say anything?"

"No."

Claire made a face. "What a weird coincidence."

It *was* weird, and like most lawyers and cops, I distrusted coincidences, because they rarely were. But this one, clearly the real thing, evoked a vague sense of disquiet—as if there were some reason why I happened to overhear that conversation.

That's ridiculous, I told myself. Knock it off and enjoy the vacation.

Chapter Three

"Dad, check out these anemones. They're the most intense lime-green I've ever seen!" It was Claire, and she was crouched next to a tide pool south of where we were staying. The skies had cleared, so we'd grabbed our backpacks and were hiking along the beach toward Cape Arago, a postcard-worthy headland jutting into the Pacific. The suspension bridge connecting the mainland with the cape had long since fallen into the sea, and the abandoned lighthouse, visible from our deck, stood on the islet like a sentinel refusing to desert its post.

"Oh, and the sea urchins. Look at them! Deep violet." Claire looked up at me, her eyes shining with wonder and enthusiasm. This wasn't the first time we'd explored Oregon's tide pools, but she always had the same reaction. She was born with a deep affection for the natural world, and I loved her for it.

A couple of small, multicolored sculpins darted across the pool, and Archie nearly pounced. "Whoa, Big Boy," I said, laughing, "leave the fish alone." Drawn from one pool to the next, we were eventually pushed back toward shore by the incoming tide. The north swell that appeared the day before had intensified. Offshore, ten-foot waves broke like thunderclaps, the whitewater raking across a garden of craggy rocks and sending plumes of spray high into the air. I pointed toward the horizon, sharply etched against an azure sky, unobstructed. "Look, Claire, it's almost like you can see the curvature of the earth from here."

She shaded her eyes and looked westward. "You're right. Aren't you glad you came, Dad?"

I took a deep breath of sea air and exhaled. "Yeah. I'm glad. Except for my place in Dundee, this coastline's my favorite spot on the planet."

She gave me that look, and I knew a lecture was coming. "Well, then you need to come down here more often and not spend so much time at the Aerie, Dad. I don't want you to become some kind of work-obsessed hermit."

I probably blanched a little but managed a smile. "No worries." Brave words, but I knew deep down she had a point. I wasn't going to revert to that uptight L.A. prosecutor I was before her mom died, but she was right about the hermit bit. Sometimes I felt I could manage best with just a dog and a daughter living her own life. Relationships of the romantic type, I had learned, could be painful.

She kept her sapphire eyes on me. They sparkled in the sunlight. "How's that woman in Portland you've been seeing?"

She was referring to a city councilwoman named Tracey Thomas I was casually dating. "Oh, she's fine. We, uh, see each other now and then, when our schedules allow."

Claire frowned. "*When your schedules allow?* How romantic."

I shrugged. "Neither of us feel rushed. As a matter of fact, Tracy suggested we take a hiatus for the next few weeks, her way of respecting your visit, Claire."

"That's nice but not necessary. Have you heard from Winona?"

I looked out toward the horizon. Winona Cloud was my ex-significant other. She moved from Portland out to the Warm Springs Reservation to work for the Confederated Tribes. "No, not directly. But I hear she's cutting a wide swath through the male-dominated culture on the rez."

Claire laughed. "Not surprised at all. I think you should—"

A wave rolled in, forcing us to scramble. I took the opportunity to change the subject. "What about you? You've been mum on your social life lately."

She smiled, the kind that says I thought you'd never ask. "Well, not too long ago I met a guy I really like."

"Tell me about him."

A bit of color rose in her face. "His name's Gabriel Silva. He's from Argentina, but he's been living in the U.S. for a long time."

"What's he doing here?"

"He has a small consulting firm in Boston that teaches businesses how to become sustainable. He's brilliant, Dad." She went on to sing Mr. Silva's praises—not only brilliant, he was a rock climber, a mountain biker, and, like Claire, an environmental hawk.

"Sounds like an interesting guy. Are you seeing a lot of each other?"

"Well, he's in the middle of a start-up, and I'm traveling between Harvard and the Gulf Coast a lot."

"How romantic."

She stopped and looked at me, trying to look indignant. "Well, this is different."

"*Really?*" I tried not to laugh.

She shook her head as a guilty smile spread across her face. "Okay, I concede the point."

That made us both laugh.

Back at the beach house that night, Claire made a huge salad, I fried up some fresh rockfish crusted with Parmesan, and she crashed not long after we finished the dishes. I poured myself a Rémy Martin and sat down in front of the bay window in the living room. A waxing moon had followed the sun into the Pacific, and the ocean was now a dark shadow against the faint violet glow of the horizon. I sat gazing at the void while absently stroking Archie's broad back and sipping the cognac.

Yeah, Claire was right, I told myself. This is just what the doctor ordered.

————

The fair weather held, so we spent the next morning down on the beach, reading and using our cell phones to stay connected to the world. Claire was heading up a long-range study of the impact of the Deepwater Horizon oil spill on Gulf Coast wetlands. New data had arrived, which required her to join a fifty-minute conference call. I listened with one ear, marveling at her command of the complex subject matter.

That's my baby girl, I said to myself with no small amount of pride.

I'd managed to clear my court appearances for the next two weeks, and there were no new messages awaiting me that morning. Absence from my Dundee office did mean, however, that I was jeopardizing new business, never a good idea for a struggling one-man law practice. And the fact that I also did a day a week of *pro bono* work in downtown Portland didn't help my bottom line. But with the help of my early retirement pension from my years as a prosecutor for the city of Los Angeles, I made it work for Archie and me.

After lunch, I drove into Coos Bay to pick up the book I'd ordered. Coffee and Subversion was busy, at least on the coffee side of the house. The woman with magenta hair waved to me from the book side, which was nearly deserted. "Your Nesbø's in."

"Be right there." I ordered a double cappuccino, wet. It came in a big, thick mug and was finished with a heart-shaped medallion of milk floating on top, the signature of a skilled barista. I crossed over to the book side to browse the stacks—everything from Tolstoy to Márquez—and when I finished my coffee, approached the sales counter. "Great selection of books here."

The woman's streaked hair was unruly but with a purpose.

She cracked a rueful smile. "Thanks. I just stock things I've read or would read if I had infinite time." She glanced over at the customers deeply absorbed in their digital devices. "If people read books like they do their smartphones, I'd be a millionaire by now."

I laughed. "You're bucking the tide with an independent bookstore."

The rueful smile again. "Story of my life."

I paid cash for the book, and she handed it to me with a Coffee and Subversion bookmark in it. "I'm guessing you're not from around here. Where are you and your, ah, companion staying?"

"My daughter," I corrected, showing a slight smile. "We're staying south of Yoakam Point, on Sunset Lane. Vacation for both of us." I offered my hand. "I'm Cal Claxton."

She looked a little embarrassed but met my eyes and shook my hand with a firm grip. "Aurora Dennison, but everyone calls me Rori. Where are you from, Cal?"

"Dundee."

"The wine country. You a vintner?" She smiled, suggesting a playful side. "I love a good Oregon pinot."

I laughed again. "Me, too, but no, I'm a lawyer not a vintner. I've got a one-man law practice there. My daughter's visiting from Massachusetts, and we both love the coast, so here we are."

Her smile turned wistful. "It's nice you can spend time together like this." The comment rang with emotional subtext, but I had no clue what it was.

"Yes, it is. She doesn't get out to Oregon very often." I hesitated for a few moments, then said out of curiosity more than anything else, "Uh, yesterday, I happened to overhear you talking about a man who drowned over on the Millicoma River."

She swung her eyes to mine and locked on them. "Howard Coleman. You know him?"

"No. My daughter and I were fly-fishing on the river two days ago. We found his body and called 911."

Her eyes got huge. "*No*. And then you came in here and heard Skip Feltzer and me talking about it?"

"Yeah. It was such a bizarre coincidence I thought I'd mention it. Have you told your grandson?"

She raised her eyebrows. "You *were* listening, weren't you? No, I haven't told him yet. He's, ah…away."

More subtext. "Well, I don't envy you the task. My daughter actually found the body. It was pretty traumatic for her."

"I can imagine." She studied me for a moment as if turning something over in her mind. "I'm taking a break now, Cal. Can I interest you in another cappuccino? I'm buying."

I could have easily made an excuse. After all, Claire was waiting for me back at the beach house, but curiosity got me again. "I never turn down a cup of coffee." I followed her over to the bar. The decision seemed innocuous enough, but at the same time I had a feeling that having coffee with Rori Dennison would have consequences.

How right I was.

Chapter Four

Rori Dennison was a handsome woman. Sure, a lifetime of coastal living was evident in her face—the weathered complexion, deeply set laugh lines, and nests of fine wrinkles adjacent to striking, slate-blue eyes—but the result somehow enhanced her appearance, a face not spoiled by beauty, you might say. And there was something about her bearing, too, and the set of her jawline that told me she didn't suffer any fools, a trait I valued highly.

"What kind of law do you practice, Cal?" She handed me a cappuccino after insisting I take a seat while she fetched our coffees.

"I'm a jack-of-all-trades. Have to be in a one-man practice in a small town. I also spend a day a week in Portland doing *pro bono* work." She raised her eyebrows again. "Anybody who stops in off the street, indigents, homeless people. They have legal needs, just like the rest of us."

"That's quite a commitment."

I sipped some coffee. "My way of giving back, I suppose. It's never boring, either."

Her eyes registered curiosity. "Giving back seems to be going out of style these days." She paused, but I didn't respond because

I wanted to hear what she had to say. "We have a growing population of homeless people here in Coos Bay. I guess I don't know where they get legal help."

"The need usually goes unmet unless they're being prosecuted. Then they have access to a public defender."

She puffed a derisive breath. "Public defenders. They're not worth the powder to blow them up. Our criminal justice system's rigged for the rich." She took a sip of coffee and abruptly changed to the subject I figured was on her mind. "Was Coleman really tied up like Skip said?"

"Yes. It appeared to be an execution." She winced. "Your grandson knew the victim?"

"Yeah. He and Kenny have some history, and it isn't good history."

"What happened?"

She hesitated. "Howard Coleman was a jailhouse snitch. He lied in court, which helped convict my grandson of murder. Kenny got a life sentence without parole. He was *sixteen* at the time, just a kid, a beautiful kid. They tried him as an adult."

"I'm sorry to hear that, Rori. Did you appeal?"

"Oh, yeah. We appealed. And when we lost we filed a Petition for Review with the Oregon Supreme Court, but they refused to hear it. Then we tried both a Federal appeal and a Writ of Habeus Corpus with the Supreme Court, but those went nowhere." She looked around and managed a wan smile. "Now I'm damn-near broke. My husband—God rest his ornery soul—left me a pile of money, but this shop's all I've got left."

"Have you talked to the Innocence Project people?"

"Yeah, they, ah, did review Kenny's case, but they said they didn't think they could help us." She shrugged. "There's no DNA evidence or anything like that. And Kenny confessed. It was coerced, and he recanted once we got him a lawyer." She eyed me carefully to gauge my reaction, and when I simply nodded, she went on. "I pleaded with the Innocence folks, but it didn't do any good." By this time, her eyes burned with conviction. "That boy's innocent, Cal. He didn't kill anybody. And I'm not giving up on him."

"When did this happen?"

She closed her eyes and ran the fingers of both hands through her hair. "Four years ago. Two years ago, when he turned eighteen, they transferred him from the juvenile facility to the state prison in Salem." Her eyes filled. "Now he's in with grown men, and he's still just a kid."

I shook my head. "How's he holding up?"

She looked past me and gritted her teeth, forcing back tears. "He's a good-looking kid, you know? But he's big and strong, and he's a fighter." Her voice grew husky. "Prison's truly hell on earth."

"I know. It's good he's a fighter." I paused, my mind going back to the sense of connection the coincidence engendered, however ephemeral. "Is there any reason to believe Howard Coleman's murder is related to your grandson's case?"

"Probably not. Coleman's lifestyle finally caught up with him, most likely." She allowed the wisp of a smile. "I should be considered a suspect, you know. God knows I had a motive to kill the lyin' son of a bitch."

A couple of shoppers were cruising the book aisles by this time, and one was standing at the counter with a couple of books. Rori stood up and smiled apologetically. "Sorry to cry on your shoulder, Cal. Coleman's death really stirred me up." She offered her hand, and when I took it she squeezed. "Thanks for listening."

I left Coffee and Subversion that day feeling stirred up myself. I was touched by the depth of Rori Dennison's commitment to her grandson, and I had questions. Lots of questions. And that was always a dangerous thing.

———

"What took you so long?" Claire asked, a little annoyed. "I packed us a snack and a thermos of coffee. We need to get on the road if we're going to make the falls today." She was referring to Golden and Silver Falls, our destination for a mellow afternoon hike. The second- and third-tallest waterfalls in the Coast Range, they were sure to be booming this time of year.

"Sorry. Got to talking to the woman who owns the bookshop, the one with the colorful hair."

"About the body?"

"Yeah, that and other things."

"She seemed interesting."

I smiled. "She's that, for sure."

We took Route 241 east out of Coos Bay into the Coast Range, and as I drove, we talked about what Rori told me. When I finished describing what happened to Kenny Sanders, Claire said, "Are you kidding me? He got life at *sixteen*? That's horrible. I didn't know Oregon tried juveniles as adults."

"They didn't until '94, when voters passed a ballot initiative requiring it for certain crimes like rape and murder."

"Do juries decide the penalties?"

"Yeah, but only within a narrow range of choices. For aggravated murder, they can choose death, life without parole, or life with the possibility of parole after thirty years."

"What did the kid do?"

"I didn't get any details, except that he confessed, then recanted. She said it was coerced."

"*Coerced?* Is that a thing?"

"It can be, especially for someone young and naive. Trust me, law enforcement knows a lot of dirty tricks."

"Well, even if he did it, a sixteen-year-old doesn't have anything close to an adult brain yet. How can he be tried as an adult? That's draconian."

"I agree. The other side of it is that the murder must have been egregious for the jury to opt for no parole."

"Still, a kid can be rehabilitated, even if he killed someone. His grandmother says he's innocent. Does he have any chance of ever getting out of jail?"

I shrugged. "It doesn't sound good. They lost their appeals, and apparently the Innocence Project passed on it."

"There's an Innocence Project in Oregon?"

"Yeah. I don't know any of their lawyers, but I hear they're good."

"Why did they pass on him?"

"I'm not sure. They decided they couldn't help him, for whatever reason. They don't have a lot of resources, so they have to prioritize. There might be one avenue of appeal left—the Supreme Court ruled recently that juvenile offenders can only be denied parole when they're judged to be beyond redemption. That could provide grounds for a last-ditch appeal. The issue would be what factors were considered by the sentencing court."

"Did you tell the grandmother that?"

"I didn't, but she probably knows. Trouble is, the appeal would only provide eligibility for parole in the distant future. She wants exoneration, not a parole hearing when her grandson's fifty."

Claire sat back in her seat and crossed her arms. "Sickening."

At the trailhead parking lot, Archie bounded out of the back seat like an escaping prisoner. We let him run and sniff for a while before snapping on his leash. The short hike to Silver Falls proceeded through towering old-growth Douglas firs mingled with alders and maples, all growing in a green sea of sword ferns and salmonberry. As a special treat, the whole scene was overlaid with a spray of white trillium. Claire bent over one of the delicate blossoms for a closer look, then turned to me, beaming. "These just bloomed, Dad, probably this morning."

I laughed. "I ordered it up just for you, sweetheart."

Silver Falls cascaded over a rocky dome, then halfway down its one-hundred-and-sixty-foot descent it was transformed into a fine mist that billowed up at the base like smoke. We moved in close for some pictures, then quickly out again to keep from getting soaked by the dew, laughing the whole way.

After hiking the steep trail to the top of Golden Falls, we took a break. Fed by a swifter, more voluminous creek, the higher falls plunged over an upper tier before hurtling down a sheer, rocky embankment. I gave Arch some water while Claire poured us coffee and squeezed peanut butter from a tube onto crackers, our go-to trail snack. "*Bon appétit*," she said, handing me a cracker.

We ate in silence for a while, the sun gently warming us and the steady thrum of the waterfall like a mantra. Claire took a deep breath and exhaled slowly. "Mom would have loved this place. Wish we would have done more hiking back then."

"Me, too," I said as my chest tightened a little. "She was busy teaching, and I was busy being an asshole."

Claire brought her eyes up to mine and didn't smile at my self-deprecating remark. "I didn't mean that as criticism, Dad. It wasn't your fault, what happened to Mom."

I'd heard that from my daughter many, many times. She forgave me for being a selfish jerk, who was so self-absorbed that he misjudged the depth of her mother's depression. But I hadn't forgiven myself. I looked away. "Yeah, you're right—your mom would have loved this place."

Claire started to respond but was cut off by the sharp cry of a bald eagle that swooped down not fifty feet from us and then banked into a sharp turn, showing the full spread of its wingspan and eliciting a couple of startled barks from Archie. Claire leaped to her feet. "Oh, Dad! Isn't he magnificent?"

I jumped up, too, and we stood watching as the big raptor glided out of sight. After the excitement, Claire didn't come back to the subject of her mother. I was thankful for that. Whoever said time heals all wounds was dead wrong.

———

That night, after dinner, Claire said, "You've been really quiet, Dad. You're not upset about what I said up at the falls, are you? That was dumb of me."

"It wasn't dumb, and I'm not upset about anything. I, uh, I guess it's this Kenny Sanders thing. Finding the body on the river and then learning about the connection to him. I don't know, it's just hard to shake, for some reason."

She looked at me and sighed. "I think that woman convinced you that her grandson's innocent. If that's the case, maybe you should talk to her again. There might be something you can do to help the kid." I looked back at her, surprised she would grant me such permission. She smiled, and I saw her mother's face for a moment. "You won't be good company unless you do, Dad."

She was right, of course.

Chapter Five

"Remember, check the IDs of *everyone* who signs. We don't want any glitches in these petitions," Rori Dennison said to a group of people assembled in front of the community bulletin board at Coffee and Subversion. Although she wore jeans and a peasant blouse, she had the bearing of a commanding general. I'd just entered the bookstore the next morning and was standing at the back of the crowd. A young man with a nose ring and inked-up forearms handed me a sheet of paper that read:

Stop the LNG Export Terminal
at Jackson Point

We, the undersigned, request that our state take decisive action to block the proposed liquified natural gas terminal and pipeline connection at Jackson Point. If our state government is as committed to combatting climate change as it says, it is madness to pipe LNG from the fracking fields of Colorado across southern Oregon to Coos Bay, impacting 485 rivers, streams, and wetlands along the way. This project threatens our water, our air, our wildlife, and our fishing and tourism industries.

STOP THIS ENVIRONMENTAL CATASTROPHE, MADAM GOVERNOR!

Rori answered a bevy of questions, and then the group filed out of the coffee shop, each carrying a thick stack of petitions and an obvious fervor for the mission. Without seeing me, she went into the back of the shop with two other people without seeing me, so I migrated over to the stacks to look around. I found myself browsing through the poetry section, where I spotted a worn copy of Silvia Plath's *Ariel*, my wife's favorite book. I opened the slender volume and read the one that had touched her most, the title poem describing a horse ride for the ages. At the time, it never occurred to me that Nancy and Sylvia were kindred souls, suffering from the kind of sensitivity that makes it difficult to cope in this world. I closed the book and started to put it back.

"Hello, Cal. Welcome back." I turned around and Rori smiled, eyeing the book in my hand. "One of my favorite books of poetry."

"It was my wife's favorite book, period." Her brow raised slightly, acknowledging either the significance of that statement or my use of the past tense, or maybe both. "A little too bleak for my taste," I added.

"It was Plath's way of keeping her demons at bay." *A lot of good it did her*, I thought but didn't say. Rori continued, "I'm kind of embarrassed to admit it, but I googled you last night, Cal. Felt like an invasion of privacy. You've been involved in some interesting cases over the years."

I nodded, realizing we were headed in the same direction. "As a matter of fact, I was thinking about your grandson's case last night and had a couple of questions."

A wry smile. "Coffee's on me again."

The book aisles were empty, so after we got our drinks Rori told the barista—a young man named Anthony—to watch both sides of the house. As she led me through a back door, I said, "You really fired up the troops out there. How's the LNG fight shaping up?"

"Horrible," she said, as she stopped and turned to face me, her eyes blazing. "We got our asses kicked on a local ballot measure to stop the thing last year. The corporate interests poured a ton of money into it, and we couldn't begin to compete. We're *so* divided here. God knows we need the jobs, but setting aside the global-warming issue, siting a mega facility in an earthquake and tsunami zone's plain stupid. Look what happened at Fukushima, for Christ's sake."

"Where does the governor stand?"

Rori's laughter rang with sarcasm. "We're not sure. It's an election year."

She turned back, and I followed her into a small space that doubled as a storeroom and office. Boxes of books, most of them used, and some framed photographs lined one wall, and a series of shelves holding bags of coffee beans, napkins, and other supplies lined the other. She took a seat at a battered metal desk, and I sat down across from her.

"Looks like your shop is headquarters for the opposition."

A look of pride crossed her face momentarily. "It is. For the LNG fight and a lot of other causes. I used to sit on the sidelines and grumble, but after what happened to Kenny, I got woke, as they say." She laughed again. "But don't get me started."

A photograph of a woman and a young boy sat on a cluttered table behind the desk. Ten or twelve, the towheaded boy looked straight at the camera with bright, eager eyes and a broad smile. With an arm slung around the boy, the woman had a more practiced smile and eyes that expressed love and pride but hid something, too. Pain, maybe.

I looked at the photograph. "Is that Kenny?"

"Yes, with his mother, Krysta." Rori looked away. "Krysta died of ovarian cancer a year after Kenny was convicted." She hesitated a moment, then looked back at me. "The cancer got diagnosed late, and I don't think she had the will to resist. The conviction took the fight right out of her."

"What a shame. What about his father?"

She shrugged. "His biological dad's out of the picture. He took off after Krysta got pregnant with Kenny, and we never saw him again. It was good riddance. The only thing he ever mastered was rolling a joint. She married again when Kenny was ten. She and Walter split up shortly after the trial. Just as well. Walter Sanders wasn't much of a husband, or a father, either. Money was his thing, money and prestige."

"Tell me about the crime."

She sipped some coffee, set the cup down, and leaned forward. "The victim was Walter's business partner, a guy named Sonny Jenson. They owned a company that dealt in real estate and other businesses." She hiked a corner of her mouth up in derision. "Seemed like they were always one deal away from hitting it big back then. Somebody killed Sonny at his home. His wife found the body in the garage. Beaten to death. When I saw the first photo at the trial, I had to look away. It was god-awful."

"Murder weapon?"

"A blunt object. Could've been a hammer from his tool rack, but it was never recovered, and his wife couldn't say whether one was missing or not. He was in his garage, and someone apparently surprised him."

"Any evidence tying Kenny to the scene?"

"Well, they found his fingerprints in a couple of places in the garage and on a bloody gardening glove that they made a big deal of. Kenny cleaned Sonny's pool and did yardwork there, so *duh*. What did they expect?"

"They lifted a print from a glove?"

"It was cloth on the top and smooth rubber underneath. There were two prints on the rubber side. One was Kenny's, and the other was too smeared to identify. The glove was apparently used to wipe the killer's hands, maybe the murder weapon, too. We argued that Kenny's print was already on the glove."

"It must have been a messy scene. Did they look for Sonny's DNA on Kenny?"

"Yes, and they found *nothing*. His car was clean, too. Turns out he went surfing the next morning without a wetsuit, and they used that as an excuse for not finding anything on his body. And Krysta did the wash that Saturday morning like she always did. They used that excuse, too."

"Anything missing from the house?"

"Yeah. Some cash, his wedding band, and a bunch of his wife's jewelry. None of that stuff ever turned up."

"How was Kenny implicated?"

She drained her coffee, combed her hair with the fingers of one hand, and frowned. "It was a Friday night. Kenny was out delivering a package at Barview on the west side of the bay at the time of the murder. The customer never showed, and no one saw him out there. The deputy sheriffs picked him up the next day." She sighed deeply. "He never got out of jail after that."

"Deputy sheriffs? Sonny lived outside the city?"

"Yeah, Crown Point, on the east side of the South Slough. So the murder fell in Sheriff Stoddard's jurisdiction, not the city's. Anyway, those bastards grilled him for twelve hours straight and got him to sign a confession. We got him an attorney the following day, Kenny immediately recanted the confession, the damage was done."

"Was the attorney local?"

"Lincoln City. A lawyer named Arnold Pierce. Walter, Kenny's stepfather, found him." She laughed bitterly. "Pierce was an incompetent ass. We tried to repair the damage on appeal, but we failed."

"Why did the cops suspect Kenny in the first place?"

She sighed again. "He'd been working for Sonny for six months or so. They, ah, got into an argument over the amount of money Kenny was owed. Kenny shoved him, apparently, and then keyed Sonny's new Prius on his way out. Sonny called the cops, and Kenny got arrested. But Walter intervened. That was a month before the murder."

"Where does Howard Coleman fit in?"

"Coleman was in jail for an assault charge of some kind when Kenny got arrested. He and Kenny shared a cell for a day or so. He testified that Kenny bragged to him that he 'beat some dude to death and robbed him.'" Her eyes narrowed down, and I could feel the heat of her brooding anger. "Coleman got a reduced sentence after that."

"Any other witnesses?"

"A woman saw a young man get out of a Honda like Kenny's at a Jiffy Mart near Sonny's home at about the time of the murder. She picked Kenny out of a lineup."

I fell silent for a few moments before meeting Rori's eyes, which were fixed on me. Her expression was half defiance and half supplication. I said, "From twenty-thousand feet, it's a pretty damning picture. Kenny had the semblance of a motive, he apparently couldn't prove he wasn't there, and he certainly had the means. Why are you so sure your grandson's innocent?"

Rori didn't miss a beat. "Sure, he's my blood, so I'm going to be supportive. But, my God, if I felt Kenny really killed Sonny Jenson I wouldn't be talking to you." She hesitated, seeming to search for the words. "If that beautiful daughter of yours were accused of some horrendous crime, you'd know whether she did it or not, right? I mean, I can sense you two have a close relationship." I nodded. She had *that* right. "Well, that's the way it is between Kenny and me. I *know* he didn't do it, Cal."

I was moved but not convinced. After all, angry male teens were capable of unthinkable violence these days, although assault rifles and not hammers were usually the weapons of choice. But

Rori's analogy to Claire resonated with me. "I'm no appellate attorney, Rori, and it sounds like there aren't any viable appeals that haven't already been tried, but it might make sense to have a fresh pair of eyes look at the evidence and talk to some of the principals involved. Maybe some facts got overlooked. It happens. Of course, the case is cold, so it's a long shot at best."

Her face brightened. "You would do that?"

I looked her in the eye. "I'd want to talk to Kenny first."

She caught my drift and smiled with confidence. "Sure. Of course. You'll realize immediately that you're talking to an innocent young man."

"I'll call the prison to request a visit as his attorney. You need to give Kenny a heads-up that I'm coming and explain that I just want to go over the case with him. Don't promise anything."

"Okay, I can leave him a message on the prison's voice mail system. Um, what will you charge, I mean if you decide to take his case?"

I shrugged. "Nothing until I talk to him. If we decide to go ahead, I'll need a retainer, say, a thousand dollars. When that runs out, we'll review the bidding. I'm still on vacation, too, so I'm not proposing a full-time job here." Rori extended her hand, and we shook on it. "Good. Now, what can you tell me about Howard Coleman?"

She rolled her eyes. "He was a few bricks short of a full load, that's what. Drove a truck when he wasn't selling drugs or carousing. He did love to fly-fish"—she looked at me and smiled—"so he must have had some redeeming virtues. Lived off and on with a woman named Sissy Anderson. Last I heard she was waiting tables at the Fishmonger in North Bend."

"Who'd Howard drive for?"

"Sloat Trucking. Biggest in the area." A knowing smile. "Some of its drivers have been known to move more than timber." I gave her a blank look, and she added, "Drugs."

She answered a few more questions before we said our goodbyes.

I'm no adrenaline junkie, but I admit I left Rori Dennison that day feeling a sharp sense of anticipation. If Kenny Sanders convinced me he was innocent, then the hunt would be on for the real killer. At the same time, I knew my offer of help had built an inflated sense of hope in Rori. I could see it in her eyes. The thought of failing her and Kenny brought my pulse back down.

Call it a standoff.

Chapter Six

Waterdrops shed by Claire's unfurling fly line sparkled like jewels in the sunlight. She snapped her forearm forward, and the line reversed course, carrying the bright yellow bass popper forty feet in front of her in a graceful arc. "Nice cast! Now let the popper sink a foot or two… That's right. Now strip some line. Quick jerks. That's it… Nice… Okay, bring it in and cast again. There's a big old bass down there somewhere, I can feel it."

It was two days later, and I was coaching Claire on the finer points of fly-fishing for smallmouth bass. We were on the lower Umpqua River, above the tidewater zone at Reedsport, and this was her go at smallies, who strike a fly with a ferocity that belies their name. It was a breezy, sun-dappled day, and the river ran smooth and deep past banks crowded with alders and maples. Our plan was to mix a little pleasure with a trip inland to the State Penitentiary, where I'd arranged a meeting with Kenny Sanders that afternoon.

Always fascinated with my work, Claire had lobbied to sit in. "I can take notes and give you a second opinion on the kid," she argued.

I valued her judgment and having a notetaker would free me up during the interview, but this was a sensitive area. "I don't know, Claire," I responded. "I'd have to declare you my legal assistant to get you in there, and I can't lie about that."

"I've got a flexible schedule right now, Dad. I could stay and assist you until you decide what you're going to do." She gave me that smile. "I'll be the best damn assistant you've ever had."

There were potential attorney-client privilege issues that would have to be addressed, but how could I turn down an offer like that? I agreed, and since I had a contact at the prison I was able to expedite her background check.

Claire caught on fast to the bass fishing and must have hooked into and released a half dozen big olive green and bronze beauties before we called it a morning. We changed out of our fishing garb and followed the river inland on the Umpqua Highway. For my money, that river valley was one of the prettiest in Oregon—an emerald green topography of rolling hills, river drainages, and dense forests punctuated with small farms and the occasional vineyard.

After putting the Coast Range behind us, we took I-5 north, passing the turnoffs to Oregon's two main college towns—Eugene, and then forty-five miles later, Corvallis—before exiting the interstate in Salem. Like a fortified island in a two-hundred-acre buffer zone, the State Prison lay just a mile and a half from the Oregon State Capitol, if flown by a crow. We found a shaded parking spot, and after a short walk, Archie resigned himself to a wait in the car. He knew the drill.

For a prison, the three-story administration building wasn't that ugly, sporting what looked like a fresh coat of dun-colored paint with dark trim, arched windows, and an entrance with a double-sided staircase and actual landscaping. After signing in and showing our driver's licenses and my Oregon Bar card, we passed through security and were led across a courtyard in the shadow of a twenty-five-foot concrete wall. Glimpsing an armed guard watching us from above, Claire said "whoa" under her breath.

We were shown into a windowless conference room that adjoined the maximum-security wing, which housed the most violent offenders, including better than thirty condemned to die by lethal injection. Since the current governor was honoring a death penalty moratorium put in place by her predecessor, these prisoners were in limbo. Claire's laptop was allowed in for note-taking, but we'd been stripped of pens, pencils, and keys.

A few minutes later, Kenny Sanders was brought in and shackled to a steel chair across from us. He was tall, at least six three, and despite his loose-fitting denim uniform, I could see he was ripped. He had Rori's slate-blue eyes, a round face, and a downy blond mustache and goatee that fell well short of making him look older. After I introduced Claire and myself, he rested his eyes on my daughter for a couple of beats. She shifted in her seat and glanced at me. His look wasn't salacious, more like that of a man who'd just arrived at a blooming oasis after a long slog in the desert. Judging from Claire's expression, she wasn't offended, and I wasn't, either.

He swung his gaze to mine and without blinking said, "Grandma Rori said I'm supposed to convince you I'm innocent. How does that work?"

"I don't want you to try to convince me of anything, Kenny. Just tell me the truth about what happened. If I think I can help you, I'll give it a try."

He shrugged, looking unimpressed. "I've run all my appeals out. What could you possibly do?"

"That's a fair question. Maybe nothing. I won't know until I get all the facts on the table, and it starts with you. Are you willing to help me?"

He shrugged again. "I got nothin' else to do."

I leaned in. "Let's start with Howard Coleman. You know he's dead, right?"

"Yeah. Grandma told me. Said you two found his body. That's pretty weird, huh?"

I nodded. "How did you make contact with Coleman after you were arrested?"

Kenny shrugged. "For the first couple of days they put me in with the general population. He was in there, too."

"Did you talk to him?"

"Yeah, but he's the one who, out of the blue, came up to me and started shooting the breeze the second day. I thought it was a little strange at the time. I mean, why did he pick me out? There were lots of guys in that cell."

"Did you talk about Sonny's murder with him?"

"Hell, no. I didn't say a word about it to anybody in that jail."

"Any idea why someone would kill Coleman?"

Another shrug. "There's a tight Coos Bay–North Bend network in here. Maybe a year ago, I heard he was heavy into the fentanyl and heroin business on the coast. Maybe he stepped on somebody's toes?"

"Okay, let's go back in time. Tell us about the fight you had with Sonny Jenson."

"*That?* It was a joke, man. He was supposed to be this model citizen and all, but he was a bastard to work for. Always nitpicking and bitching, but he got majorly pissed when his pool had a pea-green algae bloom. He tried to blame it on me, but I'd been telling him to buy more chlorine for weeks. So he says he's not going to pay me."

"What did you do?"

"I told him that wasn't fair, that I wanted my money. He said I couldn't talk to him like that, got right in my face and pushed me hard, told me to get out. I shoved him back and he went into the pool, wearing his Rolex and carrying his cell phone. He came up sputtering, and I told him I quit. Okay, when I left I decorated his Prius with a key." Kenny showed a sly smile, as if relishing the memory. "That hybrid was his pride and joy. Mr. Environmental Consciousness."

"You didn't hit him?"

"Hell, no. He didn't have a mark on him, but he called the cops and said I not only scratched up his car but that I physically assaulted him. All I did was shove him back. Luckily, my stepdad was his business partner. But Walter wouldn't have done a damn thing to help if my mom hadn't stepped in."

"That's the whole story?" He nodded. "Do you know of anyone who would've had a reason to kill Sonny?"

Did his eyes widen ever so slightly? I wasn't sure. "No. As I said, he had this do-gooder reputation, at least that's what he wanted people to think. I knew better. He was two-faced. Maybe somebody else knew that, too."

I paused for Claire to finish typing. "Tell us about the night of the murder, where you were, what you did."

"I was getting ready to meet my girlfriend when a job came up. I used to deliver drugs now and then to make extra money for college." He paused to gauge my reaction. I didn't give him one, although I was annoyed that Rori had left the drug dealing out. He continued. "I drove down to Barview, but the guy never showed."

"And nobody saw you there?"

"I don't think so. I waited in the parking lot of a little market there. I thought it was a little weird, but I had had no-shows before."

"Did you take the order on your cell?"

"No. A dude named Jerry Crawford gave me the job in person. He was an ecstasy supplier. I only sold that and weed. No hard shit."

"Did Crawford corroborate your story?"

Kenny laughed. "No. He claimed he didn't even know me."

After getting Crawford's full name, I said, "Is he still in the area?"

"Nah. I heard he moved up to Seattle."

"Any reason to think he set you up?"

Kenny twisted a lock of his beard between his thumb and forefinger. "He was no friend of mine, but I don't know why he'd do that."

"Who was *his* source?"

"He never said. Maybe someone at Sloat."

"The trucking company?"

"Yeah, you know, they sometimes have a little extra room in their trucks."

"That's what your grandmother told me. Didn't Howard Coleman drive for Sloat?"

Kenny shrugged. "I don't know."

"What about the witness who put you in the vicinity of the murder scene?"

"Marion the Librarian?" He exhaled a breath in frustration, and I caught Claire suppressing a smile. "Her name's Ellen Dempsey. Volunteers at the library or some shit. She picked me out of that lineup, said I was at the parking lot of the Jiffy Mart in Crown Point." His eyes flared ever so slightly. "She was mixed up or lying. I wasn't anywhere near there."

"Did you have a cell phone with you that night?"

He shook his head. "My cell crapped out the week before, so I didn't ping any towers, if that's what you're asking."

"Okay. Tell us about your arrest and the interrogation."

He looked away and blinked rapidly to stave off the tears, and when he looked back the tough-guy veneer was gone. "Stupidest thing I ever did, that confession. Cost me my freedom, every-thing." His voice got thick. "I still…can't explain it."

"Try," I said, nodding encouragement.

He twisted his beard again. "So, two county deputies came by the next afternoon and asked me to come down to the station. Said they had some questions but didn't tell me anything else. No big deal, I figured, so I drove down there and walked in without a worry in the world."

"Then what?"

"Two dudes named Wilson and Drake got me in a conference room and started in on me. Dumb and Dumber. At least that's what I figured at first. They told me about the murder, said they just wanted to get a statement from me. I was shocked as hell. I mean, it was Sonny Jenson. I knew him. They went right to the run-in I had with Sonny, and I told them everything that happened. I remember Drake saying something like, 'You must have been really angry to shove him in the pool and mark his Prius up like that, right?'" Kenny sighed and shook his head. "I should have seen where he was going with that, and I should have been more respectful of the dude. I mean he was dead. But reality hadn't sunk in yet, you know?"

"Sure. I can understand that."

"Anyway," Kenny went on, "I said, 'Yeah, Sonny was an asshole. I was pissed at him.'" Shame and disgust washed over his face. "They used that quote at the trial and kept coming back to it."

I nodded, glancing at Claire, who was capturing every word and gauging Kenny's body language with quick glances.

"Wait, it gets better," Kenny went on. "I made my next mistake when they asked me where I was the night before." He shook his head and swung his eyes from me to Claire and back again. "I should have told the truth—that I was out dealing. But I told them I was just riding around, no place in particular. *Stupid*, huh?"

I shrugged. "I can see why you didn't want to admit what you'd been doing."

"Yeah, whatever. So they jumped on it. They were, like, you were riding around *alone*? What sixteen-year-old does that? And I had to admit no one could back up my story. Arnold, my attorney, had me tell the truth later, but then Crawford denied it, so I was up shit's creek. Still, I wasn't worried at the time, because I hadn't been near Sonny's place. Drake ducked out after my dumb lie, and I caught a glimpse of him talking to Sheriff Stoddard. He kept ducking in and out of the rest of interrogation like he was taking orders or some shit."

"About what time did Drake talk to the sheriff the first time?"

"I don't remember exactly. Maybe two hours in."

"Did they video or record your interrogation?"

"Nope. Wilson took notes. That was it. They said at the trial that their system was down, which was bullshit. So Drake comes back in looking all grim. He says, 'This isn't looking good for you, Kenny. We just found your fingerprints on a bloody glove in the garage. You were there, weren't you?' I said, 'Yeah, I was there, but not last night. I worked there for six months, you know.' Then they started in on me again, made me go back over everything in detail, over and over. I'm getting tired. I'm famished. But they just kept hammering on me."

"Did you ask for a lawyer?"

"Yeah, sort of. Somewhere along in there I said, 'You guys really think I killed Sonny Jenson? Maybe I should get a lawyer.' Wilson pipes up, 'You can do that, Kenny, but it's just going to make you look even guiltier. Work with us to clear this up, we're almost there.' Drake goes out and talks to Stoddard again. He comes back in and says, 'We've got a warrant to examine your car and the clothes you were wearing last night. We're going to find a lot of Sonny's blood, aren't we, Kenny?' I told them they were crazy, and they started in all over again."

"Did they bring you anything to eat or drink?"

"Some water a couple of times. No food."

"What time did they bring the first water?"

"I don't know. I lost track of time. I kept asking when we're going to finish, when I could go home. They kept saying 'we're getting close, Kenny.'" He twisted his beard and smiled with one side of his mouth. "Yeah, close to breaking me. By this time, they're trying to get me to describe what happened in the garage, you know, suggesting how I might have clipped Sonny with a hammer or something and robbed him. Asking where I put the wallet and jewelry and stuff. I'm telling them they're full of shit, but they keep going over it again and again."

"What happened next?"

"Drake goes out to powwow with Stoddard, and when he comes back he says, 'Look, Kenny, we don't need a confession.

We've got everything we need to convict you. And we'll try you as an adult, so you'll be looking at the death penalty.' By this time, I'm barely listening, tired, confused as hell, and scared shitless. Drake says, 'If you cooperate, things will go a lot better for you. Whataya say? Get it off your chest, and this'll all be over.'" Kenny paused and closed his eyes.

"What did you say?"

"Nothin'. I felt defeated, like they had me, and it was my fault somehow, you know? Like I shouldn't have been out dealing, I shouldn't have lied about it, I shouldn't have shoved Sonny in the pool... I was this bad kid, and I deserved this." He exhaled a deep sigh. "And I would have done anything at that point just to get them off my back. *Anything.*" He shook his head with a look of utter bewilderment. "I can't explain it, man. They brought a statement in, and I signed it. Didn't even read the fucker."

Claire gasped audibly at that point.

I went back over everything, filled in some more blanks, then wrapped it up, telling Kenny I'd be in touch. He looked at me, and a faint smile formed on his lips. "So I passed the test?"

I glanced over at Claire—whose expression made it clear she was in his camp. My gut was made up, but my head wasn't all the way there. "Yes, I've heard enough that I want to move ahead. What happened to you is disgusting, but I won't kid you, Kenny. The odds are against us. And I've got a lot of ground to cover before I'll know what, if anything, can be done."

He nodded, and I saw the same glimmer of hope I'd seen in Rori's eyes. "Thank you. All I want is a shot, Mr. Claxton."

The room fell silent while we waited for a guard. Finally, he said, "Grandma Rori told me you're staying down by Yoakam Point. How's the surf been?"

"It was big earlier in the week, maybe eight, ten feet, with a stiff offshore breeze blowing the tops off the waves," I said.

His eyes softened with a deep longing I understood instinctively. I kicked myself for painting such an appealing picture.

"Was anybody out at Bastendorff?"

I hesitated, and Claire cut in, looking at me. "That's a beach north of us, on the other side of the point." She turned to Kenny. "You used to surf there?"

"Yeah, I did." His gaze shifted past us to something far away, although there was nothing but a cement block wall behind Claire and me. "God, I'd love to be in the water again," he said in a barely audible voice. The door rattled open at that point, and a guard unshackled him and took him away.

Chapter Seven

Archie saw Claire and me approaching the car from halfway across the prison parking lot and started in with a high-pitched whine and little yelps of sheer excitement. He was a good sport about waiting in the car, but it was clear we had exceeded his patience level. I called Rori and filled her in while Claire took Arch for a short walk. Rori thanked me, and I warned her to keep her hopes and expectations in check. "I know," she said. "I've been down this road before, but this feels different, somehow."

I had a feeling, too, although I didn't share it with her. Mine centered more on that sensation you get with the first step onto a slippery incline.

We stopped at a city park on the way out of Salem, and after retrieving a dirty, chewed-up tennis ball from the trunk and locating a grassy field devoid of other dogs, we set about playing a game Archie never tired of—fetch the slobber ball. As Claire and I took turns tossing the ball as high and as far as we could, we kicked around what we'd just heard from Kenny Sanders. At one point, Claire said, "What really struck me were the mistakes he made during the interrogation. I could just see a sixteen-year-old boy screwing up like that, and he was so ashamed of his mistakes. If he was trying to play us, he would've been making all kinds of excuses for his behavior, but he just laid it out there." She scowled and shook her head. "And then they trapped him with his own guilt and told him a confession was his only way out. I was skeptical about coerced confessions going in but not anymore. That was pure manipulation."

I chucked the ball, and Arch gave chase, catching it about four feet off the ground on the first bounce with the agility a wide receiver could only dream about. "I agree. Two experienced investigators played him like a fiddle. My take is that once Wilson and Drake suspected he lied about his whereabouts, they made up their minds they had their killer. It sounded like the sheriff had them turn up the heat, and their tactics after that were textbook for how to wring a confession out of a naive suspect."

Claire nodded. "They rationalized their behavior by telling themselves he was guilty, so anything goes."

"Exactly. And the heat was on, because Sonny was a high-profile citizen."

Claire rolled her eyes. "Dad, I know you're not an appellate attorney, that it's specialized work, but can't someone bring the interrogation tactics up in an appeal? They acted like the Gestapo."

"It was probably already adjudicated and apparently didn't go anywhere. The appellate courts start with the presumption that the original verdict was arrived at fairly, that the interrogation tactics were not coercive. The appeals attorney has to come up with incontrovertible evidence that the tactics used were out of bounds, and that's a very heavy lift, since there's only Wilson's notes for a transcript leading up to the signed confession. It's Kenny's word against two adult detectives and the sheriff."

Always a good sharer, Arch brought the ball back, stood in front of Claire, and dropped it. She faked a forward throw and threw it behind her, which didn't fool him for a moment. "What about Marion the Librarian?"

"That's a problem, but eyewitness accounts are overrated. I need to know exactly how that lineup was conducted. But, again, if Wilson and Drake manipulated her somehow, it would be damn hard to prove." I paused for a moment, recalling Kenny's reaction. "To be honest, that was the only part of his account I wondered about."

"Why?"

I shrugged. "I caught something around his eyes when the subject came up."

"Oh, a tell. How cool. I didn't pick it up. You think he lied to us?"

"In general? No. About the librarian? Maybe. I need to talk to her."

Claire frowned. "And the only other witness is dead."

"Which is where we came in." Arch brought the ball back, a manic gleam in his eye. He didn't drop it for me, though, making me tug on the slobbery thing before he released it. I threw it into a stand of trees and high grass off to our right to give him a challenge.

"So, what do we do now?" Claire asked.

I watched Arch root around in the grass for a while. "If Kenny didn't kill Sonny Jenson, then someone else did. Maybe it was a violent robbery, but the odds are someone in his family or circle of friends and acquaintances did it. That's where I intend to focus. And it can't be just some alternate theory for the murder, either. It has to be new, rock-solid, exculpatory evidence to give us any chance at all."

Claire fixed me with her sapphire blues. I knew that look. "I'm glad I came, Dad. This isn't right. I want to help."

Chapter Eight

"I thought you were on vacation, Calvin," my good friend and private investigator of choice, Hernando Mendoza, said the next morning.

"I am, but I stumbled into a case that looks interesting. Probably won't amount to much."

His baritone laugh exploded through my cell phone. "I have heard that one before."

I sketched in Kenny Sanders's situation. "Look, Nando, all I need you to do is find an address and phone number for a guy named Jerome Crawford. He's probably in his early- to mid-thirties. Used to live and work here in Coos Bay or North Bend and has since moved up to Seattle. I'd like to talk to him, if possible."

"Very well. I will search for Mr. Crawford. How is Claire?" Nando, it turned out, was quite fond of my daughter, and Claire returned the affection, often referring to him as her Cuban uncle. "Surely she is not encouraging this activity during your time together."

"She's fine, and as a matter of fact she's hell-bent on helping me."

Nando laughed again. "A Ph.D. for an assistant. You have come up in the world, Calvin."

———

Claire and I drove into North Bend for a late lunch at the Fishmonger that same day. Where to begin an investigation was always an issue, but I've had luck with the lovers of people I'm interested in. They always know things others don't. "Is Sissy Anderson working today?" I asked the hostess as she gathered a couple of menus before seating us. "We'd like to be served by her, if possible." The hostess nodded, seated us, and after saying something to a waitress across the room, sent her to our table.

Rail thin with spiky russet hair and sharp features, Sissy poured our waters and regarded us warily with pale blue eyes. "What can I do for you?"

"I'm Cal Claxton, and this is my assistant, Claire. First, let me say we're very sorry for your loss." That was a gamble, because I had no way of knowing whether she and Coleman were on or off at the time of his death. She nodded faintly, her eyes registering obvious pain. "We'd like to speak with you for a few minutes, perhaps when you get off this afternoon."

She stood upright. "About what?"

"About Howard Coleman. We're representing Kenny Sanders."

Her eyes narrowed down. "I already talked to the sheriffs, and I got nothin' else to say to you or anybody else. Now, what can I get you to eat?"

I folded, sensing it was futile to press her. We went ahead and ordered, and when Sissy sashayed off, Claire looked at me and shook her head. "Jeez, Dad, I've told you before that sometimes you need a lighter touch. Let me handle this." Sissy served up our lunch in stony silence, and when we finished eating, Claire said, "I know you have things to do, so go ahead. I'll order a coffee and wait around for her to get off. I'll text you when I'm done."

I wished her luck and drove over to Coffee and Subversion, which was doing a nice late afternoon business on both sides of the house. When Rori saw me, she pointed toward the back room. "Get a coffee, Cal. I'll be there as soon as I can." I ordered a double cappuccino from Anthony, and when he served it up, he said, "This is on the house, Mr. Claxton. We're so glad you're taking on Kenny's case. It means the world to Rori and all of us."

I was a little taken aback that word of my involvement had leaked out, but I managed a cordial nod. A few minutes later I stood sipping my coffee and browsing the framed pictures on the wall of Rori's office. Shots of Krysta and Kenny at various ages were interspersed with larger family groupings, several of them taken on and around a fishing boat called *Skipjack*, a stout-looking, oceangoing craft with an upswept bow.

"That's my dad's boat, at least it was." Rori had come up behind me. "He was a third-generation Coos Bay fisherman." She pointed at another shot of her standing in front of the boat, struggling to hold a silver salmon nearly as long as she was tall. A big man wearing a baseball cap and sporting a dark beard stood next to her. "That's me with Dad when I was thirteen. I crewed for him summers. Fishing's hard, dirty work, but I loved it."

"Is he retired?"

A grim smile. "He was, but it was forced. The salmon runs became so depleted he had to sell *Skipjack*. Died of a stroke a year later." She looked at me straight-on. "That's why we're so desperate for jobs around here. We didn't take care of our fish or our trees." She laid a hand on my arm. "But enough of this. Tell me what the next steps are while I write you a check."

I filled her in on my plan, as unformed as it was, and at her insistence went back over everything I'd told her on the phone, including that her grandson was in reasonable spirits and looked good physically.

"That's reassuring," she said. "He stays fit to protect himself. He's under constant pressure to join one of the white suprem- acist groups, and of course the black and Latino gangs hate anyone with blond hair and blue eyes." She allowed the thin- nest of smiles. "I told him sometimes you gotta go along to get along, but he's determined to stay on his own. I worry about him constantly."

"He seems mentally strong, Rori. That's crucial." It was as much comfort as I could offer. I knew how dangerous it was inside, how the weak were mercilessly exploited, how prisoners were forced to take sides for protection. Making it as a loner was tough, making it as a twenty-year-old loner, ws nearly impossible.

She forced a smile and twisted the fingers of one hand in the other. "I still worry."

I had her give me the contact information she had for Kenny's stepdad, Walter Sanders. She said, "By the way, Walter called last night and wanted your cell number. I gave it to him. I guess the word's out that you're going to bat for Kenny. Funny thing, he said he wanted to talk to me about Kenny. That's a new attitude for him."

"By the way, I was surprised that your barista, Anthony, knows about my involvement."

Rori shot me a guilty look. "I told him. Guess I shouldn't have."

"Going forward, we need to keep this on a need-to-know basis, Rori."

The guilty look lingered. "Agreed, but that ship's probably already sailed, Cal. News travels fast in this town."

She also gave me a cell phone number for Sonny Jenson's wife, Twila. "What can you tell me about her?"

Rori's eyes softened. "Twila was crazy about Sonny, took his death really hard."

"What's she doing now?"

"She sold their place on Crown Point and moved into town. Has an art gallery on Anderson near the museum and a beach house off Seven Devils Road, south of here. She's an artist, still painting."

Rori had no contact information for Kenny's attorney, Arnold Pierce. "He's still in Lincoln City, far as I know. Nobody's missed him around here." A quick Google search turned up nothing.

"What about the appeals attorney?" I asked next. The failed appeals were water under the bridge, but I did want to touch base at some point, time permitting.

"Her name's Mimi Yoshida. She has an office in North Bend." Rori scrolled through her phone contacts and read off the number.

It wasn't until I jotted the name and number down that a bell rang. "*Mimi Yoshida?*"

She nodded, the surprise in my voice causing one of her eyebrows to tilt. "Well, her first name's Mimori, but she uses Mimi. We lost those appeals, but I don't blame her. Once you're convicted, the system's pretty much rigged against you. She's a good attorney, Cal."

I thought of the remnants of the name on the business card I'd taken off Howard Coleman's body—"Mi i Yo da." It fit perfectly. "Duly noted," I replied, not wishing to explain the source of my reaction. I glanced at my watch. "Uh, I've got some time right now. Would you mind calling her to introduce me and see if I can drop by for a quick chat?"

She obliged, Mimi was available, and a meeting was arranged. Before I left I said, "One other thing. When you next talk to Kenny, you need to tell him I can't help him unless he tells me *everything.*"

She looked surprised. "Was he holding back?"

"On a couple of points, maybe." I held her gaze for a moment. "That goes for you, too, Rori. You should have told me Kenny was pushing drugs the night of the murder."

She broke eye contact, and her look turned contrite. "Of course. I'm sorry, Cal. It won't happen again. I just—"

I held my hand up. "I can't help you unless I know everything."

———

Google Maps and I found Mimi Yoshida's law office—a converted Craftsman home—just off Virginia Avenue in North Bend, a couple of blocks from the Coos County Courthouse. She had a one-person operation like mine, relying on a buzzer to announce visitors. "Make yourself comfortable. I'll be right with you," a voice called out from behind a partially closed door at the other end of the waiting room. She entered shortly after I took a seat. Petite, with luminous dark eyes set in an oval face of remarkable symmetry, she approached with an outstretched hand and an air of confidence.

After introductions and some small talk, I got right to the point. "Were you, by any chance, in contact with Howard Coleman, the man who was murdered on the Millicoma River?"

Her head retracted slightly. "Why yes. Why do you ask?"

"My daughter and I discovered his body. We were fly-fishing that day. I found a business card in his fishing vest with the remnants of your name and phone number on it."

Her hand moved reflexively to her mouth. "Oh, my God. That must have been horrible. And now you're representing Kenny Sanders." She looked puzzled.

I explained how I happened to overhear Rori talking at the bookshop about Howard Coleman and how I felt drawn to Kenny's case. When I finished, I smiled. "It was quite a coincidence, and now this."

She smiled back. Mine was sheepish, hers knowing. "Jung called it synchronicity," she said. "Buddhists believe there are no coincidences, that everything happens in relation to everything else. I think you're wise to follow your instincts."

I shrugged. "Time will tell, I suppose. Can you tell me about your business with Coleman?"

"I had none, actually. He called about ten days ago and set up an appointment." She winced perceptibly. "We were supposed to meet today, as a matter of fact."

"Did he indicate what he wanted?"

"All he said was he had a legal matter to discuss. When I asked what it was, he wouldn't say."

I paused for a moment, taking the comment in. "Do you think he came to you because of your connection to Kenny Sanders?"

"Perhaps. Arnold Pierce has left the state, so he may have turned to me, although I only handled the appeals, of course." She showed the knowing smile again but leavened it with modesty. "After all, synchronicity seems to be at work here."

"Do you know where Arnold Pierce is?"

Her face registered something just short of disgust. "He got disbarred last year. Gross incompetence, I heard. I don't know where he is." She looked at me. "Our appeal was strong, Cal. We provided the court with documentation of the length of the interview—eleven hours and forty-three minutes—proof that the Sheriff's Office ordered no food or drinks for Kenny during that time, and we had a neurologist from OHSU testify regarding the teenage brain's lack of full development. And, of course, Kenny completely recanted the confession the day after he was arrested." She shook her head in disgust. "It wasn't enough for the appellate court. They let the decision stand."

She began describing the appeals, but I was much more interested in the crime itself. I listened politely and cut in at the first opportunity. "What's your take on the original trial?"

"Circumstantial. There was one witness who put Kenny in the vicinity of the crime, and Kenny had a previous confrontation with the victim, but there was scant physical evidence connecting him to the actual murder scene. And the witness from the jail, of course"—Mimi rolled her eyes clear to the ceiling—"they added him because they knew their case was weak."

"What about the fingerprint on the bloody glove?"

"It was a jump ball from an evidentiary standpoint. The prosecution argued Kenny used the cloth side of the glove to wipe the murder weapon clean of prints. Arnold Pierce countered that Kenny used the glove while gardening. The jury apparently believed the prosecutor's theory. Pierce's cross of the crime scene tech was a joke."

"I understand Walter Sanders and Sonny Jenson were business partners. What can you tell me about that?"

"Not much. They were partners in a company called Condor Enterprises, kind of a mixed bag of businesses. A couple of years after Sonny's death, they sold some key parcels of land to Bexar Energy, the Canadian company behind the LNG project. I think they made a killing, but I don't know the details."

"Did Walter have an alibi the night Sonny was killed?"

"I think so. You can check the discovery. I have all the files. I don't think it came up at trial. Pierce argued it was a robbery gone bad."

"What about Sonny's wife, Twila? She have an alibi, too?"

"I believe so."

I sat back in my chair. "Anything else you think I should know?"

She squinted, as if in thought, then furrowed the smooth skin of her forehead. "The sheriff. His name's Hershel Stoddard. He was up for re-election a couple of months after the trial in a tight race. That arrest and conviction put him over the top. I think he engineered Howard Coleman's testimony." She paused, her eyes registering anger. "And the District Attorney, a guy named James Gillespie, never should have put Coleman on the stand. He suborned perjury, in my opinion."

"Did you pursue that angle?"

A pained look spread across her face. "I would have, but we didn't have the funds to hire an investigator." She shook her head. "Stoddard's running again for sheriff as we speak, unopposed this time."

A client of Yoshida's arrived, but she had him wait while she helped me cart three boxes of files covering Kenny's case to my car. As if on cue, Claire texted me that she was ready to be picked up. I gave Mimi a card, thanked her, and as I was leaving said, "I'm curious. Why are you practicing law here on the coast and not in Portland, where there's a bigger demand for appellate attorneys?" I could have added, "and where you could triple your income."

She smiled, but it failed to hide the displeasure the question caused her. "My grandparents had a truck farm northeast of here. They were interned at Tule Lake during the war and lost two hundred acres of prime land, their house, everything. My grandmother died in the camp." The corners of her mouth lifted again. "I wanted to honor their memory and show my family belongs here in Coos County, too."

I smiled at Mimori Yoshida. "That's a fine reason, indeed."

———

On the way back to the Fishmonger I thought about Mimi's reference to synchronicity. As a practicing cynic, I believed there was plenty of chaos in the universe, that not all things happened for a reason, at least one a mere mortal could discern. However, I had to admit that in this case events conspired to draw me in, and now it seemed crystal clear why—to free an innocent kid facing a lifetime of incarceration.

Maybe the Buddha was on to something, I conceded.

Chapter Nine

Claire was standing outside the Fishmonger when I pulled into the parking lot, and I knew from the look on her face that she had gotten Sissy Anderson to talk. It was the same self-satisfied look I got when she beat me at Scrabble, which was hardly justified since nearly everyone beat me at Scrabble. "How did it go?" I said as she hopped in the car, and we began threading our way through North Bend toward the beach house.

She laughed. "It didn't, at least at first. I waited for an hour while she and another waitress got the place ready for the dinner service. I think the fact that I waited that long convinced her I really wanted to talk. Finally, she brought two cups of coffee over and sat down. I told her about you, Dad, how you're willing to step up for the little guy, that both of us felt Kenny Sanders was innocent, that we wondered if Coleman's murder was somehow connected to Kenny's case. She listened, but I didn't think I was getting through till I mentioned finding his body." Claire snapped her fingers. "She started to cry, and I held her for a while. She dropped her defenses after that."

My gut clenched a little. "It's as if Coleman wanted her to talk."

"Yeah, something like that—anyway, that's when she told me Coleman felt bad about Kenny."

I braked hard as the huge cab of a logging truck changed lanes in front of me like a sports car. "Because he lied at the trial?"

She nodded emphatically. "She said he lied so he wouldn't have to serve so much time, but he never believed his testimony would convict a young kid like that."

I puffed a breath. "The lies we tell ourselves. Then maybe that's the reason he contacted Yoshida. He was going to fess up, get it off his chest after all this time."

Claire looked confused. "Who's Yoshida?" I told her about my meeting with Kenny's appellate attorney and the appointment Coleman had scheduled for this very day. Her eyes got big, reminding me of when she was a little girl. "You think he was murdered to silence him?"

I shrugged. "What else did Sissy tell you?"

"Well, she said he was finally making some good money, and they were talking about buying a house and getting married." Claire swallowed a lump of emotion. "She loved the guy a lot, Dad."

"Did she say anything about his work?"

"I pressed her on that. All she would say was that he was driving a truck."

"For Sloat, right?"

"Yep." Claire gave me a look. "That company keeps popping up."

We were nearly to the bridge at the South Slough. A brisk westerly breeze kicked up, flecking the bay with white caps and flooding the car with a delicious ocean scent. "It does, indeed. What else did you learn?"

"When I asked her who she thought killed Coleman, she began to shut down again. I pressed her, and she finally said, 'Claire, if I told you who I suspected, it would put you in danger, too. And I like you.' I said, 'Why don't you go back to the sheriff if you know stuff?' She laughed at that, Dad. She said, 'Because I know what's good for me, that's why.'"

"What did you say to that?"

"I told her she didn't have to face this alone, that we could help. That was basically it. She knows a lot more. I'm sure of it."

"How did you leave it with her?"

"We exchanged cell numbers, and I told her I'd check back to see how she's doing. She didn't say no." Claire smiled a little self-consciously. "I like her, too, her grit."

"Excellent, Claire. That was damn fine investigative work." I was proud of my daughter, but the mention of her being in danger chilled the pit of my stomach. That was definitely not what I had in mind when I accepted this job.

———

As the sun descended that evening the wind died, and the ocean glassed off to a pane of deepest blue. The fog bank that loitered offshore for the past couple of nights had finally burned off, and we were treated to a sunset whose colors morphed from shimmering gold, to rose, to violet, before dying in a shroud of deep purple. I was busy in the kitchen cleaning and shelling a batch of razor clams we'd picked up in Charleston. Claire—who was on the phone with her boyfriend—called me into the living room to witness every color change.

The stress of that day was sloughing off nicely.

I had linguini at the boil and was sautéing the clams in olive oil, butter, garlic, and white wine when she came into the kitchen. "We need a salad and garlic bread," I said before asking, "How's Gabriel?"

"Oh, he's fine." She smiled shyly. "Says he misses me." She began extracting ingredients from the fridge.

"Do you miss him?"

The smile again. "Yeah, I do. But I, ah, told him I might stay here even longer now that I'm assisting you. We're crunching data right now, and I can do that anywhere. I don't have to go back to the Gulf until June."

I looked up from the skillet. "You've really helped, Claire, but now that I've accepted Kenny as a client, you shouldn't feel obligated to stay past our planned two weeks."

She wrinkled her brow. "I can't just trot off knowing Kenny Sanders is sitting in that prison, Dad. It's obscene."

"I know you feel strongly, Claire, but—"

She held up a half-peeled cucumber as if to throw it at me. "If you stay, I'm staying, Dad. You need help. Sissy Anderson might be the key to this, and I know I can get her to talk."

"What about Gabriel?"

She smiled again. It had a hint of slyness around the edges. "Absence makes the heart grow fonder, right?"

By the time the linguini with razor clam sauce was ready, Claire had built a killer salad and had taken the sourdough baguette, slathered in garlic butter, from the oven. The question of her possibly staying longer was settled, so we moved on to other, safer topics as we enjoyed the meal.

My feelings were mixed. She *was* the best damn assistant I'd ever had, but there was a troubling aura of violence surrounding this case. *We'll see how it goes*, I told myself.

———

My cell riffed a digital blues number shortly after dinner. "Mr. Claxton?" a gravelly voice said. "This is Walter Sanders. I'm Kenny Sanders' stepdad. Do you have a moment?"

Ex-stepdad, I thought but didn't say. "Sure. What's on your mind?"

"Aurora told me you've taken up Kenny's cause. I think that's commendable. I'd like to meet with you to discuss how I can help."

I told him I had a flexible schedule, and we agreed to meet in two days, when he returned from a business trip. When I tapped off, Claire said, "Who was that, Dad?"

"Kenny's ex-stepdad. He wants to get involved in the investigation."

Claire raised an eyebrow. "The guy who left Kenny's mom wants to help now?"

"That's what the man said."

She smiled conspiratorially. "Well, that's interesting."

———

Around two the next morning, Archie awakened me with a salvo of furious barking. I got up, followed my dog down the stairs, and went out on the front porch, holding him by his collar. My car looked undisturbed, but I tensed up when something moved in the shadows beyond it. It took me a few moments to realize it was the breeze stirring some of the gnarled cedars on the lot. Archie finally stopped barking and pulling at his collar. "What was it, Big Boy?"

He looked up at me and whimpered his equivalent of "I don't know."

As I returned to my bedroom, it occurred to me just how isolated this property was.

Chapter Ten

"He is dead."

"Who's dead?" I said to Nando, ignoring his annoying habit of beginning a phone call as if no time had elapsed from the last one. It was nine the next morning, and Claire and I were out walking on the beach with Archie.

"Jerome Crawford. He died of a fentanyl overdose about six months ago. You were right. He was living in Seattle, near the university. The police report said it was accidental. A friend of mine at Seattle PD confirmed it was a typical overdose, nothing suspicious. Is this a problem, Calvin?"

"No, I don't think so. It was a shot in the dark to begin with."

"What else can I do for you, my friend?"

I thought for a moment. "Nothing at this point, but I'm starting to turn some rocks over, so stay tuned."

"Very well. How is my favorite environmental warrior?"

I gazed down the beach. Claire was dancing thigh deep in the frigid surf in an attempt to coax Archie into the water. My dog was having none of it. Unlike most Aussies, the only water Archie liked was the kind he could drink out of a bowl. I wasn't even sure he could swim. I laughed. "She's fine. Staying a while longer to give me a hand in this investigation."

The line went quiet for a few seconds, a tacit indication of Nando's disapproval. "Noble endeavors can be the most dangerous. Be careful, Calvin."

———

Claire's job that afternoon was to find out everything the internet could tell her about Condor Enterprises, the company Walter Sanders and Sonny Jenson owned at the time of Sonny's death. I wanted that information before I met with Walter. I confess to an ulterior motive here—I figured a shit job like that might dampen her enthusiasm for an extended stay. Not that I didn't love her company. Far from it. But the image of Howard Coleman's hog-tied body kept coming back, reminding me of what Nando said.

My job was to interview Marion the Librarian, also known as Ellen Dempsey. I reached her at the North Bend Library, and she agreed to speak with me during her lunch hour, suggesting we meet at the Mediterranean Café across the street from her place of employment. Arriving early, I stopped to read a plaque on a bronze statue as I walked up Union Avenue to the café. Louis J. Simpson—scion of an early timber and fishing magnate— founded the fair city of North Bend, I learned, and bequeathed a large swath of oceanfront land, including Cape Arago, to the state. That was back when timber and salmon seemed inexhaustible, and the earth was a degree and a half cooler. I looked at the beneficent face and wondered where Louis would have come down on the LNG controversy. Would he see the gas from coal tar as the next natural resource to exploit, or would he favor protecting the bay and its watersheds and tempering the planet's fever? I had no answer.

I was halfway through a cup of coffee when Ellen Dempsey entered the café wearing a pink blouse like she'd mentioned on the phone. The blouse had pictures of puppies on it, which she hadn't mentioned. Mid-fifties, her no-nonsense face framed in a helmet of silver hair, she marched straight up to me and introduced herself. After ordering lunch—dolmathes for me and a lamb gyro for her—I thanked her for coming, but before I could say the next word she teared up. "My heart goes out to that young man, Mr. Claxton. I think it was a travesty that he was tried as an adult." I nodded encouragement, and she brought her moist eyes up. They were clear and intelligent. "But I told the truth at the trial. I saw Kenny Sanders in that parking lot that night."

"Why did you notice him?"

"I was the last customer out of the Jiffy Mart before they closed and was getting in my car when he drove up. He got out, and just for a second I thought it might be my nephew, Andrew. They're both tall and blond. I didn't say this at the trial, but that's really why I remembered him. Anyway, he went up and rapped on the door, but they didn't let him in." She shook her head and allowed a weak smile. "I remember thinking he probably wanted to buy one of those stupid energy drinks."

"How close were you to him?"

"Oh, I was parked across the lot, so maybe forty, fifty feet."

"Did you recognize the make of the car he was driving?"

"Not at the time. I'm hopeless when it comes to cars. But I was able to pick it out—a blue Toyota Camry—at the Sheriff's Office from a book they showed me. That make and model matched what Kenny was driving at that time."

"What caused you to come forward, Ellen?"

"I saw his picture in the paper and thought I recognized him. I knew from the newspaper account that the murder happened around the time and place I saw him, so I called the sheriff's office."

I had her take me through the way Wilson and Drake conducted the lineup from which she identified Kenny. I found no fault in the process—such as putting him in with a group of men with significantly different ages and/or physical characteristics—but when she finished, I said, "Did you see Kenny *before* the lineup?"

She paused for a moment. "Why, yes, I did. When I came back the next day for the lineup, they happened to bring him in handcuffs down the hall where I was sitting. I didn't say anything, of course. It was just a coincidence."

I exhaled a breath, shaking my head. "That was no coincidence. They *wanted* you to see him. That exposure predisposed you to pick him out of the lineup. It was a trick, guaranteed to make his the only familiar face in the group."

Her eyes expanded as she took that in, then her expression grew resolute. "It may have been a trick, Mr. Claxton, but I identified the right person. I'm sure of it." She welled up again. "I didn't want to have any part of that trial, but I felt…I felt it was my civic duty to tell what I saw, what I was *positive* I saw."

"Do you think Kenny Sanders killed Sonny Jenson?"

Her lips started to quiver, and tears sprang from her eyes. "That's just it. I don't, Mr. Claxton, I don't." She pushed away from the table and walked out just as our plates arrived. The stuffed grape leaves were delicious, but I ate only one before I paid the bill and walked back to my car.

———

"I'm sorry, but I'm going to have to ask you to leave," Rori said to a burly man with a shaved head and a beard resembling a worn Brillo pad. I had driven over to Coffee and Subversion to talk to her, and the man walked in just ahead of me. Her eyes were narrowed down, her face a hard mask of determination. "This is a no firearms zone. *Out.*"

Burly smirked, and when he turned to face Rori I saw the semiautomatic in a holster strapped to a belt buried in his stomach flab. "Oregon's an open carry state. You're impinging on my Second Amendment rights."

Rori stepped up and got right in his face, the magenta streaks in her hair like flames. "And this is private property, so take your pop gun someplace else or I'll call the cops."

Burly stepped back a full pace, his face contorted with indignation wrapped in hatred. "I have a God-given right to carry this sidearm, bitch."

Rori laughed and closed the space between them again. "You wouldn't know a God-given right if it bit you on the ass. Now get out of my store."

"Fucking libtard," he mumbled before turning and executing an ignominious retreat.

Rori turned to me and shrugged. "I get these open carry boobs all the time. They usually put up a better fight than that."

My turn to laugh. "Next time tell them how you really feel."

She joined in the laughter, and after Anthony made us coffees, we went to her office. She studied me as I took a seat, saying, "You look serious, Cal. What's up?"

"I just finished talking to the librarian, Ellen Dempsey." Rori's face tightened. "The detectives pulled a sly one on her." I described the walk-through ploy and the potential impact on an unwitting witness like Dempsey. Rori's face relaxed a little. "That's the good news." I met her slate-blue eyes. "The bad news is I'm concerned that Kenny lied to me about not being at that convenience store."

"What do you mean?"

"Despite the sheriff's clumsy attempt to manipulate her, I found Dempsey's account credible. She got a good look at the person from about fifty feet and picked out the make, model, and color of the car he was driving. She thought at first he was her nephew, so it stuck in her mind. She wasn't under any stress at the time, which accounts for a lot of misidentifications. No wonder the jury believed her." I paused to let it sink in. "Did you talk to Kenny about telling me everything?"

"Yes. I spoke with him yesterday. He got the message, Cal."

"Good. I'm going back to see him as soon as I can arrange it."

Recovering her composure, she said, "You're not doubting his innocence, are you?"

"Something's off about this, and I need to know what it is." She started to respond, but I cut her off. "Kenny mentioned that his supplier, a guy named Jerry Crawford, might have been getting his drugs from someone working at Sloat Trucking. What can you tell me about that?"

"Like I told you before, some of the truckers are involved in the drug trade, but, you know, there's a lot of that on the Oregon coast. Max Sloat runs the company with an iron fist and spreads a lot of money around the city and county, too. She's never been accused of anything as far as I know."

"She?"

"*Maxine* Sloat. Took over the company from her dad about fifteen years ago after he died in a boating accident. He and Maxine went out fishing, and only Maxine came back." She paused for a moment. "My dad hated her old man. The talk—no, it wasn't talk—the *whispers* were that he started abusing Max's younger sister after his wife died. Anyway, Max took over the business and quadrupled it. Surprised the hell out of everyone." Rori smiled and shook her head. "She's a piece of work."

"Did Arnold Pierce dig into the Crawford angle? I mean, he sent Kenny off that night on what might have been a wild goose chase to ensure he wouldn't have an alibi."

Rori's face grew hard again. "Arnold didn't follow up on much of anything. But I was less involved at that time. Stupid me thought Kenny was being well represented. Maybe you could talk to Crawford?"

"Can't do that. He died of an overdose six months ago."

"Oh. Another dead witness."

"Yeah. Unfortunately."

We left it at that, and as I was leaving Rori took my hand in both of hers and squeezed it. "Cal, Kenny didn't kill Sonny Jenson. You've got to believe that."

I left without saying anything. I didn't like playing the hardass, but I disliked being lied to even more.

Chapter Eleven

The wind died off that afternoon, the Pacific glassed over, and another big swell marched in from parts unknown, maybe Siberia. When I arrived back at the beach house, Claire announced, "We're going over to Bastendorff Beach to eat and watch the surfers. I've got food, beer, and everything else we need packed up and ready to go, except for firewood. We can stop and get some on the way." Archie loved picnics and danced around as if he understood every word Claire said. Or maybe it was just the word "food" he picked up on.

A broad, sandy cove connecting Yoakam Point to the south jetty of the Coos Bay inlet, Bastendorff was one of the best surfing venues on the coast, according to my daughter. We arrived in the parking lot at the same time as a battered van that promptly disgorged two young men and two young women—twentysomethings in wet suits carrying surfboards that looked surprisingly short. As we unloaded, Claire smiled a greeting. "Surf looks good today. Are you guys local?"

They all nodded, and one of the girls said, "Best spot on the coast, especially with a north swell like today."

Claire held the smile, which few mortals could resist. "Did you by any chance surf with Kenny Sanders?" The question came out of the blue, surprising me as much as them. A young man with a chiseled jawline and dark hair pulled into an unruly ponytail spoke first. "We all did. Kenny wa—*is* one of my best friends." His eyes moved to me, then back to Claire. "Are you the two Rori Dennison hired to get him off?"

Claire shot me a look that said "how the hell did he know that?" She hadn't heard that news in Coos Bay travels fast. "Yes, we're representing him," she answered.

"That's cool," chiseled jaw said. The others nodded in agreement.

Claire quickly added, "You think he's innocent?"

Chiseled jaw didn't hesitate. "Damn straight. I grew up with Kenny. He never killed that dude. He doesn't have a mean bone in his body."

"Yeah," one of the young women interjected, "the only thing Kenny Sanders ever killed were the waves here at Bastendorff."

"Best damn goofy foot who ever surfed here," the other young man chimed in.

Claire got chiseled jaw's name— Stu Foster—and gave him a card she fished from her wallet. The smile again. "I'd like to ask you a few questions about Kenny. Call me at that number when you can talk." Foster said he would, and the look on his face made it clear he would keep his word. The smile.

As we followed them down to the beach, I said to Claire, "Nice work."

"I figured we might learn something from him."

"Agreed. By the way, what's a goofy foot?" I grew up in Southern California, but the surfing bug never really bit me.

She laughed. "A surfer whose stance is left foot back, right foot forward, which means that if he's going to his right, like the break here, he has his back to the wave. It's harder to surf that way if you're going right." She looked at me and added, "Did Stu's response make you feel a little better?"

I already briefed her on my talk with Marion the Librarian, and she knew it had shaken my confidence in Kenny's innocence to some extent. I exhaled a long breath. "It shouldn't have, but it did. Funny. We come out here and run into Kenny's best friend just when I needed it. What were the chances?"

Claire laughed again. "Synchronicity, Dad. The universe's winking at you. They seemed straight up to me, and I don't think they would've defended Kenny out of loyalty alone."

My gut said the same thing.

The sun got lower, the waves got bigger, and finally there were just a handful of surfers still out, including the four we'd met. Paddling out was harrowing enough, but surfing the sheer green walls was a profile in physical courage—a near free fall at the takeoff, followed by a game of chicken as they cut back and forth, staying just ahead of the collapsing wave that threatened to engulf them. The juxtaposition of that raucous, joyous scene with the image of Kenny locked in a cell was stark and discomforting, and I was sure Claire was having similar thoughts.

We'd found a good spot on the beach, made a fire ring with loose boulders, and soon had a blaze going. By the time the sun set and the surfers had all paddled in, we were sipping cold beer and cooking shish kabobs made with marinated chicken, onions, peppers, and mushrooms. Archie had snuggled in next to Claire and was watching her every move with doleful, coppery eyes, a shameless ploy to con a couple of chunks of chicken. He succeeded, of course.

By the time we finished our meal, the sun had extinguished itself in the Pacific, leaving nothing but a thin, blood-red line above the horizon. Claire extracted a notebook from her backpack and squinted into the rapidly fading light. "Okay, here's what I've got on Condor Enterprises. It's a weird mash-up of businesses, sort of a mini-conglomerate, if there is such a thing. Sonny Jenson started a company fifteen years ago and grew it to a fleet of five fishing boats harbored in Charleston, three motels strung along the coast, and four laundromats. He and Walter Sanders joined forces in 2012 and named the company Condor Enterprises.

Walter is a real estate broker, and they started investing in land in Coos and Douglas counties."

"Mimi Yoshida told me they sold some land to the Canadian company pushing the LNG pipeline—Bexar Energy, I think it's called. She said they made a lot of money on the deal."

"Exactly." Her face twisted up like she'd licked a lemon slice. "Nobody should make money on that fracked gas time bomb. California and Washington both turned the terminal down. If Oregon goes ahead, the facility will be the largest greenhouse gas polluter in the whole state just to refine the stuff to natural gas, and then it gets shipped and burned in the Far East."

I winced. "You and Rori need to talk."

"I've read her stuff. It's spot-on. But it looks like the Feds are behind the project now, so they may get steamrolled. Anyway, Condor did cash in. In 2016—three years *after* Sonny was murdered—they announced the sale of five hundred and twenty-five acres of land at Jackson Point to Bexar, the Calgary-based oil and gas company pushing the deal. That rounded out a key piece of acreage needed for the facility. Condor also sold them a number of parcels in southern Oregon on the projected route of the pipeline, if it gets built."

"Did Twila Jenson keep her share of Condor?"

Claire shrugged her shoulders. "I don't know. It's privately held, of course, and I couldn't find anything relating to its current ownership."

"What do Condor's holdings look like now?"

She laughed. "Way different. The fishing boats, laundromats, and motels were liquidated. Now it's a string of adult video and novelty shops, video lottery joints, and several payday loan businesses. I googled a couple of the adult shops." The lemon face again. "They're beyond gross."

"Did you run across anything of interest on Sonny?"

"Sort of. Kenny may have thought he was an asshole, but he was a contributor to the Boys and Girls Club, started a sailing club for kids, that sort of thing. From all outside indications, he gave the impression of a model citizen, just like Kenny said."

"What about Walter Sanders?"

"Nada. The man keeps a low profile."

At this point, we were working on dessert—roasted marshmallows. I liked mine golden brown and Claire preferred hers flambéd. Archie wasn't interested. Claire peeled some charred skin off hers and popped the soft white core in her mouth. "So what do you think?"

I studied the smoldering embers for a couple of beats. "I'm wondering where Condor got the money to buy all that land. I mean, their original holdings didn't sound capable of spinning off that much cash, and banks usually shy away from real estate speculation."

"Good point. I hadn't thought of that."

"The shift in their business focus is curious, too."

Claire skewered another marshmallow and hoisted it over the embers. "Right. It's definitely not the direction Mr. Civic Responsibility would have liked."

I bit into a perfectly cooked marshmallow and nodded. "Thanks to you, I'll have some good questions for Walter Sanders and Twila Jenson." I looked straight at my daughter, whose face was partially illuminated by the glow of the fire, the visible portions reminding me more of her mother than I would have wished. Suppressing a grin, I said, "If you hang around, there'll be more of this kind of shit-work research, you know."

Her laugh rang with a tease. "Nice try, but you can't scare me away that easily." The unshadowed portions of her face grew resolute. "I'm committed to this project, Dad. And you need me."

I smiled across the fire ring, not wishing to start a fight I would surely lose.

Chapter Twelve

The next day broke clear and calm. To the south, the whitewashed lighthouse was the only vertical feature on the low rock surface of the cape, whose tabletop flatness gave it the appearance of a man-made structure. The sky and the ocean were so near the same deep blue that it was hard to distinguish one from the other. The view was wondrously disorienting.

We were up early and took a long walk on the beach, during which Archie once again kept a wary eye on the crashing surf. Claire laughed when he retreated from the incoming surge, not even willing to get his paws wet. "He's such a wuss when it comes to water, isn't he, Dad?"

I chuckled. "Yeah. He's been that way since he was a pup. If we're out jogging, he'll go around puddles, and if it begins to rain, he starts lobbying to turn around."

"Of course, you just keep soldiering on, right?"

"Hey, it's Oregon. If we waited around for the sun, we'd never get anything done."

Back at the beach house, I was cooking breakfast when Claire's phone chirped. It was Howard Coleman's grieving girlfriend, Sissy Anderson, inviting Claire to lunch in Charleston. "I think she's trying to decide whether she can trust me," Claire opined after accepting the invitation.

We just finished breakfast when Walter Sanders lit up my cell phone. "I'm going to be out your way later this morning, Mr. Claxton. You're in the Phillips's house, right?" I said I was, not surprised he knew where we were staying. This was Coos Bay, after all. "I could stop in if you're going to be around." I told him that would be fine.

When I tapped off my cell, I turned to Claire and grinned. "Not a bad start to the day. People are coming to us."

Claire spent the morning out on the deck crunching data and making phone calls. I checked my messages at my Dundee office and returned a half-dozen calls. My neighbor to the north in the Dundee Hills, Gertrude Johnson, who was also my accountant, called midmorning. To call Gertie a fiscal conservative would be understating it, so not surprisingly she didn't like it when I told her I might extend my stay. "You sure you want to do that, Cal? Your billable hours are in the shitter."

"I've got a client here," I countered, wondering once again how she always managed to put me on the defensive. I went on to explain the situation Claire and I found ourselves in.

"Well," she said when I finished, seemingly unimpressed with the humanitarian aspects of the case, "at least you're spending some time with your daughter, although it doesn't sound like quality time to me. What are you billing out at?"

"Uh, that hasn't been decided yet."

She cleared her throat. "Figures. Okay, Cal, but keep in mind you've got a quarterly tax payment due next month and the work on your office roof is scheduled for next week." I told her not to worry, that I was on top of things, but when I hung up, my stomach did a slow half twist. I knew Rori Dennison couldn't afford my full rate and extending my stay could also mean the loss of other, more lucrative business. I walked out on the deck and watched the waves pounding the rocks at Yoakam Point for a few minutes, which made me think again of Kenny Sanders sitting in prison on this beautiful day.

Find a way, I told myself.

———

A couple of quick barks from Archie told me my guest had probably arrived. I opened the front door just in time to see a man flick a lit cigarette into the yard as he got out of a forest green Land Rover. He turned to look at me through mirrored Ray Bans and produced a practiced smile that radiated from his tanned face. "Mr. Claxton, I'm Walter Sanders." He swept his arm in a grand gesture and turned up the wattage, revealing a narrow gap in his front teeth that gave his smile an unintended leering aspect. "Love this place. Best views on the coast, and you're above the tsunami zone. If it ever comes on the market, I'm buying it."

I invited him in, and we made small talk while I brewed us each an espresso, which we carried out to the west-facing deck with Archie following. A soft breeze had materialized, and we could hear the rhythmic thrum of the surf mingled with the squawks and caws of seagulls. He took a sip of his coffee and waited for me to initiate the discussion. I sat there without speaking. He'd called me, so the ball was in his court. He was trim with thinning hair and small, close-set eyes. Finally, he showed his bleached white teeth. "So, I heard you were taking up Kenny's cause, and I wanted to thank you, first of all, and offer my help."

I drank some coffee. "What did you have in mind?"

"Well, I doubt you're working *pro bono* here. Perhaps I could help out with your fee. I mean Rori can only sell so many used books."

"She'd appreciate that, I'm sure."

"What, ah, arrangements have you made with her?"

"She's given me a small retainer. We haven't discussed my fee going forward." I cringed a little inwardly. Why did I always put off discussions of money with clients? I could see Gertie shaking her head. "If you want to help financially, you should discuss it with her."

"Fine. I'll do that."

I sipped some more coffee and eyed Walter over the rim of my cup. Never a trusting soul, Archie had taken up a spot at the corner of the deck, affording a clear view of our guest. His chin rested on his white paws, but his coppery eyes were wide open.

"I take it you've had a change of heart regarding Kenny?"

The gapped, too-white teeth again. "Well, you know, Cal, it was a shock to lose my friend and business partner, and my marriage to Kenny's mother was on the rocks." He lowered his gaze. "I, ah, took the easy way out, I guess. Not my finest hour."

His use of my first name irritated me for some reason. "And now you want to help Kenny. Why?"

He brought his eyes back up, but they avoided my gaze. "I think I should have been more supportive, and I want to make up for it, if possible. Kenny's a good kid. How's he making out?"

"Okay, considering. I'm seeing him tomorrow for a second interview." I paused. "If it wasn't Kenny, then who do you think killed Sonny?"

He shrugged. "I don't know. Maybe a burglary gone bad? After all, Twila's jewelry was cleaned out and never showed up. They're a lot of meth heads here on the coast, Cal."

The first name again. "It looks like Condor Enterprises landed on its feet after your partner's death. Is Twila Jenson an active partner?"

His eyes registered a note of surprise. I knew more than he thought I did. "Fortune has favored us, Mr. Claxton. Mrs. Jenson is not active in the management of the company."

"A silent partner, then?"

A forced smile with fewer teeth. "We don't discuss our ownership. You know how that works."

"Of course. Uh, I'm still getting caught up on the facts of the case. Where were you the night Sonny was killed?"

He held the smile, but his eyes narrowed perceptibly. "Am I a suspect?" I didn't answer. "I was in Newport on business. You can check the motel records."

"I will." At this point, Walter turned the tables and began probing me about the nascent investigation. The only things I shared were that I believed Kenny was innocent, that his confession was a travesty, and that I intended to take a fresh look at all the evidence. As I showed him out, I said, "I'm sure Rori will appreciate your offer to help. As I said, you need to work that out directly with her. You do understand, however, that she's my client and, as such, I can't discuss the details of the case with you."

"Of course," he responded.

After he left, I called Rori and told her that Walter Sanders would probably offer his financial assistance. I told her I would work for two hundred dollars an hour plus expenses, that the time I had in so far was gratis, and that I would let her know when the retainer was consumed. She agreed to the terms, then said, "I don't think I can take money from Walter, Cal."

"Why?" I was pretty sure I knew the answer but asked the question anyway.

"It's tainted, that's why. He got a lot of his money by selling land to Bexar Energy. How can I lead the effort against the LNG terminal and take his money?"

"Hear him out, Rori. He said he had a change of heart regarding Kenny. If the man wants to help, I'd let him."

She sighed heavily into the phone. "I'll listen, but...don't worry, Cal. I'll pay you no matter what."

"I'm not worried, Rori. Look, if you have to carry this alone, we'll work something out, okay?" I could hear Gertie's tsk-tsk. Always a pushover, that was me.

"Thank you."

"And keep in mind that Walter isn't entitled to any information about what I'm doing."

"Of course. You don't suspect him, do you?"

"Should I?"

A pause. "Never liked the man, to tell you the truth, but according to Arnold, Walter was up the coast that night on business."

"Was there any animosity between Sonny and him?"

"Not that I know of."

"We'll see if his alibi checks out. The way Sheriff Stoddard seized on Kenny, my guess is his investigators didn't spend much time looking anywhere else."

———

I'd just finished a call confirming our next interview with Kenny when Claire returned from her meeting with Sissy Anderson. "You're back early. How'd it go?"

She plopped down in a chair across from me and brushed a strand of hair from her forehead. "Whew. That was interesting. The poor woman. She's really a mess. She spent a long time telling me about Coleman's funeral. Only a handful of people showed up, and she couldn't get any of his friends to be pall-bearers. She was really hurt, Dad."

"Maybe they were afraid, given the way he was killed."

"She didn't say that, but it's possible. I felt horrible, tried to comfort her as best I could. We ended up skipping lunch and ordering drinks. She told me Coleman had gotten involved with a couple of guys who're brothers, real lowlifes, to use her term. I asked if they worked for Sloat Trucking, too. She said she thought one did, but she wasn't sure. She wouldn't tell me what they were involved in."

"Kenny already did—the fentanyl trade. Names?"

"I'm coming to that. First, I asked if she'd told the sheriff about them. She said she hadn't. She said she'd gotten a death threat by phone, something like 'keep your mouth shut or you'll die like your boyfriend.'"

I winced inwardly at the threat. The stakes just went up several notches. "Why is she talking to us, then?"

"I told her we'd keep what she told us in confidence. I also think she's wary of the sheriff because of what Howard was into.

Maybe she's afraid of being implicated. Anyway, I get around to asking their names. She starts to answer, then looks across the room and gets this horror-stricken look on her face. 'Oh, shit,' she says, 'speak of the devil. One of them's here. Go out the back, through the kitchen, *now*.' I did what she told me." Claire made a face. "Didn't get any names."

"Did this guy see you?"

She shrugged. "I don't think so."

"Did you see *him*?"

"Just a glance as I was getting up. He was right out of central casting—big guy with stringy, dark hair and inked-up neck and arms. I called Sissy when I got down the road, but she didn't return my call." Claire leaned back and exhaled. "So, what do you think, Dad?"

I got that cold feeling in my stomach again. "I think Sissy Anderson knows a hell of a lot, and now I know why she's not talking to the sheriff. And I think it was no coincidence that one of Coleman's business associates was at that restaurant. The word's obviously out that we're nosing around."

"I'll get the names, Dad, and I'll find out what else she knows. I think she was going to really open up."

I latched onto her eyes. "I also think it took at least *two* men to kill Howard Coleman." I let that sink in. "We need to be very careful, Claire."

What I didn't say was that I decided to find a way to get Claire back to Harvard just as soon as I could figure out how to do it.

Chapter Thirteen

Big drops of spring rain thumped down on the skylight in my bedroom, awakening me early the next morning. I made my way to the kitchen, with Archie following closely behind, and after feeding him I ground some deep roast beans for a double cappuccino. An incoming front had stalled, leaving the Pacific oddly undisturbed except for a fine, crepe-like texture imparted by the rain. By the time Claire got up, I'd finished my second cup, and an hour later we loaded Archie into the back seat and headed for the State Penitentiary to interview Kenny for the second time. The sodden skies, the steady rain, and the feeble, gray-suffused light seemed to cast a pall on our departure that morning. I didn't pay that feeling any heed, but perhaps I should have.

"So, how's Gabriel?" I asked as we turned off Highway 101 at Reedsport and began threading our way into the Coast Range. Claire had been on the phone with him a long time the night before, and now she seemed a bit withdrawn.

"He's okay, I guess."

"Just okay?"

She sighed. "He said my work on the Gulf was important, that I shouldn't compromise it by staying here with you."

This was thin ice. I proceeded cautiously. "Any truth to that?"

I could feel the heat of her glare on the side of my face. "Maybe in some abstract way, but that isn't the point, Dad."

"What is the point?"

"The point is, it's *my* decision to make, not his. I'm a big girl. I don't need any mansplaining."

"Does he do that, talk down to you?"

"There've been a couple of instances, but this is the most conspicuous. I cut him some slack earlier." She smiled. "He's from Argentina, after all."

"No slack this time?"

"I hung up on him."

"Oh. Do you think that was wise?"

She shrugged. "I don't know. I just resent him trying to tell me what to do." I glanced over at her. Her brow was scrunched up, and she was chewing on her lower lip. "Do you think I screwed up?"

"Hard to say. I understand why you were upset, but maybe a little 'splaining of your own would have helped him understand where you're coming from. Maybe he's never encountered someone as fiercely independent as you, Claire."

She nodded and went silent, obviously mulling the situation over.

———

The rain let up on the west side of the Coast Range, and by the time we reached the prison it was little more than a mist, although the cloud ceiling remained low and ominous. In the weak light, the administration building looked more institutional and decidedly less inviting than on our previous visit. We cleared security and then waited for better than thirty minutes before two guards brought Kenny in. Claire sucked a quick breath, indicating she was as shocked at his appearance as I was. His eyes were hollow, his hair and beard disheveled, and he bore the purplish-yellow remnants of a bruise covering most of his left cheek and the pink outline of a stitched-up gash above his right eye. He also walked with a slight limp.

"Top of the morning," he said, forcing a thin smile. "How are things in the free world?"

"What happened to you?" I said, dispensing with formalities. "That bruise and gash look nasty."

"Clumsy me, slipped and fell. But the STM team thinks some-body beat me up. They—"

"What's an STM team?" Claire cut in.

"Security Threat Management. They, ah, maintain order around here. Anyway, they wanted me to name names. They have a hard-on for the white supremacists." He chuckled. It rang with bitterness. "But snitching's not good for your health."

"So you didn't tell them anything?" Claire said.

"Nope. I want to keep breathing." He sighed and fidgeted with his beard. "I just found out yesterday that I lost my job in the commissary. I'm back to cleaning showers and latrines. I'm supposed to"—he made quote marks with his fingers in the air—"think it over. If I continue to stonewall, I could get time in solitary. But they have a nicer word for it—segregation."

"*What?*" Claire said, looking at me with pure disbelief. "They can't do that, can they?"

I nodded, and Kenny just laughed, eyeing Claire. "This ain't a gentlemen's club."

"So, what faction of the white supremacists are trying to recruit you?" I asked.

"The EK, European Kindred. They pretty much run the show in here. They beat me just to soften me up. 'You're young,' they told me. 'You'll see the light soon enough.'"

"What did you tell them?" Claire said, her eyes wide.

"I spit in their faces, and that got me the pretty bruise to go with the cut above my eye and a couple of kicks in my knee." Kenny pointed at his cheek and laughed. "It was deep purple a couple of days ago, but no busted bones."

I leveled my eyes at him. "So you're not going to bend, I take it."

He looked at me, and I saw Rori in his eyes. "No, I'm not going to bend. I reject their ideology, and I told them so."

A surge of admiration for him was swamped by a wave of anxiety. Kenny had a survivor's instinct and a backbone of steel, but was it enough?

Claire said, "Can you intervene, Dad, get him some protection?"

Before I could answer, Kenny's hand shot up like a traffic cop's. "*No*. No legal intervention. That's worse than being a snitch. A guy tried that two years ago. Word leaked out in no time. I watched them carry him out under a bloody sheet."

A few moments of silence followed as reality set in for Claire and me—Kenny Sanders was on his own in prison, and the only way to help was to get him out. We moved on to the questions we had for him, which encompassed going over his story again in some detail. Nothing of interest surfaced on the first pass. Claire asked if he had heard anything from the Coos Bay network about who Howard Coleman was working with in the drug trade. He hadn't. When asked if he knew much about the business Walter Sanders and Sonny Jenson were involved in, he said, "Walter didn't talk about business around the house."

"Were they getting along?" I asked. "Any tension that you were aware of?"

He shrugged. "They weren't best buddies or anything. It was always about the money with them, but I wasn't paying much attention, to tell the truth." He smiled with half his mouth. "You know, just your typical teen—sex, surfing, and rock 'n' roll."

I circled back to my principal interest—Marion the Librarian's testimony. "I talked to Ellen Dempsey about her court testimony." I leaned in and focused on his face. "She's positive that was you she saw at the Jiffy Mart. I gotta tell you, Kenny, she was very convincing."

The words seemed to brush him back. He tried a defiant look, but it came out defensive. "So?"

"Were you there or not, Kenny? Cut the bullshit. We can't help you unless we know the truth."

He exhaled a long sigh, closed his eyes, and when he reopened them, they had softened. It seemed a weight had been lifted from his shoulders. "Okay, she was right. I stopped there to get a can of Crunk." I must have looked puzzled, because he added, "An energy drink. I was on my way over to Sonny Jenson's."

Claire gasped. I said, "Why?"

He shook his head and swept his eyes from me to Claire and back again. "You'll never believe me."

"Try us."

"I decided to stop by and apologize before the drug run. I'd been thinking it was the right thing to do. Sonny never should have acted like he did, but I shouldn't have shoved him in the pool and scratched his car. That was juvenile, man. Grandma Rori was on my case to do it. She has a way of getting in my head."

"What happened?"

He sighed again, and a tear broke loose and slid down his bruised cheek. "Sonny has a long driveway. I didn't want to just drive up and make a big entrance, you know? So, I parked around the corner. I sat there for a while and finally decided to go through with it. I was out of the car when I heard a car coming out of his driveway."

"Who was it, Kenny?"

Another tear broke loose. He scrubbed it off his cheek with a fist. "My mom."

"Your mom," I echoed, trying to keep my voice calm. "Did she see you?"

"No. She turned right on Stanton and headed off."

"What did you do?"

"I got in my car and left."

"Why?"

He looked at me like I'd just asked the dumbest possible question. "I wasn't going to apologize to some asshole who's porking my mom."

"Why did you come to that conclusion?"

"Walter was out of town, and she told me she was going to her yoga class that night."

"That was it?"

"No. I walked in on them once at a party at his place. They looked all guilty. I let that one slide. They'd both been drinking."

"So, your mom was having an affair with Sonny Jenson?"

"Yeah, I think so. Don't blame her much. Walter was such an uptight prick."

"Did she kill Sonny?" Claire said.

He turned and glared at her. "*No*. Not a fucking chance. She was kind to a fault, generous, a vegan who wouldn't eat anything with eyes. No, she couldn't have done it."

I leaned in again. "But you lied to protect her."

"I did. I figured nothing good would come of me saying anything. I just put it out of my mind like it never happened, and then the roof fell in on me the next day."

"Did you talk to her or your grandmother about it?"

"No. Not a word to either of them. And they never brought it up with me."

"Did your grandmother know about the affair?"

He shrugged. "I don't know. She and Mom were pretty tight."

I leaned back and studied him for a few moments. The room was quiet, and the still air smelled of disinfectant overlaid with body odor. "Why tell us this now?"

"Because I believed you when you said you need to know everything. I just needed a push, I guess. You're my last hope."

"What if we conclude your mother did it?" Claire said.

He looked at Claire and showed his first genuine smile. It brimmed with confidence I hadn't seen before. "You won't. Somebody else killed Sonny, not her and not me."

"Is there anything else you haven't told us, Kenny?" I asked.

He swung his gaze back to me. "No. Nothing. I swear."

That's where we left it, and as the guards reappeared, Kenny asked again about the surf conditions on the coast. Claire answered, mentioning how we'd run into some of his friends, including Stu Foster, at Bastendorff. As he was being led away, he turned back to us. "Tell them I miss them and to ride some waves for me."

———

The rain picked up again, and the somber sky matched our mood on the return trip. A beat-up, dark-colored Ford Explorer was well behind us but caught my eye. It occurred to me I'd seen a similar looking car earlier that morning on the way to Salem. We kicked Kenny's interview around, and at one point Claire said, "So, can a dead person be charged with murder?"

"No. A person must be capable of mounting a defense to be chargeable. A dead body can't do that. But we can investigate whether or not Krysta Sanders killed Sonny Jenson."

"And if we find something, what then?"

I puffed a breath. "I'm not completely sure. But having a dead perpetrator muddies the water, for sure."

We drove on in silence for a while. The traffic was sparse except for the cab of a logging truck right behind me, looking for an opportunity to pass on the winding road that followed the course of the river. Was it just me, or were these trucks without their double load of timber always driven like Indy race cars? That seemed to be the case, and I would have pulled over to let this guy pass, except there were no pullouts along that narrow stretch of highway.

We came to a downward slope with a sharp bend that followed the river, a section of white water visible straight ahead in the thin light. The road was slick with rain, and I braked the Beemer as I approached the turn. I glanced in my rearview mirror. The logging truck, which had backed off my bumper, now came at us like a runaway freight train. I realized with horror that if I continued braking he was going to hit us. Between the river on one side and the steep embankment on the other, there was no place to go, so I hit the accelerator knowing full well I probably wouldn't make the turn.

Too late. "Look out!" I yelled just before the massive cab hit us. The crunch of metal, Claire's scream, and Archie's yelp rose up in one agonizing sound as my old Beemer launched off the bumper of the truck like a sharply struck cue ball, skidded off the highway, and down the embankment into the rain-swollen river.

My head smacked into something that didn't give, and total blackness ensued.

Chapter Fourteen

A voice cut through the black shroud enveloping me. "Dad, Dad, are you okay?" I opened my eyes and saw Claire's face through a pink film. Her eyes were wide and her hair a wet, tangled mass. I tried to lift my head, but the effort caused my pink-filtered world to take a nauseating spin.

"Stay down, Dad. You've got a big gash on your head. I'm going up on the road to flag someone down. You're still half in the water. *Don't move.*"

I groaned. "Are you okay?"

"Yeah. I'll be right back. *Stay where you are.*"

I tried to sit up, but the nausea only intensified. "Where's Archie? Where the hell's my dog?" But Claire had set off up the bank, and I got no answer. I slipped back into darkness again.

Time ceased, but when I heard voices I fought my way back to consciousness. The effort felt like scaling Half Dome. "How you doin', Buddy?" a strange, deep voice said. "I'm holding a cloth against your head wound to stop the bleeding. Try not to move."

I opened my eyes. A big man with a friendly face knelt next to me. Claire stood behind him with a worried look. "Dad, Dave stopped to help. He called an ambulance."

I forced myself up on my elbows, ignoring the nausea. "You okay, Claire?" I repeated.

"Yes, Dad. I'm okay."

"Where the hell's Archie?"

Her face crumbled. "He got swept downriver. I'll find him, Dad. As soon as I know you're taken care of. Don't worry."

I tried to stand, but the effort sent the world spinning again. "He can't swim, Claire!"

"We don't know that, Dad. I'll find him."

I turned my head enough to see the car and waited out a wave of nausea. Submerged nearly to the roofline, the Beemer had done a one-eighty and sat rocking in the swiftly moving water, the trunk pushed into the back seat. "You saw him go?"

"Not exactly. He was knocked into the front seat between us. Thank God the current helped me open the door, and when the water began to pour in, he just froze. I had to push him out to get at you." Claire looked down and teared up. "That's the last I saw of him." She raised her eyes, her face filled with guilt and remorse. "You were unconscious, Dad. I had to get you out of there."

Her words were like a hot knife in the heart. "Claire, I understand," I managed to say. "How the hell did you get me out?"

She shook her head with a look of bewilderment. "It's all a blur now. By the time I got your seatbelt off, the water was neck high. I crawled over you and grabbed your head to keep it above water. When I kicked away from the car, I almost lost you to the current, just like Archie."

"No. Archie's not lost." I pointed downriver. "Go find him, Claire. Now."

My daughter shook her head defiantly. "Not until I get you in an ambulance."

———

By the time I reached the hospital in Reedsport, my mind was clearer, although I was racked with a throbbing headache and an abiding fear my dog was lost. A nice surgeon named Dr. Patel stitched me up—eighteen closely spaced sutures—and told me that I had to stay overnight for observation in view of the concussion I'd sustained. I was still on a gurney in the hall when a Douglas County deputy sheriff approached, took a detailed statement, and told me where my totaled BMW would be towed.

"No," I told him, when he pressed me about the truck cab that hit us, "I didn't get a license plate number. All I know is that it was humongous, just the cab, no trailer or load of timber. Dark blue or black, I think, massive bumper. Driven by a man, no passenger."

"Can you describe him?"

"No. All I got was a quick glance when the cab first came up behind me. He was wearing shades, I think, and a cap." I paused for a moment. "There was something weird about the cap—it had something sticking up from it." I made a circle with my thumb and index finger and held it above my forehead. "Like this."

"An action cam? He was making a video?"

I shrugged and shook my head. "Who knows? There was plenty of action, that's for sure."

"Do you remember anything special about the truck?"

I paused, closed my eyes for a couple of beats, then shook my head. "Sorry. All I can tell you is that it was huge, dark blue or black."

"When did you first notice it behind you?"

"Maybe fifteen miles out of Reedsport. Came out of a dirt road, I think, and stayed right behind me. I didn't think anything of it, and I sure as hell didn't think it could blow me off the highway like that."

The deputy shook his head. "Those trucks are designed to haul forty-five tons of logs. He swatted you like a fly."

"I think it was deliberate. The driver held back until I braked before the curve, then he accelerated to make contact. I also suspect a Ford Explorer might've been involved, although I'm less sure of that. It may have followed us to Salem and back to tip off the truck." I described what I'd noticed and went on to tell the deputy about the investigation Claire and I were conducting in Coos Bay.

"You think this was in retaliation for your investigation?"

"Could be." The deputy asked a few more questions, took some notes and left, promising to stay in touch. He was polite and professional, but I had the distinct impression he thought my story might have been hatched in my recently bruised brain.

They trundled me to a room in the hospital, and after the nurses left I got up and started pacing. I felt trapped—no phone, no transportation, no word from Claire, and a headache that lingered. I'd refused the opioids they offered, preferring to keep my head clear, and the acetaminophen I did take barely touched the pain. Claire finally arrived two hours later, and when I saw the look on her face, my heart sank.

She hugged me gingerly, her eyes wet with tears. "We haven't found him yet, Dad. I had to come to see how you are." She examined my sutures and made a face. "How are you feeling?"

"Fine," I snapped.

"Good. A deputy's taking me back upriver so I can keep searching." She handed me my cell phone. "I retrieved this out of the car. It's dead. So's mine. We'll need new ones right away."

"What about your computer?"

She made a face. "It's gone, too, but I'm fully backed up on the cloud. There's still plenty of light, Dad. I'll find Archie."

"*We'll* find him," I said. She started to object but thought better of it. She knew her dad.

She turned around while I slipped on my still-wet clothes. "Come on, let's get out of here."

———

The deputy escorting Claire offered to help in the search, but he got a call, so he handed us a GPS tracking device, and said he'd find us downriver when he got free. "I'll be back," he promised as he dropped us off where Claire had stopped her previous search. "Good luck."

The trail along the river alternated between wide and unobstructed to nonexistent. We worked our way downstream, calling out Archie's name periodically. But we heard nothing in response except the slosh and clatter of the river, sounds which had lost every bit of their charm for me. It was close to nightfall, and we were miles from the crash scene when the deputy sheriff finally reappeared. We were both exhausted. I was still fighting nausea, my head pounded, and my legs felt like rubber.

After apologizing for not showing up earlier, the deputy said, "Don't worry. Your dog probably got out somewhere and is lost. Aussies are good swimmers."

Claire and I exchanged worried glances. I said, "One big problem is that his tag has my phone number on it, and my phone is dead."

"Don't worry, people around here love dogs. If someone finds him, they'll probably call us if no one answers your phone."

We reluctantly gave up the search for the night and got a couple of motel rooms in Reedsport after devouring a meal at the diner next door. The motel clerk was able to arrange for an Uber to pick us up the next morning at first light. Claire fussed about the dressing on my head wound, which was stained with soaked-through blood. I told her we'd worry about that after we found Arch, but I failed to mention that my head still pounded like a bass drum. The sleep I managed that night was punctuated by a vivid dream. In the dream Claire crept into my room, and as I lay there, kissed me gently on the forehead. I saw her looking down at me surrounded by an aura of soft light I knew to be the spirit of her mother. When I awoke and opened my eyes, my cheeks were wet with tears.

I was pulling on my mud-stained jeans at five the next morning when it hit me. I rushed over to Claire's room and pounded on the door. When she opened it, I said, "If Archie's alive, I know exactly where he is!"

The Uber driver pulled over at the curve where the truck hit us. I told the driver to wait while I worked my way down the rocky bank to the water's edge with Claire following. A shelf of intermittently exposed rock roiled the current in this section of the river. The opposite bank, maybe thirty yards away, was heavily wooded and lined with dense vegetation. I cupped a hand to my mouth. "Archie. Are you over there, Big Boy?" I called out. "Archie."

Two sharp barks came in immediate response. Claire gasped and clutched my arm with both hands. "Hey, Archie, we're here. Show yourself." The bushes moved, and my dog appeared on the bank, barking, squealing, and wagging his entire backside.

He barked again, and then, before we could stop him, plunged into the river and started swimming.

"Oh, shit!" I yelled and started moving downstream, where the current was pushing him. But his head stayed up, his stroke was strong, and although he veered off at a forty-five-degree angle, he made steady progress, bobbing and weaving through the exposed rocks. I waded into the water and, when I finally grasped him by the collar, let out a sigh of relief.

Behind me, Claire said, "So, you can swim, after all." This set us both into a fit of uncontrolled laughter.

The Uber driver wasn't happy about taking a wet dog on board, but we promised him a generous tip. We were down the road when Claire said, "Okay, how did you know he'd be there, Dad?"

"It was simple. He's a smart dog, right? If he'd gotten out on *our* side of the river, he would have come right back to the crash scene. He didn't. So, he either drowned or got out on the other side. If he got out on the opposite bank, he would still come back to the crash site, right? It was the last place he'd seen us. While we went downstream looking for him, he came upstream looking for us. And we missed each other."

Claire rubbed Arch between his ears. "Why didn't he swim across and wait for us at the crash site?"

I laughed. "He can swim, but he still hates the water. It took seeing us to get him to go back in, I guess." We rode in silence for a while, with Archie between us. My head still ached, but my daughter and my dog sat next to me, safe and sound.

The world was right-side up again, and the shock of having almost lost everything dear to me was slowly replaced with a cold fury and a grim determination to find out who did this and how it related to the Kenny Sanders case. Vacation was over, and this would no longer be a part-time job.

Chapter Fifteen

The front moved on, and the slanting rays of the rising sun glittered on the water like schools of silvery bait fish. Claire was still asleep, and Archie and I were down on the beach for a slow walk the next morning. The swell had lessened somewhat and was now bearing in from due west, the waves breaking with sharp, crisp claps that carried in the morning air. I didn't see any snowy plovers, so Arch was off leash. To his credit, he'd learned to ignore the gulls who were out in full force, squawking and cawing as they swirled around looking for breakfast. I watched my dog maneuver along the waterline, keeping his paws dry as usual. If he was traumatized by the car crash, he didn't show it. That was no surprise. Archie lived in the moment, and at this moment he was enjoying a beach walk on a clear, brilliant morning.

I, a less centered being, was deep in thought instead of relishing the beauty of my surroundings. The question of what the hell to do next was front and center in my mind.

When I got back to the house, I was surprised when the landline in the kitchen rang. "How is the Oregon coast, my friend?" a familiar voice greeted me in a suspiciously cheery tone for this early in the morning.

"It gets more interesting by the minute. Where did you get this number, Nando?"

"Your daughter called me last night. She said your cell phones were lost in an incident. I am calling to learn more about what happened and offer my help. The people who did this to you need to be taught the severest of lessons. How is the head wound?"

"It's on the mend, and Archie's good to go, too."

After I described in detail what happened, Nando said, "You are sure that the logging truck hit you deliberately?"

I paused for a moment. "I've been mulling that question over all morning. But, yeah, I'd bet the Aerie on it. He waited till I braked for the curve, then came on like a guided missile. I looked at a map last night. That curve was the perfect spot to put us in the river, and it had no guard rails."

"You were coming back from the State Penitentiary. How did the interview with the young man go?" I gave him the highlights, and he said, "If this boy's mother killed her lover and is now dead, why would someone want to kill you? It makes no sense."

"There's obviously more to this, but right now I have no clue what that could be. I've barely scratched the surface here."

He chuckled again. "Judging from the response, I would say you have scratched more than the surface. I'm craving some time at the beach, Calvin. I can come tomorrow, and we can talk face to face." I agreed, and he added in a serious tone, "Did you bring your Glock to Coos Bay?"

"No. I was expecting a peaceful vacation." The truth was that the weapon, which Nando gave me several years ago, sat gathering dust most of the time. I wasn't good with a gun and in fact had never fired the damn thing. But he had a point. The beach house was isolated.

"I will stop by the Aerie and pick it up for you. You keep it in a shoe box in your closet as I recall."

Archie and I turned around and headed back after the conversation ended. The sun had climbed in the morning sky and was warm on my neck. I was glad Nando was coming. To be honest, I wasn't sure how long it would have taken me to ask for help. My daughter was clearly a step ahead of me.

———

After breakfast, we hired another Uber to get into Coos Bay and spent a frustrating hour and a half getting new cell phones. I walked over to Coffee and Subversion while Claire went on to run additional errands. By the time Rori arrived, I'd already had one of Anthony's stellar cappuccinos. Rori came in through the back of the store, and when I turned at the coffee bar to greet her, she saw the bandage on my head. Her eyes widened. "My God, Cal, what happened to you?"

"It's a long story. Grab a coffee, and I'll fill you in." A few minutes later, after we sat down in her cluttered office, I took her through what happened to Claire, Archie, and me coming back from the State Prison. When I finished, her eyes were even wider, her face horror-stricken.

"You think it was attempted murder? I mean those truckers drive like there's no tomorrow through the Coast Range."

I ticked off the reasons, adding, "And whoever did it must have known we were going to be on the Umpqua Highway that day. Walter Sanders knew about the trip, because I mentioned it to him the other day. And Anthony asked me how Kenny was when I walked in this morning, so he knew, too." I looked at her and waited.

"Yeah, I did mention you were going back to see Kenny. I didn't think that was any big secret, and besides, Anthony's like family."

I absently ran my fingers along my bandaged stitches. "He said he mentioned it to his drinking buddies at his favorite watering hole. They're all caught up in this thing, rooting for Kenny, you know."

Rori's expression turned guilt-tinged. "Oh, God. So half of

Coos Bay–North Bend knew about your planned trip. I'm sorry, Cal."

I waved the apology off. "I screwed up, too, but tight lips from now on, okay?"

"It won't happen again."

"Did you and Walter Sanders work something out?"

Her expression grew resolute. "He offered to pick up half your expenses. I thanked him but said no. I couldn't do it, Cal. His money's dirty."

"That's a generous offer, Rori. Are you sure?"

She nodded emphatically. "Positive."

"Well, I'll, uh, work with you on my fee."

"That's kind of you to offer, Cal, but I'm good for every cent. Walter asked a lot of questions about what you're up to, and he got pretty frustrated when I didn't tell him anything."

"Good. He'll probably keep trying, you know."

"Oh, I don't doubt that. As he was leaving, he said he cared about Kenny and wanted to be kept in the loop." She smiled with bitterness. "You arrive on the scene and suddenly he cares about Kenny? What a crock." She paused for a moment. "How's my grandson?"

When I finished describing the beating he'd taken, her eyes were brimming with tears. "Can anything be done to protect him?"

I shook my head. "Not as long as he won't cooperate. He told us that seeking legal help for protection was considered worse than snitching. He wanted no part of it."

She buried her head in her hands. "Oh, Kenny, my baby boy," she uttered between sobs.

I let her cry for a while, feeling helpless. Finally, I said, "There's more, Rori."

She looked up at me, wiped tears from her eyes, and seemed to gird herself. "Sorry. What else did he say?"

"He admitted that the librarian, Ellen Dempsey, told the

truth—he did stop at the Jiffy Mart. He was on his way over to Sonny Jenson's."

Rori flinched like she'd touched a live wire. "*No.*"

"Yes. He said he was going there to apologize at your behest."

Her face registered fear and disbelief in equal measure. "Did he…did he go in?"

"No, because someone pulled out of Sonny's drive just as he arrived—your daughter, Krysta."

Color drained from her face. "*Krysta?* Oh, no. That can't be."

"What do you know about this? I want the truth, Rori. Kenny said Krysta and Sonny were having an affair."

She seemed to gather herself, then exhaled deeply, reminding me of Kenny when he finally unburdened himself. "Krysta was seeing Sonny, that's true." A wan smile. "She always told me the truth, that girl. I said it was a stupid mistake, but she didn't listen. I kept her secret and figured I'd take it to my grave. But I didn't know she'd been with Sonny *that* night, I swear."

"Where did you think she was?"

She paused and tapped her lips with a finger. "I thought she was home. She was supposed to go to yoga that night but said she wasn't feeling well. I was in an LNG meeting and stopped by afterwards to see how she was. She was home and seemed fine."

"What time was that?"

"Oh, near eleven o'clock."

"So, you can't dispute Kenny's account."

Rori hesitated. "No…I guess I can't. But Krysta never told me she was with Sonny that night."

"So, both you and Kenny concealed information that would have made her a prime suspect. Why shouldn't I conclude that she killed Sonny?"

Rori stared off at the wall for a few moments, then swung her gaze back to me. "Krysta wanted to come forward, admit she was having the affair. Maybe she was trying to work up the nerve to admit where she was that night. But I talked her out of it. I figured it would just slide by and not be a factor in the trial."

"That's what Kenny thought, too."

"But did Krysta kill Sonny? *No.* Not a chance in hell. Krysta had a hard time swatting flies. And I saw her that night. She didn't seem the least bit upset. Trust me, if my daughter had just finished beating a man to death, I would have sensed something."

We sat in silence for a long time, both of us wrapped in our own thoughts. I said, "Is there anything else you haven't told me, Rori?"

She dropped her gaze, scratched at her desk with a fingernail, then looked up. Her face was placid, but her eyes burned with conviction. "I'm deeply sorry about this, Cal. No, there's nothing else. And considering what happened to you and your daughter, I won't blame you if you decide to walk... But I hope you don't."

We sat looking at each other, the only sound the faint hissing of the espresso machine in the other room. Finally, I got up. "I've got things to do. I'll be in touch. Keep the faith."

I left Rori Dennison with a relieved look on her face. Yes, I was angry that she and Kenny hadn't been square with me, but she needn't have worried about my dropping the case. I had skin in this game now. Getting run off the road into a river does that to a person.

Chapter Sixteen

I found Claire in the book stacks when I came into the front of Coffee and Subversion after talking to Rori. Carrying a couple of books, she looked at me skeptically. "You don't look so hot, Dad. How do you feel?"

"Still got the headache. Did you get us a car?"

"Yeah. A Subaru, four-door sedan. Solid as a tank. Got a new laptop, too." She shot me a stern look. "Our next stop's a medical clinic. I want you to get checked out, Dad. There's one on Woodland Drive in North Bend."

She paid for her books, and as we got underway I told her about my discussion with Rori, and how she had confirmed the affair between Krysta and Sonny Jenson. "I'm not that surprised," Claire said. "Kenny's a perceptive kid. That changes things, doesn't it."

"Right. But neither one of them thinks Krysta Sanders was the killer."

"No surprise there. But she had means and opportunity. And, of course, anyone involved in an illicit love affair can easily acquire a motive."

"Such as?"

"Rejection, betrayal, jealousy. Any one of those would do the trick."

"You think Krysta would let Kenny take the fall for her?"

Claire shrugged. "I would hope not, but I don't know what kind of mother she was."

"Walter Sanders would have a motive, too, if he knew about the affair," I added.

"Of course, and don't forget Twila Jenson." She gave me a conspiratorial grin. "The plot's thickening, Dad."

It was great working with such a bright colleague, but to be honest, my daughter was obviously enjoying this sleuthing more than I would have liked.

———

"Mild traumatic brain injury," I said to Claire as we left the clinic. "Nothing to do for it except rest. I'm not tired, and my headache's easing off some, so I'd like to stop at Sloat Trucking on the way back."

"Okay," Claire said with some reluctance. "Sissy Anderson called while you were with the doctor. I told her what happened on the Umpqua Highway, and she wanted to talk at her place. I'll drop you off and swing by to see her. You can text me when you're done at Sloat."

Fifteen minutes later, we waited while a logging truck hauling two empty, full-length trailers pulled onto the road, its diesel engine whining, its twin exhaust stacks on either side of the cab belching dark smoke. "Just drop me here. I can walk in," I said to Claire. We were just off the Cape Arago Highway on Grinnell. A sign above a wide entry gate proclaimed, "SLOAT TRUCKING, PROUDLY MEETING THE SOUTH COAST'S TRUCK-ING NEEDS FOR THREE GENERATIONS." As the truck cleared the gate, I spotted a dispatcher in a booth inside the gate eyeing me. "Better wait to see if I can bluff my way in."

I put a faded ball cap on to hide the bandage covering my head wound. "See you soon. Be careful."

"*Me* careful?" she said, her face pinched with concern. "You could be going into the lion's den, Dad."

"No worries. I just want to walk around, look at some trucks in the yard, maybe pop in to see Maxine Sloat, if she's available. I like unexpected visits, and if someone working for her was in on the attempted murder, our cover's blown anyway." I got out and waited on the curb as two more trucks lumbered out.

"Can I help you?" the dispatcher called out from the booth.

I walked over to him, wearing my best smile. "I'm a truck nut. Have been my whole life. Just wanted to walk around for a while, check out some of these beauties."

Gray-haired with a neatly trimmed mustache and goatee, the man smiled back. "I'm the same way about trucks. I'm really not supposed to let you in but go ahead. Don't be too long." He handed me a visitor's badge. "Watch your step in there. And be sure to check out the new T-340s at the end of line. They're somethin.'"

"Wow, you have a T-340? Thanks. I owe you one, buddy." I flicked a thumbs-up to Claire, then sauntered in, not having the slightest idea what a T-340 was and wondering what it was about boys, men, and trucks.

The yard spanned several acres, with a gleaming row of massive trucks parked on one side and an industrial-sized wash station and maintenance building on the other. The door to the maintenance building was wide open, and inside I saw mechanics in blue coveralls swarming over trucks on hydraulic lifts and in various stages of disassembly. A two-story office building, with cars parked in front and on the side, sat toward the back of the lot, and the area behind the building looked like the place where old trucks went to die.

The line of trucks was a mixed bag—bright red trucks made by Freightliner, with the Sloat logo on the side, and others of various makes and colors with the name of the owner on most of them. The latter were contracted to Sloat, I figured, and parked in the yard by their owners when not in use. I stood next to the hulking machines, feeling like one of the Seven Dwarfs. No wonder we wound up in the river, I said to myself, as the crash played back like a bad dream, and the ache in my head went up a notch.

I worked my way through the trucks, standing in front of the various makes, and when I came to the first one made by Peterbilt, I stopped dead and the back of my neck began to tingle. I closed my eyes, and it all rushed back in crystal clarity—the huge radiator sectioned by a half dozen vertical dividers, the broad steel bumper, and the narrow rectangular headlights mounted on the fenders. An unmistakable geometry. *A Peterbilt hit us.* I was positive. I pulled my cell phone out and called the deputy who'd interviewed me after the crash. He didn't pick up, so I left him a message. Now they'd know what make of truck to look for.

I went through the rest of the trucks, but there wasn't a dark blue or black Peterbilt to be found. I cut across the yard to the maintenance complex and wandered along, smiling to the mechanics with my visitor's badge displayed on my chest. No dark blue or black Peterbilts were being worked on, either. I asked a mechanic working next to a bottled water dispenser for a drink, figuring it would ease my headache a bit. He said sure and after I drained a paper cup, I saw something that caught my eye—a big spool of fine gauge, multifilament steel cable. I walked over and examined it. "What's this used for?" I asked him.

"We use it to tie flags on, hold tarps down, all kinds of things. It's flexible but strong as hell."

"Damn, I need to get some of this stuff for my workshop. Could you cut a piece off for me?" The mechanic obliged, I thanked him, putting the coil of cable in my pocket.

It looked damn familiar.

I walked over to the office complex next, noting the hulking, cherry red Dodge Ram truck parked in a slot reserved for "Max Sloat." I was on a roll, so I wasn't surprised when Max's assistant told me she'd be free in a few minutes if I wanted to wait.

When you're hot, you're hot.

I remained standing in the outer office and browsed the pictures on the wall, mostly early nineteen-hundreds-era shots of spindly logging trucks and men standing around felled old-growth Douglas firs, smiling like they'd just bagged a big-game trophy. The pictures, like those of the bountiful salmon harvests of that era, always gave me a twinge of sadness. Those resources were harvested like they were in endless supply. It turned out they weren't.

The office door opened, and a woman's voice said, "Now, run along, Ronnie. If you ever do that again, you'll never drive for me or anyone else on the coast. Is that understood?"

A heavyset man with a dark beard and a spiderweb tattooed on his neck slunk out of the office, but not before saying, "Yes, Ms. Sloat. I understand." He glanced at me as he hurried past, his forehead, ears, and neck a blushing red.

Max Sloat appeared at the door and looked at me. Nearly my height, she wore a khaki work shirt, jeans, and heavy boots. She had short, dark hair parted on one side, rounded, ruddy cheeks, and inquisitive, unadorned eyes that appraised me with obvious curiosity. "And you are?"

I introduced myself. "I represent Kenny Sanders. He's the young man who—"

"I know who Kenny Sanders is, and I heard he had a new lawyer," she interrupted as she turned and walked back to her desk with a swagger you couldn't miss. She must have been a good bowler judging from the trophies displayed on a low table along one wall. "I only have a few minutes, but come in." As she sat, I noticed a tattoo on her left forearm that said "Annie" with a heart on either side. "That kid murdered one of Coos Bay's finest citizens. What do you hope to accomplish at this late date, Mr. Claxton?"

"His freedom. I'm convinced he didn't kill Sonny Jenson."

"A jury of his peers decided otherwise." Her smile dripped with derision. "How quixotic of you, Mr. Claxton."

I kept a level expression. "If by quixotic you mean I'm questioning incompetent lawyering, a coerced confession, a lying witness, and a sixteen-year-old boy given a life sentence, then, yeah, just call me Don."

A faint smile creased her lips. "I see. How could I possibly help you? I know nothing about this."

"The lying witness, Howard Coleman, drove a truck for you. He was found murdered in the Millicoma recently. I'm sure you know about it."

"Oh, that was horrible what happened to Howard. We've been cooperating with Sheriff Stoddard." She smiled in an offhand way. "I guess I'd forgotten about his connection with the Kenny Sanders trial."

"I'm wondering if I could have access to Howard Coleman's driving logs and any information about anyone he might've driven with, that sort of thing." *It never hurts to ask.*

Her face hardened. "Why would that be of any concern to you and Kenny Sanders?"

"I'm not at liberty to say."

An icy smile. "We've provided information to the sheriff, but here at Sloat we respect the privacy of our drivers. I'm sure you understand."

That answer echoed what Walter Sanders had told me. "Not really. You own the company. You can do what you want." Her expression didn't change, and I persisted. "I'm also interested in learning about any contract trucks you might have had running on the Umpqua River Highway the day before yesterday. The truck I'm interested in is a Peterbilt, dark blue or black."

"My hands are tied, Mr. Claxton."

My face got hot, and my headache throbbed even more. I took my hat off, exposing the bandage that covered my head wound. "These are not arbitrary questions. My daughter, my dog, and I were forced off the highway and into the Umpqua River two days ago by someone driving the cab of a logging truck." I pointed at the bandage. "And I got eighteen stitches as a souvenir. I'd like to know who did it."

"I'm sorry to hear that, but what leads you to think one of my trucks was involved? After all, my drivers are well trained, and the company has an outstanding safety record."

"You're the biggest trucking company on the South Coast. Seemed like a good place to start."

She paused for a moment, and I could almost hear the wheels spinning in her head. "Tell you what, Mr. Claxton, I'll make some inquiries. Give me your card. If I turn up anything, I'll call you." She forced a smile, then glanced at her watch. "Now, you'll have to excuse me, I've got another meeting."

At the door, she stopped and rested her eyes on me. They were steel gray with a dark blue rim around the irises. "You *really* believe Kenny Sanders is innocent?"

The question surprised me. "I wouldn't have taken the case if I didn't."

Something stirred behind her eyes, too subtle for me to read. "I see," she said in a voice that barely carried to my ears. "I never considered that a possibility." With that, she opened the door.

I left Sloat Trucking that day feeling good about the Peterbilt truck identification and the cable that looked a lot like what was used to hogtie Howard Coleman. Max Sloat, on the other hand, was a bit of an enigma. Was she cleverly stonewalling me, or would she actually help? And what about her obvious interest in the possibility that Kenny Sanders was innocent? More questions for which I had no answers.

Chapter Seventeen

I'm not sure who was happier to see Nando—my dog or my daughter. Beaming a smile, Claire hugged him, and Archie did a little squealing, butt-wagging dance around my friend when he arrived just before noon the next day. Always at the sartorial cutting edge, Nando wore a silk shirt of rich colors and floral design, linen trousers, and open-toed leather sandals. He handed me a hefty grocery bag. "I stopped on the way and picked up a few items for lunch, including some fresh halibut." He smiled, the one that always lights up the room. "Calvin, I am hoping you will make me a very happy man by making Cuban-style fish tacos for lunch."

I laughed and told him I'd try.

"Wait till you see the view from the deck," Claire said. She took his hand and led him through the house. I stayed back to check the shoebox he'd set down next to his leather bag. It held the Glock. The clip was full, the gun heavy in my hand and slick with a film of oil. Nando had obviously cleaned and loaded it, which didn't surprise me. I stashed it up in my bedroom and put up the groceries—fish, mangoes, avocados, tomatoes, red onion, cilantro, limes, hot sauce, and tortillas—before joining them on the deck with three Mirror Pond Pale Ales in hand. The sun was out, but a mass of gray fog lurking to the north threatened to cut the fine weather short. "The Oregon Coast is very different from the coast of Cuba," Nando said as he looked off toward the lighthouse, "but seeing the ocean always makes me homesick."

We talked in general for a while—Nando with the goings-on in Portland and Claire with her impressions of Harvard and her work on the Gulf, documenting what happens when you inundate delicate wetlands with crude oil. It wasn't a pretty picture, even eight years later.

By the time we got around to the business at hand, the fog had swallowed up our view and sent the temperature into steep decline. I fired up the outdoor gas grill, we retreated into the kitchen, and I handed out food prep duties. Claire and I began laying out the Kenny Sanders case for Nando. At one point he shook his head. "It does not look good for the young man. If he didn't do it, his mother probably did, and she is dead."

"We're both convinced Kenny didn't do it," I responded, placing the halibut in a marinade of olive oil, lime juice, and spices I found in the cupboard. "And I'm having a hard time imagining his mother went to her grave knowing her son was doing a life sentence for a crime she committed. It doesn't compute for me."

"I hope Kenny's mom didn't do it, but I'm less sure than Dad," Claire chipped in.

"Okay," Nando said, "setting them both aside for now, we are left with the stepfather, the wife of the victim, or some random hoodlum who is still out there. What do we know about the wife and stepfather?"

"Very little," Claire said. "The investigators seized on Kenny immediately, so there was scant follow-up on other suspects. Dad and I both read the police reports. The stepfather, Walter Sanders, said he was in Newport on business, and motel records there confirmed he'd checked in the afternoon of the murder. That was corroborated by his credit card receipt."

"So his alibi's nonexistent," I said, as I started to assemble the mango and avocado salsa. "That's a straight shot, less than a hundred miles. He could have easily driven to Coos Bay, done the deed, and driven back to the motel that night."

Nando nodded. "Motive?"

"His wife was having an affair with the victim, but we don't know if he knew. He also took Condor Enterprises in a different direction after Sonny's death." I described the move to video poker parlors, adult shops, and payday loan businesses. "Maybe Sonny didn't want that. He was seen as a straight arrow, civic-minded."

"What about the widow, Twila Jenson?"

"We don't know if she knew about the affair, either."

"Her alibi's tighter," Claire said. "She found the body but claimed she was in her studio apartment in Coos Bay at the time of the murder."

"Doing what?"

"Painting and listening to opera, according to the report. A security camera on the building shows her entering four hours earlier, then leaving twenty-five minutes before she found the body at a little after eleven."

"How precise is the time of death?"

"Very," I said, wrapping the tortillas in foil and sticking them in the oven to warm. "Sonny Jenson's watch was shattered at 8:32 p.m. Body temperature and blood coagulation were consistent with that time."

"The back door of the building was self-locking, so if she snuck out it would have locked behind her, meaning she would've had to re-enter from the front, where the camera was."

Nando snorted. "Please, she could have taped the lock like the famous Watergate burglars."

"Of course. But the detectives also noted that the video showed she wore the same clothes coming and going—a white blouse and tan slacks. Her clothes were examined. They had some paint on them, but no blood. It was a bloody murder, so unless she somehow carried an identical set of clothes, it seemed unlikely she could have done it."

I slipped out the door to put the fish on the grill, and when I returned Nando was waiting with another question. "No leads on strangers?"

"None. The detectives didn't interview anyone else except the witness who put Kenny near the scene. There's another, less defined angle, though. We know that Howard Coleman, the man who testified against Kenny, drove a truck for an outfit called Sloat Trucking. We also suspect he might've been ready to talk about his testimony."

I explained the appointment Coleman made but never kept with Mimi Yoshida and the possibility that the truck that knocked us into the river could have been driven by one of Sloat's drivers. I looked at Claire. "Tell Nando what you learned yesterday from Sissy Anderson."

"Sissy was Coleman's girlfriend. They were on again, off again, but she loved the man dearly. She told me Coleman entered a business arrangement with two brothers about eighteen months ago. An arrangement that was spinning off enough cash that they were planning to buy a house. She thought one of them drove for Sloat, too, but she wasn't sure."

"And Kenny Sanders told us he heard via the prison grapevine that Coleman was involved in the fentanyl trade," I said.

"That's right," Claire added, "but Sissy claimed she didn't know what the business was. I'm not sure I believe her. Anyway, she thinks these guys killed Coleman."

"Because he was going to talk to Yoshida?" Nando asked.

"She doesn't know or wouldn't say," Claire said. "I caught a glimpse of one of them at a restaurant, but Sissy didn't know his name. The other's name is Robert, but she's never seen him. She's afraid of these guys."

We broke off the discussion at this point to retrieve the fish from the grill and build our tacos. After Nando took his first bite, he raised his bottle. "Even in an unfamiliar kitchen, you excel, my friend." I thanked him, and we ate in silence for a while. Nando said, "I do not have a good feeling about this. The stack of hay has too many needles."

Claire laughed. I added more hot sauce to my taco. "I agree. It's complicated." I looked at Nando. "How long can you stay?"

"I have told my employees I'm taking a beach vacation. I am at your disposal, Calvin."

I glanced at Claire, then back to my friend. "Thanks, Nando. Why don't you start by seeing if you can get a line on the two brothers?"

He drew his face into a scowl, revealing a side he didn't show that often. "It will be a pleasure to find the persons who put you in the river. One could be named Robert. One could be driving for Sloat Trucking. They may be in the fentanyl drug trade." He turned to Claire. "And you saw the one who is not Robert." After she described him, Nando shrugged. "I have started with less."

"Claire," I said, "why don't you provide some research help for Nando? I'm sure he's going to be searching some of his databases. Also, why don't you go back over everything in the sheriff's report on Walter Sanders, see if there's any way to crack his so-called alibi? Dig deep. Don't assume anything. And one other thing—see what you can find on the death of Max Sloat's father, Millard Sloat. He died fifteen years ago in some kind of boating accident." Claire flashed an annoyed look. "Just a hunch," I countered. "Indulge me."

A half hour later, I left Nando and Claire huddled over her computer, with Archie in the corner watching them both. My job that afternoon was to first meet with Twila Jenson and then with Sheriff Hershel Stoddard.

As I headed north on the Cape Arago Highway, I fought off a feeling of frustration. It seemed like we were stuck at base camp instead of climbing the mountain, but at least we had the semblance of a plan now.

It was a start.

Chapter Eighteen

I offered to meet Twila Jenson at a coffee shop, but she insisted I come to her house. She told me it was a town house in Coos Bay, but it was more like a town mansion. Located on a multiblock knoll on the southeast side of town called Telegraph Hill, the street side of the place had a deceptively low profile, but when she opened the door and ushered me in, a view of the Isthmus Slough and Coos Bay beyond it boomed out from a floor-to-ceiling glass wall running the length of the sunken living room.

"Stunning view," I said after introducing myself.

"Thank you, Mr. Claxton. I never tire of it."

"Call me Cal."

She smiled. "And you can call me Twila, Cal." She had black hair with stylish pewter streaks, dark eyes, and a hesitant smile that had a slight tilt to it. I followed her down four thickly carpeted steps to the living room and took a seat, keeping my cap on to obviate the need to explain my head wound. Wearing stretch pants and a silver colored sweater, she tucked her bare feet under her as she took a seat. Out of nowhere a young Latina woman appeared balancing two tall glasses of iced tea, a plate of sliced lemons, and a bowl of sugar on a lacquered tray.

Twila thanked the girl, turned to me, and smiled again. "I

thought you might be thirsty." I nodded thanks and took the glass she offered me. "Now, let's get this over with, shall we?"

I cleared my throat. "I appreciate your agreeing to meet like this. I'm sure this is still a painful subject for you, so I'll keep my questions as brief as possible."

Her smile crumbled, but she held her composure. "Thank you. I believe the best therapy is to face the past. It's the only way to move forward." The words were there, but her voice lacked conviction.

I started with some bland background questions, jotting a few notes as we conversed. The exchange didn't become interesting until I said, "How serious was the dispute between Kenny and your husband, the one that wound up with your husband in the pool and his car keyed?"

Her smile was edged with disdain. "That was nothing. Sonny made a big deal out of it to teach Kenny a lesson about controlling his temper."

"He had Kenny arrested for assault."

"Yes, but he never meant to press charges. In fact, I think he and Walter were in it together, you know, a life lesson for the boy. Sonny liked Kenny."

"Why didn't this come out at the trial? The incident was cited as a key motive for Kenny."

She sighed and closed her eyes for a moment. "I really don't know. You'll have to ask Walter."

"No one asked you?"

"No, they didn't. I was given a wide berth by the sheriff. The grieving widow and all."

"Was anything bothering your husband in the period leading up to his death, or was he having difficulty with anyone?"

She hesitated, then exhaled slowly, her eyes never leaving my face. "He and Walter were arguing over the direction of Condor."

"What were they arguing about?"

"Walter had some valuable insider information on the LNG

thing, and he wanted to cash in. Sonny was against it. He didn't think the project was the best thing for Coos Bay."

"How serious were these arguments?"

"They were both hardheaded, so pretty heated, I guess. I believe a lot of money was at stake."

"This didn't come out in the course of the investigation?"

"Not that I know of. No one asked me about it, and it wasn't that unusual for them to be bickering, to tell the truth."

My pulse ticked up, but I held a neutral expression. "What was the nature of the insider information?"

She paused for a moment, furrowing her brow. "Walter somehow found out the preferred route of the pipeline from California, which was being held in secret. He probably bribed someone on the inside of Bexar. He wanted to buy up key parcels—easements, outright property sales—and then resell them to Bexar." She curled up one side of her mouth. "You know, good ol' real estate speculation."

"What was the outcome?"

She rearranged herself on the couch. "Well, Walter eventually got his way, of course, and made a lot of money. Bexar wanted those parcels, even though they hadn't gotten final approval for the project."

"Got his way? You mean when your husband died?" She nodded. "What about you? I assume you inherited Sonny's share of the company."

A wan smile. "I sold my share several months after the funeral. I was even more adamant than my husband. I wanted nothing to do with that LNG abomination."

I kept my eyes on her face. "Who did you sell to?"

She hesitated for what I took to be a crossing-the-Rubicon moment. "A woman named Maxine Sloat. She owns a trucking company in town. Her lawyer worked out the terms with mine." She shrugged. "I suppose I could have held on and made more money, but I really didn't care. I sold our big place on Crown

Point and bought this place and a beach house. I also signed a lease on space for an art gallery"—she looked at me and smiled sarcastically—"and then I moved on."

I took a first drink of my tea to gather myself. "Why are you telling me this now, Twila? Do you have doubts about Kenny's guilt?"

A deep sigh. "I was in shock at the time, and with the confession and all, I guess I thought he was guilty."

"And all?"

"Oh, I guess that woman who saw him in the vicinity, and the fact that my jewelry was stolen. It was passed down from my grandmother to my mother, then to me." A wistful smile. "Some fine pieces and high sentimental value as well. That seemed like something an inexperienced kid would do. You know, go for the shiny objects."

"None of the jewelry has turned up, right?"

"Unfortunately." She raised her eyes and exhaled a deep sigh. "The truth is, I've been self-absorbed since Sonny's death. But I'm coming out of it. Kenny was so young then. How could he have done something like that?" She paused and dabbed a tear from her eye with a curled index finger. "Will this information be of use to you?"

I figured she knew full well the incendiary nature of her revelations but let it slide. "Yes, all pertinent facts help. We're fighting an uphill battle here, since most of the issues in the case have already been litigated. Would you be willing to recount this under oath?"

She hesitated for a couple of beats. "Yes, if I had to."

I took another sip of tea. "I understand you're a painter," I said, shifting the subject, "and that you were painting at a downtown studio the night of the murder." I stopped short of mentioning the affair between Sonny and Kenny's mom, Krysta. *Save it for another time*, I told myself.

She smiled knowingly. "Oh, my turn to be a suspect? Yes, at that time I was renting a studio apartment in the Tioga, which I used as my artist studio. It had a view of the bay and good light in the afternoon. I was painting that night."

"Was the back exit of the Tioga accessible to you?"

Her expression turned blank. "Well, I don't know. I never tried it."

"Did anybody else in the building use that exit?"

Another blank look. "Not to my knowledge."

She was beginning to look uncomfortable. "Fine," I said, cutting off the questions. "I appreciate your help, Twila. If you think of anything else, you can reach me at this number."

I got up and handed her a card, and as she showed me out I stopped in front of a large painting hanging in the hallway. It had a haunting quality to it, representational enough for me to recognize the setting, yet the sky and the water swirled with an almost Van Gogh-like abstraction. "I think I know that vista," I said. "Bastendorff Beach, looking toward the south jetty, right? Is this your work?"

She smiled with genuine modesty. "Yes. An earlier piece." A half laugh. "My paintings are darker now, or so I'm told."

"Well, it's beautiful."

———

I was brimming with news but running late for my appointment with Sheriff Stoddard, so I called Claire while driving south on Highway 101 and had her put the call on speaker so Nando could hear as well. When I finished filling them in, Claire said, "Cui bono, Dad. Who stands to gain? Sonny's in the way of an LNG deal that Walter wants. Sonny dies, and Max pops up as Walter's partner."

"And they both make the boatload of money," Nando added. "How considerate of the young man to get rid of Sonny for them."

"Yep, if what Twila told me is true—and I have no reason to doubt her—both Walter and Max are prime suspects. Listen,

Claire, go back and see if you missed anything on Condor's real estate holdings and dealings with Bexar Energy. We need the whole picture—money, timing of transactions, that sort of thing."

"I'm on it," Claire answered. "Meanwhile, we've already downloaded rap sheets on all felons in Coos, Douglas, and Curry Counties between twenty-five and forty-five named Robert who are not in jail, all forty-seven of them. We're going to try to find which ones have brothers next. Stay tuned."

"We are hoping Robert has a record," Nando added. "It is the only way to narrow the data set."

I wished them luck, and just as I merged onto OR 42, signs urging me to vote for Sheriff Hershel Stoddard began appearing, a testament to his grassroots support, I supposed, since the guy was running unopposed. My cell phone riffed. "Cal? Walter Sanders here. How are you today?"

"I'm fine, Walter. What's up?"

"How's the investigation going?"

"It's going." I waited as a car passed, unwilling to divulge anything.

"I, ah, talked to Rori about helping out with the legal expenses, Cal. Made her a damn generous offer, but she turned me down flat. Seems my money's tainted or something. Listen, Cal, I still want to help. Maybe you and I could work something out, you know, just between us."

"I'm late for an appointment right now and don't have my calendar," I told him. "But that sounds interesting. I'll get back to you later today." He thanked me and signed off. There was no way I could accept a dime from Walter in light of what I'd just learned from Twila Jenson, but I now had new questions to ask him.

I spent the rest of the drive thinking about how to approach Sheriff Stoddard. On the one hand, I had information that might inform his investigation of Howard Coleman's murder. But how much to tell him? I recalled Mimi Yoshida's warning that he engineered the coerced confession from Kenny. And Sissy Anderson was counting on us to keep her information in confidence. Then there was what I'd just learned from Twila Jenson—that was too fresh to share with anyone outside the investigation.

I would play it by ear, I decided, erring on the side of caution.

It must have been a slow day at the county seat, because I scored a parking place right in front of the Sheriff's Office, a drab, two-story structure connected by a pedestrian bridge to the county courthouse. After checking in, I took a seat in front of a low table on which three tattered magazines were scattered—*Sports Illustrated*, *Men's Health*, and *People*. I picked up the *SI*, which was two years old, and leafed through it until a deputy appeared and escorted me through a security check, down a long hallway, and up one flight of stairs to Stoddard's office.

Tall and lean with sandy hair, pale blue eyes, and a chin neatly cleaved as if by a scalpel, Stoddard wore a crisp, tan uniform and greeted me with a robust handshake. "What can I do for you, Mr. Claxton?"

"A couple of things, Sheriff." I reached into my windbreaker and pulled out a coiled piece of the steel cable I'd picked up at Sloat Trucking, explaining that, in my opinion, it closely resembled what was used to tie Howard Coleman's hands and feet.

"That's very interesting, Mr. Claxton," Stoddard said when I finished, his tone borderline patronizing. "Are you suggesting the cable's unique to the Sloat maintenance shop? There's probably a lot of that in use around the bay."

I shrugged. "That could be, but I thought your investigator could check it out."

"Of course. I'll pass it on to Detective Rice. Thanks for—"

I put a hand up. "There's one more thing." I went on to tell him the story of how I'd been forced off the Umpqua Highway by a logging truck, that it was being investigated by the Douglas County Sheriff's Office, and gave him the name of the officer in charge of the investigation.

When I finished, Stoddard said, "I'm glad you, your daughter, and your dog are okay, Mr. Claxton. Are you suggesting the two crimes are connected?"

"Yes, I think they could be."

Stoddard leaned in and placed his elbows on the desk separating us. "How so?"

"It's a hunch more than anything. Howard Coleman was killed by at least two men, and the attempt on my life was by two men, one in a logging truck. Coleman drove for Sloat Trucking, right? And I spotted the steel cable at Sloat Trucking. Maybe one or both of the killers work at Sloat."

Stoddard straightened in his seat, and his forehead grew lines. "What were you doing at Max Sloat's yard?"

"Trying to get some information about the situation. She was uncooperative."

"Why would these men—if there were two—attack you, Mr. Claxton?"

"Good question." I met his eyes. They were direct and unblinking. "As you know, Coleman was involved in Kenny Sanders' conviction four years ago. By sheer coincidence, I became Kenny's attorney recently. I'm trying to prove he's innocent." Stoddard's face stiffened. It was clear he didn't know about that. Apparently, the Coos Bay grapevine didn't extend into the county. "I think the attack on the Umpqua was in response to my taking the case."

He leaned back and seemed to take a more careful look at me. "Do you have any other evidence to support this claim?"

I shook my head. "No, nothing more than the timing, but I'm working on it." I stopped there and held his probing gaze. "Anyway, that's why I stopped in, Sheriff. Now you know as much as I do."

Suddenly more interested, he took me back over the story, asking more detailed questions, most of which I couldn't or didn't answer. When we finished, he said, "I'll pass this on to Detective Rice and have him contact you. I'll also make sure he gets with Douglas County to get their input on the hit-and-run."

"That works for me," I said as we both stood and shook hands. "Maybe you and Douglas County can sort this out."

When I got to the door, Stoddard said, "Can I give you some advice, Mr. Claxton?"

I turned back to face him.

He smiled, but his eyes didn't participate. "You're an attorney, so you probably won't listen, but if I were you, I'd think carefully about representing Kenny Sanders. That was a righteous conviction, and we won every damn appeal. People around here think he's right where he belongs—in the State Penitentiary. Don't waste your time on him."

I wanted to tell Stoddard exactly what I thought of his open-and-shut case, but this wasn't the time or the place. I walked out without responding.

On my way to the beach house, I mulled over the conversation, reasonably satisfied that I'd gone about as far as I could go without revealing the bigger picture of how Howard Coleman's murder might be related to Kenny Sanders.

But one nagging question kept recurring—was the advice Sheriff Stoddard offered me just that, or was it a veiled threat?

Chapter Nineteen

After dinner that night, Claire got a call and immediately retreated to her room, with Archie tagging along. The fact that her ears turned a shade of red when she looked at the screen before answering tipped me that it might be a call from Gabriel. She'd had that ear-blush tell since she was a little girl, and her mother and I made good use of it when she was growing up, without her ever knowing. A devious trick, admittedly, and it occurred to me that I should fess up one of these days, although I knew I would pay a heavy price.

Armed with glasses of Rémy Martin, Nando and I retired into the living room and sat down below the Jackson Pollock. The glow of the setting sun faded, and the sea became a deep, black cavern. The search for Robert had progressed. Out of the forty-seven felons with that first name, seventeen had at least one brother, although our data on family members was sketchy and incomplete. Those names were now circulating with Nando's contacts to see if any of them were in the drug trade. It was a long shot, but we had to start somewhere.

Nando inhaled the rich aroma of the cognac, took a sip, and said, "I had a look around this house. The windows on the first floor have locks that are not easily defeated, and the doors have solid deadbolts. Keep everything locked."

"I intend to. I've checked out the neighborhood. If someone wanted to approach the house unseen, the best method would be from Lighthouse Beach. There's a steep, narrow gully leading down to the beach at Yoakam Point. They would probably use the trail access at the highway—there's a trailhead marker there. Then they would descend via the gully to the beach and come back up at our staircase."

"It makes sense," Nando said. "Your best intruder alarm has four legs. And when you're home during the day, keep the Glock downstairs just in case."

"Will do." The chances of needing a gun in broad daylight were slim, but it was a disquieting thought. "And whatever plans get made, Claire's never going to be here alone."

"That would be very wise, Calvin."

Our conversation drifted off to other topics and finally came around to how I got myself into this situation. Like Gertie, Nando always considered the financial implications of his actions, a trait I sorely lacked. At one point he said, "What if this case drags on? This is a very nice place, but you cannot stay here indefinitely without jeopardizing your livelihood."

I shrugged. "I know. The original plan was a two-week vacation, and it's been, what, twelve days? I can spend another week or so working full time on this without any major blowback in Dundee and Portland. After that, I'll have to go to plan B."

"Which would be?"

"I haven't gotten that far."

He looked dubious but managed a smile. "Well, in that case, we will have to make fast work of it."

"Right. And this isn't about finding some new avenue of appeal. That would take too long, and time's not Kenny Sanders' friend. This is about finding who really killed Sonny Jenson and proving it." I drank some more Rémy and exhaled a long breath. "We need a break or two to have any chance at all."

———

Claire came into the kitchen the next morning, her eyes tinged red and the tone of her voice making it clear she was upset. Nando looked at me and raised his eyebrows. Never one to postpone the inevitable, I said, "Was that Gabriel who called last night?"

She shot me a lethal look. "Unfortunately."

Nando said, "Gabriel? Who is this person who has upset you?"

She looked at me, then swung her eyes to my friend. "He's, ah, *was* my boyfriend in Cambridge. We broke up last night."

"What happened?" Nando said, his face filled with obvious concern.

Claire turned her head and glared out the kitchen window. "Machismo. That's what happened."

"*Vaya cabrón.* Where is Gabriel from?"

"Argentina."

"Ah, the Argentinians, they have this problem. It is well known."

"And Cubans don't?" she spat.

I swallowed a laugh, and Nando put his hands up, looking a little cornered. "It is less of a problem in Cuba, where many strong women live."

Claire looked at me. "Gabriel doesn't get it. He thinks I'm unprofessional for taking this hiatus to help you. 'Your work's too important,' he told me. Okay, I get that, but it's not his call. God forbid I should make my own career decisions, right? Then last night he reminds me that I'm supposed to meet his parents next week." She hit her forehead with the heel of her hand, a mock blow. "I completely forgot, and I can't make it now, anyway."

I cringed. "You're surprised he got upset?"

Her eyes swelled in exasperation. "Of course not. But I am surprised that after I explained *again* how important this was to me, he still seemed pissed."

"You can still make it, you know."

Daggers flew from her sapphire eyes. "I'm staying here as long as you do, Dad. Helping Kenny's the right thing to do. Meeting somebody's parents is not that big a deal."

"Even if they've come all the way from Argentina?" Nando ventured.

Claire shot him the same withering look. "They didn't come to Boston just to meet *me*."

I started to comment but was saved when Claire's cell went off. She was an integral part of this effort, but on the other hand I didn't want her to blow up a relationship that obviously meant a great deal to her. She glanced down at the screen anxiously and then walked into the dining room to take the call, looking disappointed. When she returned she said, "That was the surfer we met at Bastendorff, Stu Foster. He wants to meet me for coffee this morning. I told him okay."

"Good," I said, more relieved that she had something to focus on than excited about what she might learn from Kenny's friend. "It's worth a shot."

———

Claire left about ten that morning to meet Foster, and by then I'd left Walter Sanders a voice mail indicating I had a flexible schedule that day. Meanwhile, Nando worked the phones for a good hour—without learning anything new, it turned out— and then found an image online of a dark blue Peterbilt logging truck that I agreed looked like the one that knocked us in the river.

"I am going to have this printed out and then ask around the area of Coos Bay–North Bend this afternoon. I will ask about two brothers who might own or be associated with such a logging truck," he explained. "Even if the Douglas County Sheriffs have done something similar, people are not always comfortable talking to the law."

"Good idea." I pulled up a map of Coos Bay–North Bend on

my computer and showed him where Sloat Trucking was located. "Hit the bars and eateries in and around this area," I suggested.

After Nando left, Archie was bugging me for a jog, so I took him down the weathered staircase to the beach. Although the day was clear and the lighthouse on Cape Arago shown brilliant white in the sunlight, I zipped up my jacket against a stiff breeze that threatened to kick up whitecaps. But the plovers were out foraging breakfast in the wet sand, so I clipped a leash on Archie before heading off towards the Cape. We hadn't gotten far when I heard someone call out.

I turned around and saw a man waving from the deck of our place. I headed back, and after closing half the distance, realized it was Walter Sanders. I was glad he showed up, because with both Claire and Nando gone I was without a car. But it still irritated me that he'd come to the beach house again without being invited.

"I'll say it again, one of the best views on the coast," Walter said as I neared the top of the stairs, his gap-toothed smile in full bloom, his Ray Bans gleaming in the sun. Archie had gone ahead and stood on the deck, looking at our guest with his head cocked in canine scrutiny. Obviously no lover of dogs, Walter acted as if Archie were invisible, a gesture not lost on my dog. "Hope you don't mind my popping by again, Cal. I was out this way and figured why not?"

I gestured at one of the deck chairs, and when he sat I took a seat beside him. He would get no coffee this time. "What's on your mind, Walter?"

"How are you and your daughter? I heard you had a terrible accident on the Umpqua Highway."

"We're both fine."

He glanced at Archie for the first time. "Was the mutt with you?"

I nodded, biting back a caustic comeback. "We're all fine, except for my car."

"Good, good." He shook his head and put his Ray Bans in his

shirt pocket. "Those damn truckers are a menace on the highway. Look, Cal," he continued, making eye contact, "you know why I'm here. I want to help out Aurora and Kenny. The kid carries my name, for Christ's sake. Over the years, I, ah, I don't know…I've come to believe he didn't do it."

"I appreciate that, but I don't need to tell you Rori's a proud woman. You need to give her a little more time. Maybe she'll come around."

"Why can't I just pay you directly? You can take it off her bill."

"Something like that needs to be transparent. Let's give it some more time."

He sucked a tooth and nodded. "Okay, okay. How's the case coming?"

"Slow but sure. We've pretty much ruled out a robbery gone bad," I lied.

His eyes registered surprise. "How have you done that?"

"Investigative work." He leaned in, waiting for me to elaborate. Instead, I said, "This suggests Sonny Jenson was killed by somebody he knew, somebody with a good reason."

"*Really?* Sonny didn't have any enemies, you know."

By this time, Archie was lying down facing Walter. His ears were up, his big, coppery eyes on our guest. "Around the time of his death," I continued, "did you and Sonny agree on the direction of Condor Enterprises?"

He looked at me, his face suddenly wary, but his eyes never quite met mine. "Why do you ask that?"

"Just trying to fill in the big picture."

"Well, we had our differences, but nothing major."

"But after his death, you steered the company in a very different direction. Would Sonny have agreed to that?"

"We moved in that direction after he was gone. So, the question's moot."

"I see. He was an outspoken opponent of the LNG project. Would he have agreed to the land speculation deal you engineered?"

A sarcastic laugh. "You make it sound nefarious. You've been listening to Rori too much. It was smart business based on a lot of due diligence. Like everybody, Sonny had his price. When he saw what we stood to make on that deal, he came around."

"Oh, so he agreed to it? When was that?"

"Right before his death."

"You must have needed a lot of cash to pull that off. Did you take on a new equity partner?"

His face hardened, and the muscles along his jawline flexed. "We financed some of it, and my business associates are none of your business. Look, Cal, I suppose you have to ask these questions, and I'm answering as best I can, but I draw the line at my business affairs."

"Your equity partner, if you have one, is a person of interest, Walter."

He glanced at his watch and got up. "I've got to run."

I walked Walter to the front door. Normally the perfect gentleman, Archie didn't bother to join us. He knew where he stood with Walter Sanders. "Uh, one other question," I said as he started down the steps. "We have information that suggests Sonny was having an affair with someone. Do you know anything about that?"

He'd just put on his Ray Bans, so I couldn't see his eyes, but his jawline flexed again before he produced a smile that fell well short of full wattage. "Sonny Jenson was having an affair? Mr. Upstanding Citizen? I wouldn't know anything about that, Cal." He turned and got into his Land Rover. "The offer to help's still on the table," he called out before pulling out.

I watched him drive away. Did he know about the affair between Sonny and his own wife? I wasn't sure, although the inability to hide the sarcasm was telling.

I joined Arch back on the deck. "Whataya think, Big Boy? Was Sonny Jenson a holdout on the LNG deal like Twila said, or did he cave like Walter just told me?" My dog sat up, giving me his full attention. "And why doesn't Walter want me to know about Max Sloat?"

Archie listened politely, then whimpered a couple of times. I laughed. "Okay, I haven't forgotten. I still owe you a run on the beach."

Chapter Twenty

I cleared the phone messages from my Dundee office, moved a court date at the McMinnville County Courthouse, and had just finished up a semi-contentious call with Gertie Johnson when Claire breezed in.

"How'd it go with Stu Foster?" I asked.

She shrugged. "Probably a bust. But he's a nice kid. Going to community college, knows a lot about environmental issues." She smiled with a tinge of embarrassment. "He came on pretty strong, too."

I laughed. "*What?* His main interest was you, not the case? That's a shocker."

"Something like that. I played it straight with him, had him go back over everything he could remember about the time leading up to Sonny's death. That didn't produce anything of interest until we got to Walter Sanders." She drew her face into a look of disgust. "Probably more salacious than useful—but he told me Walter was—"

My phone interrupted us. I didn't recognize the caller, but Claire paused, nodding for me to take it.

"Cal? This is Anthony, you know, Rori's barista. Um, she asked me to call you. She's been arrested."

"*Arrested?* Where is she?"

"Handcuffed to a Bexar Energy limo in front of City Hall. Can you come?"

———

We were there in seventeen minutes. While Claire parked the car, I worked my way through a gathered crowd and spotted Rori sitting in the back seat of a squad car with the windows up. Anthony stood behind the car looking distraught. I nodded to him, then told a uniformed officer, who had one foot propped on the bumper, that I was Rori's lawyer. He agreed to roll the window down so I could speak to her.

"What's going on, Rori?"

Wearing a T-shirt that said *No Dinosaur Farts in Coos Bay* across the front, she pushed a length of magenta hair off her forehead with both hands, which were manacled together. "You missed all the fun, Cal. Bexar Energy's meeting with the City Council today. We were picketing, then I decided to attach myself to one of their limos."

"Why?"

"*Publicity*. The bastards are trying to fly under the radar."

"How did you, uh, attach yourself?"

"I bought some handcuffs at one of Walter's sex shops. The rest was easy. Took the cops a while to unhook me." She laughed, a gleeful bark. "Walter sells pretty high-quality stuff."

"Listen, Rori, I—"

"Jesus Christ, Rori, what the hell were you thinking?" a voice boomed from behind me.

I turned to face a man wearing a police uniform and a badge with "Chief" embossed in blue letters on it. Rori peered out at him. "Hello, Maynard. I'm just trying to let people know what's going on in their fair city." She flashed a smile. "The *Coos Bay World* got some nice photos and even interviewed me before your guys arrived with the bolt cutters. I want people to think about the LNG project, not just let it happen."

"Well, goddamnit, this is no way to get people to think."

"*Oh, really?*" Rori countered. "Ever hear of civil disobedience? It's about the only tool we have left, Maynard. And what are you going to charge me with, anyway—felony limo attaching?"

I stifled a laugh, and when the police chief swung his glare to me, introduced myself. He shook his head and said to both of us, "I convinced Bexar not to press charges." He turned to the officer next to the patrol car. "Cut her loose, Jimmy." Then he looked back at Rori. "You're welcome."

———

I joined up with Claire, who was disappointed she missed all the fun. We gave Anthony and Rori a ride to Coffee and Subversion and sat in the back of the coffee bar while a throng of pro-testors relived the encounter and hailed Rori—who sported a skinned elbow and a bruise on her cheek—as their fearless leader. Apparently, she hadn't told anyone about her plan with the handcuffs, and a timely call placed by Anthony made sure a reporter was there to catch the whole drama.

As the last of the group drifted out, Nando called, and I gave him directions to the shop. When he arrived, I introduced him to Rori, and we gathered in her office, leaving Anthony to mind the front.

"God, I need a drink," Rori said, producing four glasses and a bottle of Maker's Mark from her desk. After pouring us each a generous amount, she raised her glass. "To Kenny," she said, as her eyes opened up like a couple of floodgates. She sighed, swiped the tears from her cheeks with the fingers of both hands, and sniffed. "Sorry. I'm a little emotional at the moment." She looked at me. "Are we making any progress, Cal?"

I brought her up to date on my discussion with Twila Jenson.

"So, in addition to the possibility that Walter knew of his wife's infidelity," I said in conclusion, "Sonny stood in the way of the LNG deal that Walter had cooked up. At least, that's what Twila Jenson told me."

"A double whammy," Nando quipped.

Claire said, "Last night I went back over all of Condor's real estate transactions I could find during that time. It looks like they bought at least three million dollars' worth of land and resold it to Bexar for better than eight million a couple of years later."

Rori smirked. "Financial gain would be one hell of a motive for Walter. I wish to hell I'd known that was his intention at the time."

I nodded. "Max Sloat invested in Condor *after* Sonny's death, but she could've already been secretly working with Walter Sanders."

"That would give her the same financial motive to get rid of Sonny," Nando added.

"Right. And this is where Howard Coleman's murder might come in—Sissy Anderson thinks one of his killers could be driving for Sloat Trucking." I looked at Rori. "Sissy doesn't want anyone to know she's cooperating with us, so don't share that." Then I turned to Nando. "Any luck tracking down our truck driver?"

"Perhaps. At a little bar on Robeson Road, a couple of miles north of the truck yard, a waitress told me of a man who drives a Ford Explorer and occasionally a dark colored Peterbilt cab like the one we're looking for. A regular customer, at least he was until the last week or so, pays with cash, no credit cards, tall with graying hair and tattoos from his fingertips to his armpits."

"Robert's brother?" I said.

"Yes, I am thinking the same thing. The description is not inconsistent with the man Claire saw, but this man is probably older, judging by his graying hair."

"Okay, so Robert's the *younger* brother. Sounds like the older brother might be lying low after the attack on us. Since he frequents a bar not far from Sloat Trucking, it's likely he's the brother driving for Sloat. Anything else?"

"Yes, the waitress, Joyce, has my business card and has promised to call me if this man reappears."

"Excellent." I looked at Rori. "It turns out Walter has a skeleton in his closet." Gesturing toward Claire, I said, "Tell them what you just told me about your meeting this morning."

"I had coffee with a guy named Stu Foster, Kenny's best friend at the time."

"I know Stuart," Rori said. "He was one of my favorites."

"Well, he told me Walter was, um, seeing a sixteen-year-old girl at the time of the murder."

"Oh, God. That sounds like something Walter would do." Rori said, her face flushed with revulsion. "No wonder Krysta decided to have an affair. What's her name?"

Claire glanced at me, and I nodded the go-ahead. "Kathy Harper," she said. "I'm going to see if she'll talk to me about the period leading up to the murder."

Rori shook her head, her look morphing into bewilderment. "She was a cheerleader at Marshfield High. A year behind Kenny, I think. Just a beautiful young kid. Did Kenny know about this?"

"No," Claire answered. "Stu said this didn't come out until after Kenny went to prison."

Rori shook her head again. "Kathy Harper. Maybe she'll have a Me-Too moment."

I met Rori's eyes. "This is hearsay. No leaks."

Rori lowered her eyes. "Of course."

The room fell silent, and Rori poured herself another shot of bourbon, downing it in one swallow. I said, "We've made progress—we have three potential suspects for Sonny's murder— Walter Sanders, Maxine Sloat, and Twila Jenson. We also have a good lead on the two brothers responsible for killing Howard Coleman, a key witness in Kenny's trial."

"These two will lead us back to Sonny's killer," Nando said. "Howard Coleman was killed to shut him up."

"That's our best theory, but there's no guarantee it's right. Right now, all we have are motives and suspicions. What we need, what we must have, is hard evidence."

"Like what?" Rori asked.

I shrugged. "Oh, the murder weapon with a print on it would be nice," I said in jest. "The forensic evidence at the crime scene has been dealt with in the trial and appeals. We need something new, something incontrovertible."

That's where we broke it off. As we filed out of the office, Rori said to me, "Cal, I'd be depressed as hell about our chances, but this is quite a team you've assembled. That daughter of yours is sharp as a tack, and Nando,"—she blew a breath for emphasis— "what an impressive man. Maybe I'm naive, but I feel hopeful right now."

I put my hand on her shoulder. "Hope beats despair every time, Rori."

I told myself the same thing, knowing full well what a tough road lay ahead. Suspects and theories were one thing, but hard evidence after four years was quite another.

Chapter Twenty-One

"Am I still a suspect?" Twila Jenson said teasingly. It was the next morning, and I'd called to ask for some additional time to "clear up a couple of questions."

"Of course," I said with mock seriousness, returning the tease. No reason to set her on edge.

"I'm at my place on Seven Devils Road. This is a painting day. We can chat here, if you don't mind talking while I work."

"That's fine with me." I jotted down her address and told her I'd see her within the hour.

The rest of Team Claxton was already on the move. Sissy Anderson had left a voice mail asking Claire to stop by her place, and as a precaution, we decided Nando should go with her. Before they left, Claire covered my stitches with a narrower, less obtrusive bandage that made me look less like a wounded warrior.

I took Arch for a quick walk, then ushered him into the car. I wasn't leaving him alone at the beach house, either. He hopped in with enthusiasm, despite my warning that he might have a long wait in the car. I took the Cape Arago Highway to Cottrell Lane, a narrow road that wound its way through an area—once thickly forested with Sitka spruce, western hemlock, and Douglas fir —that had been ruthlessly harvested, the leavings of the clear-cut stacked in huge piles like funeral pyres. I drove through the devastation, shaking off a feeling of anxiety at the thought of losing our virgin forests.

At Seven Devils Road, I headed south until it became a dirt road ten miles later. After crossing a one-lane bridge over a narrow creek two miles in, I spotted Twila's place. Painted dark green with a cupola promising a view of the sea, the two-story house stood alone on an isolated, wooded lot. A black Lincoln Navigator with heavily tinted windows was parked in front on a circular drive with an ornate birdbath in the center. Twila was at the side of the house, tending a bed of rambling nasturtiums that had yet to bloom.

I let Archie out to stretch his legs, and when Twila saw him, he shamelessly worked his magic on her. "Oh, he's so handsome," she cooed after we exchanged greetings. "I love dogs. Bring him in, Cal." Today her hair was wound in a careless bun, and she wore a pair of paint-spattered coveralls. She looked down at them in a self-deprecating way. "Excuse the outfit. I forget these are on half the time. I'm a messy painter."

"A walking Jackson Pollock," I quipped.

She showed the tilted smile although her eyes failed to join in, reflecting instead the melancholy I sensed in our first meeting. Having lost my wife, I knew the feeling. Archie and I followed her into the house, which was tastefully decorated in pastel shades and comfortable-looking overstuffed furniture. Her studio was in the cupola, a glass-fronted, rectangular box jutting from the roof and accessible from the second floor by a spiral staircase. We climbed the stairs, followed by Archie, who made quick work of it in a show of his athletic prowess.

"Well, that's the first dog that's ever made it up here," Twila said as Arch summited, found a spot in the corner, and plopped down with his back to the wall, gangster style. "I call this my crow's nest." She moved some brushes and paint tubes so I could sit down. "Excuse the mess. I'm a pack rat. Never throw anything away."

"No problem. The view's stunning." An aria played softly in the background. "Is that Maria Callas?" I knew just enough about opera to proffer a guess of who owned that soaring soprano voice.

Her eyes came to life. "Yes. "Mi chiamano Mimi" from *La Boheme*." She smiled demurely. "I'm an opera fanatic. So was Sonny." Her look turned wistful. "We had season tickets in San Francisco. Never missed a performance. I still go." She took a seat in front of her easel and gazed out at the ocean. "The light's so gorgeous today, I dropped everything to paint."

I had to agree about the light. Obscured by fine mist, the sun bathed the ocean in a rich, silvery glow. Now and then the mist would part, revealing a deep blue sky, and the ocean responded by morphing from silver to turquoise in that brief moment.

Twila had covered a long, rectangular canvas with swirls of a matching silver hue and was in the process of adding silhouetted cypress trees that seemed to float through a silvery mist. "The wind doesn't shape the coastal trees by actually bending the branches," she said as she worked. "The buds on the side exposed to the salt and wind shrivel and die, while those on the sheltered side develop and grow away from the weather." She sighed, showing a wan smile. "I identify with those trees."

"They're survivors," I offered. I watched her paint for a while, engrossed, and not particularly anxious to break the tranquil mood.

She said, finally, "Is your investigation making any progress?"

"Yes and no. Theories abound, but hard evidence is scarce." Seizing the opening, I continued, "Walter Sanders told me your husband decided to go along with the LNG deal just before he died."

She kept painting, her eyes on the canvas. "That's absurd, and Walter knows it. Why would he lie about that?"

Good question, I said to myself. "He said the money was just too tempting."

She dipped the fine-tipped brush in black acrylic and continued to paint. "Well, Sonny wasn't averse to making a buck, but like I told you, Cal, he hated the LNG proposal. Walter is either misinformed or lying."

"Sonny wouldn't have agreed to something or signed any papers without you knowing?"

"Not a chance. He kept me apprised of all the Condor dealings. We were close, a team."

I paused while she dabbed at the canvas. "You were painting on the night he was killed. Was that typical, I mean you two not hanging out together on a Friday night?"

She managed a tight smile. "When I'm inspired, I make it a point to paint. Sonny was very understanding about that."

"A happy marriage, then."

"Very." She dipped her brush again and turned her attention back to the canvas, the bent silhouettes of the trees forming an intricate, lace-like pattern.

"What were your husband's plans that night, I mean, while you were at the Tioga? Do you remember?"

Her brush stopped in mid-stroke. "He was doing what he loved, woodworking. He was making a bookcase out of some gorgeous old walnut he had shipped in from North Carolina." She looked at me, her eyes suddenly shiny in the ambient light. "That's where I found him, in the garage that doubled as his workshop." She swiped a tear and began painting again. "Sonny was a wonderful man."

I felt a stab of guilt for bringing her to tears. "I'm sure he was. You're kind to help me like this, Twila. Just a few more questions and I'll get out of here."

She looked at me, her face resolute. "That's quite alright, Cal. I want to help. Don't hold back on my account."

While she focused on the canvas, I took her back over her previous comments about the quarrel over the LNG deal and details of the sale of her share of Condor Enterprises. Nothing new surfaced, and by the time I finished that line of questioning,

Maria Callas had moved on to other operas and most of the morning mist had burned off. I stood up and Archie sprang to his feet, his stump of a tail wagging anxiously. He'd had enough art and music.

I paused at the staircase. "Is there anything else you can think of that might be important?"

She put her paintbrush down and absently brushed back the hair that had fallen from her bun. "No, Cal, but if I do, I'll contact you immediately." She paused for a moment, then, "Do you think Walter had anything to do with Sonny's murder?"

I met her eyes and held them. "Do you?"

She sighed deeply. "God, they had their issues, particularly near the end, but I never..." Her voice trailed off and she looked away. "How could he?"

"Was that a question or an accusation?"

Her eyes filled again, and she didn't answer. I decided to leave it there. We spiraled back down to the second floor, then took the stairs to the first with Archie leading the way. The entry hall on the way out was lined on either side with family photos, portraits, and memorabilia. I was stopped by an oil painting of a woman who had the same off-kilter smile as Twila.

"That's Grandma Elenore," she said. "I know, I know. I look just like her." She pointed to a beautiful, multi-strand jade necklace around her grandmother's neck and smiled. "When you crack the case, Cal, I'd like that necklace back."

———

I drove away with mixed feelings. On one hand, the case against Walter Sanders was strengthened, but I did wonder if Twila was all that innocent as she slowly but surely painted him into a corner. And was she really unaware that her husband—Mr. Upstanding Citizen, to use Walter's term—was screwing the wife of his business partner? I wasn't so sure. There was something else, too—I could sense the sorrow she was living with. And for that, my heart went out to her.

A wave of impatience and frustration washed over me again. I still hadn't uncovered a single piece of physical evidence. Without that, I might as well be trying to figure out how many angels can dance on the tip of Twila's paintbrush.

Chapter Twenty-Two

When Arch and I got back to Sunset Lane, Nando's Lexus sat in the beach house driveway, gleaming in the morning sun. A tribute to my friend's fastidiousness, I'd never seen a speck of dirt on that car. "In Cuba," he remarked to me once in a moment of candor, "I took a job in a big hotel because that's where the good food was, food I could sneak to my family. Those were hard times, Calvin. Is it any wonder I enjoy the finer things in life?"

Now an avowed capitalist, my friend had switched from communism with the zeal of the newly converted. In addition to being the best PI in Portland, he dabbled in real estate and owned a janitorial business. Nando hated bureaucrats and regulations and cut corners wherever he could, but I trusted him implicitly, and when it came to doing the right thing, I'd never known my friend to flinch.

I found him and Claire out on the deck. With the mist burned off, the sky and the ocean vied for the richest, most beautiful shade of blue. "We picked up some smoked salmon and bagels," Claire said. "Saved you some."

I scooped out the last flesh from half an avocado shell and spread it on a bagel, squeezed lemon juice on it, then layered on a slice of red onion, a slice of tomato, and a generous portion of salmon. "How did it go with Sissy?"

Claire looked at Nando then back at me, her eyes alight. "Amazing, Dad. She's got evidence that Max Sloat was involved in the distribution that Howard Coleman and the brothers were running."

I set my bagel down. "*Evidence?* What kind?"

She fiddled with her computer for a moment, then pointed at the screen. "I took a picture of it and uploaded it. There are seven pages."

The photos revealed what appeared to be a handwritten tally sheet of some kind, inscribed in cramped but legible printing. Each sheet had three columns headed by HC, RB/DB, and MS. The rows were delineated by dates, the most recent being ten days before Howard Coleman was murdered and stretching back nearly six months at roughly two-week intervals. The entries in each column were dollar amounts. I studied them for a few moments then looked up and smiled. "HC stands for Howard Coleman, RB slash DB for the two brothers, RB being Robert, DB his sibling, and MS stands for Max Sloat."

"*Bingo,*" Claire said, her eyes wide with excitement. "And now we know the initials of both brothers. The dollar amounts are interesting, too. If you total across each row, you'll find that MS always gets twenty percent of the take for that date."

"A management fee, I am thinking," Nando said.

"Right," I responded, looking at Claire. "That fits with what Kenny said about Sloat's trucks hauling more than timber. It looks like she's taking a cut for providing cover for their fentanyl distribution."

"I asked Sissy about that," Claire added. "She said the timber industry is so vital to the region that law enforcement gives them a wide berth, or it may be that Max Sloat's paying off Stoddard or some of his deputies to turn a blind eye. In any case, no way Sissy's showing this to Stoddard."

"Where did she find it?" I asked between bites.

"She said she found it in the only book he owned—his deceased mother's Bible—but she may have had it all along. She wants us to use the information but doesn't want it to get out that Howard was distributing such nasty drugs."

Nando chuckled. "A lot of cash accrued in Howard's column, north of one hundred and fifty thousand dollars by my counting. Perhaps Sissy would like to retain this money."

"That could be," Claire said, "but she also wants justice for Howard in the worst way, and she sees us as her only hope. She's gotten some death threats, too, Dad—phone messages telling her to keep her mouth shut about Coleman's business dealings."

Nando showed a knowing smile. "She has the temper and fire of a Latina. I am reminded of some women I knew in Cuba. And she has an impressive arsenal—a double barrel shotgun and a couple of handguns, including a sweet, chrome-plated Sig Sauer P-320. It would be a mistake to underestimate this woman."

We kicked around the possibilities this new information suggested but quickly realized we had more theories than facts to back them up. After we had shaped a particularly complex conspiracy involving the various players, Nando smiled and said, "There is another explanation." We both looked at him. "Howard Coleman was discovered skimming money from the drug operation. Max Sloat had the brothers kill him, or they did it on their own. The simplest solution is generally the correct one—what philosophers refer to as the Razor of Occam."

I expelled a breath in frustration. "In other words, no connection to our case. Point taken. We don't know enough yet."

"So, what do we do next?" Claire said, looking equally frustrated.

"We've got to find Robert and his brother," I said. "And we can't neglect Walter Sanders or the possibility that Walter and Max were both behind Sonny's murder." I went on to describe my meeting with Twila Jenson and the fact that she said her husband wanted nothing to do with the LNG deal.

"That motive stays alive," Claire said.

"Have you heard back from the young woman Walter was carrying on with?" I asked.

"As a matter of fact, Kathy Harper called back when I was headed over to Sissy's. I kept it vague, said I was assisting an attorney and wanted to ask her a few questions about that time, background stuff. She became wary immediately. 'I'm busy with a two-year old,' she told me. 'I'll think it over and call you back.' I'm not sure she ever will. Women, especially women in a close-knit community like this, are still reluctant to come forward."

That afternoon Claire and Nando planned to continue the hunt for the two brothers, but first Nando called his office assistant, Esperanza, to ask her to alert his contacts that Robert and brother D shared a last name beginning with the letter B. "That should narrow down the field even more," he said when he clicked off.

I went back out on the deck and opened a file folder marked "Millard Sloat" that Claire had prepared for me. It contained a fifteen-year-old article from the *Coos Bay World*, headlined "Local Businessman Lost in Boating Mishap." It went on to describe how experienced sailor Millard Sloat and daughter Maxine ended up fighting for their lives in the frigid water just off Yoakam Point after a sneaker wave nearly flipped their boat. Miraculously, Maxine was able to save herself and get back in the boat. She then spent an hour and a half looking for her father before giving up and motoring back in.

Another article dated seven months earlier announced the funeral arrangements for Annie Sloat, the younger daughter of Millard and sister of Maxine. Attached to that was Annie's obituary, which described a quiet young girl of fifteen, who loved books and animals. The cause of death wasn't mentioned, but Claire had written in the margin, "Rori told me she hanged herself." I recalled the tattoo on Max's forearm—her sister's name bracketed with red hearts, a touching tribute. The final item was the obit of Millard's wife, who died of cancer four years before the boating accident. In the margin, Claire had written, "Spousal loss a known trigger for sexual abuse of a family member...?"

I sat back and thought about what I'd just read. The tragedies that had stalked the Sloat family weighed on me, and the suggestion that the elder Sloat had abused his younger daughter was revolting. Then a thought occurred to me—Claire, Archie, and I had something in common with Millard Sloat and Howard Coleman. Millard and Howard both died watery deaths, which was exactly what our attacker intended for us. Bizarre coincidence or something more sinister?

I didn't have an answer, and despite the deck being awash in brilliant sunlight, a cold chill snaked its way down my spine.

Chapter Twenty-Three

"I'm working late tonight," Max Sloat said. "I suppose I could spare a few moments then. I'll tell Manny to let you in. Does seven work?" I told her it did, pleased she had taken my call. She chuckled. "Manny got his butt chewed for giving you a visitor's badge last time. Passing yourself off as some kind of truck aficionado was devious, Mr. Claxton. What other tricks do you have up your sleeve?"

"None, I assure you," I said in a light tone. "I'll wear a short-sleeved shirt just to prove it." I clicked off, and my stomach tightened a couple of notches. Who was I dealing with here— someone who's simply taking money from a drug operation or a stone-cold killer with a penchant for death by drowning?

Claire and Nando called later that afternoon, and we agreed to meet for a quick bite at a little fish house in Charleston, the High Tide, ahead of my meeting with Sloat. "We did not turn up any new sightings of the Brothers B," Nando said as he read through the menu, "and when we checked in with Joyce, the waitress at the bar where we think brother DB hangs out, she suddenly had no desire to speak to me. But luckily the story does not end there."

Claire smiled. "I'd been waiting in the car while Nando went in to talk to her. When he came out, I said, 'Maybe she's worried about being seen with you. After all, you do stand out in a crowd. Let me try.' So, we waited a few minutes, and then I went in and got her to tell me what happened."

Nando looked at me. "She has the velvet touch, this daughter of yours."

"I know."

Claire went on, "Joyce said that DB came in two nights ago, but a buddy of his pulled him aside, and then he left in a big hurry. DB's friend must have seen Nando the first time, assumed he was a cop. Anyway, the guy gives Joyce a look that almost stopped her heart, you know, the keep-your-mouth-shut-or-else look."

"But she talked to you, anyway," I said.

Claire shrugged. "I said she'd be helping an innocent man get out of prison, that it was time for women to stop letting men push them around." Claire looked at me, her jaw set in that defiant, stubborn line I'd known since her childhood. "That's all it took, Dad. Joyce's tough. All the women around here seem to be."

"Good work," I said. "The good news is that the Brothers B may still be in the area. The bad news is DB won't be popping into that bar again any time soon."

Nando slapped his menu down on the table and twisted his face into a scowl. "Always the bad news following the good. What we need is some good news that travels alone."

I couldn't have agreed more.

———

"Thanks a lot, man," Manny said, as he opened the side gate at Sloat Trucking for me. "Because of you I'm stuck on the fucking swing shift for the foreseeable future."

"I'm sorry," I told him in a tone meant to convey my sincerity. "I didn't mean for that to happen."

Sloat's Dodge Ram, the only car left in front of the office building, sparkled like a polished cherry in the strong overhead lights. *Maybe the world can be divided into people who keep their cars obsessively clean and those who don't,* I thought as I climbed the stairs and knocked on the office door.

"I'm on a short fuse, but come in, Cal," Max said, echoing how she greeted me the last time we met. She was dressed the same, too, except for the Pendleton shirt that replaced the khaki Carhartt.

Pleased to hear we were now on a first name basis, I followed her strong, purposeful strides into her office and took a seat in front of a massive, cluttered desk that stood like a bulwark between us. Like the Ram truck, her bowling trophies gleamed in the overhead lights, dust free. "Like I mentioned on the phone," I began, "I've got a few issues I was hoping you might help me with. I—"

"You still think Kenny Sanders is innocent?" She interrupted, her tone impatient.

"More than ever. But I'd—"

"Who do you suspect?" She interrupted again, her eyes wide with curiosity, her intent clearly to dominate the conversation.

I showed a patient smile. "I can't discuss that. If you don't mind, I'd like to circle back to Howard Coleman. You were, uh, going to make some inquiries about any connection between him and someone who might drive a dark-colored Peterbilt truck."

Her steel-gray eyes narrowed a fraction, and she waved a hand dismissively. "I didn't find anything. We must have a couple of dozen Peterbilts on the books, nearly all dark-colored. None of them was running for us the day you had your accident."

"Thanks for checking. I'd still like to see your records," I added, just to gauge her reaction.

She huffed a breath and shot me a look of exasperation. "Look, Cal, my truckers work their butts off just to eke out a living here on the coast. This ain't exactly a booming economy, in case you haven't noticed. If they happen to be working something on the side—you know, a little black-market weed or cigarettes, that sort of thing—that fits with their delivery schedule, I'm not gonna pry. And I'm sure as hell not sharing any information voluntarily. They expect that from me."

I smiled at her brazen openness. "Do you take a cut?"

Her eyes flashed at me, like light off gun metal. "No. I'm strictly legit."

"Of course. Let me ask you about something else—your relationship with Condor Enterprises. You were brought in to help finance the LNG real estate deal, right?"

She blinked a couple of times, not a good poker move. "Who told you that?"

I gave her the patient smile again. "It's not exactly a national secret, Max. I'm curious. Why the sensitivity around your partnership in the company?"

She paused, obviously deciding whether to respond or not. Finally, "Well, the LNG thing has the whole area divided in half, and the businesses we diversified into are not without controversy. A lot of my trucking customers are real straight arrows. Walter doesn't really give a shit what people think, so we decided he'd take all the heat."

"When did you enter into negotiations with Twila Jenson to buy her share?"

"Oh, a few months after Sonny died. I don't remember exactly."

That tallies with what Twila told me, I said to myself. "Did you have any discussions with Walter Sanders prior to Sonny's death?"

"No. None." No hesitation whatsoever.

"Did you know Sonny was against the LNG deal you wound up helping finance?"

She hesitated. "Now that you mention it, Walter did tell me Sonny was a holdout, but like I said, that was after the fact." She shook her head. "Doesn't surprise me. No disrespect for the dead, but Sonny Jenson was a fucking hypocrite."

"Hypocrite? How?"

She twisted her mouth into a scowl. "Oh, you know, always

playing the quintessential good guy around Coos Bay, anything to make him look good, get his name in the paper."

"Mr. Upstanding."

"Yeah, right. But he wasn't all that innocent. Hell, I'll bet the reason he balked on the LNG deal wasn't out of love for the environment. It was a big play. He probably didn't have the *cojones* to risk the money." She caught herself and a look of dawning recognition spread slowly across her face. "Are you suggesting Walter had a reason to get rid of Sonny? Is *he* a suspect?"

I ignored the question. "What else did Walter tell you about Sonny?"

She looked to the side for a moment, then returned her gaze to me. "He told me Sonny was having an affair."

"With whom?"

She paused as a sardonic smile formed on her lips. "With his wife, Krysta. I told you Sonny was a hypocrite."

"When did Walter tell you this?"

"After he left Krysta, maybe a year after the trial."

"Did he tell you anything else?"

Max shrugged. "No, not that I recall. I think I've already said too much about my partner."

"Why are you being so open?"

She studied the clutter on her desk for a few beats. "I don't know. First off, Walter's a big boy and can take care of himself. And I don't owe him a damn thing. If nothing else, that kid deserves to have the truth told about what happened. I think there was a rush to judgment."

That exchange pretty much ended the session. As I started toward the door, I noticed a photo on the wall of a thinner, younger Max standing with her arm around a teenage girl who apparently inherited all the beauty genes in the Sloat family.

"That's Annie, my kid sister," Max said. "She passed fifteen years ago."

"I'm sorry for your loss. She's lovely."

"Yeah, well, she was a beauty inside and out."

I looked around at the photos on the wall and didn't see any of her father, Millard. "Your dad left you quite a legacy. I imagine he'd be proud to see what you've built."

She drew her lips into a tight line and looked away. "If he is, it's not mutual," she said in a voice I had to strain to hear. "He's not mourned by me, Cal."

"I heard something about a boating accident."

"Yeah, he drowned right off Yoakam Point." The sardonic smile again. "Makes you believe in poetic justice." With that, she opened the door and let me out without another word.

Chapter Twenty-Four

When I arrived back at the beach house that night, I found Claire on a conference call in her room with the door shut and Nando waiting for me with his bag packed. "I have a property closing tomorrow morning, and I need fresh clothing," he said. "How did it go with the madam of trucking?" When I finished describing the meeting, he stroked his chin and lowered his thick eyebrows. "So, Maxine continues to deny any knowledge of the Brothers B, an obvious lie."

"Yep. No surprise there, if our interpretation of the tally sheets is right. She did admit some of her truckers might traffic in dope but played it down as black-market marijuana, something she turns a blind eye to."

"Such innocence. And she tells you Walter Sanders knew about his wife's indiscretions."

"Yeah, that was a big surprise."

Nando flashed a knowing smile. "It seems Maxine is trying to point us in Walter's direction."

"Right. Just like Twila Jenson." I closed my eyes and massaged the bridge of my nose for a moment. "Who to believe? Max and Walter both have secrets, and we've got nothing tangible on either one of them." I exhaled a long breath and looked at my friend. "Maybe this is a fool's errand, Nando."

He shook his head. "It is not. You look tired. Get some sleep. I'll see you tomorrow night."

"We haven't talked about your fee yet."

He picked up his bag and opened the front door. "I am on vacation."

———

Claire had already eaten, but Archie's doleful look made it clear he hadn't. I fed him and then threw a quick meal together—a three-egg frittata made with some asparagus spears, the remaining smoked salmon, and a generous amount of grated Gruyere. A bottle of Mirror Pond worked nicely for a beverage. After cleaning up, I wandered back to Claire's bedroom and knocked.

"*What?*" The response had an edge to it.

I opened the door and looked in. She was sprawled on the bed with her laptop, surrounded by sheets of paper. Her eyes were red, her cheeks tear-stained. "You okay?"

She looked away. "No."

"What's wrong, sweetheart?"

"Everything."

I sat down on the edge of the bed. "Want to talk about it?"

She stayed mute for a long time, staring at the seashell-patterned wallpaper across the room. Finally, she said, "It's Gabriel."

"What did he do?"

"It's what he didn't do. He hasn't called or anything."

"I thought you broke up."

She snapped her laptop closed and looked at me, tears welling from her eyes. "Oh, Dad, I thought he was the one. Now it's all screwed up."

"Do you love this guy?"

She sighed, sat up against the headboard, and swiped the tears from her cheeks. "Did you know you loved mom, I mean, right away?"

I smiled as the memory rushed back, vivid, undiminished. "It was lights out for me the first time I saw her. I was on campus, the Bear's Lair, wolfing down a sandwich at one of those little stand-up tables. She came up and asked if she could share the table. I introduced myself, but all I got back was her first name and the fact that she was an art history major."

Claire smiled, and her eyes regained some sparkle. "Tell me what happened? I've heard this before, but it's been a long, long time."

"I spent a week or so eating lunch there every day, just hoping to see her again. Finally, she reappeared, and when I went up to say hi, she didn't even remember me." Claire laughed out loud. "But I did get her last name and a phone number."

"What attracted you to her?"

I paused for a moment, savoring a feeling I hadn't allowed myself for a very long time. "The whole package, but if I had to name one thing, her eyes." I looked at my daughter. "Your eyes."

"I'm not as pretty as she was."

I laughed. "Oh, yes you are. You got *everything* from your mom, well, except for your broad shoulders with freckles and being five-foot-ten."

"And your brain. I'm not prone to depression like Mom was. I don't get depressed. I get angry."

"And now you're angry with Gabriel."

She folded her arms across her chest and stitched her brows together. "Not so much angry as disappointed." I waited for her to continue. "I don't think he gets it. I'm not going to compromise my independence. Women can't afford to do that anymore, Dad."

I nodded. "Give it some time. If he really cares about you, he'll come around."

She looked away. "That's what I'm afraid of, that he won't. Did you and Mom go through any rough patches early?"

I laughed. "Oh, yeah. We broke up twice before we ironed everything out. Relationships hardly ever ramp up smoothly, Claire."

She exhaled a long sigh, signaling that this particular conversation was over. I'd ventured about as much advice as I dared. My daughter kept her own counsel, and I knew it. We sat there in silence for a while, and I thought I could hear the muffled roar of the surf, but it was probably just some random buzzing in my ears.

———

Later that night, after the light went out in Claire's bedroom, I poured myself a Rémy Martin and carried it into the dark living room. The moon, a waxing gibbous, hung low on the horizon, its reflected light beating a shimmering path back to the shore. I sipped the cognac and took some deep breaths to calm my mind. I ached for Claire, hating to see her in anguish over an affair of the heart, which was, of course, the worse kind of pain. My heart was like an old leather football that had been punted around, but hers was fresh, full of hope and expectation, and dangerously vulnerable.

Maybe she'll fare better than me, I said to myself. One can always hope.

My thoughts turned to the Kenny Sanders case as I absently watched the moon sink below the horizon, extinguishing the lighted path. It was an apt metaphor. The momentum I'd felt just a few days earlier seemed to be extinguished as well. What we had was an embarrassment of motives without anything tangible to latch on to. My spirits sank with the moon until I thought of Claire. "Don't get depressed," I said out loud. "Get angry."

It was good advice.

———

By the time I finished the Rémy, the sea was dark, and my eyelids were heavy as lead. I drifted off, knowing full well that Archie needed a walk, but I was too far gone to act on the thought. A troubling dream set in. My dog was growling, a low, guttural sound signaling danger. Like a free diver coming up for a breath, I surfaced from the dream only to realize I wasn't dreaming. Archie stood at the sliding door leading out to the deck, his hackles raised, his throat rumbling.

Thump, then thump again. The muffled sound seemed to come from the north end of the deck. I came fully awake as the hair on my arms and on the back of my neck stood at attention.

Where the hell did I put the Glock?

Chapter Twenty-Five

I'd left the Glock in the nightstand drawer in the bedroom. In pitch blackness, I took the stairs two at a time and came back down brandishing the weapon, a cold block of highly engineered steel in my hand. Archie hadn't moved. I flattened myself against the wall next to him. "What is it, Big Boy?" I whispered. He looked up at me and whimpered a couple of times, a signal that he wanted out to investigate. Only the south end of the deck was visible from our vantage point. Nothing moved in the onshore breeze except the shadowy branches of the gnarled cedars beyond the deck.

Thump, then thump again. The sound came from the direction of the gate that closed off the stairway down to the beach. Archie's growl went up an octave. "Easy, Big Boy." I slipped from the living room into the dining room, where a window afforded a view of the north end of the deck, then I moved along the wall and peered cautiously out the window. Thump, thump. The sound again, but this time I pinpointed its origin—the unlatched gate was catching in the breeze before the attached spring snapped it back.

I breathed a sigh of relief, although I did wonder how the gate became unlatched in the first place. Had Claire left it that way?

I would inquire in the morning. Meanwhile, I switched on the floodlights that illuminated the deck and watched for several minutes before venturing out to relatch it.

That night Archie didn't get his walk, and I slept with the Glock sitting next to me on top of my barely read Joe Nezbø like a bodyguard.

———

Ominous shadows of wind-swept cedars tumbled through my dreams that night, and when I got down to the kitchen the next morning, Claire was gone. A note on the table said,

> Meeting Kathy Harper in Coos Bay at 9. Wish me luck!
> Claire

I fed Arch, drank a double cappuccino and headed down the outside stairs to the beach, with Archie leading the way. The cool breeze that kicked up the night before was still blowing, but the sky was achingly clear, and the slanting sunlight seemed to dance off the Pacific. Halfway down the stairs, Arch stopped to sniff an ugly brown spatter on the edge of a stair tread. I pushed him away instinctively.

Nothing else caught my eye on the way down the stairs, and the soft, uneven sand at the base of the steps didn't reveal any footprints, nor would I have expected it to. The plovers were out foraging in the wet sand, so I tethered my dog and walked north toward Yoakam Point, where a narrow gully—more of a trench, really—afforded access to Lighthouse Beach from the bluff above for those willing to make the steep climb. The base of the gully was littered with rocks, but the sand there was firmer. I saw what looked like fresh footprints between some of the rocks—by the spacing it looked like two sets of prints, one following the other. The footprints led down to the high tide line and disappeared, making it impossible to tell whether they headed north or south.

As I studied the prints, Archie found another brown spatter, this one more voluminous. It looked like partially dried spittle. With Archie scrabbling ahead, I started climbing up the trench. I didn't see anything of interest except for three more brown patches that Arch stopped to sniff—two in the gully and one on the trail leading out to the Cape Arago Highway. I got down on my hands and knees, leaned in close to one of the patches and reluctantly took a sniff.

Ugh! Chewing tobacco. No question.

Twenty minutes later I was back at the beach house, completing a full circle. After finding a safety razor in a kitchen utility drawer and emptying a small aspirin bottle, I went back to the first patch of spittle I'd seen on the stairs and used the blade to scrape it into the bottle. Then I called Captain Harmon Scott at the Portland Police Bureau.

"Oh, shit," Scott said, "that friendly greeting means you want something, Claxton."

"You owe me, Harmon, and you know it."

"The hell I do."

"All I need is for you to run the DNA of a sample. See if it's in the system. I need a name."

"Oh, is that all? You know I can't do that."

"Yes, you can. Come on, Harmon. This is life and death stuff. I'm not kidding."

"Jesus, it's always the same with you, Claxton. I heard you were on vacation."

"I am, but, uh, something's come up."

The line went silent, and I feared he'd hung up. Finally, he heaved a sigh. "I suppose you need it like yesterday."

"How did you know that? I'll overnight the sample to you. It's a wad of spit and tobacco juice. I think it belongs to someone who tried to kill my daughter and me."

"Some vacation. Okay, I'll see what I can do. A priority job done off the books, that's gonna take a shitload of persuading."

"Who better? Thanks, Harmon."

"We're flat even now, understood?"

———

Claire breezed in an hour later, and while I cooked brunch, she described her meeting with Harper. "She's a nice woman, married now with a two-year-old and holding down a teller job at a savings and loan. I told her that as part of Kenny's defense, we were conducting routine interviews of his friends at that time. She said she was shocked by the news and remembers that time vividly. She answered my questions and made it clear she never believed Kenny committed the murder."

"Did she say why?"

Claire smiled. "Yeah, she said Kenny was a surfer, that he took all his aggression out on the waves at Bastendorff. She thought it was a robbery. 'Whacked-out meth heads' was the term she used. But when I mentioned Walter Sanders, she slammed the brakes on. 'Kenny's stepdad? I hardly knew the guy.' We danced around that for a while. Finally, I told her we had reliable information that she was seeing Walter around the time of the murder. Talk about a deer in the headlights. She looked terrified, Dad. 'I'm married now,' she said. 'I have a little girl. I don't want to stir up the past. And, besides, how could I possibly help you?'"

"What did you tell her?"

"I said we were in fact-finding mode, and her cooperation could be vital in helping Kenny get out of prison. I also told her we'd do everything in our power to keep her information confidential."

"Good. You didn't promise anything."

Claire laughed and shot me a look. "I know better than that. Kathy said she needed some time to think, that she'd get back to me. I left her with a gentle reminder that a lot of her sisters were coming forward these days."

"Do you think she'll cooperate?"

Claire shrugged and made a face. "Hard to say. "Coming forward's one thing—and the right thing—but facing the consequences is daunting. Women who speak truth to power still run the risk of having their lives blown apart."

"Point taken." I paused. "Listen, Claire, there's something else—did you leave the gate to the beach stairs open?"

"No, not that I know of. Why?" I explained the trail of tobacco juice Archie discovered and the two sets of footprints I'd seen. She said, "The Brothers B were *here*? Last night?"

"That's my conclusion."

She picked up the aspirin bottle, peered at it, and said, "Nice of one of them to leave his calling card." A wry smile. "At least we know we're not dealing with master criminals, Dad."

I had to laugh, although I had a more serious message in mind. "Not master criminals but dangerous as hell, Claire. Listen, I think you should—"

My phone riffed. "Take it, Dad," Claire said, her look making it clear she knew what I was about to say and didn't want to hear it.

It was Rori Dennison. "Cal, it's Kenny. He's been stabbed."

Chapter Twenty-Six

"He's a lucky fellow," the surgeon said, a small woman with a quick smile and intense, dark eyes and a name tag that read N. Nguyen. She'd taken Rori's hands in hers, a spontaneous show of compassion I didn't expect to see at a prison infirmary. "The blade missed his heart and lungs and only nicked one of his vertebrae. I repaired most of the damage. His body will do the rest."

Relief flooded Rori's face. "Oh, thank God." Her magenta hair was in a magnificent tangle as she bent slightly to accommodate the surgeon's diminutive stature. "When can we see him? We have visitor clearance."

The surgeon hesitated. "Let's see how he feels when he comes out of the anesthesia. Why don't you wait, and I'll let you know?"

The time crept by, and it was nearly the end of visiting hours when the surgeon returned. She was smiling. "He's an amazingly strong young man. You can go directly to the recovery room." She put a finger up. "*But*, only ten minutes."

I gestured in Claire's direction and said to the doctor, "We're his legal team. We'd like to speak to him separately, if that's possible."

"Okay. Five minutes each."

Rori was allowed in first and returned obviously sobered by the visit. "He looks awful, and they have him manacled to the bed, but I got a smile out of him. He wouldn't talk about what happened, said he didn't want to worry me." She rolled her eyes. "Like I'm not going to worry. He's glad you're here, Cal. I think he might open up to you." Her eyes filled, and a tear cleared her lower lid and traced a path down her cheek. "How can he go back into that hellhole?"

When we entered the room, Kenny looked at Claire first and managed a faint smile. "An angel. Have I died and gone to heaven?"

Claire suppressed a return smile. "No such luck, Kenny."

To me, he said, "Hello Mr. Claxton. Thanks for coming." His cheeks were hollow, and his blond beard and slate blue eyes stood out against skin that was white as the sheets on the gurney.

"How are you feeling?" I asked.

"Not so hot, but it beats the alternative."

"What happened?"

He sighed a weak breath. "I was out in the yard when a group of EKs kind of drifted over, a few at a time so I didn't notice. Then they surrounded me to block the view, and bam, I had a shiv in my back before I could do anything." He closed his eyes and grimaced. "Worst pain I've ever felt. They left it in me." His mouth curled up on one side. "I guess they figured I mean what I said about not joining them."

"You know it was somebody in the European Kindred?"

"Positive." He glanced at Claire, then back at me. His eyes seemed sunken compared to the last time I'd seen him, but they burned with intensity. "But that doesn't mean shit in this place." He grasped my arm with surprising strength, then grimaced in pain and let go. "I can't go back in there, Mr. Claxton. They won't miss next time. If I go back, I'm a dead man."

I resisted the temptation to promise something I couldn't deliver. "Can you give us some names, something to work with?"

"I already told Security that it was the Kindred. They know all the players, but they can't do squat. It's my word against theirs, and nobody else will talk, even if they saw it." He looked at me, his eyes suddenly desperate. "Can you do anything? People get transferred to other prisons, but I don't know how they do it. I can't go back in there, Mr. Claxton."

"I know that, Kenny. We'll find a way," I said, although I didn't know the ins and outs of moving prisoners around in Oregon. "Meanwhile, you're safe here in the infirmary, and the doc says it'll be a while before you're ready to go back in."

That seemed to calm him somewhat. "How's the investigation coming?"

"We're making steady progress," I said, "but we still have a lot of dots that need connecting."

"We've hired a top-notch private investigator from Portland to help us out," Claire chimed in.

He smiled. "Good." A nurse appeared at this point and shooed us out. As we were leaving, he said to Claire, "How's the surf been?"

"We had a nice swell yesterday, but it was blown out this morning. Onshore wind."

Kenny smiled. "Damn on shores. They screw everything up this time of year."

Claire and Rori went out to the parking lot to give Archie a much-needed break. I joined them ten minutes later, after talking to a clerk in the Prison Services Office about prison transfer procedures. "Kenny needs to talk to his counselor about filling out a transfer request called a 1206. That goes up the line for approval. As his attorney, I can provide a letter in support of his request," I said as we pulled out of the parking lot and headed for I-5.

"How long would that take?" Rori said, her voice filled with concern. She knew better than me how slowly the prison bureaucracy moved.

"They were vague on that. If approved, the move can take place rapidly, but there're two catches. First, there has to be an opening, and Oregon prisons are overcrowded, and second, transfer of someone doing a life sentence needs the approval of the DOC Director." What I didn't say was that the clerk also told me that that kind of approval was rarely, if ever, granted.

"Where would he go?" Claire asked.

"The clerk said the only option is the prison at Pendleton in eastern Oregon."

"*Pendleton?*" Rori said. "Jesus, Cal, that's hundreds of miles from here."

"I know. It's a stopgap until we get him out, Rori. He says he can't go back in here, and I believe him."

Her expression turned contrite. "Of course. I didn't mean it that way. It's just that it's eastern Oregon. They're probably more skinheads over there than here at Salem."

"Yeah, I didn't think of that, but it's still our only option."

Claire said, "He can start over there. It'll buy us some time, if nothing else. We'll contact Kenny tomorrow and get the ball rolling on the transfer."

Rori agreed, and we drove on, shrouded in discouraged silence. We'd already discussed the case on the way to the prison, and the truth was we were spinning our wheels. And now the timing was even more imperative. It wasn't just Kenny's freedom at stake but his life. The transfer would keep him safe, at least temporarily, but the best scenario would be to get him out before he went anywhere. The doc hadn't given us any timing, but he'd probably be well enough to go back into the general population in two weeks, if not sooner.

I marveled at the absurdity of it. *Two weeks.*

I didn't need any more incentive for this case, but there it was.

Chapter Twenty-Seven

"I am cooking dinner tonight," Nando announced when Claire and I arrived at the beach house after dropping Rori off. He was back from Portland, and we couldn't help noticing the two large pizza boxes sitting on the kitchen counter. "We are having my specialty—thin crust pizza with fennel sausage, roasted onions, basil, and Calabrian chiles."

Claire looked closer at the boxes, and a smile bloomed on her face. "Oh, bless you. Ken's Artisan Pizza. You have good taste, Nando."

I laughed, and Nando maintained a straight face. "Okay. I confess I brought them from Portland, but I plan to reheat them perfectly, so they do not become soggy. This requires considerable culinary skill."

While we ate pizza and drank beer, Claire and I brought Nando up to date. Most of the discussion centered on Kenny's stabbing and the time pressure that placed on the investigation, but after I described the night visitors we'd had, Nando said, "You were right about the approach to the beach house the Brothers B would take, Calvin. These men are relentless. And nice work on the tobacco juice."

Claire said, "We can thank Archie for that. He found those

loogies first." On hearing his name, Archie's ears popped up, and his jaw dropped open in a doggy grin.

Laughter all around. Then Nando grew serious and started to say what I'd intended to, "Claire, this has become a very dangerous situation. I—"

Claire shot a hand up. "*Stop*. It's dangerous for *all* of us." She turned from Nando to me and put her hands on her hips. "Don't patronize me, damn it. I'm not some helpless damsel in distress." Her eyes flashed. "I'm the one who pulled you out of the river, Dad. Remember? Treat me like an equal, *please*."

Nando and I sat there searching for something to say. Claire was my only child, my baby, but she was right, of course. We were both acting like condescending jerks. I glanced at my friend and heaved a sigh. I was, indeed, hoisted on my own petard. "Alright. I can't argue with that. We all need to recognize the threat level's at maximum." I looked at Claire. "And I don't want you off on your own—down to the beach or into town, whatever—unless you clear it with me or Nando. Okay?"

"Fair enough."

Looking a bit relieved, Nando said, "We need to address the threat. Calvin, if you are right about last night being a reconnaissance run by the Brothers B, we can be sure they will be back, and probably very soon."

Claire asked, "What should we do?"

"How quickly can Harmon Scott turn the DNA sample around?" Nando said.

I shook my head. "I didn't get any promises, but if he's able to sneak it in at the head of the queue, the lab can do the analysis in two days. But that's a huge if."

Nando nodded. "I agree. We cannot assume we will get any near-term help from Scott. And my sources have turned up nothing so far. So, we need a plan." He stroked his cheek and chin with a big hand. "In Cuba, my father used to say, 'If you want to catch sharks you must chum the waters.'"

He described a plan, and we kicked it around. I didn't like it. It was a long shot and seemed risky, but I had to admit I didn't have a better idea. "Okay," I finally conceded, "we'll try it for a couple of nights."

Claire described her conversation with Kathy Harper next. "One thing stood out," she concluded. "Before Kathy shut down when I mentioned Walter Sanders, she said she remembered the events around the time of the murder well. I've got a feeling she might know something relevant."

"Then, you must persuade her to talk," Nando said.

"Working on it."

After dinner I brought us back around to Sonny Jenson. "I know we favor Max for the murder because of her financial motive, her connection to the Brothers B—"

"And the fact that she may have murdered her father," Claire interjected.

"—Yeah, that, too. But we can't rule out Walter. He had the same financial motive, a flaky alibi, and may have known his wife was sleeping with Sonny."

"*If* we can believe Max about that," Claire added.

"Right. So, what does this suggest we should be doing besides trying to find the Brothers B as soon as possible?"

"Excellent question," Nando said. "Both Max and Walter have secrets, and it's quite possible that even if Walter was not in on the killing, he suspects her guilt. Perhaps we should drive a wedge between them to get Walter to give her up."

"Or, vice-versa," Claire chipped in.

I tipped my beer bottle at them both and flashed a broad smile. "Yes, the thin end of the wedge. Excellent idea."

We came up with a couple of ideas, although we realized we weren't quite ready. More work was needed, a full court press.

———

A blanket of wet fog greeted us the next morning, and the only evidence of the Pacific out beyond the beach house was the muffled thrashing of the surf and the intermittent squawking of seagulls. After breakfast, Nando was ready to set out for the Umpqua Highway with his Peterbilt truck photo in hand. "The Peterbilt appeared behind you from a dirt road about fifteen miles east of Reedsport," he said. "This suggests the Brothers B had some familiarity with the terrain. I am going to scour the area for possible witnesses. Somebody living or working along that stretch of highway could have seen something. A truck that big is hard to hide."

Archie, Claire, and I left soon after that for the North Bend Library. Claire had research and data analysis work related to her Gulf Coast study that needed immediate attention. After dropping her off, my next stop was Coffee and Subversion to check in on Rori and get one of Anthony's double cappuccinos.

Stirred by Rori's act of civil disobedience, a raucous crowd had gathered for another day of collecting signatures for the Stop the LNG Petition. Rori was up front, giving last minute directions. Little half-moons of discoloration showed below her eyes, but she spoke in a firm, clear voice. "We need at least another five thousand signatures before this petition will have any impact on the Governor. Stick to the script and be enthusiastic but not discourteous."

"Like when you handcuffed yourself to that limo?" someone called out, causing the group to erupt in applause, cheers, and laughter.

She waved them off, smiling a bit sheepishly. "That needed doing. Corporations like Bexar don't want people to know what they're up to. They'd rather you read about the fait accompli in the paper when it's too late." She flashed a look of determination and raised a fist. "Now get the hell out of here and collect those signatures."

"Are you okay?" I said, as we sat having coffee after the throng departed. "You look a little tired."

She shrugged. "I didn't get much sleep last night, but that's nothing new." She sipped her coffee and looked at me. "What are you up to today?"

"I just dropped Claire at the library. She's doing postdoc stuff. I left a voice mail for Kenny earlier this morning with instructions for how to get the ball rolling on the transfer." Rori nodded enthusiastically. "Then I'm off to see Twila Jenson. She called this morning and said she had something important to give me."

"Did she say what?"

"No, and I didn't press her on the phone." I paused. "One thing I haven't asked you, Rori—do you think she knew about her husband's affair with Krysta?"

Rori studied her cup for a few moments, then looked up at me. "I saw no hint of that, and she was terribly grief-stricken after Sonny's death—depressed, really. Took her a long time to recover. That would be a hard thing to fake." She looked at me. "You don't suspect her, do you?"

"Nobody's ruled out at the moment."

"Well, she seems to have gotten her life back on track, and her painting's gotten a lot better—darker but more interesting." She paused and held my gaze with sad, tired eyes. "Do we have a prayer, Cal?"

"Yes. We do. Stay positive."

That admonishment applied to me as well.

Chapter Twenty-Eight

Twila Jenson was at her artist getaway off Seven Devils Road, so I headed south again. By this time the sun had vanquished the fog, and Archie had his head thrust out the back window of the Subaru with a big doggie grin, proving he wasn't immune to that universal canine compulsion for rushing fresh air. It made me laugh. It always did.

"How's the painting going?" I said when she came to the door.

She rolled her eyes. "It's always a struggle." Then she knelt down and made a big fuss over my dog. I followed her down the hall, and as I passed the portrait of her grandmother wearing the jade necklace, I was struck again by the resemblance.

With a view of the ocean through a scattering of pines, the kitchen sported an AGA cast iron range, a ceiling rack holding an assortment of copper pots, and some striking seascapes on the walls. She offered me tea. Her hair was down, brushing her shoulders, and her dark eyes were devoid of makeup. I said yes to the tea but apparently without sufficient enthusiasm.

"Oh, dear. You're a coffee drinker, aren't you? I don't own a coffee machine. I'll make the tea strong."

Archie took stock from a corner while she brewed the tea, and we chatted about the weather. A haunting soprano voice drifted down from the cupola. "Who's that singing?" I asked.

"Renée Fleming." Her face brightened somewhat. "Did you see her sing *Danny Boy* at John McCain's funeral?" I shook my head. "That's a shame. It was incredibly moving. She's performing on opening night in San Francisco later this month—*La Traviata*."

"Are you going?"

She handed me my tea in a delicate porcelain cup and saucer. "Wouldn't miss it. I'll be at the Fairmont." She allowed a smile. "The opera's an excuse to play dress-up." She took a few sips, then looked up and asked, "Are you making any progress on the investigation?"

"Yes, but we've had a setback."

I told her about Kenny's stabbing, and by the time I finished her eyes glistened with tears. "Oh, that poor boy. Surely they'll allow him to change prisons."

"I'm told it's not easy for someone with a life sentence. We'll see." I paused and drank some of my tea. "You, uh, said you found something that might be important?"

She dabbed her eyes with a tissue, her face noticeably paler than the last time I'd seen her. "Yes, I have, and now I feel even better about my decision to share it with you." She managed a smile. "I told you I was a pack rat." She put her cup and saucer down and walked over to a counter where a file folder lay. She turned and looked at me. "I'm embarrassed to admit it, but I had Sonny's clothes hanging in a closet in the Coos Bay house until recently. It was just too hard to throw them out, to admit he was really gone, you know?"

"Yes, I do know."

Her eyebrows arched at my comment, but she continued her train of thought. "Well, I finally got around to some housecleaning. His clothes are now at the Goodwill." She smiled with a little less effort. "When I sold the house, I had everything packed up, moved, and stored in a spare bedroom in the Coos Bay house. Never looked at the damn stuff until yesterday." She picked up the folder and handed it to me. "I found this in a box of his office files. I thought it might interest you."

The tab on the folder had LNG handwritten on it. I opened it and withdrew a map, which I unfolded and laid on the kitchen table. A heavy red line traced a route from the California border through southern Oregon and terminated at Jackson Point on Coos Bay. I looked up. "The proposed route of the pipeline."

Twila nodded.

I leafed through the rest of the papers in the folder—a series of detailed plat maps of the same area, showing property lines and proposed easements, along with a listing of names, addresses, and phone numbers with dollar amounts and comments next to each, indicating "yes," "no," and "maybe." Finally, several pages of financial calculations were appended, suggesting some very attractive profits, depending on assumptions made. "This looks like the business case and supporting data for Walter's real estate deal."

"Yes, that's what I thought."

"Did the investigators see this at the time of the murder?"

"No, I don't think so. They went through Sonny's files, his computer, his calendar, but this had been tucked into an unmarked folder. I was tossing all the folders out when it literally fell on the floor. Those detectives weren't very thorough. I'm not surprised they missed it." She pointed at the folder. "There's, ah, a note in the back from Sonny to Walter that you should see."

I found the note, read it, then looked back at her as my heart pumped a little faster. "This is a copy. Did Sonny send the original to Walter?"

"I assume so, but he never said a word to me. That's definitely his signature."

"This is important evidence, Twila. I'd like to take some photos of the file with my phone, if you don't mind." She readily agreed, and after I finished, I said, "I think it's better that the file stays in your possession to preserve its integrity. I want you to keep it in a safe place. Don't add or remove anything, don't show it to anyone, and don't discuss it with anyone without checking with me first. Can you do that?"

"Yes." She paused, and her eyes narrowed down. "Do you think Walter and Max Sloat were behind my husband's death, Cal?"

"I can't say at this juncture, but what you just showed me certainly demands follow-up." That's all I could give her.

She'd lost whatever color was left in her face, and when she closed her eyes, her lower lip trembled. "God, I thought this was all behind me," she said in a barely audible voice. She reached out, put her hand on my arm as if to steady herself, and got up. "More tea?" I said yes and after she filled my cup, she added, "You, um, said a while ago you knew about loss. What did you mean?"

I exhaled a breath. "I lost my wife. It's been over a decade now. She was a painter like you, watercolors mainly, and she taught art at Occidental College in L.A. She suffered from depression and committed suicide. Pills. So, I have some inkling of what you're going through. We, uh, find ways of blaming ourselves in these situations."

She put a hand to her mouth, her face registering a mix of surprise and compassion. "Oh, I'm so sorry to hear that, Cal. That makes us kindred spirits, I guess." She raised her eyes to mine. "I hope you don't blame yourself."

I shrugged. "It's a process. The same goes for you."

She looked away, focusing on something in the distance. "Well, you know, it's what got left unsaid, what could have been, that sort of thing. We always assume we have all the time in the world." A deep sigh. "God, I want justice for Sonny, and I want justice for Kenny Sanders. It's just that…all this drama is ripping the scab off the whole festering wound."

I felt a stab of guilt. "I know it's painful, Twila, but it's cathartic, too. You're doing the right thing, and that will help you regain your footing in the long run."

She nodded slowly, as if considering my words with great care. The conversation drifted off to her love of opera and painting, and after we finished our tea, she showed Archie and me to the door.

Chapter Twenty-Nine

I texted Claire that I was on my way to the library and got this text in return:

> Hey, finished up. Thought of Twila since you were with her, so I walked over to the Tioga Building to have a look at the layout. Pick me up there.

The Tioga Building, I'd learned, was on the National Register, and along with its counterpart, the Egyptian Theater, had elegantly anchored downtown Coos Bay during its halcyon timber and fishing days. At nine stories, the Tioga was still the tallest building on the Oregon Coast and boasted a four-story sign out front that proclaimed its name in retro neon. This is where Twila was painting the night of the murder. She'd been picked up on a security camera coming and going through the front of the building. Claire, I assumed, was assessing the feasibility of an exit out the back, an item on our to-do list.

She was standing outside the building when I drove up, and after she hopped in, said, "Okay, the front of the building is retail—a seafood restaurant and an antique store—and the elevator up to the apartments is further back. There's a rear exit down a hallway next to a set of public restrooms and the fire stairs. It's a one-way emergency exit with a sign that says using it will activate an alarm."

"So, she couldn't have snuck out that way," I said.

"Not likely, unless it wasn't an alarmed exit four years ago, and the police report is vague on that point. I asked around at the restaurant and the antique store, but nobody'd been around that long except one waiter, but he wasn't working today. I asked one of the other waiters to have him call me." She shrugged. "Anyway, I'll get a definitive answer on that. It'd be nice to eliminate a suspect." She paused as I turned onto Ocean Boulevard. "How'd it go with Twila this time?"

"She showed me a file that proves Walter was pushing the LNG deal with Sonny and that Max was completely in on it." I handed her my phone. "I took photos of the file and told her to hang on to it. The first three shots are of a note Sonny wrote to Walter dated nine days before he was killed. Check it out."

Claire tapped on the screen and squinted at the small print of the typewritten note—recorded in three separate photos—

Walter,

I've looked over your proposal, and I think you're being conservative. There's the potential to make even more money. Bexar may be anxious to lock in the properties and easements, and your asking price might look like chump change to them. I don't know and don't wish to know how you determined the pipeline route, and I appreciate the fact that whatever you paid was not charged to Condor.

Having said this, let me be clear. As a managing partner in Condor Enterprises with a fifty percent equity stake, I don't agree to proceed with this. First and foremost, I'm against the proposed LNG facility at Jackson Point based on environmental and safety considerations. You know the arguments by now. Second, what you are proposing may be illegal and is certainly highly unethical. Third, setting aside the legality and ethics, there's a considerable risk that Bexar may balk at buying the properties before they know for sure if the project is approved or if the powers that be decide on a change in the pipeline route. Do you really want to bet the company on this?

One final point—if you and Max decide to go around me somehow, I will divulge everything I know publicly to stop you. We'll talk, of course, but I wanted to set this down in writing so there's no misunderstanding. Incidentally, Maxine called me yesterday, and the discussion devolved into a shouting match. Tell her that threatening me will get her nowhere.

Sonny

"This is incredible, Dad," Claire said after reading the note. "Did Sonny actually send this to Walter?"

"I assume he did. The note was a copy, and Twila said it was definitely Sonny's signature. It was stuck in the back of the file, which apparently was overlooked when the investigators went through his office. Twila found it by accident yesterday while she was doing some housecleaning."

"Wow. And nine days after Sonny sends the note, he's dead, and the LNG deal eventually goes through, enriching both Walter and Max. Motives on steroids."

"And there's evidence of a direct threat from Max," I added.

"If Walter received the letter, he must have worried it would surface, right?"

I nodded, slowing down for a truck loaded with timber. "The cash stolen the night of the murder came from Sonny's home office, which suggests the killer could have been looking for the note. The fact that it wasn't found isn't surprising. The investigators missed it, too."

"Is this enough? I mean, can Max and Walter be charged, or Kenny's case reopened?"

"No. This is the first hard evidence we have, and it goes strongly to motive for both Walter and Max. But we still have no direct evidence linking either one of them to the murder scene."

Claire slumped back in her seat and crossed her arms. "Then how does this help us?"

"Well, in the absence of a smoking gun, which we do not have, the note and the supporting file showing the huge financial stake might give us the ability to squeeze Walter, get him to talk."

"Assuming Max did it and Walter knows it," Claire said.

"That seems to be the most likely scenario. Walter must know something or suspect something. That's why he's been cozying up to me and Rori, to find out how much we know. And we'll have even more leverage if you can persuade Kathy Harper to come forward. It's not likely he'll want that to get out."

Claire looked at me, alarm in her eyes. "Oh, Dad, this feels so tenuous. What if we don't find a smoking gun?"

"We will, Claire. We're getting damn close." She regarded me for a moment longer and nodded, but I'm not sure she bought the optimism. Maybe I didn't buy it, either.

———

We stopped for a game of slobber ball with Archie at a soccer field and then drove on to the Portside Restaurant in Charleston, where we'd arranged to meet Nando for dinner. We arrived first and scored a table with a view of the bay, although an offshore cloud bank spoiled our chance to see a dramatic sunset.

Nando arrived a half hour later. "This private detective work is difficult," he said as he took a seat, his face in a pout. "I was unsuccessful today." The waiter appeared, and he ordered a Dos Equis. "It's hard to believe, but people in the Umpqua Valley seemed suspicious of a Cuban man asking a lot of questions."

He cast his eyes down. "And even my secret weapon didn't work so well."

He paused, and Claire took the bait. "What is it?"

He laughed, pointed an index finger at his mouth, and smiled broadly. "*This*. It disarms many, especially the women."

"But not today?" I asked.

He waved a hand in disgust. "No. No one saw anything, or, if they did, they weren't about to share it with me. But I am not finished. I am going to search the area around the Millicoma River next, where you and Claire found the body of Howard Coleman. Somebody could have seen something there as well. I will need another day or two, at least."

A waiter appeared, and after we ordered I told Nando about the LNG file and Sonny Jenson's note to Walter Sanders. When I finished he smiled with approval. "This will provide the thin end of the wedge, Calvin." He turned to Claire. "And I agree with your father that Walter will be even more willing to talk if he thinks we might reveal his dalliance with the young cheerleader."

Claire rolled her eyes. "Jeez, guys, I don't need any more pressure."

By the time we finished our meal, we had turned to the shark-chumming plan we hatched the night before. Nando said, "We have been away from the beach house all day. As we discussed last night, the only reason for the Brothers B to case the place is in preparation for some kind of attack."

"It's possible," I said. "And I doubt they realize we're on to them."

Claire laughed. "Well, they're not exactly the brightest lights in the harbor."

"Please," Nando said, shooting her a look, "hubris is dangerous. As we discussed last night, if the brothers are intent on attacking us, they will most likely deploy themselves somewhere around the beach house. They could ambush us as we enter, or they could even hide inside, hoping to make it look like a robbery in either case."

"There's not much cover on the outside of the house, so assuming we're right, they'll opt to strike from inside," I added.

"Agreed. And leaving the two most readily accessible windows on the deck unlocked should make it an easy choice for them."

Claire made a face. "The thought of them waiting for us in the house creeps me out." She looked at Nando with a dubious smile. "Using thread is so low-tech. You think it'll work?"

I stifled a laugh.

Nando smiled. "Sometimes low-tech is best, Claire. They will approach using the stairs from the beach. They will not notice the fine thread I placed low across the gate." He looked at his watch. "Now, we have more time to kill. Let's go into the bar."

———

At a little past midnight, we set off for the beach house. Nando took the lead in his Lexus, and Claire, Archie, and I followed in the Subaru. We pulled over a couple of blocks from the turn-off to Sunset Lane, and Nando walked back to our car. "Okay, I am going in now. Once I confirm they are not lying in wait outside, I will check the thread. If they are inside, I'll pull back and we can call the sheriff to report a burglary in progress."

I tensed up as he strolled into the darkness, because checking the outside was the most dangerous part of our scheme, and Nando insisted on doing it. "It was my idea," he said when I raised the question. "I will take the risk."

We sat in silence in the Subaru as time dragged by. Fourteen agonizing minutes later my cell phone riffed.

"All is clear. There are no sharks in the tank."

Chapter Thirty

"I'm okay, I guess, but my back hurts like hell every time I move," Kenny Sanders said.

"That's good, Kenny. If you're able to move, it means you're on the mend," Rori responded. It was the next morning in her office at Coffee and Subversion. She'd arranged a call with Kenny, and her speakerphone was turned on so that Claire and I could listen in.

Kenny laughed softly. "Yeah, well they've gotten the message here about opioids being addictive. Either that or they're cutting costs on medications."

Rori wrung her hands. "Well, I've got a lot of confidence in your surgeon, Dr. Nguyen. If you have a problem with pain, ask to see her."

"It's okay, Grandma, I'm just bitching. Got nothing else to do right now, and, besides, I'll probably heal faster without taking a bunch of drugs."

"Kenny, this is Cal," I cut in. "Have you been able to start the transfer request procedure?"

He laughed again, more strongly this time. "Yeah, I told them I wanted to get the hell out of here. They sent a dude from security right away. He, ah, told me I was wasting my time, that the DOC

Director would never approve a transfer for a lifer like me. He told me not to worry, that they're taking steps to, quote-unquote, neutralize the threat to me." He laughed again. "I think a transfer request makes the STM look bad."

Rori shifted in her seat and shook her head emphatically. I asked, "What did you say to him?"

"I told him they couldn't *neutralize* shit, and they knew it. I said if they don't get me out of this prison I'll be a dead man walking, pure and simple."

"He doesn't have the final say on this, Kenny. Did he give you the transfer request papers?"

"Yeah, I have them."

I spent the next twenty minutes helping Kenny fill them out. When we finished, I said, "Okay, Kenny, you need to submit this as soon as possible and insist on written confirmation that it's been received. Meanwhile, I'm going to draft a letter in support of your request and send it directly to the DOC Director. The sooner we get this done the better, so don't sit on it, okay?"

"That's right," Rori said, "get it in today. We're gonna get you out of there."

Before we signed off, Kenny said, "Hey, Claire, I need a surf report."

She laughed. "I knew you would. Bastendorff's glassed off this morning with a north swell running four to five feet. Perfect conditions. I'm sure Stu Foster and your buds are out there ripping it up."

A long pause, then in a thick voice, "I'm picturing that in my mind. Thanks, Claire."

———

We were discussing the call when a sharp, double knock sounded that elicited a single bark from Arch. I was closest to the door, so I opened it. "Well," Walter Sanders said with a smile that showed most of his bleached white teeth, "the whole Free Kenny Sanders team. Anthony said you were all back here." He glanced at Archie. "Even the mutt." My dog assiduously ignored him.

"What do you want, Walter?" Rori said in a voice laced with annoyance.

He walked into the office before answering, which didn't surprise me. "I just stopped by to say hi, Aurora, and see how things were going." He introduced himself to Claire before turning back to Rori, who remained sitting behind her desk. He chuckled and upped the smile intensity. "I saw that article in the *Coos Bay World* about you. Nice cuffs you were wearing. They looked familiar."

Rori remained stony-faced. "They should have. I think we got a lot of mileage out of—"

He waved her off. "I didn't come here to argue about the goddamn environment, Aurora. As a matter of fact, I've become a believer in global warming."

Rori barked a laugh dripping with contempt. "Oh, that's rich. You're a believer now, after making a killing on the LNG proposal?"

He shrugged and opened his hands. "It was *business*, for Christ's sake. That project's backed by Washington, so you know damn well it's going to get approved, no matter what the Governor says or does. Somebody was going to make that money. And we took a hell of a risk." He turned to me and changed the subject. "How's the investigation going, Counsellor?"

I locked my eyes on his, figuring it was time to insert, if not the thin end of the wedge, at least a suggestion of what was to come. "We're getting a handle on what actually happened leading up to the murder, who was involved, and who had something to gain from Sonny Jenson's death. People have a lot of secrets in this town, Walter."

His eyes flared, and he produced a brittle smile. "Sounds like you're making real progress. That's great news."

I held his eyes but didn't say anything. He finally looked away. Rori said, "This is a race for Kenny's life, Walter. He was stabbed a couple of days ago." She explained the situation with the white supremacists. "He's recovering, but he's a marked man if he goes back into the prison".

"That's awful, Rori." He said it as if he meant it, then looked at me. "Surely there're legal steps you can take."

"We're looking at our options."

"I've said this before, but let me know if there's anything I can do to help." He glanced at the door, suddenly looking uncomfortable, like the uninvited guest he was. "Well, I'm sorry I interrupted your meeting. I'll leave you to it." He nodded to Claire. "Nice meeting you."

As he opened the office door, I said, "If you think of something else, or remember something you might have forgotten, this would be a *very* good time to come forward, Walter."

"I'll keep that in mind," he said without looking back.

I shut the door. Claire smiled. "Dad, I think you scared the crap out of him."

"I meant to."

Rori looked at me, her face taut, her eyes narrowed down. "Do you have more on Walter now? Is he involved in this somehow?"

I showed my palms in defense. "I've told you everything I can right now, Rori. You're going to have to trust me."

She pursed her lips. "Of course. When are you going to put it all together?"

I exhaled. "Patience. There're a lot of moving parts."

She looked off to the side, scowled, and said, half to herself, "If Walter's mixed up in this, I swear, I'll take a filet knife to him."

Claire shifted in her seat. I said, "Come on Rori, I don't need another client right now."

We waved to Anthony on the way out, and once we were out on the sidewalk, Claire made a whistling sound. "I sure wouldn't want to get on the wrong side of Rori Dennison."

"Me, neither. You can tell she's a fisherman's daughter."

Our next stop was the medical center in North Bend, where I finally got my stitches removed.

"Oh, that's a badass scar," Claire said, laughingly, when I rejoined her in the waiting room. "Gives your face real character."

"Just what I needed."

"Let's get lunch at the Fishmonger," Claire suggested when we reached the Subaru. "I should check in with Sissy. We haven't talked in a couple of days."

It was a bright spring day, and the restaurant was filled with good aromas and humming with customers. When Sissy saw us, she pointed to a small table near the back. When she brought our menus, she spoke to me first. "How's that head injury, Mr. Claxton?" She had one hand on a bony hip and her face looked borderline gaunt beneath spiked-up hair, but her bearing appeared anything but weak.

"It's fine." I pointed at the thin, pink scar just below the line of my hair. "Got the stitches out today."

"Good." To Claire she said, "Hey, girl, been thinkin' about you. Did you read my mind?"

Claire laughed. "Of course. Are things okay?"

She rolled her eyes. "Still getting threats." She looked at me. "When're you going to catch those bastards?"

"Soon, I hope. How are they threatening you, Sissy?"

"Mostly phone calls, you know, one of them talking through a sock or some damn thing. I just laugh at them."

"They're cold-blooded killers, Sissy," Claire said. "You need to be very careful."

"*Mostly?*" I said. "What else besides phone calls?"

"Oh, they drove by late and shot out one of my windows. Probably drunk. They ain't gonna kill me." She smiled with a hint of slyness. "They think I know more than I do and that I wrote one of those 'read this if I'm killed' notes."

"When was the drive-by?" I asked.

"Two nights ago."

"Is there anything we can do to help you?" I asked.

She cast her eyes down and shrugged. "Nah, I can take care of myself. Just catch 'em, Mr. Claxton. Howard deserves justice." She glanced in the direction of the kitchen. "I need to get my butt in gear. What can I get you?"

We ordered, and Sissy sauntered off. Claire looked at me. "That drive-by was the same night we had our visitors."

"Right. The master criminals were multitasking."

Claire sighed. "I'm worried sick about Sissy. What do you make of the threats? Do you think she's right about the Brothers B being afraid to kill her?"

"Maybe so. I mean, you'd think they would have tried something by now if they weren't."

Claire nodded. "I get why they wouldn't fear her going to the sheriff—you know, she could implicate herself, and there's all that money she and Howard stashed. But wouldn't they worry about her working with us?"

"Good point. Maybe they didn't make the connection the day the older Brother B saw you with Sissy. But they know we're looking into Coleman's death."

"Or, they could just be flat-out afraid of her," Claire added. "She's a hell of a lot tougher than she looks."

I smiled. "Nando would agree with you."

Claire shook her head with a puzzled look. "It's a weird stasis between the Brothers and her, but I still worry, Dad."

"Me, too."

Chapter Thirty-One

Back at the beach house, Claire immediately got involved in a phone call related to her postdoctoral research, and I started to work on the letter in support of Kenny's transfer. Sometime after four I had the letter drafted and my phone messages cleared. A lot of the calls had to do with delaying some cases and putting off potential clients looking for legal representation back in Dundee. This was *not* a sustainable situation, I reminded myself. I also put a call into Harmon Scott to see how the DNA sample was faring. He didn't pick up, and I didn't leave a message. Better not to annoy him with a voice mail.

I'd gone out on the deck to catch some sun when Gertrude Johnson called. "Hello, stranger," she began. "How's it going down there?"

"We're making progress. How's the homestead look?"

"Still standing, last I checked, but the weeds own your garden now."

I felt a stab of guilt-tinged disappointment. My vegetable garden was not to be this year unless I solved this case damn soon. "That hurts. Put a couple of tomato plants in your garden for me, would you?"

She chuckled. "Sounds like you're not wrapping up down there any time soon."

I exhaled in frustration. "This case has kind of mushroomed on me, Gertie. I'll get back as soon as I can. It's been what, seventeen days? Hell, I planned on two weeks, so I've only been AWOL three days so far."

"Okay, you're the boss," she said with a notable ring of resignation. "Hug Claire and stay safe, you here?"

"Roger that." I tapped off with a vague feeling of anxiety. I told Rori Dennison I'd reduce my rate to a hundred twenty-five dollars an hour after she refused help from Walter Sanders, a fact I'd yet to mention to Gertie. I'd be faced with postponing and losing better-paying business back in Dundee pretty damn soon.

Nando came back around five that afternoon. "A waste of gasoline and good shoe leather," he replied when I asked how it went. "The Millicoma River region is sparsely populated, and nobody I talked to recalled seeing anything around the time of Howard Coleman's murder." I opened us each a beer, and we went out on the deck to wait for Claire to finish up. A fresh breeze blew off the Pacific, and the afternoon sun cast a glittering silver sheen on the water. Nando took a long pull on his beer and looked south, toward the Cape Arago Lighthouse. "In Cuba, that lighthouse would still be in operation. Americans throw things away too soon."

"It's scenic but obsolete," I said. "It's all GPS navigation now. Satellites."

He puffed a breath. "Always the technology. Where will it end? In Cuba, people are still driving American cars made in the fifties and sixties."

"Plenty of vintage cars in the states. Maybe you should trade your Lexus for one?"

He laughed at that. "Yes, how quickly we are corrupted with material things."

Claire joined us not long after that, and at sunset, with Archie in tow, we made a big show of leaving the beach house in both cars, thus opening the gates of the shark tank once again. Nando announced he was taking us to the Captain's Cabin, the seafood restaurant on the first floor of the Tioga Building in Coos Bay. His treat.

Claire said, "I was there the other day. It's pricey, Nando."

He waved a dismissive hand. "Not a problem. It is my treat tonight. After all, am I not getting a free room on this vacation?"

Claire looked at him. "*Vacation?*" We all laughed at that.

Nando ordered the South African lobster tail, and Claire and I feasted on the sushi-grade, seared yellowfin tuna. He also sprang for a 2016 Domaine du Nozay Sancerre that paired nicely with our seafood. After dinner, we took Archie for a long walk on the boardwalk that ran along the bay on the east side of the city. We then put him in the back of the Subaru and returned to the Tioga to kill more time at the restaurant bar. We got some looks when all three of us ordered Irish Coffees without the Irish. It was close to midnight when we headed back toward the beach house with Nando leading the way. Time to check the shark tank.

Nando pulled over about an eighth of a mile north of the Sunset Lane turnoff and I followed in behind him. I rolled the window down as he approached. "Okay, same plan as last night," he said as he racked the slide of his Sig Sauer to chamber a round. "Perhaps the sharks have taken the chum tonight. We have rolled out the welcome mat, after all."

"Be careful, Nando," I said. "Remember, come in from the south side where the cover's a little better."

"I plan to. If the Brothers B are inside the house, as we hope, they will have concealed themselves for an ambush, which makes it unlikely they will see me checking the thread."

If, I thought but didn't say, as I watched my friend disappear into the shadows.

Too far from the ocean to hear the surf, Claire and I waited, listening to the soft rustle of the fir trees in the breeze and the intermittent chirping of crickets in the understory. Nine minutes later, the evening's tranquility was shattered by three gunshots, *pop…pop, pop.* The reports caused Archie to shift nervously in the back seat and whimper.

"*Oh, shit,*" I said. I snatched the Glock from the glove compartment, chambered a round, and got out of the car. At that moment I felt like I was being ripped in half, as that old saw about the best laid plans ricocheted around in my head like a mocking taunt. Part of me demanded I stay with Claire to protect her, and yet I couldn't leave Nando alone in a firefight in which he was almost certainly outnumbered two to one.

Sensing my indecision, Claire looked squarely at me, her expression unwavering, "Go, Dad. Nando needs your help." She pulled her phone out. "I'm calling 911."

"Okay. Keep the car doors locked, the engine idling, the lights off. If anyone approaches the car you don't know, get the hell out of here. Run them over if you have to."

Claire nodded with her ear to the phone. "Go! Now! And be careful, Dad!"

With my adrenal glands at flood stage, I sprinted into the darkness. When I veered off onto Sunset Lane, I bent low and kept moving, staying in the shadows of the spindly cedars lining the unlighted street. As I approached the driveway of the beach house, three more shots rang out. The muzzle flash of the first report came from a spot halfway down the drive, probably Nando. The next two came from the north corner of the house—separate flashes indicating two shooters. The Brothers B. With my heart practically beating out of my chest, I stayed low, moving along the tree line until I was within several feet of the first shooter. It was Nando, I was sure of it. He was lying prone behind a large landscape boulder adjacent to the driveway.

"It's me," I said as I slid in next to him. He grunted and squeezed off another shot, which elicited a return volley. Bullets thudded into the boulder and one grazed the top, sending a spray of basalt chips over us. Then the scene went silent, except for the noise of my ragged breathing. I'm not sure how much time elapsed. It seemed like a lifetime. I whispered, "I think they're gone. Probably took the stairs down to the beach." Nando grunted again. "Let's pull back to the cars," I said. "We can't leave Claire and Arch alone."

Nando grunted, made it to one knee, then rolled over on his back. "You go," he said in a hoarse whisper. "I am hit." His head lolled to one side, and he went limp.

"*Nando,*" I whispered. I shook his shoulder, but he was unresponsive, and I drew back a hand wet with blood. "Oh, no." With my heart in my throat, I checked his neck and caught a weak, rapid pulse. As I took my cell out to call Claire, I heard sirens wailing in the distance. "They're gone," I told her. "Call 911 again and request an ambulance. Nando's hurt." She gasped. "Then bring the car. Hurry."

I peered over the boulder and saw no movement at the house. I ripped my jacket off and put it under my friend's head. Using the flashlight on my phone, I tried to determine where he'd been hit. Upper arm or shoulder, judging from the blood, which wasn't a steady flow. At least he wasn't bleeding out, I concluded.

An equal measure of fear, anger, and guilt washed over me. So much for the best laid plans.

Chapter Thirty-Two

A county sheriff patrol car arrived first. By this time, Claire was cradling Nando's head in her lap and holding my T-shirt against his left shoulder and chest to staunch the bleeding. It wasn't immediately apparent where the bullet entered, and I hoped it wasn't near his heart. In any case, he was coming in and out of consciousness.

"Help's on the way," she said over and over. "Hold on, Nando, hold on."

He gritted his teeth and moaned, a sound that was somehow reassuring. "She's right, Nando," I said, crouching next to him. "We're going to get you out of here."

As the patrol car drew near, I stood out at the end of the driveway and waved to make sure they could see I was unarmed. Both deputies approached cautiously with their service weapons drawn. Claire had pulled the Subaru in and left the lights on so that she and Nando were bathed in light. "My friend's been shot," I said. "Home invasion. An ambulance is on the way."

The shorter deputy hurried back to the car and extracted a first aid kit. The taller one said, "Where's the shooter?"

"There were two." I pointed at the house. "I'm pretty sure they took the stairs off the back deck down to the beach. They probably went north. There's a narrow gully you can take back up to the road at the Yoakam Point trailhead. They might be driving a dark, late model Ford Explorer. We surprised them when we came home."

Tall one called the information into the next car on its way to the scene. By this time, the shorter deputy had relieved Claire, whose blouse was stained with Nando's blood. She was crouched next to our friend and continued to talk to him. Tall one pointed at our guns, which I'd laid out on the driveway in plain view. "Whose weapons are those?"

"Mine and Mendoza's," I said.

"You were both armed?"

"Yes."

He nodded. If that raised a question in his mind, he didn't ask it.

The ambulance arrived a few agonizing minutes later, and when Nando was finally on his way to the Bay Area Hospital, I breathed a sigh of relief. It felt like the first breath I'd allowed myself since he'd been shot. Was he going to make it? He had to.

———

"Forced into the Umpqua River, and now your house is invaded?" Sheriff Hershel Stoddard said. "I'm afraid you're getting the wrong impression of the South Coast, Mr. Claxton." Claire had just been interviewed, and now it was my turn. Stoddard had come from home and was sitting in on the talks, which were being held at the hospital while we waited for Nando to get out of surgery. Apparently, the sheriff thought the late-night events warranted his direct involvement.

"You can remedy that by catching the bastards who did it, Sheriff."

He lost the grin. "How's Mendoza?"

"He's in surgery. That's all we know at this point."

Detective Rice, lead investigator on the Coleman murder, also caught this case and was conducting the interviews. When I finished answering his questions, Stoddard said, "Help me with the big picture here, Mr. Claxton. You think the two men who were breaking into your house are also involved in Coleman murder and the attempt on your life on the Umpqua Highway?"

"I do," I answered. "I believe Coleman was killed to keep him quiet about the Kenny Sanders case. I—"

"There's no evidence of that," Stoddard shot back. "You—"

"Let me finish, Sheriff," I said, feeling the heat rising in my neck. "You wanted the big picture." The sheriff nodded curtly. "I have evidence that Coleman was getting ready to talk before I arrived in Coos Bay." I met the sheriff's eyes. "After all, what he did to that sixteen-year-old boy was reprehensible. Apparently, the man discovered he had a conscience."

Stoddard's eyes flashed. "What? Telling the truth's reprehensible?" His tone rang with righteous indignation.

I laughed bitterly. "Coleman would've sold out his own mother for a reduced sentence, and you know it." By this time, my neck felt hot as a stove. "I'm not sure which was a worse injustice, Sheriff—arranging Coleman's deal or coercing a confession out of a scared, naive sixteen-year-old. How can you look yourself in the mirror?"

Stoddard stood abruptly. "We're done here," he said, and stomped out of the room.

I got up to leave, but Rice shot me an embarrassed look and stayed seated. "The old man's sensitive as hell about the Kenny Sanders case."

I laughed again with even more bitterness. "He won the last election by sending an innocent kid to prison for life. The truth should come out."

Rice frowned and ran a hand through curly, dark hair. "Yeah, well, just between me, you, and the fence post, I think he's conflicted about the case."

"*Conflicted?* He told me it was a righteous conviction, that I shouldn't waste my time defending Kenny Sanders."

Rice's eyes did a roll. "That was candidate Stoddard talking. I never said the man lacked ambition, but I know for a fact he's had second thoughts about the case."

I sat back down and regarded Rice more carefully. "Why are you telling me this?"

He shrugged and looked back with intelligent, unblinking eyes. "I've got the Coleman murder and now this home invasion case. I'd like to clear them both. Could you, ah, finish connecting the dots?"

"Well, the rest is simple. When I arrived on the scene and took on Kenny's case, I became a threat to whoever really killed Sonny Jenson. This person dispatched the same two thugs who killed Coleman to take care of me. They failed on the Umpqua Highway and they failed last night. Find the two thugs, and you'll solve your cases."

He kept his eyes on me. "There's more, isn't there?"

I paused. Rice was sharper than I thought. Could I trust him, which, by inference, meant I had to trust Stoddard as well? I thought of Nando, in surgery at that moment, and the vulnerability of Claire and me. God knows we needed help. I decided to risk it.

"One of the killers drove a truck for Max Sloat. He's a contractor with his own rig. He was delivering drugs as well as timber. The other killer's his younger brother, and their last name starts with B. The younger brother's named Robert. We don't know the older brother's first name, but it starts with D." I paused again. "One other thing—I'd strongly advise your forensic team to scour the scene for any tobacco-stained spittle around the point of the shooting and back on the deck and down the stairs. We know one of the brothers chews. You'll want his DNA."

Rice's jaw dropped a little, but he didn't ask me to explain. Instead, he scribbled down some notes, and after asking several more questions said, "Thanks, Mr. Claxton. This could really help."

I stood to leave. "If you catch the Brothers B, you'll help Kenny Sanders, too, Detective."

He stood and offered his hand. "For what it's worth, I admire what you're doing for that kid. I never bought the conviction and was glad it was Drake who caught the case, not me." He met my eyes, and his lips edged up at the corners. "I'm on a knife-edge here, but I'll do what I can to help."

I shook his hand, holding his steady gaze for a moment. "Thanks, uh..."

He smiled. "Call me Chet."

I smiled back. "Call me Cal. Thanks, Chet. Kenny Sanders needs all the help he can get."

———

An ally, I said to myself as I left the hospital conference room. Didn't see that coming.

Chapter Thirty-Three

Nando was still in surgery, and Claire and I were wired, so after taking Archie for a walk along a grassy stretch adjacent to the hospital, we went back in and got some bad coffee from a machine. An understanding nurse had given Claire a blue pullover to wear and a plastic bag to stash her blood-stained blouse. I had just finished telling Claire about my interview with Rice.

Claire furrowed her forehead. "How can you be sure Rice's on our side, Dad?"

I shrugged and sipped some coffee. "Gut feel, to be honest. We've got to trust somebody. Rice can crack two big cases if he finds the Brothers B, so we share the same goal. And I think what he told me about Sheriff Stoddard—that he acted more out of ambition—aligned with my read of the guy."

Claire scowled. "That doesn't make what Stoddard did to Kenny Sanders right."

"Of course not, but it suggests he's not part of a murder conspiracy."

"But he might try to delay or obfuscate until after the election," Claire pointed out.

"Good point," I said, impressed as always with my daughter's insight. "That's a valid concern."

Two and a half hours later we got the word that Nando was out of surgery and out of danger. "Any gunshot wound is serious, and this was no exception," the ER doc told us, "but it was a small caliber bullet—a twenty-two—and it missed the subclavian artery. We got the bullet out in one piece, so no fragments were left behind. The less fortunate news is the bullet lodged in the brachial plexus, a bundle of nerves serving the shoulder. That's what incapacitated him. The pain was so intense he went into shock almost immediately."

"Will his arm and shoulder be okay?" Claire asked, her eyes puffy and etched in worry.

"That remains to be seen. At the very least, your friend is in for a lengthy bout of physical therapy to regain full motor function."

———

Around six a.m., we were finally allowed into the recovery room for a short visit. "I am sorry, Calvin," he said as we entered his room. "I screwed this up."

Claire sucked a sharp breath at the sight of him. I said, "Nonsense," while trying to hide my shock at seeing his pallid skin, chalky lips, and drug-dulled eyes. "How are you feeling?"

"How is it said?" He asked, ignoring my question. "Timing is everything? I got to the edge of the drive just in time to see the shadow of one brother going in a side window."

"A *side* window?" Claire asked. "It was locked."

Nando nodded and mumbled something inaudible in Spanish. "I know. The idiots missed the open window right in front of them and had to break in. Anyway, I waited, and nothing moved, so I figured the other brother was already inside. He wasn't, and he saw me before I saw him." Nando exhaled a slow breath. "I was stupid and careless. I am sorry."

"No," Claire said. "Don't you dare blame yourself. We all signed off on the plan, Nando."

He shook his head and grimaced. "The plan was good. Just a few more minutes, and they would have both been in our trap. *Al mejor cazador se le va le liebre.*"

I exhaled a breath. "You're okay. That's all that counts. And now every cop on the coast is looking for the Brothers B."

He gripped my arm with his right hand. "I'm sure the sheriff has taken your gun and mine for ballistic tests. Listen, there is a Smith and Wesson and an extra clip in the glove compartment of my Lexus. I brought it along, just in case. Get my keys from the nurse, get the gun, and use it to protect yourself and Claire. And move my car off the highway. I am worried it will be stolen."

"Don't worry," I said, "we'll take care of your car."

For the first time, Nando glanced down at his left arm, covered in bandages and bound tightly to his body, leaving only his fingers exposed. "The fingers don't work so well," he said, showing a weak smile. "They are not saying much about the arm yet, except that the bullet struck some nerves." He looked up at me, and I saw something in his eyes I'd never seen before—fear. "This better not harm my salsa dancing, Calvin."

Claire laughed despite herself. I said, "It would take more than a gunshot wound to do that, Nando."

We'd just left Nando's room when Chet Rice called to say the beach house was cleared and that the BOLO he'd issued on the Brothers B hadn't turned up anything yet. "I, ah, also talked to the old man. We're going to station one of our units on Sunset Lane at night for your security."

"Maybe your gut-check was right, Dad," Claire remarked after I told her what Rice said, "but I don't think the Brothers B would dare show up at the beach house again. Look at the reception they got last night, and now they're on the run." Claire's reaction was a relief, since I worried my daughter wouldn't be comfortable staying there going forward.

How silly of me.

I had another concern—how would the owners of the beach

house react when I told them what happened? I wasn't looking forward to that discussion. Would they tell us to clear out? That would sure as hell complicate things.

———

"*What?*" Claire said, her eyes suddenly round as saucers. "We'll be right over." We'd just finished breakfast at a little diner near the hospital when the call came in. "That was Sissy," she said after she clicked off. "More multitasking by the Brothers B—they killed her dog last night."

Sissy Anderson lived in a small mobile home community on Ocean Boulevard, a collection of double-wide trailers, most of which sported additions, carports, and foundation plantings that implied permanence, not mobility. Sissy's weather-beaten mobile home was set off by a picket fence needing paint and a sign adjacent to the front door that warned off solicitors. A Harley-Davidson motorcycle sat in the carport next to a road-worn Camry. She answered the door, her eyes red and swollen, and invited us in.

"You want some coffee?" she said. "I just made a pot." We said we did and followed her into a small kitchen. She filled three mugs with steaming coffee, set out cream and sugar, then turned to us and sobbed once before catching herself. "Howard wasn't enough. They had to kill Murphy. What the hell did he do to anyone?"

"What happened, Sissy?" Claire said.

She chewed her lower lip for a moment. "Murph, um, pretty much roams the neighborhood, you know. People around here love him. Didn't show up for his supper last night, which didn't worry me too much. Anyway, it just gets dark, and I hear a car pull up in front, then take off, leaving a patch of rubber. I went outside..." Tears welled up and streamed down Sissy's cheeks... "He was in a garbage bag on the front lawn, shot through the head."

"That's horrible. We're so sorry this happened," Claire said. She looked at me. "They drove to the beach house next."

Sissy swept her tearstained eyes from Claire to me. "What happened there?" When I finished describing the events of the night before, her face was stone hard, her lips pressed into a thin, straight line. She looked at me. "So, they shot my dog then drove to your place. Those lowlife bastards. Nando's arm, how bad is it?"

"We don't know yet. We're hoping he'll regain the full use of it."

"He's a good man, that one," she said, then turning to Claire added, "like your father." She sipped some coffee and stared straight ahead. "Who's going to stop them?" she asked the room.

I hesitated, searching for an answer that would satisfy. Claire filled the vacuum. "We are, Sissy. Listen, the Brothers B seem to combine actions, right? Two nights ago, they came in and shot up this trailer, then drove over to our place to check out the approach. This time, the same pattern, except they came in for the kill. Why would they do it that way unless they lived a fair distance from the bay? Could it be that multitasking minimized their time on the road?"

She turned to Sissy. "You've gone through Howard's belongings and so has Rice. Maybe you both missed something. Something with an address or location on it, you know, that points to someplace a good distance from here—the Coast Range, maybe the Umpqua Valley?"

Sissy shrugged her narrow shoulders. "To tell the truth, I still haven't gone through all his stuff yet. Hell, I should sell his Harley, but I can't bring myself to do it." She sighed. "Now, Murph's gone, too."

Claire reached across the table and took Sissy's hand. "I know how hard this is, Sissy. Would you mind if I take a quick look through Howard's belongings? I'm a fresh pair of eyes. Maybe I'll spot something that was missed."

"Now?"

"Yes, now. People and animals are getting shot. You can be right there with me. Anything personal, you just say the word."

Sissy chewed her lower lip some more. "Well, I—"

Claire's sapphire eyes had fire in them. "Sissy, do you want to stop these guys or not?"

Sissy agreed, and the two of them went into a back bedroom. Meanwhile, I poured myself another cup and called the owner of the beach house. "Hey, Cal," he said, after I provided a cursory explanation and promised to fix the broken window. "No problem. The house is fully insured. I'm just glad you and your daughter are okay, and I wish your friend a speedy recovery."

All lawyers should have such easygoing clients.

Claire and Sissy returned to the kitchen thirty minutes later. Judging from the look on my daughter's face, the search hadn't turned up anything significant. "Rice took photos of all Howard's credit card transactions for the past year, but I've got his receipts." She held the stack up. "Nothing else caught my eye."

Looking unimpressed, Sissy crossed her arms and glanced at me. "Why don't we cut to the damn chase? We know Max Sloat's behind this, right? I mean, those two dimwits sure as hell aren't acting alone."

I shook the comment off. Sissy didn't need to know what we knew. "We don't have any proof of that," I cautioned. "But I can tell you that Detective Rice is showing some interest in Sloat."

She shot me a wary look. "I shared that tally sheet to help you catch the two brothers, not get me in trouble with the law."

"We've kept our promise of confidentiality, Sissy, but I can't control where Rice might take his investigation. If he comes back with more questions, you better not lie to him."

Sissy expelled a breath and studied the floral pattern on the plastic tablecloth in front of her for a long time. "What does it matter, anyway?" she said, finally, more to herself than Claire and me. "Howard's gone. Now Murph's gone."

Claire took her hand again. "Don't lose faith, Sissy. We'll get to the bottom of this."

That's where we left it. More promises made.

Chapter Thirty-Four

After leaving Sissy's place, I dropped Claire at Nando's Lexus so she could drive it back to the beach house. As soon as she pulled in the driveway, I extracted the S&W and the extra clip from the glove compartment. She went immediately to her bedroom and crashed, but I felt too agitated to sleep, so Arch and I went out on the deck. Cool and soothing on my cheek, the breeze coming off the Pacific failed to disturb its surface, a mirror-smooth expanse of turquoise shading to cerulean blue out toward the horizon. I slouched down in a canvas chair and flopped an arm onto the broad back of my dog, who'd lain down beside me. The lighthouse stood stubbornly on the cape, a reminder that some things had at least a modicum of constancy. I envied that structure, yearned to be that inanimate, uncaring tube of brick and plaster. *Nando's right*, I realized, as my eyelids grew heavy. Things change too damn fast. I can't keep…

I don't know how long I was asleep before a sound awoke me. Distant at first, it grew louder and louder, like an approaching patrol car, except that instead of a siren I heard the digital excuse for a blues riff. I made a mental note to change the damn ring tone on my phone.

"Yeah? This is Cal," I growled.

"Top of the day to you, too, Sunshine. It's Harmon Scott. I've got something for you."

My head cleared in a millisecond. "Great, Harmon. Give me the headlines."

"Not on the phone, my friend. Sorry. I'm overnighting a package to you. I called to confirm your address down there."

"You got a hit."

"Yes. What address do you want me to use?" I gave him the beach house address, barely able to contain my excitement. "How's the vacation going?" he asked.

I exhaled a long breath into the phone. "Let me put it this way. Your package can't come soon enough, Harmon."

Whatever sleep I'd managed to get, it was enough. I popped up and went into the kitchen, clearheaded and suddenly ravaged by hunger. I made a double cappuccino first, then toasted four slices of wheat bread and proceeded to build a couple of sandwiches, using a can of locally packed albacore tuna, some jalapeños, a little mayo, and, of course, some fresh lemon juice. As I ate, Arch sat beside me, watching my every move with his big, doleful eyes. A true denizen of the Northwest, my dog loved albacore tuna.

"Okay, Big Boy, you win." I dug out a nice chunk from the can and dropped it in his dish. It was gone in one gulp.

With my energy restored, I called Rori to inquire whether she'd been in contact with Kenny. "He called this morning," she said. "He's feeling a little better, although his voice didn't sound strong at all. He said he's heard nothing about the transfer request."

"It's too early," I said. "I expect they'll take some time to respond." I went on to describe our encounter with the Brothers B the night before.

"Oh, what next?" she gasped, when I told her about Nando. "Where is he?"

"Bay Area Hospital. We're going to visit him later this afternoon. We can swing by the shop and pick you up." She agreed, thanking me.

I made another cappuccino and sat at the kitchen table deep in thought. Although I'd given Rice most of what I had on Max Sloat, it still might not have been enough for him to justify seeking a search warrant to force her to open up Sloat Trucking's books. Not that I expected him to find an obvious paper trail connecting her to the older Brother B. Max was too smart for that.

I thought about Walter Sanders. Nando and I were planning a good cop, bad cop party for him, but now I was missing my bad cop. Could I play both roles? It was worth a try. I reached Walter's voice mail and left a message for him to call me.

I just punched off the call when Claire staggered into the kitchen, bleary-eyed, hair in a tangle. I made her a coffee and fixed her a tuna sandwich. As she began eating, I told her the good news—that Scott had gotten a hit on the tobacco juice DNA—and we talked about next steps. Between hungry bites, she said, "After we visit Nando, you can drop me at the library. I need an hour or two to go through Coleman's credit card receipts."

"That'll work," I said. "If Walter doesn't call me back, I'm going to cold call him at his office, anyway. That reminds me, what about Kathy Harper? Any way you can work your charms on her, get her to meet with us?"

Claire made a face. "We've been playing text tag. She's agreed to at least meet, but she's been evasive. I think she's afraid."

"Afraid of what?" I asked. "Could Walter be threatening her?"

Claire shook the question off. "My guess is it's closer to home. It's probably still about her husband and family." Claire's look turned sour. "And, she's the victim."

———

"I know firsthand how bad the food is in this hospital, so I brought you a little something from the shop," Rori said to Nando, setting a bakery bag down. "Almond croissant, *pain au chocolat*, and pumpkin bread, baked this morning." We had just descended on my friend, who had regained some color but still looked like a shadow of himself.

Nando showed a weak smile. "Thank you, Rori. That is very kind of you." He looked at a nurse who was adjusting a drip medication, then back at Rori and winked. "I will have to hide this from Gloria, here. She is not to be trusted."

The nurse laughed and rolled her eyes dramatically as she left the room. "You're the one not to be trusted, Hernando," she called over her shoulder.

Rori stepped up to Nando's bed and began a tearful apology, but he cut her off in mid-sentence. "What happened to Calvin and Claire and now to me is not your fault, Rori," he told her. "I came here because my friends were attacked, and I see now that the people behind these acts are afraid the truth about your grandson's innocence will be exposed. I am honored to work on his behalf."

Rori was dabbing her eyes when Sissy Anderson came through the open door, surprising all of us. After greetings were exchanged, Sissy looked at Nando with obvious shyness. "I just came here to see how you're feeling. I'm sorry about what those two brothers did to you."

Claire shot me a look and suppressed a smile. Nando's Latin charms were in clear evidence.

Nando seemed touched. He said, "Thank you, Sissy. This is nothing compared to the loss you suffered."

An awkward silence followed, after which we kept the banter light with Nando sprinkling in jokes—mostly at my expense. After a short time he began to tire. Sissy stayed silent the whole time and was the first to leave. Judging from her demeanor, the grief she'd suffered was turning into seething anger.

———

I hadn't heard back from Walter Sanders, but I dropped off Claire at the library and drove over to the headquarters of Condor

Enterprises. Located on North 6th, just east of Tremont, the reception area of the building was on the second floor to show off an expansive view of the Bay. An attractive young woman greeted me from behind a marble top desk. "Can I help you?"

"Yes. I'm Cal Claxton. I'd like to see Walter Sanders."

"Is he expecting you?"

"Well, I called earlier. If you could just tell him I'm here, I'd appreciate it."

"Of course," she said with a look that made it clear people didn't just pop in on Walter. As I stood there, she relayed my message, and a long pause ensued as she listened intently. Then she shot me a different, more attentive look. "Have a seat, Mr. Claxton. Mr. Sanders will be right with you."

I sat down, put my briefcase aside, and hauled out my phone to check my email while I waited. "Hello Cal," Walter Sanders' voice boomed out a few minutes later, stirring me from a fatigue-induced stupor. "To what do I owe the honor?" Looking like he just stepped off the campaign bus, he wore a pinstripe suit, powder blue button-down shirt, solid red tie and his best bleached-white, gap-toothed smile.

I stood up and smiled reflexively. "I wanted to update you on the investigation."

"Great," he said, upping the smile ante. "I hope it's good news. We can talk in my office."

Why do I find this man so annoying? I said to myself as I followed him down a hallway. By the time we reached his corner office, I realized it had a lot to do with the phony affability he used to mask an aggressive nature. That and the narrow gap in his front teeth that bugged me for reasons I couldn't begin to fathom.

Chapter Thirty-Five

The seat Walter offered me in front of his desk afforded a nice view of the bay, which was more green than blue in the afternoon light and corrugated by a stiff breeze blowing east to west. The office smelled like a combination of air freshener and cigarette smoke and sported an oval glass desktop of impressive breadth and thickness, upscale leather furniture, and an obligatory bragging wall of photos and certificates attesting to his business prowess and social outreach. A large, well-executed seascape hanging on the opposite wall spoke to his good taste in art.

I sat down and pointed at the painting. "Is that a Twila Jenson?"

He beamed a proud smile. "Yes. One of my favorites." His face clouded slightly. "She painted that before Sonny died. I'm glad she's painting again, but her stuff's a lot moodier now, not so much to my taste. A shame." He swung his eyes from the painting to me. They were eager. "So, what's the latest?"

I opened my briefcase and pulled out a file folder stuffed with papers. Most of the papers were blank, but I didn't let on to Walter. A thick file suggested lots of facts and evidence, the impression I wanted to impart. This was a bluff, pure and simple.

"We're getting close to wrapping this up," I lied, "and I've got some concerns about your situation. Since you offered to help Rori out, I figure I owe you this."

His head recoiled slightly, as if my words had buffeted it. "*My* situation?"

Here goes, I said to myself, feeling like I was about to take the first step on a high wire. Playing Walter off against Max would either split them—which is what I was after—or unite them against a common enemy—me. "We have mounting evidence that your business partner, Maxine Sloat, is behind the murder of Sonny Jenson."

His forehead became a crosshatch of deep furrows. "You're kidding."

"No, I'm not kidding. Max wanted in on the LNG deal, but Sonny was in the way."

He raised a corner of his mouth dismissively. "That's nonsense. I told you Sonny bought in."

I opened the file, removed a single sheet of paper, and slid it across the glass surface to him. It was a copy of the letter Twila Jenson gave me. "Yeah, you did, but that was a lie, Walter."

He took the paper, scanned it, and swallowed, his Adam's apple bobbing like a cork in choppy water. "Oh, this. Well, Sonny sent it, then changed his—"

"Bullshit, Walter," I cut in. "You're joined at the hip with Max Sloat. I don't believe you're involved in the murder, but if you don't start telling me the truth, you might find yourself in hot water. And Max could easily turn on you, you know. Somebody's going down for this, trust me."

He leaned back in his chair and absently squeezed the fingers of one hand with the other until his knuckles went white. "Sounds like I should talk to my attorney."

"You can do that, of course, but it's going to make you look like you're involved in this. And you'll be impeding my ability to get Kenny out of prison. Helping Kenny is something you care about, right? Look, Walter, I know a lot more than I'm telling you, including the identity of others Max recruited to do her dirty work. The smartest thing you can do is tell me everything you know and make a clean break from her."

He steepled his fingers and tapped them against his lips for what seemed an age. The wind had increased, with gusts now buffeting the large window and streaking the bay with nascent whitecaps. An antique clock behind his desk marked the time with faint, audible clicks. He finally sighed and leaned forward, avoiding my eyes as usual. "There *was* something that bothered me," he said. "I mean, besides the fact that Max threatened Sonny. Hell, I chalked that up to her business style, you know, the take-no-prisoners type. But the night Sonny was killed, Max called me, said she wanted the three of us to meet, to try and iron things out."

"What time was that?"

"I don't remember exactly, sometime in the late afternoon or early evening. She asked me if Twila was painting that night at the Tioga. Yeah, I said, she is, but why? 'Because I think she's a sticking point in this,' Max says. 'It's better if she's not around.'"

"How did you know Twila was at the Tioga that night?"

Walter shrugged. "I don't remember. Maybe Sonny said something. I mean, she spent a lot of time there. Anyway, I reminded Max that I was in Newport getting ready for an important meeting the next morning, that I wasn't about to drive back to Coos Bay. She says, 'Oh, yeah, I forgot about that. Well, forget it, then.'" Walter looked at me. "I remember thinking how weird that was."

"Why didn't you mention this to the investigators?"

He shrugged. "By the time I heard about the murder, Kenny had already been picked up. I figured the sheriff must've had something on him, and then, you know, he confessed and all. It happened really fast."

"You never suspected that Max could have killed Sonny? What about the letter Sonny wrote, the one I just showed you?"

"Max asked me not to say anything about it. 'It'll make us both look bad,' she said. I told her I wouldn't but that the investigators would probably find Sonny's copy. When they didn't, I just forgot about it."

A slow bloom of anger rose inside me. "So, Max knew Sonny was alone at his house, and she asked you to suppress the letter that stated she threatened him." Walter nodded sheepishly. "Do you realize how incredibly irresponsible it was not to report that?" I continued, my voice rising. He dropped his gaze. "What else do you know, Walter?"

"That's all I can think of." He brought his eyes up and gave me a pleading look. "I'm sorry for that now. At the time, you know, word got out immediately that Kenny did it, that the sheriff had him. I guess I should have questioned it, but I did get him a lawyer, you know."

I shook my head in disgust. "Yeah, you did. A total incompetent. From where I sit, it looks like it was just too damn convenient to question it. Exposing Max might've toppled your LNG scheme, so you let Kenny take the fall."

"That's not true," he shot back.

"Let me ask you something else—why did you lie to me about Sonny wanting to do the LNG deal?"

He swallowed, and a vein in his neck appeared and began to pulsate. "I, ah, I guess I didn't trust you at that point. For all I knew you'd start blaming me for Sonny's murder."

"Only if you did it, Walter. Only if you did it." I met his eyes and managed to hold them this time. "I hope you're telling me everything. God knows, Max isn't holding back. She mentioned you were having an illicit affair at that time, and Sonny threatened to unmask you."

His eyes nearly popped out of his head. "That's a damn lie!"

I shrugged. "I haven't been able to corroborate it. Just thought I'd mention it."

His neck acquired some color. "Yeah, well, Max is running drugs through her operation. She takes a cut on all the action."

I laughed with derision. "Tell me something I don't know. For example, the names of two of the players, a couple of brothers, one of whom drives for her?"

He shook the question off convincingly. "Nah, I don't know anybody involved, but I know she's been taking a cut for years."

The office went quiet, except for the antique clock. The white-caps out on the bay were in full bloom. I said, finally, "You've been a help, Walter. I'll be in touch as this unfolds. I assume you'll hold this in the strictest confidence, particularly with Max. If you talk to her, it'll look like you're trying to coordinate your stories. You don't want that, believe me."

I left Walter sitting at his desk with what I could only describe as a dazed look on his face. I had slipped the thin end of the wedge in and whacked it hard. Was Walter telling me the truth about the night Sonny was killed? Had Max signaled her murderous intent, either acting alone or through the Brothers B? It cheered me that the next day I would know the identity of one of the brothers. A solid lead, at last. Would that be the key to untangling this thing?

I could only hope.

Chapter Thirty-Six

"So, DB stands for Darnell Barton," Nando said, the name lingering on his lips as if he were savoring it. At the Bay Area Hospital the next morning, he was cranked up a little straighter in his bed, had regained some color, and the mischievous glint in his eye had returned for the most part. However, he still couldn't move the fingers of his left hand. They were numb and tingling, a fact I had to pry out of him.

"That's right," I said. "Forty-seven years old, grew up in the Coast Range in a little crossroads called Woodell, east of here. He got eight years at Salem for aggravated assault, got out six years ago on good behavior, was rearrested for sexual assault, but the charges were dropped when the woman he assaulted decided not to testify." I handed him a printed copy of Darnell Barton's mug shot.

Nando shook his head in disgust. "A nasty fellow." He looked at Claire. "Is this the man you saw in the restaurant?"

She nodded. "The very same, only he now has longer hair and neck tats."

"He has no known current address," I went on, "but get this—four years ago, at the time of Sonny Jenson's murder, he was living in North Bend."

Nando's eyebrows raised. "Opportunity."

"Yep."

"What about his brother?"

"His name's Robert Barton, consistent with the initials RB," Claire responded. "He's forty. He lived at the same address as Darnell four years ago, but no known current address, either. They both seem to be living off the grid."

"I called Chet Rice this morning," I went on, "and told him what we had."

"What did you say about your source?" Nando asked.

"I didn't. He was happy to get the lead, didn't press me. He's got a murder and a home invasion to solve."

"What about the connection to Douglas County's hit-and-run investigation?" Nando asked.

"Rice said he would pass the information on. Between the two counties, maybe they can find these guys."

Nando pulled his brow into a frown. "I hope they do not work at cross-purposes."

I described my conversation with Walter Sanders next, and when I finished, Nando flashed a broad smile. "Ah, well done, my friend, a nice placement of the wedge. Either Max Sloat was planning a hit on Sonny, or Walter wanted you to think she was. And now we know the Brothers B could have played into the plot."

"That's right. My gut says Walter's telling the truth and wants to save his ass from being implicated. I think Max is our perp, and she probably used the brothers to actually kill Sonny."

Claire shot me a puzzled look. "Okay, I get the importance of finding the Barton brothers, because we have nothing tangible on Max, but after they're caught, then what? I mean what can be done to get them to talk about a murder committed four years ago?"

Nando showed a smile tinged with slyness. "The thin end of the wedge again, Claire. This time one brother is played off against the other. The younger brother, say, is offered leniency on the Howard Coleman and Sonny Jenson murders in exchange for testimony against the older brother and Max."

"Right," I said, "in the absence of other evidence, that's a route to prove Kenny didn't kill Sonny. Rice and Stoddard have to be willing to reopen Sonny's murder to make it happen."

Claire shot me another look. "Stoddard won't like that. Even though he's running unopposed, it'll make him look bad."

"You're right, Claire. Our only hope is that Rice will have enough courage to push it, despite what Stoddard says. He seems sympathetic to Kenny's cause."

Claire's face clouded over, and she shook her head. "Jeez, Dad, a lot of stars have to align."

"And some planets, too," I answered.

—

The wind that kicked up the afternoon before was the precursor to a front that moved in off the Pacific, stalled at the foot of the Coast Range, and laid down a gentle spring rain, the kind that soaks in instead of running off.

The last known address of the Barton brothers was a dilapidated rental house off Highway 101, just below the McCullough Bridge—a low, mile-long structure spanning the upper reaches of Coos Bay. Claire's research had determined that the owners of the house lived next door, and we'd decided to pay them a visit.

"Four years ago?" the owner asked, a Latina woman with a little girl clinging to her leg. "Oh, yes, I remember them. Two brothers." She made a face. "I did not want to rent to them, but times were hard then. My husband got injured at the mill."

Claire nodded sympathetically. "Why did you dislike them?"

The little girl whimpered, and the woman swept her up effortlessly before smiling a bit sheepishly. "No reason except they looked hard, you know? Have they done something bad?"

"We just want to talk to them," Claire said. "Did they leave a forwarding address or say where they were going?"

The woman laughed. "No. They left one night, late, without paying the rent, almost a full month's worth."

"Could you tell us when that was?"

The woman invited us into her home, an immaculate ranch with smells of spices, maybe cumin and paprika, from something cooking in the kitchen. Claire offered to hold the little girl, and the woman handed her over without hesitation. Then she sat down at a small desk along one wall, and after leafing through a ledger for that year, said, "They left the night of May twenty seventh."

Claire looked at me, her eyes wide, and turned back at the woman. "Are you sure of that date?"

"Yes, very. Is the date important?"

"Yes, it is," Claire answered, as she handed the little girl back. "Did you happen to notice any regular visitors during that time?"

The woman paused for a moment, then shook her head. "One good thing—they were quiet, those two."

"How about their cars?"

She squinted, as if trying to picture them in her mind, and stepped toward the kitchen, calling out a question in rapid-fire Spanish. A male voice answered in English, "A dark-colored Ford Explorer and a white Honda Civic."

That was the extent of what we learned, but it was enough. We thanked her, and as we were leaving Claire said, "Your home is lovely, and your daughter is very beautiful," a comment that caused the woman to break into a smile.

When we got into the car, Claire let out a little squeal of excitement. "Oh my God, Dad. The Brothers B skipped out three days before Sonny Jenson was murdered." Archie, who'd been patiently waiting for us in the back seat, picked up on the excitement, matching Claire's squeal with a couple of his own.

I nodded. "If you were planning a hit, maybe leaving the place you'd been living in and finding a hideout would make sense."

"Yes," Claire answered, "perfect sense. These aren't the kind of crooks who would hide in plain sight. That takes a certain amount of intelligence. These guys would opt to get the hell out of Dodge until the heat died down."

"Without paying the rent," I said as I pulled back onto Highway 101 and headed south. "The Ford Explorer fits, too, and maybe they're still driving the white Civic."

Claire leaned back in the car seat and laughed. "Well, one thing's for sure—they don't drive very gangster-like cars."

Chapter Thirty-Seven

The unincorporated community of Woodell lay twenty miles east of Coos Bay, at the top of an S-shaped bend in the south fork of the Coos River. Once a thriving logging town, where the Weyerhaeuser Corporation processed and deposited cut logs into the river and floated them down to Coos Bay for export, it now consisted of a Mobil gas station, a general store called McKnight's, and a very large and thoroughly abandoned sawmill. It was also the town where—according to the packet of information Harmon Scott sent—the elder Barton brother, Darnell, lived prior to his incarceration, and it was a good bet younger brother, Robert, lived there as well.

Buoyed by our success at the rental house, Claire and I decided to drive out to Woodell.

We had another, more strategic reason for the trip. In her search at the library the day before, Claire found one of Howard Coleman's credit card receipts from McKnight's General Store. Why was Coleman visiting this place, where the Brothers B once lived, just a few weeks before he died?

Southbound traffic on Highway 101 was light, and by the time we'd turned off at the base of the bay and crossed the bridge at Catching Slough, the rain had let up. Claire said, "Gabriel called last night."

"Oh?"

She sighed and focused on something across the narrow waterway for a moment. "It was good to hear his voice, I admit that." I waited. "He just started in like nothing happened between us. Maybe he just wants to be friends now, I don't really know."

"How would you feel about that?"

She puffed a dismissive breath. "No way I could stand being his friend. It's either all or nothing with him, as far as I'm concerned."

"What did he say?"

"Oh, that he was enjoying his parents' visit from Argentina but that it was taking a lot of his time to show them around." A slightly bitter laugh. "I think he was counting on me to shoulder some of that burden. You know, what I'm doing's not as important as his start-up."

"Careful that you don't assume more than what's there."

I caught her nod out of the corner of my eye. "Good point."

"Did he ask about what you've been up to?"

She laughed. "Oh, yeah. I laid it out for him, and he was shocked, to say the least." I winced inwardly. I could only imagine what kind of father Gabriel thought I was, exposing my daughter to such risk. "You know what he said?" she went on. "He said, 'I'm worried about you, but I think that what you're doing is courageous, Claire.'"

"*Well*," I said, "that sounds like he's extending an olive branch."

Another bitter laugh. "It's what he said next that got me. He said, 'I understand a little better, now.' *A little better?* That's as far as he was willing to go, Dad."

I kept my eyes on the road. "What did you say to that?"

"I thanked him for calling, and when he asked when I thought I was coming back to Boston, I said, 'When Kenny Sanders' case is wrapped up, and not a day sooner.'" She sighed again. "It was a frosty goodbye."

We drove for a while with nothing but the sound of our tires sluicing through the standing water on Coos River Road. I could have offered words of advice, but I kept them to myself. I knew instinctively this was her issue to sort out, and, besides, she hadn't asked for my opinion. One thing was clear—despite a deep reservoir of feeling between Gabriel and my daughter, it was a standoff with neither one willing to blink. Claire's response didn't surprise me. She was a strong woman, to be sure. Was Gabriel up to it? That remained to be seen.

McKnight's General Store sat well back from the highway, a weathered single-story building with a front porch running the width of the structure. A large sign, courtesy of the Pepsi Corporation, rested on the roof, promising Groceries, Sundries, and Fishing Supplies. After taking Archie for a short walk, we went in, a bell announcing our entrance. Claire took the lead at asking the questions, having clearly demonstrated her chops at that particular art form. She introduced us to the man behind the counter.

"We're investigating the murder of this man." She handed him a picture of Howard Coleman. "He was murdered on the east fork of the Millicoma River two and a half weeks ago."

Harney McKnight—an octogenarian with clear brown eyes, a drooping mustache, and a mane of silver hair—squinted at the picture. "I heard about that. Tied him up and threw him in the river." He shuddered visibly and looked up at Claire. "That's no way to die."

Claire nodded with a look of sympathy. "Back in April he bought some fishing leader and flies from this store." She handed him a copy of the credit card receipt. "Do you remember, by any chance?"

McKnight put his glasses on and looked at the receipt, then the picture again. "Well, I'll be. I was here that day—always am—but I don't remember. I'm not too good with faces."

Claire smiled. "That's okay, Harney, neither am I." She handed him pictures of Darnell and Robert Barton next. "He could have been with these two men."

McKnight looked at the pictures, then beamed a smile. "Oh, Lordy, those are the Barton brothers. I remember them coming in, and yes, they were with another man." He looked at Coleman's picture again. "That could be him, for sure. They were going steel-headin' upriver at a place the brothers knew. They're from around here, you know." His face darkened. "Are they mixed up in this?"

Claire shook her head. "No, we're just retracing Coleman's steps, is all. What can you tell us about the Barton brothers?"

"Well, not much to tell. They moved in here with their daddy after their mother died. Josiah Barton worked at the mill before it closed down completely. He was a monster. Always drunk, always brawlin' and beatin' up on his boys. Story was, Darnell tried to intervene once when the old man was wailing on Robert and got put in the hospital for his trouble. The hospital staff wondered how a sixteen-year-old kid got that beat up. When the sheriff came to investigate, Darnell claimed he fell off the roof, and Robert backed him up."

"Any idea where the brothers might be now?"

He shrugged. "Not the slightest. Their place up on Coos River Lane has been vacant for, what, thirteen years or more?"

"What became of Josiah?"

"Cheap booze ate his liver. I heard tell both sons cried at his funeral." McKnight chuckled and shook his head. "Go figure."

"What about other family members?"

He stroked his mustache and paused for a moment. "Nobody I know of on their daddy's side. The mother's maiden name was Gunderson, but I don't know where her people live."

After a few more questions, we bought some bottled water, thanked him, and left. At the car, I said, "So Coleman fished with the Barton brothers a couple of weeks before they murdered him."

Claire made a grim face. "It was probably a trial run." We got in the car, and she added, "Let's go look at where they lived."

"Why?"

She shrugged. "Just curious. I mean, we drove all the way out here." She looked at me. "You don't think they could be there, do you?"

"Nah. They wouldn't hide out in a known address, and Rice has probably sent deputies out here already. I'm surprised they didn't talk to McKnight."

The address Harmon Scott supplied led us to a narrow lane running north from the highway a mile past the general store. After passing a half dozen houses, the pavement ended abruptly and the lane, now heavily rutted, narrowed even further before dead-ending at an overgrown driveway. A rusty mailbox riddled with bullet holes stood at twelve o'clock, with "Barton" and the street number barely legible on its side. The house was visible through a scattering of second growth firs. The roof was nearly rotted through, and all the windows were blown out. A small shed adjacent to the house leaned at a thirty-degree angle, seeming to defy the law of gravity, and a rusted-out carcass of an old car squatted beneath a large alder. Affected by a blight of some kind, the alder was half dead.

"The Barton homestead," Claire said.

"What's left of it."

We stood there for a while, silently taking in the scene. Claire sighed. "Depressing. Doesn't look like anything happy ever happened here." She looked at me. "Can you imagine that kid, Darnell, saying he fell off the roof to cover for his father?" She crossed her arms across her chest and shuddered. "It makes me see him differently, Dad."

I nodded. "He probably knew nothing but violence growing up."

She sighed again, more deeply, her eyes suddenly bright with a film of moisture. "There but for fortune."

"Yeah."

"But it's no excuse in the eyes of the law, right?" my daughter added, showing a sardonic smile. "We haven't evolved to that state of understanding yet."

She was right about that.

Chapter Thirty-Eight

On our way back to Coos Bay, I checked in with Chet Rice. "We dispatched a couple of deputies early this morning to have a look at the property in Woodell," he told us. "The Bartons weren't there and hadn't been. We've circulated their names and photographs to law enforcement. I'm saying they're wanted for questioning." He paused for a moment and exhaled audibly. "I'm taking a leap of faith here, Cal. I don't have any evidence these guys have done a damn thing."

"I know. Pick them up. Trust me, you won't regret it. Incidentally, we can confirm they're not in Woodell," I said, and explained what Claire and I had been up to. "You might want to talk to the guy who runs the general store there—name's Harney McKnight. He told us Howard Coleman and the Bartons stopped in there on their way to steelhead fishing up the South fork of the Coos a couple of weeks before Coleman was murdered." I gave Rice the date but didn't tell him how I knew it.

His soft chuckle was audible. "Thanks, again. Why is it you're always a step ahead of me, Cal?"

"Hey, we're in this together," I answered. "If you catch these guys, you're a hero for solving two cases, and I have a shot at getting an innocent young man out of prison." I went on to describe how the Bartons skipped out of their rental in North Bend three days prior to Sonny's murder.

"Interesting," he responded. "But I'm taking it one step at a time. I'm set to interview Maxine Sloat later this afternoon. Maybe she's got a current address for our boys."

Claire eyed me after I tapped off the call. "Interesting? One step at a time? That sounded pretty noncommittal to me, Dad."

I shrugged, keeping my eyes on the road. "Chet Rice's got integrity. He'll come around. It's a simple *quid pro quo*, and he knows it."

At least, I hoped that was the case.

———

Back in Coos Bay, we stopped at Mingus Park to give Archie a much-deserved exercise break. At seventy pounds, Arch was on the large side for an Australian Shepherd at seventy pounds, but he still had enormous energy and a work ethic to match. His job that day was to drag Claire and me around the tree-lined trails in the park and then retrieve a tennis ball no matter how far it was thrown or how difficult it was to find. Four young boys on dirt bikes stopped to watch him go after the ball, cheering each time he made a leaping, twisting catch.

Such a show-off.

Claire dropped me at the hospital next. "Tell Nando I love him and that I'll see him tomorrow." She was off to the library. "I want to investigate the Barton and Gunderson families," she'd said. "Maybe that'll give us a lead to where the brothers are holed up."

I thought it was an excellent idea.

Rori Dennison was in Nando's room when I arrived. Her magenta-streaked hair didn't look quite as windblown as it usually did. There was a large bouquet of spring flowers next to Nando's bed, along with a hardbound copy of *Cien Años de Soledad*, Márquez's masterpiece in the original Spanish. Nando looked good, although there still seemed to be a hint of worry around his eyes.

"Calvin, my friend," he greeted me. "Catch them yet?"

"No, not yet." I hugged Rori and turned to my friend. "How are you feeling?"

He flashed his trademark smile but avoided my eyes. "Better. I am negotiating my release date with the doctors here." He glanced at the flowers and book. "The bouquet is from the gang at my PI office in Portland. They all wanted to come visit, but I said, 'Who will do the work? I might not be able to pay you next month.'" He smiled with a hint of slyness. "They decided to stay."

Rori laughed. "The book's from me."

Nando laughed. "I was telling Rori that Fidel Castro was a voracious reader. He read all of Márquez's books, and they were good friends." He gestured toward her with his right hand. "But she already knew this. I am not so voracious, but I am looking forward to reading this book."

I pointed toward his left arm. "Any movement in the fingers?"

He cast his eyes down, telling me this was the source of his worry. "No, I still can't feel them or move them." He looked up at me and forced a smile. "But it is early times."

I wanted to ask more questions, but it was clear Nando didn't want to talk about the havoc the bullet had wreaked on his arm and shoulder. Instead, he asked to be brought up to date on the case. When I finished describing what Claire and I learned earlier that day, he said, "Good detection work, Calvin. You and your daughter are quite a team." He smiled. "I would like to be a flea on the wall when Detective Rice confronts Maxine Sloat."

I laughed. "Me, too. I—"

Rori's phone rang. She looked at the screen. "That's Kenny. Excuse me." She stepped out of the room and reentered a few moments later, her face ashen. "Kenny said the request for a transfer's been denied." She held her cell up and tapped the speaker button. "He's still on the line, Cal."

"Hello, Kenny. This is Cal. What exactly did they tell you?"

"The head of the Security Threat Management Team, a guy named Corey, Phil Corey, came to my room. He said they'd identified the quote-unquote troublemakers in the European Kindred gang." Laughter. "As if only some of them are bad news. Anyway, he said they put them on notice, that the STM was confident I wouldn't have any more trouble. I laughed in his face. 'Even if I still refuse to join the EK?' I said. 'Yes, even if you refuse to join,' he told me."

"What did you say to that?" Rori asked, her voice quavering.

"I told him he had his head up his bureaucratic ass, that he was out of fucking touch with reality. If I go back in there, they'll find someone else to finish me off."

"Did he give you anything in writing, Kenny?" I asked.

"He said that I would get a written response, and that you, Cal, as my attorney, would also get something in writing. But he didn't leave anything. He said it was a courtesy visit."

Rori looked at me, her eyes filled with horror. I said, "Listen, Kenny. Do *not* worry about this. It's just round one. Once I get their statement, I'll respond. We'll get a court order if we have to."

Rori grabbed my arm with both hands and squeezed hard. "That's right, sweetheart. Don't worry. We've got your back."

"Thanks, Grandma," he answered, his voice thick with emotion. "How's the investigation going, Cal?"

"It's going well," I said. "We know what happened. Now all we have to do is trap the guilty parties."

"*No shit?* Who the hell did it?" he shot back.

I wanted to buoy his spirits, but I kicked myself for saying too much. "Not on a prison phone, Kenny. Don't worry, I'll update you in person as soon as I can."

He laughed, a couple of loud, nearly maniacal bursts. "Get the bastards, Cal. I can't live in this place anymore."

We signed off the call, the room silent, and the double meaning of Kenny's last sentence seemed to hang in the air like a reverberation. Finally, Nando looked at Rori and said, "Calvin is the best lawyer in Oregon. If Kenny needs to be transferred before we solve this case, he will find a way."

I shot Nando a thanks-a-lot look then turned to Rori, whose eyes were spilling over with a mixture of hope and gratitude. I wanted to scream, "There are absolutely no guarantees here. This whole thing's hanging by a thread," but I felt like that would crush Rori. Instead, I met her eyes. "Don't worry. We're going to beat this."

———

Hello pressure, my old friend.

Chapter Thirty-Nine

Claire was still busy researching when I left the hospital, so I drove over to the library, parked in the front lot, and used my cell phone to knock down some emails and return some calls, mostly from irate clients I'd been neglecting. I'd now missed a full work week back in Dundee, which necessitated moving several meetings and another court appearance. I felt even worse when I thought about my one-day-a-week pro bono practice in Portland. I pictured people in need coming by and reading the sign at my office that read *Closed Until Further Notice*. What would those people do? I swallowed the guilt and forced the negative thoughts down.

There's blood in the water, I told myself. Focus on the task at hand.

Claire emerged an hour and a half later. "You'll never guess who helped me today," she said as she piled in, toting her briefcase.

I laughed. "Not Marion the Librarian?"

"None other. Ellen Dempsey. What a nice person, and a damn good librarian."

I waited while Archie greeted Claire like he hadn't seen her in a week. "I like Ellen, too. She was seriously conflicted over her testimony at Kenny's trial. She told the truth about seeing him at the convenience store but never believed he was a murderer. Did you tell her who you were?"

"No. I just said I was interested in the genealogy and property history of the Josiah Barton family, most recently from Woodell, Oregon, and of his wife, a Gunderson, whose first name I didn't know. It would've taken me a week to do what Ellen did, Dad. She's a whiz at research and very professional. Didn't ask me any personal questions."

"Did you find anything?"

Claire pulled a notebook from her briefcase and opened it. "Maybe. I looked at the Barton side first. Josiah Barton was the son of Cornelius Barton and Emily Trask. They owned a small RV park on the Chetco River east of Brookings but lost it in bankruptcy. However, Emily's younger brother, Chad, still lives in Brookings and has several properties—three in town, small houses, and five acres further east on the Chetco. I took a look at the acreage on Google Maps. It's completely wooded and undeveloped."

"The brothers might know about it, right?" I said. "Maybe they visited there."

"It's possible. But where would they stash the Peterbilt truck and two cars?"

"Good point."

"On the Gunderson side, their mother Francis was the daughter of Mildred and Harold Gunderson of Port Orford. Her father was a fisherman there. Francis and Josiah married in Port Orford, and both Darnell and Robert were born there. When Francis died of an aneurysm in 1970, Josiah and the boys moved to the house on Coos River Lane in Woodell. It's the only property Josiah ever owned, but Harold Gunderson's sister still owns several plots along the coast, including twenty acres just north of Allegany."

"*Allegany?* The little town where the Millicoma River forks east and west?" Claire nodded, and I felt a faint tingling along my spine. It wasn't that far from where we'd found Howard Coleman's body. "What's the twenty acres look like?"

"There's a long dirt road in from the highway to a clearing in the trees with a house, a barn, and some smaller outbuildings. From the satellite image, it didn't appear that anyone was living there, but I don't know when the satellite shot was taken."

"The barn's big enough to house a logging truck and a couple of cars?"

"I think so."

"Hmm. That's damn fine work, Claire."

She laughed. "You can thank Marion the Librarian. What should we do next?"

I paused for a few moments as I turned off Connecticut Avenue onto Highway 101 and headed south into a stream of heavy traffic. "The easy thing would be to tell Rice, but realistically the odds are slim that the brothers are at the Allegany site, and he might drag his feet. Maybe there's a way to get in close enough and watch the place for a while." Claire shot me a skeptical look. "*Safely*, from a distance with binoculars," I added hastily.

She considered that for a moment. "The terrain's mountainous and heavily wooded. We could download a topo map of the area and figure out the best approach." The traffic slowed to a crawl, commanding my attention. Claire consulted her little screen for a couple of minutes. "There's a sporting goods store on the way to the beach house. Take the next right, then left on Broadway. It's down a mile or so on the right." I glanced at her questioningly. "Binoculars, Dad. We'll need them."

"Oh, of course." I smiled to myself. My daughter was definitely not the type to let the grass grow under her feet.

———

That evening the ocean and sky were sharply delineated, and when the sun finally vanished it left two bands of flaming gold separated by a narrow strip of radiant turquoise. I'd cobbled up a meal of leftovers, and afterward we sat out on the deck watching the show, as the turquoise turned violet and bled into the gold, and the seagulls scurried off to wherever they roost.

Claire said, "Just think, Dad—if we would've started fishing a little further down the Millicoma, I wouldn't have stumbled onto Howard Coleman's body, and we wouldn't be entangled in this affair at all." She smiled. It was tinged with resignation. "And I'd be back at Harvard and probably still with Gabriel."

"Yeah, the whole synchronicity thing's intriguing," I responded. "I mean, finding Coleman connected us with Kenny Sanders, and that seemed so, so, non-coincidental, like some deeper intelligence was involved."

Claire considered this for a while. "Deeper intelligence or just chance? I sort of see how everything's connected to everything else—butterfly wings causing hurricanes and all—but the question in my mind is whether it's random, or as you suggest, there's someone or something guiding it all."

A soft breeze off the ocean seemed to be carrying nightfall. I paused for a long time before speaking. "Here's how it looks to me, Claire. It's not the event itself. Maybe that's essentially chance. It's how we *react* to the event that counts. We could have walked away from the coincidence of my overhearing the conversation that connected Coleman to Kenny, but we didn't. We built on it, because it spoke to our consciences."

She paused for an equally long time. "Okay, I think I get what you're saying—a chance encounter becomes significant when we choose to make it so. So, looking back on it, it *appears* like synchronicity because of our actions. In other words, *we* make the synchronicity, not the other way around."

By this time, the gulls had stopped flying, and it was nearly dark. I chuckled, got up, and stretched. "Yeah, something like that. I don't have many answers, Claire, but I love the mystery of it all."

———

"This ridgeline looks promising," I said, pointing to the topo map Claire pulled up on her computer screen after we cleaned up the kitchen. "We could park at this pullout, where the trees would hide the car. It's maybe four miles from the dirt road into the Allegany property."

"I don't know, Dad," Claire said. "The ridge looks pretty steep. We'd have to do better than twelve hundred feet vertical before it levels out."

I gave her a stern look. "If we decide to do this, I'm hiking in *alone*. You'll stay with Archie in the car." She started to speak, but I cut her off. "It's nonnegotiable, Claire."

She paused as if formulating an argument, then apparently thought better of it. "Okay." She looked back at the computer image. "Once you're on the ridge, you've got a long hike, maybe three miles, before you get anywhere near the property."

"That's no problem." I squinted at the map. "At that point, it looks like I'd be five hundred feet or so above the clearing and the house."

Claire clicked out of the topo map onto a satellite image and zoomed in. She pointed with a pen. "You'd be right about here." The area was a mottled deep green, the lumpy tops of tightly spaced conifers reminding me of heads of broccoli.

I leaned in closer. "Right. There's a break in the trees a little further on." I pointed to a buff-colored gap in the broccoli. "I might get a decent view of the house from there." I looked up at my daughter, raised a hand, and she met it with hers in a high-five.

"It looks doable."

Chapter Forty

By the time we crossed the Coos River on the Chandler Bridge the next morning, the Coast Range was a purple silhouette against the light of the nearly risen sun. We followed Highway 241 northeast for twenty-five miles, crossed the Millicoma just before Allegany, and took a right on East Fork Road. Our designated pullout was five miles down on the right. I parked the Subaru behind a tight screen of fir trees, so it wasn't visible from the road. We got out, and I slipped on a day pack that held the Glock, a water bottle, a packet of trail mix, and a brand-new pair of Nikon binoculars with 8X magnification that I'd paid eighty-five bucks for.

"How many bars do you have on your phone?" Claire asked.

I glanced down. "One."

"Same here. Let's hope you get some reception up on the ridge. Remember, a text goes through easier than a call most times."

"Roger that. You've got Rice's number, right?" She nodded. I looked down at Archie, who was anticipating a hike in the woods. "You're staying back, Big Boy. Take care of her, you hear?" He cocked his head and gave a couple of whimpers in disappointment. "It'll take me maybe two, two and half hours to get into position. If the brothers are there, I'll call Rice and stay put to give him eyes on the place. If I can't get him, I'll text you and you can call him. Keep your head down, okay?"

Claire looked at me, her face tight with worry. "You, too, Dad. Don't take any chances, promise?" With that, she kissed me on the cheek.

I set off towards the ridgeline through a forest of old, second growth Douglas firs that were infiltrated with red alder, hemlock, and the occasional bigleaf maple. The going was steep and made even more difficult by a thick understory. If I wasn't scrabbling hand over hand, I was forced to move laterally to get around patches of ridiculously large sword ferns or dense tangles of salal and salmonberry.

Halfway up the ridge, I encountered a vertical basalt seam that looked like it might run continuously from one end of the ridge to the other—a natural barrier that wasn't foretold by either the topo map or the satellite image. The seam was at least ten feet high and too smooth to climb. *Shit.*

I moved along the base of the seam for maybe a mile and a half in intense frustration until I was stopped by a big, bleached out snag that had fallen years earlier. The gnarled root ball rested at the top of the rock wall. Using the branches as hand-and footholds, I worked my way slowly up the steep incline. Bark-free and smooth, the trunk was slippery as an ice rink, and when I finally hopped off at the top, I raised my fist in silent triumph.

Forty minutes later I was at the top of the ridge. I mopped the sweat off my brow with a handkerchief, took a long drink, and checked my phone. One bar. I called Claire and updated her. "So far, so good."

I made good time along the spine of the ridge and fifty minutes later saw the break in the trees up ahead—a scree field that was maybe a hundred yards across. I ducked into the tree line for better cover and moved cautiously until I got to the edge of the rockslide. From there I could just make out the barn and house across the clearing to the east.

Finding a smooth place next to a large rock, I lay down and removed the binoculars from my pack. I focused in, and a chill ran down my back when the first thing I saw was the cab of a dark, Peterbilt truck parked next to the barn. A second later I saw the Ford Explorer sitting next to the house—a dilapidated two-story house with a covered front porch. I scanned the rest of the area. No white Honda, but it could have been parked on the far side of the barn. A vivid memory of hurtling toward the Umpqua River after being struck by that truck played across my mind. I bit down a surge of rage.

Finally, I said to myself.

I checked my phone—the single bar was gone. I tried calling Claire anyway. The call didn't go through. I tried a text—

In place. Can't call from here. This is it. Waiting to confirm they are home. Stand by.

To my relief, this pinged back within seconds—

Great. Standing by. Careful.

I drank some more water and waited. The air was cool and crisp, the sun warm on my back, and the scene quiet except for the occasional birdcall. Ten minutes into my wait I saw movement down below and scrambled to attention, focused my binoculars, and then chuckled. A big doe and a tiny fawn strolled out from behind the barn and walked through the clearing before disappearing into the trees.

I ate some trail mix and waited.

Just past eight-thirty, I snapped to attention at what sounded like a screen door slamming and focused in on someone coming out of the house. I couldn't see his face, but he was tall, with long, grayish hair. Both arms, below the sleeves of a white T-shirt, were shaded with tattoos. It had to be the older Barton brother, Darnell.

He sauntered over to the Ford. *Oh shit*, I thought. He's leaving. But, to my relief, he opened the trunk, extracted a bag, and walked back into the house. I texted Claire—

> Confirm at least Darnell is home. Call Rice and explain situation. Tell him to proceed with caution. I'll keep him updated from here.

She pinged back immediately that she was on it, and fifteen agonizing minutes later this text came in from Rice—

> On our way with five squad cars. Will contact you when we arrive and before deployment. ETA forty-five minutes. You better be right about this, Claxton.

I drank more water, ate more trail mix, and waited. At 9:23, this text came in from Rice—

> At daughter's location. Our plan is to stay hidden and surround farmhouse, then order them out. Stay where you are. Advise if perps exit house prior.

Twenty minutes later, I saw a couple of deputies creeping around in the trees at the periphery of the clearing, carrying semiautomatic rifles. I sent this text—

> I see your men getting into position. No sign of either brother outside or any activity inside. You're good to go.

I tensed and waited… Another fifteen minutes elapsed before two squad cars pulled up next to the Ford in front of the house. Rice and three deputies got out and stood behind the cars. Amplified by a microphone, Rice's voice boomed out, "This is the Coos County Sheriff's Office. All occupants of this house are requested to immediately come out with their hands behind their heads." He waited. No response. He repeated the request. He waited some more.

At that point, I saw movement at the back of the house and focused in. Darnell burst out the back door, carrying a rifle, and started sprinting toward the tree line. Two deputies, one on either side of him, stepped from behind trees and ordered him to stop. He swung his rifle around in the direction of one of the men, and I heard the report of a gunshot. Both deputies opened up on him in response, the multiple shots reverberating up the hillside.

It was over in a heartbeat. They cut Darnell down.

"No, goddamn it," I screamed from my lonely perch. "I need him *alive!*"

Chapter Forty-One

I worked my way down the steep slope through the trees—careful to make sure I didn't get shot like Darnell—and when I reached the clearing had enough signal to call Claire. Darnell's body had already been covered, and there was no sign of Robert or the white Honda on the premises. "It looks like Robert's in the wind, so get your butt over here," I said after I told her what had just gone down. "Wait for me on the highway at the entrance. There's a deputy posted out there, I'm sure."

Rice was talking to the deputies who'd shot Darnell, and when he saw me, he patted them both on the shoulder and came over and pumped my hand. "Thanks for the help, Cal. You're quite the cowboy."

I shrugged. "I wasn't sure they were here and didn't want to waste your time. I, uh, saw the shooting. It was righteous. Darnell fired first."

"That's a relief," he said. He glanced over at the shooters. "Tim and Henry will be glad to hear they have a witness. These things can get gnarly. I'll need a full statement."

"Of course."

He eyed me with curiosity. "How did you find this place, anyway?"

"My daughter, Claire, found it with the help of a North Bend librarian. This property belongs to the brothers' great-aunt on their mother's side. We took a flier, thinking they might be here."

He pushed his bottom lip out and nodded. "Impressive work. It's a damn shame we killed him."

I shook my head and scowled. "Your guys had no choice. Who knew Darnell was going to react like that? Take Robert alive, whatever you do. He's in a white Honda Civic. He can't be far."

"What year?" Rice asked. I said I didn't know and waited while he called the information in. He gestured toward the Peterbilt truck. "Is that the rig that knocked you in the Umpqua?"

"Looks like it." We walked over to it, and I examined the steel bumper, pointing to a smear of paint. "That's the exact color of my old Beemer, metallic gold. They didn't even bother to remove it. Then again, those two aren't exactly shining lights of criminal intellect."

Rice chuckled. "Douglas County's going to be interested in the truck."

I looked at him and cracked a smile. "I hope there's something here for all of us."

Rice went on, "I'll apprise them. They'll probably bump your case from a hit-and-run to attempted murder now." He withdrew two sets of latex gloves from his jacket pocket and handed me a pair. "We've cleared the house and barn, and I figure I owe you a look-see."

We gloved up, and I followed him to the barn first. Stuffed with rusting, cobwebbed farm implements and tools, the poorly lit interior reeked of chemicals and mildew. Once my eyes adjusted, I pointed to a roll of small-diameter steel cable sitting on a work bench next to a scattering of tools, including a large pair of heavy-duty cable cutters. "I'll bet that's the wire they used to tie up Howard Coleman."

Rice said, "That was an early clue that Sloat trucking might be involved, right?"

I had to smile. "I was just spit-balling then. I happened to see a roll of similar cable when I was snooping around in their shop. It was just a hunch. You know how that goes."

He pointed at the cable cutters. "Those can leave a distinctive mark on the material they cut. I have the cable they used on Coleman. We might be able to prove where it came from."

At the other end of the bench, I spotted a couple of fly rod cases and a tackle box. While Rice poked around, I walked over to the fishing gear. The tackle box was open, and a handsome metal case containing a primo collection of steelhead flies sat right on top, the lid open. I eased the lid closed so I could read the name embossed on it—Howard Coleman.

I called Rice over and showed him. "They didn't just tie him up and throw him into the river, they stole his flies," he said, then added with a deadpan expression, "That's a worse crime than murder around here."

He glanced at his watch. "Let's take a quick walk through the house before the forensic team and the ME get here. I'm going to be busy once they arrive." He grimaced. "Then there's the fatal shooting—as the officer in charge, I've got a shitload of paperwork and reviews to do for that."

The dust-layered front room of the house looked like a mausoleum decorated by a centenarian spinster. The only three rooms that appeared lived-in were two bedrooms upstairs and the kitchen, which had a collection of beer and hard liquor bottles on every flat surface and a rank, garbage smell from a stack of dishes in the sink. Rice stopped at the cluttered kitchen table and pointed at a cell phone resting between a plate with dried egg on it and a half full coffee cup. "Didn't see that the first time through. Must be Darnell's." He picked it up gingerly, selected "recents," and squinted at the screen. "Yep, he called out at 10:03. That's right after we arrived. He probably warned his brother to stay away before he bolted out the back."

Our quick walk-through revealed plenty of evidence of

wrongdoing, but nothing that caught my eye vis-à-vis the Sonny Jenson murder or Max Sloat. Not that I was expecting anything obvious. We found over fifty one-kilo packages of white powder that Rice said looked like pharmacy grade fentanyl, stashed in a bedroom closet along with a suitcase full of cash we didn't bother to count. The other bedroom contained a laptop and a cache of weapons and ammunition, including a half dozen handguns of various sizes and shapes and two Colt AR-15s with large capacity magazines. A third AR-15 lay outside next to Darnell's dead body.

"Some arsenal," Rice remarked.

"What every sportsman needs," I said.

Rice hooked a pen through the trigger guard of one of the handguns, lifted it up, and smelled it. "This puppy fires a twenty-two round like the one your friend took in the shoulder," he said, "and it smells like it's been fired recently. We've got the slug they took out of him."

I nodded. "Don't bet against it being a match."

We went back outside, and Rice had me give a detailed statement on a portable recording device. Afterward, he looked me in the eye and said, "I owe you, Cal. Don't worry, I'll keep you in the loop. If we find anything that pertains to Max Sloat and Sonny Jenson's murder, you'll be the first to know."

I wanted to ask why he wouldn't tell his boss first but thought better of it. I shook his extended hand. "I appreciate that, Chet. Kenny could use a break." I took a couple of steps, looked back, and said with a smile, "Remember, take Robert alive."

I started off down the dirt driveway just as an ambulance, an unmarked black sedan, and a panel truck passed by, marking the arrival of the medical examiner and the forensic technicians. A quarter mile later, Archie saw me first and almost knocked me over with an airborne greeting, and once I regained my balance Claire grabbed me in a bear hug. "Oh, Dad, I'm so glad to see you."

I patted my dog on the head and smiled at my daughter. "It's mutual, sweetheart. I'm tired and hungry. Let's get out of here."

———

"So, they've got evidence now to charge our boys on Howard Coleman's murder, our hit-and-run, Nando's shooting, and drug trafficking," Claire said as we headed back toward Coos Bay. "That's quite a crime spree."

"Well, they won't be charging Darnell with anything now, but Robert's in the crosshairs. There's a lot to this thing, but Rice's a good cop. I think he'll piece it all together."

"What about Sonny's murder?"

"That's the question, isn't it? Either we get a break and Rice finds something at the house, linking them to Max and the murder, or he gets Robert to talk once he's caught."

"Robert's brother is dead now. Why would he admit to anything about Sonny's murder?"

I shrugged. "He doesn't have a lot to lose. Coleman's murder alone could get him the death penalty. Maybe his older brother did the actual killings. It's hard to say how he'll react once he lawyers up. One thing about lawyers, they like to make deals."

"What if they don't catch him?"

"They will. He probably went out to buy beer. How far could he get?"

We drove along the winding Millicoma in silence for a while. The river's color mimicked the sky in the bright, midday sun. After calling Sissy Anderson and leaving her a message to get in touch, Claire released a long breath and crossed her arms across her chest in that familiar pose of hers. "Maybe I should feel encouraged right now, but to be honest I don't. We've solved every damn crime but the one that counts, Dad. And the truth is, we don't have any leverage. Rice and Stoddard have it all."

I couldn't disagree. "Keep the faith," I said as much to myself as to my daughter. "We're not done yet."

Chapter Forty-Two

We stopped for clam chowder and fish and chips at a little joint on Highway 101, then swung by the hospital to check in on Nando and bring him up to date. We arrived at his room just as Sissy Anderson was leaving. "I just dropped by to wish him well," she said, showing a somewhat embarrassed smile. "Brought him some cookies."

We exchanged greetings, and Claire asked Sissy not to leave, announcing we had important news. I began describing what happened that morning at the Gunderson property, and when I finished recounting how we'd discovered the Barton brothers' hiding place and the shooting of Darnell Barton, Sissy sucked a sharp breath and started to cry. Claire enveloped her in a hug.

"Sorry," she said, moving free of my daughter, looking at each of us in turn, and forcing a bitter smile. "I don't know why I'm crying. These aren't tears for that bastard."

"It's okay to let some emotion out," Claire told her.

Nando filled the awkward silence that followed. "The younger brother, Robert?"

"He wasn't there," I answered. "Chet Rice promised to call me when they pick him up." I went on to describe the evidence that was immediately apparent in the barn and house. At the mention of the fly case with Howard Coleman's name on it, Nando—who enjoyed playing devil's advocate—pointed out that Howard could have lent his fishing flies to the brothers.

Claire said, "He has a point. We learned yesterday that they fished together on the Millicoma just a month earlier."

Sissy laughed with disdain. "Howard would *never* loan his steelhead flies to anyone, let alone those two idiots. Sure, he fished with them, but he didn't respect them."

"Well," I said, "judging from what I saw, Rice will find plenty of evidence against them. They're sloppy and he's a thorough detective." I went on to describe the money and weapons, leaving the suspected dope for last. "There was also a large amount of narcotics in the house. Rice thought it was high grade fentanyl." I looked at Sissy. "You could get drawn into this investigation in a hurry. If they bring you in for questioning, I'd advise you to get an attorney."

"You?" Sissy asked.

"No. I've got all kinds of potential conflicts." I dug Mimi Yoshida's card out of my wallet and handed it to her. "If they bring you in, call her. She's the attorney Howard was going to see before he was killed."

Sissy took the card and blew a breath in disgust. "Howard didn't say anything about fentanyl. I know that shit's bad news. He told me they were just dealin' a little black market weed. I—"

I put up my hand. "Don't tell us anything you're not willing to tell the sheriff, Sissy," I warned. "We can be questioned as well."

"Okay," Sissy said, looking chastised. "But I don't know hardly anything about the drug dealing."

"Good," I said. "The less you know the better."

Nando changed the subject. "We now know the brothers own a logging truck. This will presumably lead Rice and the Douglas County investigators back to Sloat Trucking." I nodded, and he continued. "Aside from Howard Coleman's tally sheet, which is circumstantial at best, this could be the first direct evidence linking the brothers to Maxine Sloat."

"True," I said. "I'm hopeful they'll find more direct evidence at the house. There was a cell phone in the kitchen and a laptop sitting in one of the bedrooms. I'd love to get my hands on both of them."

"Sounds like nothing has changed," Sissy said, curling her lip in disgust. "*Evidence?* Some things you just *know,* and I know Howard and my dog would still be alive if that woman hadn't ordered those two lowlifes to kill them." She swung a pointed finger around to include us all. "And she nearly succeeded in killing all three of you." Her eyes burned bright with a kind of manic quality. "She won't get away with this."

Claire said, "We're as frustrated as you are, Sissy, but we're getting close now."

I said, "Look, Sissy, this is an investigation, and we don't have any direct evidence that Max Sloat ordered *anything* at this point. You've got to trust the process."

Sissy glanced at the clock on the wall. "I've got to get to work." Emotion distorted her face, and she teared up again. "I'm sorry. I know you have your hearts in this." With that, she turned and left.

Claire frowned and shook her head. "Wow. Getting one of Coleman's killers off the board didn't move the needle much for her, did it?"

I nodded agreement, and Nando said, "She has the thing about Maxine Sloat, and Sissy Anderson is a woman to be reckoned with."

Chapter Forty-Three

Claire and I left Nando's hospital room that day on a down note. When I asked if the feeling in his left hand and fingers was coming back, he said, "Not yet."

Concern gathered in Claire's face. "What are the doctors saying?"

He shrugged his right shoulder. "Nerve recovery can be slow, that it is too early to tell. I am not concerned, though." He flashed his broadest smile, but traces of worry around his eyes gave him away. Nando was a handsome man who carried himself with the physical grace of a bull fighter. Having a useless left arm would be a devastating blow for anyone, but most especially for my friend. I cringed at the thought, and judging by the expression on Claire's face, she had the same reaction.

We left without letting on, hoping for the best.

When we got back to the beach house, I found a letter in the mailbox addressed to me from the Department of Corrections. The letter was short and decidedly unsweet, confirming that Kenny Sanders' request to be transferred to the state prison in Pendleton was denied. The letter stated that, as Kenny related, the Security Management Team at the Salem facility made a determination that the threat was no longer extant, and in view of this, the DOC Director had denied the request. The response was no surprise. Aside from the fact that lifers were seldom granted the luxury of a transfer, validation of the threat by the SMT would be tantamount to an admission that the prison couldn't protect one of its own.

Claire went out on the deck with Archie to watch the sun boil into the Pacific. I sat hunched over my computer at the kitchen table and began researching the case law for prison transfers in Oregon. After two hours I had a petition roughed out to the Honorable Donald Armstrong of the Marion County Circuit Court in Salem requesting a court order to halt the reintroduction of Kenny into the general population at the prison, pending a hearing on the merits. The refusal to grant the transfer, I argued, was an abridgment of Kenny's Eighth Amendment right to protection from cruel and unusual punishment and to his right to humane facilities and conditions, two inalienable entitlements of every prison inmate. To my surprise, I found and cited the case of a man who was beaten to death in his cell at the Snake River facility. An artist, he refused to do tattoos for a white supremacist gang. He was temporarily removed from the prison but forced to return, despite his plea to be transferred. Prevent the state of Oregon from making another tragic mistake, I implored the judge.

———

"The request for a hearing on the transfer's done," I told Rori in a phone conversation after dinner that night. "I'll send it registered mail tomorrow. I think we have a good chance of prevailing." I didn't mention the killing at Snake River, figuring that would only upset her. I went on to describe the scene at the Gunderson property, and we discussed the ins and outs of that situation.

"You and Claire must be exhausted, Cal," she told me as we wrapped up. "I hope you know how much Kenny and I appreciate all you're doing." I told her we did, and she said, "I had a visit from Walter today. It was, ah, interesting. He mentioned a meeting you had with him a couple of days ago. I think his visit resulted from that. He wanted me to know he had nothing to do with Sonny Jenson's murder."

"Oh, right. Things have moved so fast I haven't had time to update you. I put the heat on Walter, and the bottom line was that before the murder Max asked Walter if Sonny was alone that night. He said it never occurred to him to mention that to the investigators, because the case against Kenny looked so compelling. I told him it was more likely he didn't want to threaten the deal by implicating his potential partner."

"That bastard. He even broke down and cried, Cal. He said he was sorry he wasn't more supportive of Kenny at the time. Now I see why." She paused. "Do you believe him?"

"He's got a financial motive, and his alibi's a little shaky, but I haven't found anything else."

"So, it's Max along with the Barton brothers?"

"It's looking that way. We've got a ton of circumstantial evidence supporting that. Now we need solid proof."

"Oh, you just lifted my spirits." Rori paused. "When Walter left, I noticed a check on my desk. It was for ten thousand dollars, Cal. Made out to me and signed by him."

I whistled. "What did you do with it?"

"I tore it up. He can't buy his way back in with his dirty money." She released a deep sigh. "I suppose I should find it in my heart to forgive him, but I'm afraid I'm a substandard Christian."

———

The next morning Claire and I took Archie for a run on the beach, and then I mentioned needing to go to the post office to mail Kenny's hearing request. "I'll stay here with Arch," she said. "We'll be fine."

"Nothing doing," I shot back. "As far as we know, Robert Barton's still out there. You're both coming with me."

She made a pouty face but agreed. Then she bent her head and tapped out a text with lightning speed using both thumbs. I looked at her with raised eyebrows. "I'm reminding Kathy Harper that she agreed to talk to me. Maybe she can meet us somewhere. I know we're less interested in Walter now, but I'd still like to hear what she has to say."

We stopped by the Charleston Post Office, and Claire and Archie waited in the Subaru while I mailed the letter. As we were pulling out of the parking lot, a text pinged in on Claire's phone. "It's Kathy. She's agreed to meet with us. There's a small park on State Street, just off Broadway. She said she'd be at the playground there with her little girl for the next hour or so."

"You want me involved?"

"Yes." She smiled. "I want you to bring your gravitas, Dad. We need to convince her this is important, and you can answer any legal questions she might have."

We parked a half block down on State Street and cut across a soccer field to the playground, where kids swarmed over the equipment with abandon, safe in the knowledge their falls would be broken by a soft, synthetic turf. We had Archie in tow, figuring his presence would lend an air of informality to what promised to be a tense situation.

Claire spotted Kathy on a bench on the periphery of the play area. Tall, with ice-blue eyes and honey blond hair, she greeted us with a wary smile that still managed to be dazzling. "I, um, I'm still not sure I should be here," she said after Claire introduced Archie and me.

Claire showed a sympathetic smile. "We can understand that. Four years is a long time ago," she said, glancing at Kathy's cherub of a daughter snoozing in a stroller, "and you've obviously moved on." Kathy smiled with parental pride. "We're here," Claire continued, "because one of your friends hasn't been able to move on. He's in prison for the rest of his life."

Kathy's smile crashed. "You know, we couldn't believe Kenny did it, but, you know, he confessed and a jury convicted him."

"Did you know he recanted his confession the next day?" Claire asked in a gentle voice.

"Um, not really."

Claire glanced at me, while Archie calmly lay down next to the stroller like a guardian. I said, "The confession was coerced, Kathy. Kenny was young and scared, and they manipulated him. We believe he's innocent, and we're faced with the job of proving it. To do this, we need to know all the facts surrounding the case. Do you understand?"

She cast her eyes down. "I do, but I don't see how I could help." Her voice was barely audible.

Claire said, "As I mentioned when we talked last, a person of interest in the case is Walter Sanders, Kenny's stepdad. We know about the affair, Kathy. We're interested in anything you can tell us about him as it relates to Kenny or to Sonny Jenson around the time of the murder. *Anything*. Details are important."

She brought her eyes back up. "What if this gets out?"

Claire said, "Oh, come on. All your friends know about the affair. How do you think we found out so easily? Your husband, Brad—you really think he doesn't know? Be serious."

She looked stunned for a moment. "Is that true?"

Claire rolled her eyes. "It's the 'me-too' era, Kathy. Time to lose the guilt."

Kathy glanced at her daughter and exhaled a breath, as if releasing something she'd held in for a long time. "Well, Walt and I didn't talk about Kenny. That was too close to home for both of us. And he never talked about Sonny Jenson or anything related to his businesses that I remember. My God, I was only sixteen."

"When did you two stop seeing each other?" Claire asked.

"Right after the murder, actually. Two, maybe three days later." She smiled bitterly. "I was devastated. Walt told me all along that he loved me, that when I turned eighteen he'd leave Krysta and marry me. Then, boom, he breaks up with me. He said I couldn't tell a soul about us, made a big deal out of that." She drew her mouth to one side in a smirk. "I wonder why?"

"What else do you remember around the time of the murder?"

"Well, I remember we were together that night. I—"

"The night of the murder?" Claire interrupted, keeping her voice even. "Are you sure?"

"Yes, I'm sure. It was a Friday night, and word about the murder got around that Sunday, at least that's when I heard about it, and that Kenny was in trouble. That's why I remember."

"Where did you go with Walter that night?"

"Um, Walter drove in from up north, Newport, I think." Her fair complexion took on a shade of color. "We, um, went to our usual spot, a motel on Highway 101 down by Millington called the Slumber Lodge. He would go rent the room, and I would wait in the car." Another smirk. "He called it our special place."

"What time span did that cover?" Claire asked.

She paused for a moment and absently stroked her check with a hand whose fingernails were nicely manicured. Her daughter stirred in the stroller. "It was after dinner, I remember, so around seven, maybe. We, um, left the motel around eleven, eleven thirty."

Claire fixed her eyes on Kathy. "You're sure of the timing? From around seven to around eleven?"

"I'm sure. It was our last night together."

"Did Walter get any calls that night that you remember?" I asked.

She focused on something across the park for a few moments. "He was always getting calls, you know, making deals and things like that, but I never listened. I don't remember that night being any different."

"Why do you think Walter chose that time to break up?" Claire asked. "Had you argued?"

"No. We hadn't argued at all. He never gave a reason, just

said he couldn't see me anymore." She paused for a moment and stitched her brows together. "Funny, I never associated the murder with the breakup, but maybe that's what happened." Her eyes got wide. "Do you suspect Walter of being involved in this?"

"We're just gathering facts, Kathy," Claire responded, "and what you've told us is very useful." Claire went on to ask a few more questions before drawing it to a close.

I said, "Thanks for your candor, Kathy. It's vitally important that you keep the discussion we just had confidential, even from your husband. Can you do that?" She said she would. "You know," I continued, "statutory rape's a felony, and there's no statute of limitations. You could also pursue this in civil court and claim damages."

"*Damages?*"

"Walter Sanders stole part of your childhood. You could hold him accountable."

The little one started to fuss. She picked her girl up, hugged her, and smiled fully for the first time. "I hope you get Kenny out of prison. I really do."

We left on that note. When we got to the car, Claire looked at me, her eyes wide with excitement. "Oh, my God, Dad. That was so cool. I see why you do this work."

"You did all the heavy lifting, Claire."

She showed a modest smile. "And I loved how you slipped in the bit about her being able to go after that SOB in court."

I laughed. "So, what do you think?"

"She's telling the truth," Claire answered without hesitation.

"You don't think Walter got to her, desperate for an alibi, even one that might get him a rape charge?"

"Not a chance. She wouldn't lie for him."

"Even for money?"

Claire shook her head emphatically. "Even for money. She was telling the truth. The only thing I don't get is why he broke up with her right after the murder. The timing's a little weird."

"Yeah, I had the same thought. I think Walter knew his personal life might get scrutinized in the investigation, and he didn't want the affair to come out. So, he went with the I-was-in-Newport alibi."

"So, now we know Walter didn't kill Sonny with his own hands," Claire said. "But he could have been involved with the Brothers B and Max."

"My gut says that's unlikely."

Claire looked at me. "So, he's off our list?"

"For all intents and purposes."

"Well," she said, "that narrows down the field."

Chapter Forty-Four

An uneasy lull descended on our investigation at that point. In one sense it was timely, because both Claire and I had issues and obligations back in the world to attend to. Claire received a call from her boss at Harvard, an eminent professor of environmental science, who asked for an update on her continued absence from campus. She explained that the family emergency requiring her presence wasn't resolved yet, which was the truth. However, I doubt she was completely truthful about the nature of the emergency. After all, not everyone would agree that helping your father solve a cold case murder would qualify as such, even if it involved an innocent kid looking at life in prison.

She emerged from the call looking a little sheepish. "Professor Hastings is trying not to pry, but there're limits. She said she could only justify another week, given the workload on the group. If I don't get my butt back to Cambridge, she'll probably take some kind of action."

"Like what?"

Claire shrugged. "I don't know. I was afraid to ask. She might ask me to leave her research group."

I felt a jolt of parental alarm tinged with guilt. "That can't happen. It's your dream job, and other environmental scientists in this country would kill for it."

"I *thought* it was my dream job." She brought her sapphire eyes up to meet mine. "You need me, Dad, and you know it."

"This isn't about me, Claire," I shot back. "It's about your future."

She crossed her arms, and her eyes narrowed down. "What about Kenny's future? I made a commitment to you and him, and to Rori, too." A wisp of a smile spread across her lips. "This is like environmental work, Dad. I feel like I'm making a real difference here. I'm not quitting until this gets resolved."

I cringed inside. What the hell had I done? But it was clear my headstrong daughter was dug in, and there wasn't much I could say. I laughed instead. "Well, that settles it, then. We've got a week left to crack this sucker."

———

Gertrude Johnson called not long after that, wondering where in the hell my billable hours for the month were. Already two days late, I told her I'd get something to her by email and reluctantly started combing through my disorganized records. I wasn't a good record keeper in ordinary times, and these weren't that, for sure. Aside from a divorce case I'd argued before our arrival in Coos Bay, all my billable hours were for the Kenny Sanders case. And they were quoted at a steep discount to Rori Dennison, the very same Rori Dennison who would have a hard time paying me and who had just torn up a check for ten thousand dollars.

Easy come, easy go.

———

An hour after lunch, Chet Rice called. "I'm slammed on all fronts, Cal, but I promised to keep you updated. I—"

"Have you caught him?"

"Not yet, but we've got every law enforcement agency in the state looking for him and the white Honda."

"There's another family property you should look at. I should've mentioned it yesterday, but I thought you'd pick up Robert in a heartbeat." I went on to describe the five-acre plot on the Chetco River that Claire had also found. "It's wooded and undeveloped, probably the last place he'd go but worth a look."

"Got it," he said. "You won't believe this, but you, your daughter, and your dog are the stars of a video."

"*What?*"

"Our tech guy has been going through Darnell's phone and computer. Darnell uploaded a video of when he took your BMW out, the whole thing, how he waited while you slowed for the curve, then his acceleration to the point of impact. Must've had an action cam, probably strapped on his cap. A video hobbyist, apparently."

Those terrifying moments flooded back to me. "Yeah, I remember seeing something like that on his head but didn't know what the hell it was. A video, huh? Why am I not surprised?"

Laughter. "Douglas County has the video, and they've impounded the Peterbilt," Rice continued. "Darnell uploaded it, and the only fingerprints they found inside the cab belong to him, so it looks like he was the driver, not Robert. We're building a strong case on the Howard Coleman murder. We found a couple of pings from Darnell's phone at a cell tower about a mile and half from the scene on the Millicoma. That puts him there on the day of the murder. The cable and cutters from the barn, along with the cable we took from Coleman's body, are already at the state police forensic lab for analysis. There were fingerprints all over the cutters. Not Darnell's, so probably Robert's. Wouldn't be at all surprised if the lab shows they're the ones used to cut Coleman's wire."

"Obviously they were both involved in the crime spree," I said.

"Yeah, it's frustrating that we won't get the satisfaction of charging Darnell with anything, but we can sure as hell clear these cases and throw the book at Robert."

"What about Nando's shooting?"

"Promising. We lifted a set of prints from the twenty-two found in the house, and we've already got a match to the slug your friend caught."

"You're thinking the prints are Robert's?"

"They're not Darnell's. That could give little brother murder, home invasion, and attempted murder counts at the minimum. And, thanks to you, we recovered several globs of tobacco juice at the scene."

I laughed. "They'll be loaded with Darnell's DNA, I promise, and he's in the system."

Rice chuckled again. "Damn it, Cal, promise me that when this is over you'll tell me how you knew all this. I'll buy the beer."

"I like wine better," I quipped. My throat tightened a little as I asked the next question. "Any evidence that Sloat Trucking or Maxine Sloat's mixed up in this?"

"Aside from some pay stubs of Darnell's, that's a negatory. We're working with our narcotics team on the fentanyl distribution side of it. They're going to follow up with Max as well. I'll keep you in the loop."

He paused. "We did find something relating to the Sonny Jenson murder four years ago." I waited, not liking the change in the tone of his voice. "The first time Darnell used his action cam was for a bonefishing trip he and Robert took in the Bahamas. To be honest, we looked through them because the videos had some great action shots. They're both damn good fishermen. Anyway, the date stamps on the videos start two days before and end five days after Sonny's murder. I just happened to notice it. It's pretty solid evidence they weren't involved, Cal."

I went silent, thinking of when the Barton brothers left the rental house in North Bend—just three days prior to the killing.

Looks like they took off to go bonefishing. I exhaled. "You're sure about that?"

"Yeah. Every video has a date and time stamp. They don't lie, Cal."

Well, shit.

Chapter Forty-Five

"So, the brothers Barton did not commit the murder Kenny Sanders is in prison for," Nando said, sitting in a chair in his hospital room wearing a white bathrobe and slippers. He was allowed out of bed for short periods now, but his fingers still remained numb and paralyzed. He swung his dark eyes from me to Claire and back again. "This is an interesting development."

"That's right," I said, "and thanks to Claire, we also know now that Walter Sanders wasn't in Newport the night of the murder. He was at a motel south of here with Kathy Harper most of the evening."

Nando's thick, brushy eyebrows rose as he looked at Claire. "You got the young mother to talk about a difficult subject. Good work." Claire nodded, and a devious smile spread across Nando's lips. "So, enter the lady who commands the logging trucks."

"Right," I said. "Center stage. Claire and I have been kicking that around. There are two possibilities. First, the brothers, who did not kill Sonny, have no connection to his murder whatsoever, which means the apprehension of Robert will not help us."

"*But*," Claire chimed in, "we just learned Chet Rice thinks Robert's the one who shot you, Nando. So, there's that."

He shrugged his good shoulder. "They were both shooting at me. It was one or the other. I don't really care."

"The second possibility," I continued, "is what we've been working up to these last three weeks. Let's assume, for a moment, that Max Sloat decided to get rid of Sonny that night four years ago. The idiot was about to screw up a multi-million-dollar deal, after all. She confirms he's alone that Friday night by talking to Walter, goes over to his place and dispatches him with a hammer from his workshop. Makes it look like a robbery. After that, the whole comedy of errors plays out that resulted in Kenny being arrested and coerced into confessing."

Claire laughed, a harsh, derisive note. "Max was probably amazed at her good luck."

"Right. So, everything's cool for Max, and she even puts the jailhouse snitch Howard Coleman on her payroll. Why not? He did her an unwitting favor."

"Or, maybe it was part of a payoff, we just don't know," Claire interjected.

"That's right," I said. "In any case, Howard starts distributing fentanyl with the Barton brothers, and Max begins taking her cut. Everything's still cool."

Claire laughed. "Fast forward four years. Howard grows a conscience and sets up a meeting with Mimi Yoshida to atone for sending Kenny to prison. That could unravel the whole thing."

"And Max gets wind of it," I went on, "probably through the Barton brothers, who are Howard's fishing buddies as well as his partners in crime. So, she has them take Howard fishing one last time, just to make sure she's never found out."

"In which case," Nando said, "the apprehension of Robert Barton is *vital*."

"Exactly," I said, "if—and it's a big if—he knows why she had them kill Coleman."

Nando stroked his chin stubble with a big paw. "It seems likely the Barton brothers warned her about Howard's intentions, which suggests they knew about Sonny's murder. Who knows, perhaps Maxine let something slip?"

"I hope you're right. The brothers ran an exceedingly sloppy criminal enterprise, but so far Rice has found nothing that directly connects them to Max."

Nando grimaced, and with his left arm wrapped tight against his chest, used his right arm to help himself stand. His color was good, his voice strong, but the worry in his eyes was still apparent. "I like your scenario. It fits the evidence like the glove."

Claire laughed again, derisively. "*Circumstantial* evidence. We know what happened, but we can't prove it."

Nando sat down wearily on the edge of the bed, and Claire helped him get in and covered him with a sheet. He thanked her and smiled with a tinge of embarrassment as he lay his head back on a pillow. "I tire too easily. Tell me, what are the next steps?"

Claire and I looked at each other. "Other than waiting for Robert to surface, we're stymied," I answered. "When he's caught, I'm confident Rice will squeeze him hard to implicate Max and find out what Robert knows about her motives." I exhaled a breath and shook my head. "It's shaky, at best."

The room got quiet. A gurney rattled by out in the hall. Nando said, "The situation is indeed precarious. I am wondering about Walter Sanders. Has he told you everything he knows? After all, he is trying to have it both ways—casting suspicion on his partner and maintaining his secrets. Perhaps you should shake his cage once more, Calvin?"

I shrugged. "I can try, but I'm not sure it will yield anything."

Claire said, "Rori told us he came to her in a pretty emotional state yesterday. There must be a reason for that. He's anxious about the investigation for obvious reasons, and he could be worried about what Max Sloat might do to him. Maybe we can play off his anxieties."

Nando looked at me and smiled. "Your daughter makes a very good point, Calvin."

———

There's no time like the present. Claire and I left the Bay Area Hospital that day and drove directly to the headquarters of Condor Enterprises on North 6th. It was midafternoon, and the sun was a hazy silver disk behind a layer of fast-moving clouds. Claire and I both went in but were informed that Walter Sanders had left for the day. I asked the receptionist to have him call me as soon as possible. "Tell him it's urgent," I said.

Back at the beach house, Claire and I took Archie for a well-deserved jaunt on Lighthouse Beach. The plovers weren't around, so I was given permission to unleash my dog, who dashed off with reckless abandon, at least until he got near the waterline. A stiff breeze blew off the ocean, and the air had that good sea aroma. I mentioned liking the salty smell, and Claire laughed. "You can't smell salt, Dad. What you're smelling is actually a sulfide compound produced by an enzyme associated with the algae in the water."

"Oh," I said. "Didn't know that. *Sulfides, enzymes?* Somehow, that takes the romance out of it." That made us both laugh, the first levity we'd shared in quite a while.

We just got back to the house when the doorbell rang. I said to Claire, "Bet you ten bucks that's Walter Sanders. He always shows up uninvited."

I opened the front door, and there he stood. "I know, you were just in the neighborhood, Walter." His gap-toothed smile fell a little at my remark. "Just kidding. Come in." The wind had become blustery, so I led him into the living room and offered him a seat below the Jackson Pollock print. Claire joined us. I said, "Thanks for coming by on short notice, Walter. We're, uh, about ready to wrap this investigation up, and, at the request of my client, Rori, I'm giving you a chance to get out ahead of it." I locked onto his eyes. "Kenny Sanders did *not* kill Sonny Jenson. That's a settled fact. His business partner—you—and a potential partner—Maxine Sloat—both had strong financial motives to silence him. The letter Sonny wrote to you is—"

"That letter was just business, for Christ's sake," Walter cut in, holding my gaze. "Sonny loved brinksmanship. And it was Max who threatened him, not me. I had nothing to do with Sonny's death. I was cleared in the investigation. I was in Newport."

Claire let a half laugh slip out.

I said, "There you go again, Walter, lying to us. You were at the Slumber Lodge Motel that night with a sixteen-year-old girl with whom you were having an ongoing affair."

The blood drained from his head like a plug had been pulled. "I, uh, that was a big mistake, something I regret very much."

I waited, letting him twist in the wind for a while. "It does provide you with an alibi for that night. However, that would be a costly thing to have surface here in Coos Bay, considering your standing in the community and all." He looked at me in disbelief. "If you don't want the focus of attention on you, I strongly recommend you tell me *everything* you know about Max Sloat during that time."

He licked his lips, swallowed, and his small eyes seemed to retract into their sockets. "Okay, okay. About a week before the murder, Max and I were talking about that goddamn letter. Max was really pissed. She said something like, 'We should kill the bastard. I know a couple of guys.' I laughed, thought she was kidding. That's all she said, I swear."

"What happened after that?"

He exhaled. "When I heard what happened—that was before they arrested Kenny—I went to Max's place. I said, 'What the hell have you done?' She looked me straight in the eye and said, 'Are you fucking crazy? I was kidding about that. I was at my office last night. I can prove it.'"

From the corner of my eye I saw Claire lean in. I said, "*Did* she prove it?"

He shrugged with a sheepish look. "I don't know. I guess I took her word for it. I guess I believed her over my stepson. It's, ah, not anything I'm proud of. It seems so different now, looking back on it."

Claire said, "Do you know of anyone else who could speak to her alibi, one way or the other?"

Walter shook his head. "Nah. You might ask someone who was working that night at the yard. They usually have a guy at the gate, but it was a long time ago."

"That's all you got, Walter? You're not holding back anything else?" I asked.

He raised his palms in a gesture of appeasement. "That's it, I swear." In a lower tone, he added, "I wish I'd done the right thing in the first place."

As I walked him to the door, he asked me what I was going to do with the information about his affair. I bit down a strong urge to tell him exactly what I thought of his actions, but this wasn't the time for that. I said, "Nothing, unless it's necessary to prove Kenny's innocence." It wasn't the reassurance he was looking for, I'm sure. I added to his anxiety by saying, "Max Sloat knows you're a potential witness. If I were you, I would watch my back."

After he left, Claire looked at me, crestfallen. "That didn't go anywhere, did it?"

"No, not really. But at least it showed that Walter suspected Max. Hell, he accused her of doing the murder."

"But it's still not enough to charge her with anything."

"Afraid not."

She exhaled and rolled her eyes to the ceiling. "Jeez, what does it take?"

"To vacate a jury conviction, a lot, Claire, a lot."

Chapter Forty-Six

The wind, which usually dies down after the sun sets on the Oregon coast, maintained its blustery ways that night, which made for some strange noises as the cedars brushed and scraped the side of the house. About three in the morning, Archie barked—two sharp yelps indicating he didn't like one of those noises for whatever reason. I was already sleeping on the edge of consciousness—that weird, floating state between being awake and asleep—so his barks snapped me to attention with a start.

I sat up, withdrew the Smith and Wesson from the nightstand drawer, and moved cautiously downstairs, with my dog leading the way. We stood in the shadows and watched the deck through the window for a long time. Nothing moved, except tree branches animated by the wind. "Okay, Big Boy," I said, finally, "false alarm." He looked up at me as we took to the stairs, and I patted his head. "I know, just doing your job."

——

I got up early the next morning, and after a couple of cappuccinos, started cooking breakfast, a five-egg omelet to which I added nearly everything I found in the refrigerator—green onion, red bell pepper, some leafy spinach, Gruyere cheese, and some bacon I'd nuked in the microwave. An even less perky morning person than her father, Claire staggered in just as I laid the concoction out on the table along with toast and a jar of local honey.

Despite the latest admission by Walter Sanders that seemed to seal the deal on Max Sloat, our mood had shifted. Maybe it was because Chet Rice hadn't called, meaning Robert Barton was still at large, or more likely a sense that we were running out of actions *we* could take to advance the case.

Had we hit the wall? It was beginning to feel like it.

Over breakfast, we did discuss the possibility of chasing down Max's whereabouts the night of the murder. "What about that guy at the gate at the truck yard who let you in that first day?" Claire asked. "Maybe he was around four years earlier or knows someone who was."

I shrugged. "It didn't look like they kept any written records, so it would be next to impossible to prove, even if he or someone else remembered back four years. The most we could hope for would be that Max wasn't where she told Walter she was that night."

Fortunately, we stayed busy that morning. Claire was engrossed in a conference call with her research teammates regarding interpretation of some new data. From her comments afterwards, it appeared the Gulf oil spill was an even worse catastrophe than anyone imagined. "If Coos Bay only knew what they were getting themselves into," she told me, "they wouldn't touch that LNG proposal with a barge pole. The science doesn't lie."

For my part, I was engrossed in a couple of conversations with prospective clients back in Dundee. One was a high stakes divorce case—the kind I hated but always paid well—and the other an ownership dispute over a prime chunk of acreage in the Red Hills, with a southern exposure preferred for growing pinot noir grapes. I took the business. I also called Gertie to make sure she'd gotten my billable hours for the month. "Your cash flow's down forty percent," she told me. "You better transfer five thousand from your savings to your business account so I can pay your quarterly taxes." I told her I would.

The pressure to return to Dundee was up several notches. I could feel it.

———

That afternoon, we called Rori and told her we were coming into town to update her and then swing by to visit Nando. The wind finally died down, and as we crossed the Cape Arago Highway Bridge, the sun glittered like a billion silver coins on the mirrored surface of the bay. At that point, the car's Bluetooth connected to my ringing cell phone, and I tapped it on. "Claxton? This is Max Sloat. We need to talk."

"Sure," I answered, trying not to sound surprised. "Your place or mine?"

"I'm in my office at the yard."

"Fine. I'm in the vicinity, it turns out. I'll see you in ten."

When I punched off, Claire looked at me and smiled. "Synchronicity, Dad?"

A faint tingling slithered down my spine. "Maybe so."

———

"You again?" It was my favorite dispatcher leering at me at the entrance to the yard at Sloat Trucking. Claire had dropped me off and gone on to see Rori.

I smiled. "Back on days, I see."

"Only because Arnie Bloom's sick today," he fired back, without returning the smile.

"Say, I'm wondering—do you keep any written records of who comes and goes around here?"

He shook his head. "Just the trucks, no humans." He handed me a badge. "The boss is expecting you."

I made my way across the yard, which bustled with activity, and took the stairs next to Max's cherry red truck, which appeared even shinier than the last time I'd seen it. Only one person waited in the reception area—a red-headed man who looked like he could bench press a logging truck as well as drive one—and when Max's assistant told me to go right in, Red gave me the stink eye.

Max looked up from her desk as I entered, her eyes locked on me, her lips drawn together, thin and ruler straight. "What the fuck's going on, Claxton? I just got through dealing with two Douglas County Sheriff deputies, who wanted to know all about a contractor I use occasionally. They said he was involved in a hit-and-run, the one that put you in the Umpqua. I hardly knew the driver and sure as hell can't be responsible for what he does when he's not working for me. The deputies had warrants and took copies of all my records around that time, like I might be involved or something. They acted like a bunch of goddamn Nazis."

I stood in front of her desk and waited, sensing she had a lot more to say.

Her neck took on a little color. "That's not even half of it. Some detective named Rice and some other dude from the Coos County sheriff's office showed up to question me about Howard Coleman's murder and fentanyl trafficking involving that same driver." She stood up and shook her head. "Had to call my lawyer at that point. We're going in this afternoon to chat about that." The color reached her cheeks. "Then to top it off, my business partner's acting all weird, like I had something to do with Sonny Jenson's murder."

I said, "Those are serious crimes. You'll be doing the community a real service if you can shed more light on what happened."

She placed her thick arms on the desk and leaned forward, glaring at me, now red faced. "This is all your doing, isn't it?" I shrugged. "You come into town—Mr. Do-Gooder, trying to rescue a confessed murderer—and start turning rocks over and stirring things up and—"

"You can't go in there!" the voice of the assistant called out, just as the door to the office burst open and Sissy Anderson walked in.

Sissy registered surprise at seeing me but quickly turned her attention to Max, her eyes burning with ferocity. "Hello, Maxine. I just stopped by to tell you you're not getting away with killing Howard and my dog."

The assistant came in behind Sissy. Red stood behind him. "Shall I call someone, Max?" the assistant said, concern in his eyes.

Max laughed. It rang with a mixture of disdain and arrogance. "No, Wendell. You two go on out, I'll handle this." She looked back at Sissy with genuine curiosity. "What in the name of hell are you talking about?"

Sissy stepped forward and faced Max. "I'm talking about your having Darnell and Robert Barton tie Howard up and throw him in the Millicoma River. Cold-blooded murder. And my dog, they shot my dog, for Christ's sake." She jerked a thumb in my direction, and when she spoke next, her chin trembled. "And they forced this man and his daughter into the Umpqua and shot his—"

"Shut up." Max's voice was sharp and threatening. "You're talking like a crazy woman." She looked at me and laughed again, with bitterness this time. "See what I'm talking about? This must be pile-on-Max-Sloat day." Then she turned her glare back to Sissy. "Now, get out of here, or I'll throw you out myself."

The room went silent as the two women faced each other. In an attempt to de-escalate the situation, I said, "Sissy, why don't you and I go outside and talk this over?"

Without taking her eyes off Max, she said, "Stay out of this, Cal. I just want her to know she's not going to get away with—"

Before Sissy could finish the sentence, Max stepped around the desk and pushed the smaller woman hard in the chest. "I said get out, you dumb bitch. Out."

Sissy staggered back and collided with the table on which Max's bowling trophies sat. Struggling to recover her balance, she grasped one of the trophies in her right hand, and without even looking, whirled around and swung the thing. The marble base of the trophy caught Max square in the temple. She dropped like a puppet with its strings cut.

"No!" I screamed as I rushed over and knelt next to Max's crumpled body.

Sissy dropped the trophy, covered her mouth, her eyes huge orbs. "Oh, Jesus, I didn't mean…"

Wendell came in, looked at Max, then at me, his face a study in stunned disbelief. "What the hell happened?"

"She's badly hurt. Call 911. Now!" Wendell hurried out, but not before eyeing the bloody trophy at Sissy's feet.

Max's eyes were half open, and she reached a hand up as if to pull me closer. I leaned in. She tried to speak but her mouth moved without making any sound. I got closer still, and her eyes opened wide, locking onto mine. In a hoarse whisper, she said, "I never did what she said, Cal. I never killed anybody but my old man, I swear."

With that, her hand flopped down onto her chest, her eyes fluttered closed, and she became still.

Chapter Forty-Seven

I thought Max was dead, but I found a weak pulse in her neck. Red had entered the room and stood staring at us, frozen in shock, his mouth agape. "She's alive," I said. "Go out to the gate to make sure the rescue team knows exactly where we are. Every second counts. And have somebody call the sheriff." He rushed out as well, relieved I'd given him something to do. I turned to Sissy, who still stood next to the trophy she'd dropped on the floor. Her eyes were wet, her face pale, and her knees shook perceptibly. I nodded my head toward a chair behind her. "Sit down before you collapse."

"Is she going to die?" she asked in a tremulous voice as she collapsed into a chair.

"I don't know. Listen, Sissy. The sheriff will be here soon. They're going to arrest you. Don't say *anything* about what happened until you get a lawyer. Not a word. Do you understand?"

She nodded and looked down at the trembling palm of her hand then back at me in disbelief. "God, I didn't mean to, it just happened, Cal. I didn't even think. She shouldn't have pushed me like that."

"I'm going to call Mimi Yoshida for you as soon as I can, Sissy. You're going to need an attorney."

It was an agonizing wait for the ambulance. Max remained unconscious during that time, while Sissy bit her nails and sobbed quietly. Wendell brought a first aid kit from the shop area, and I doubled up a couple of compresses to staunch the bleeding at the site of the wound, which had become an ugly hematoma the size of an orange. I was prepared to give Max CPR, but to my relief, her weak pulse stayed stable.

When the paramedics arrived and loaded her onto a stretcher, I followed them out to the waiting ambulance. A sizeable crowd of workers from the yard had gathered. They were solemn-faced, some dabbing tears. Others near the ambulance asked if she was going to be okay and what had happened. It was clear to me that Max Sloat wasn't just the owner and the boss, she was, if not beloved, certainly well-liked by her employees. I was surprised and moved by the outpouring of concern.

Two sheriff's deputies arrived just as the ambulance departed. They first questioned me, Wendell, and Red, then arrested Sissy on the spot. She was handcuffed and led out to a patrol car they'd parked next to Max's truck. Word had apparently gotten around about what happened, so when Sissy appeared a smattering of angry shouts rose up from the crowd.

At that point my cell riffed, and when I answered Claire said in an anxious voice, "Dad, are you okay? I'm outside the gate with Rori. They're saying Max Sloat got hurt in a fight of some kind."

"Yeah, I'm okay. She's badly hurt, and I witnessed it. Wait for me. I'll explain when I get out of here."

I had no sooner disconnected when Chet Rice called. "Cal, I just heard that somebody damn near killed Max Sloat."

"I know. I was with her when it happened."

"You're kidding me. Who did it?"

"Howard Coleman's girlfriend, a woman named Sissy Anderson."

"What happened?"

"There was a scuffle, and Max got clocked with a bowling trophy."

"Ouch. Were you working with this Anderson woman?"

"Yes, we had some contact. She knew the first name of one of the Barton brothers—Robert. That got the ball rolling for us."

"Is Sloat going to make it?"

"I don't know. She took a hell of a shot to the temple. She was conscious for a short time and then when out like a light. I thought she died."

"Well, I hope she pulls through. This is a big enough clusterfuck as it is."

"You're right about that," I said, the implications too fresh for me to comment any further. "Uh, what's the latest on Robert Barton?"

Rice sighed into the phone. "We've had reports of at least twenty-three suspicious white Honda sightings. None have panned out. That may be the most common make and model in the state. Robert's gone to ground, I'm afraid. *But*, you were right about the tobacco juice spittle. It was loaded with Darnell's DNA. That puts him at the scene of the Nando Mendoza shooting. You give good tips, my friend."

I called Mimi Yoshida next and apprised her of the situation. "I'd be happy to talk to Sissy," she said after I finished. "Where is she?"

"She was arrested and carted off to the Sheriff's Office ten minutes ago. I told her I'd call you."

"Okay. I can leave right now."

I sat down in the reception area to wait for the detailed interview I knew was coming. My emotions were churning, not just from the shock of witnessing the violence and the fact that the victim was our key suspect. Another concern gnawed at me at a deeper level—what was I to make of the last thing Max said to me? It felt like a deathbed declaration, after all.

I was still processing that.

———

I paced around for a half hour before finally talking to the investigator in charge of the case, a colleague of Chet Rice's named Drake. "We'll want you to come to the office to read over and discuss your statement and sign it," he told me when we finished. "We'll text you a time." I said that would be fine, and when I finally escaped the truck yard, I found Claire, Archie, and Rori waiting across the highway in the Subaru.

I got in and heaved a sigh before giving them a quick summary of what happened. When I finished, Claire looked at me with incredulous disbelief. "I don't get it, Dad. Why on earth would Sissy do that? What possible good did she think would come from such a confrontation?"

I could only shrug. "I think she was angry and totally frustrated. She wanted to put Max on notice. When Max shoved her into the trophy table, she just reacted. It was spontaneous. I don't think there was any premeditation toward violence at all."

"So, it was self-defense?" Claire asked.

I had to chuckle. "That, I'm afraid, is a question that's going to be vigorously adjudicated. My guess is Sissy will be charged with aggravated assault. I called Mimi Yoshida, and she agreed to represent her. Mimi's with her now."

"Good," Claire responded. Then her face clouded over. "What if Max dies?"

"Sissy will be looking at manslaughter at a minimum."

My daughter's face grew even darker. "What about our investigation? It'll be crippled, won't it?"

"*What?*" Rori said, who so far hadn't realized the threat this posed to our effort to free her grandson. "You can still prove Max killed Sonny, even if she's dead, right?"

"We can gather evidence," I said, "but we can't take her to court. Our judicial system doesn't allow dead people to be charged with a crime. This, uh, complicates things, Rori."

I could feel the heat of Rori's gaze on the back of my neck. "How bad is this, Cal?" Her voice was low and filled with trepidation.

"We'll find a way, Rori."

That's what I told that brave and loving woman, but for the first time, I had a sense that Kenny's exoneration might be a bridge too far. Perhaps it was Max's statement that weighed so heavily on me—did she tell me the truth before slipping into unconsciousness? Was her father the only person she ever killed? I wasn't sure, and I wasn't about to share my doubts with anyone at that point.

Chapter Forty-Eight

Two days later at the beach house the clouds were low and thick over the slate-colored water, and for some reason the gulls were not their usual noisy selves. I had just returned from the sheriff's office and was out on the deck sipping a coffee and talking to Nando on my cell phone. "So," he was saying, "Esperanza and George are driving down today from Portland to pick me up. George will drive me back in my Lexus. How does my car look?"

"Well, you know, there's a lot of condensation at night, so it's a little streaky, I guess."

"Then we will have to wash it."

"Of course. What are the docs telling you about your arm?"

"It is still the early days. I will begin physical therapy in a week."

"Any movement yet?"

"No." He paused there, making it clear he didn't wish to discuss the prognosis for regaining the use of his left arm. "What is the latest on Maxine Sloat? She is just down the hall from me, but my nurses are not telling me a thing."

"She's still in critical condition," I said. "They've induced a coma because of the swelling in her brain. She has a shot at recovering, but it's going to take a long time."

"I see. Are you leaning guilty or innocent?" my friend asked next. I'd told him about Max's near-deathbed statement to me and how conflicted I felt about it.

I sighed into the phone as the look in Max's eyes at that moment unspooled in my mind yet again. "She's still our best suspect, but I have profound doubts now. Of course, it's moot since we don't have anything concrete one way or the other."

"What about Sissy?"

"Her bail hearing's tomorrow. They've charged her with first-degree assault, which means they must prove she acted with intention. I think that's a stretch."

Nando chuckled. "So says the star witness."

"Unfortunately."

"Well, I wish her the best." He paused. "I hate to leave you and Claire, my friend, but there appears to be nothing more I can do here under the circumstances."

"No worries. We're packing up today, as well. Claire has booked a flight back to Boston in four days."

Nando chuckled. "She agreed to that?"

"Well, I told her that if they finally find Robert Barton or a new lead develops, I'll let her know and we can decide if she needs to rejoin me."

"She is an excellent investigator, Calvin."

"I know, but she's also an excellent environmental scientist, and the world needs more of those right now, don't you think?"

"Ah, I see your point. How does she feel about it?"

"Mixed. She's so committed to Kenny Sanders and Rori, she's having a hard time letting go."

"Claire has a good heart, my friend. You have raised her well."

I exhaled a breath. "Anyway, I'm going back to Dundee. I'll keep my hand in, but not full time, obviously."

"What did Aurora say about this?"

"I haven't told her. Haven't gotten up the nerve yet. She's going to take it hard. And I'm still waiting for a date on the hearing to get Kenny transferred." I blew another breath. "I've got to win that, Nando, but I think the deck's stacked against me."

"You will win it, Calvin. You should not be ashamed, my friend. You have laid everything on the line for that boy and his grandmother."

"Yeah, well, there's not much to show for it, is there?"

———

"I'm such a pack rat, Dad. What should I do with these shells and rocks I've collected?" Claire asked as she came out of her room later that morning. "I can't take them with me."

I was vacuuming in the living room in front of the Jackson Pollock. "Put the keepers out on the deck."

Her cell phone buzzed at that point, and she had a conversation I didn't hear. When she finished, she motioned for me to turn off the vacuum. "That was the waiter at the Tioga Building." I must have looked puzzled. "You know, the old timer there. Anyway, he apologized for taking so long to get back to me. I'd forgotten all about him. So, three years ago, he said, the owners of the restaurant had that emergency door put in because a couple of customers went out the back without paying."

Three years ago?

"Yes, he was positive about that. And I asked him about the use of the back way out before the door was installed. He said he didn't know whether residents used it or not." She looked at me. "What do you think, Dad? Synchronicity?"

I shrugged. "Okay, that means Twila could have gone out and come back through the back exit and avoided the security camera in the front of the building, but the video of her final exit showed her wearing the same clothes she entered with, and no blood stains were visible. So, we're back to the same problem— she was awfully tidy for having just bludgeoned her husband with a hammer."

Claire nodded and started back to her room. I turned the vacuum back on, looked at the paint-spattered Jackson Pollock, then turned the vacuum back off as everything clicked into place.

"*Of course*," I said out loud, "the *coveralls*. I saw her wearing them at Seven Devils. That's how she did it!"

Claire stopped and turned around. "Did what?"

"Kept her husband's blood off her clothes, that's what. She must have worn them that night. We've been all wrong." I paused for a moment, my mind racing, then pointed at her phone. "Look up the San Francisco Opera, opening night. It's René Fleming in *La Traviata*. When the hell is it?" Claire started to speak, but I cut her off. "Just do it."

She looked up from her screen a few moments later. "It's tomorrow night, Dad, but—"

"Good. It's not too late."

Claire looked at me like I'd just gone crazy. "What's not too late?"

I looked back and laughed. "She's a pack rat like you. And she likes to dress up for the opera. She told me that, too."

Claire narrowed her eyes down. "That doesn't help, Dad."

I laughed again. "It's so out there, I'm embarrassed to say. Bear with me." I rushed into the kitchen, where my cell phone was charging, and called Nando. "I need a huge favor."

"Of course, Calvin."

"I need your best camera guy. I need a close-up of someone, from the waist up. High resolution, and they can't know they're being photographed."

"Is that all? This is what we do. My best man is Ramón."

"That's not all. I need Ramón to get on a plane either tonight or early tomorrow morning for San Francisco. The subject is staying at the Fairmont Hotel and will be going to the opera tomorrow night. He needs to catch her either when she comes out of the Fairmont or at the opera. It will be a busy scene."

Nando paused. "How important is this?"

"Very, or I wouldn't ask you."

"Then you will need Felix as well. It will take a spotter and a camera man to ensure the job is done properly. We will need several photographs of the subject in order to be able to pick her out." He paused. "This bears on the case, *verdad?*"

"Yes, but trust me, Nando. I'll explain later."

"Very well. Unfortunately, Esperanza is on her way here. Send the photographs to my account at the office, and I will instruct Ramón how to access them. Give us several shots. Felix is a good face man, but he needs reliable input to spot his prey."

I disconnected and said to Claire, who stood next to me with a perplexed look on her face, "Get your computer. We need to find some good headshots of Twila Jenson and send them to Nando. Also, we need to go through the files we were going to take back to Mimi Yoshida and find the insurance pictures of the items that were supposedly stolen at the time of the murder."

Claire crossed her arms and gave me a hard look. "*Only* if you tell me what's going on."

I explained my epiphany, such as it was, how that damned Jackson Pollock painting had triggered the whole thing. Thirty minutes later we had found three good photographs of Twila on her website and one in the Coos Bay World digital edition—a full-length shot of her standing next to a painting in her gallery—and sent them on to Nando's office.

I leaned back in my chair and took a breath. "Whoa, that was intense. Thanks for the help, Claire."

She nodded. "Do you think you're right, Dad?"

I shrugged and smiled with a tinge of sheepishness. The rush had worn off and doubts were setting in. "I might be howling at the moon, Claire. I just don't know."

There was nothing to do but wait.

Chapter Forty-Nine

Our bags were packed, and we spent the next day in limbo except for a meeting with Mimi Yoshida to give her my full account of the bowling trophy incident and additional background on our relationship with Sissy Anderson. "I'm not surprised at the first-degree assault charge," she told us as we sat in her office in North Bend, "Gillespie's an aggressive DA."

"Do you think he'll allow her to plea down?" Claire asked.

"Too early to tell for sure, but he's got to be thinking about it in light of what your dad witnessed. There's risk in overcharging someone. He could lose the case entirely if he can't prove Sissy came with the intention of hurting Sloat."

"I think he'll come around," I offered.

"Of course, if Sloat dies, all bets are off," Mimi added, a reminder I knew would upset my daughter.

Claire winced visibly. "When can I see Sissy?"

Mimi smiled politely, but her dark eyes flashed a warning. "You can't. You could be involved in this case if it ever goes to trial."

"Oh," Claire said, blinking back a tear. "Of course."

———

When we left Mimi's office, Claire suggested we stop by Coffee and Subversion to see Rori, but I argued against it. "I don't know what in hell to tell her right now, Claire. She's probably expecting me to say I'm scaling down the investigation and going back to Dundee. Let's wait to see how the Hail Mary comes out. Maybe we'll have something new to tell her."

Claire shot me a stubborn look. "If there's more work to be done, I'm staying, Dad."

That's my daughter, I thought but didn't say.

———

On the way back to the beach house, we stopped in Charleston and got the fixings for paella—some local pink shrimp, chorizo sausage, rice, an onion, a bell pepper, some outrageously expensive saffron, and a sourdough baguette. I was on edge, and so was Claire. Cooking a big meal—perhaps our last at the beach house—might relax us, we figured.

After taking Archie for a long walk on Lighthouse Beach, Claire set to work chopping as I peeled the shrimp. Although neither one of us said so explicitly, it was understood that while we cooked, we wouldn't discuss the case but simply wait to see what came back from San Francisco. The paella came together beautifully, and while it simmered on the stove, we rewarded our hard labor with a glass each of a nice pinot I'd brought from the Aerie—a 2012 Le Petit Truc.

The wine put Claire in a wistful mood. "I wish I would have gotten some of Mom's artistic ability. I would love to paint like her. Her watercolors are so, I don't know, so delicate and calming, at least the early ones."

"Yeah," I said, "She had a wonderful gift. And she was a great teacher, too."

My daughter looked at me. "Why don't you hang some of her paintings in the Aerie, Dad? I don't get it. It's been a long time since she passed, and they're all still up in the attic."

"I know. I, uh, they bring back so much. Looking at those paintings is like staring into your mom's eyes again, Claire. It's difficult."

Her sapphire blue eyes locked on me. "You should do it, Dad. It'll be cathartic, trust me. And it would brighten up the Aerie. God know the place needs it."

I stirred the paella and stayed silent for a long time. Finally, I nodded. "Okay. I'll consider it if you agree to help me place them."

She smiled. "Deal."

———

When it got to be ten thirty, and nothing had come in from Ramón and Felix, we both began to worry. Then, at ten forty-five, a series of images pinged into my email account with this note—

Sorry for the late reply. We missed the subject at the Fairmont and at the entrance to the opera but caught her coming out. We hope these photos are what you are seeking.

Sincerely,
Ramón & Felix

I clicked on the first photo, a large crystal-clear image in which Twila Jenson appeared to be looking directly into the camera. I regarded it for a moment then thrust a fist into the air. "Yes!" I pointed at the jade necklace draped around her neck. "That necklace has got to be the one that belonged to her grandmother. I saw it in a painting at her place. She told me it was her favorite piece of jewelry, and I figured that if she had it, she'd wear it to the opera."

"She couldn't bear to part with it," Claire said. "I don't blame her. It's magnificent."

"Yes, I think that's it. The opera was too big a temptation, and San Francisco probably seemed far enough away for her to chance wearing her jewelry." I gestured at the file folder holding the insurance photos, and Claire slid it over to me. I opened it and found a close-up of the necklace, a three-tiered piece consisting of delicate beads of jade strung on gold. It was a perfect match with the one she was wearing.

Claire, who stood behind me at this point, clutched my shoulder with a hand. "She took the jewelry to make it look like a robbery. She killed him, Dad."

I let out a breath in disgust. "I misread her completely. I thought what she was exhibiting was depression from grief. I even felt sorry for her, offered some advice. Of course, it was all about the guilt. I mean, she bludgeoned her husband to death and let Kenny take the fall. Why the hell didn't I see that?"

"There's a fine line between grief and guilt, Dad. They can both lead to depression."

I shook my head. "Maybe so."

Claire patted my shoulder. "But you figured it out." She laughed. "Well, with a little help from Jackson Pollock and some well-timed synchronicity."

We went through the rest of the photos of Twila Jenson at the opera. The last one showed a clear image of her right wrist, which bore a lovely diamond bracelet, a dead ringer for one she'd reported missing.

"Frosting on the cake," Claire quipped.

Sitting below the Jackson Pollock, we talked far into the night, and when Claire finally started off to bed, we had the semblance of a plan for the next day. "This will be interesting," I said as she walked away with Archie trailing her. "We're not out of the woods yet."

And we weren't. Not by a long shot.

Chapter Fifty

The next morning broke bright and clear, and the Pacific got its color back along with a horde of hungry, cawing seagulls that dived and swirled out beyond the deck. I got up first and took Archie for a run on the beach, and when we got back, I made Claire and me a stack of French toast with the last of the eggs and sourdough bread. Over breakfast I said, "I left a voice mail for Chet Rice to call me."

"Good," Claire said with a wry smile. "I know where Twila's hiding the jewels."

That raised my eyebrows. "Where?"

"At her place on Seven Devils Road. It's remote, you know. She's hiding damning evidence, so she'll want psychological security." Claire smiled again. "She probably has them in a wall safe or some cool place like that."

I had to chuckle at my daughter's enthusiasm. "Good point. It's no given that I can convince Rice to go for a search warrant, and he'll need a green light from Stoddard. Then, there's no guarantee a judge would grant one based on the photographic evidence alone. And that's all we've got at this point."

Claire's smile crashed. "With the law, there's always a catch."

———

Rice didn't call back until late that afternoon. I explained I needed to see him right away, that I had significant new evidence in the Sonny Jenson case. "It's visual," I said. "We need to meet face to face. I'm going to need your help."

"Sorry, Cal, I'm slammed the rest of the day and tied up tonight. Got a meeting at the state forensic lab early tomorrow. Looks like they got a match on the cable and cutters we found in the barn. I can meet you tomorrow afternoon, earliest."

I had no choice but to agree. He was right, after all. His priorities lay with nailing the Barton brothers. New evidence in a four-year cold case? From his perspective that could surely wait.

———

Time passed that day at glacial speed. At mid afternoon, Claire, who had been busy at her computer most of the day, wandered out on the deck. "Do you think Twila's back from San Francisco yet?"

I shrugged. "Maybe."

"I was just thinking, you should update her on the Sloat incident, right? I mean, she's been cooperating and all. You owe it to her."

"Talk to her?"

"Why not? You can get a face-to-face read, if you do. Maybe she'll reveal something. She's conflicted, right? And there's no risk of tipping our hand."

"Beats sitting around here," I agreed.

———

Twila Jenson answered on the third ring. "Well, hello, Cal." I could hear water running in the background. It sounded like she was drawing a bath.

"How was the opera?" I said brightly.

She paused for a couple of beats. "It was, ah, quite good. I just got back from San Francisco not more than an hour ago."

Her voice was flat and tinged with wariness. I instantly regretted making the call. But there was no turning back. "Say, I was wondering if I could stop by. There have been some significant developments in the investigation that I wanted to discuss with you."

The pause was longer this time. Finally, she sighed heavily into the phone. "You're a busy little beaver, aren't you? That man with the camera outside the opera. He was photographing me. I saw him. You must have sent him."

"What man?" I said, trying to project total innocence. But I knew she had me.

"You're cleverer than I thought, Cal. I'll give you credit for that."

I caught something in her voice, a note of resignation. I decided to go for it. "I know what you did, Twila, and I know how you did it. And I know you're carrying a lot of guilt around. Isn't it time to unpack it? Living a guilt-ridden life is no life at all."

The line went quiet, except for her breathing. Finally, she said, "Well, you have a point there. It is no life at all. Goodbye, Cal Claxton." With that, she disconnected.

"*Shit. Shit. Shit,*" I said, staring down at my cell phone in disgust.

"*What?*" Claire said, who'd been standing by as I made the call.

"She made Ramón at the opera. He wasn't as good as Nando advertised." I stood there for a moment before it hit me—her, "goodbye," rang with existential finality. "Come on," I said. "We're going to Seven Devils Road."

"Why?" Claire asked, following me out the front door. When I didn't answer, she said, "How do you know she's there and not in Coos Bay?"

"I don't, but she just got back in town. She's probably putting her jewels away, right?"

Chapter Fifty-One

We left Archie whining at the front door of the beach house, and by the time we crossed the one-lane bridge on Seven Devils Road twenty-six minutes had elapsed. "She's there," I said when the house came into view with the Lincoln Navigator parked in front. I wasn't sure what to expect, so I said to Claire, "Wait here. I'm going to check it out." Claire nodded. I went to the door and knocked loudly. Nothing. I knocked again. No response. I let myself in and called out her name. Deathly silence.

The first floor was deserted. I took the stairs to the second, calling out her name. The door to the master bedroom was ajar. I opened it, looked in, then entered. The door to the bath was shut. I went to it and knocked. Silence. I tried the door. Locked. *Shit!*

Kicking a door in is not as easy as it looks in the movies, but it finally yielded in a splintering crash after several tries.

"*Oh no,*" I said when I saw her, naked in an elegant, clawfoot bathtub filled with pink water. Her head was tilted back, her left arm draped over the edge of the tub and her right submerged. I pulled her arm out of the water. The wrist was slashed deeply and efficiently and was leaking blood at an awful rate. I took my belt off and tied a crude tourniquet around her upper arm. Then I stripped a blanket off the bed, and after scooping her out of the bath, wrapped her in the blanket and hustled her downstairs.

Claire gasped when she saw us. I opened the rear door of the Subaru and managed to get in, holding Twila in my arms.

"Is she alive, Dad?"

"Yes, I think so. Drive, Claire. The hospital." I wrestled my phone free of my jeans pocket, scrolled down to Rice's number, and punched it in with my thumb. He picked up. "Chet. Listen. I've got Twila Jenson in my car. She's slit her wrist. We're way down on Seven Devils Road. Can you have a deputy meet us at the Cape Arago junction? We need a police escort to the hospital, or she's not going to make it. We'll be in a burgundy Subaru sedan. I can't talk now. I'll call when we get to the hospital."

He said he'd take care of it. Next, I loosened the belt on Twila's arm and applied pressure with two fingers on her brachial artery just above the elbow to stanch the bleeding. She groaned, telling me she was still alive.

Claire did a great job driving, pushing the Subaru to high speed where she could but not being reckless. That daughter of mine. A county patrol car was waiting in the right lane as we swung onto Cape Arago Highway. Claire flashed her lights, and the white SUV pulled out in front of us with its blue lights flashing. The escort parted the traffic beautifully, and when we arrived at the emergency entrance, a doctor and two attendants were waiting at the curb with a gurney.

When Twila finally disappeared through a set of swinging doors, I heaved a sigh of relief. Claire looked at me, her face ashen, tears in her eyes. "Do you think she'll make it? She can't die, Dad, she just can't."

"I know, Claire." I took her in my arms and hugged her. "I think we caught her in time, but we'll just have to wait now."

"Not again," she said.

———

We plopped down in the waiting room after scrounging around for things to read. Rice called thirty minutes later, and although I didn't want to present my case over the phone, I had no choice but to sketch in the situation. When I finished, he said, "Jesus, Cal, if you're right, this is huge."

"I'm right, but I need you to help me prove it. We need a warrant to search for the jewelry, Chet."

"Let me think about it," he said. "I'll want to see the pictures, of course. Approaching my boss is going to be tricky, to say the least."

"I'll call you in the morning. If you're religious, pray for Twila Jenson."

Claire and I went down to the cafeteria and bought the last two sandwiches in the case. I got a coffee, figuring I wasn't going to sleep that night anyway, and she got an orange juice.

Two and half hours later, a stern-faced nurse came into the waiting area and asked for me. "The patient you brought in is insisting on seeing you." She allowed a thin smile. "I think she wants to thank you for saving her life."

I turned back to Claire and gave her a thumbs-up as I followed the nurse to a recovery room. Twila Jenson's eyes were closed. She had a large bandage on her right wrist but was otherwise unencumbered with tubes, wires, and fluorescing screens. I cleared my throat, and she opened her dark eyes, the lids at better than half-mast.

"Hello, Cal," she said with a wan, crooked smile. "You should have let me die, you know."

"Not on your life, Twila." I returned her smile. "How are you feeling?"

She looked off to one side as if pondering the question. "Strangely enough, better than I've felt in a very long time. I thought I wanted to die, but now I'm not so sure. I feel like I need to put my burden down, so to speak."

"What burden is that, Twila?" I said, my voice as soft as I could make it.

She showed the smile again. "You know what I'm talking about. I killed my husband and stood by while a young kid took the blame. I didn't plan it. I just flew into a rage." She brought her eyes to mine. "I'm tired of carrying that guilt, and I'm so sorry for what I've put Kenny Sanders through, deeply sorry." She sobbed a couple of times and tears broke loose.

I stepped closer and handed her a tissue from a box on the table next to the bed.

She dabbed her eyes and looked pensive. "You know, it was weird. When you showed up with your dog and your daughter, all eager to help Kenny, I tried to throw you off the scent, but I knew at some deeper level I was going to break." She shook her head. "You were just too...too goddamn decent, I guess."

I sat there for a moment in silence. "It takes courage to do the right thing, Twila. You won't regret this. Can you tell me what happened that night?"

She brushed a lock of streaked hair off her forehead with her left hand. "Before I cut myself, I, ah, left a video selfie confession on my phone. It's probably still in my bedroom at Seven Devils. I wanted to make sure Kenny would be exonerated."

"That's good, Twila, but I'm guessing it wasn't very detailed. Would you mind taking me through the events of that night? It's important. Trust me."

She nodded. "Okay. I'll try. I was painting but had left a couple of tubes of paint and some brushes back at the house. I went out the back way of the Tioga to get them."

"Why did you come in via the front entrance earlier but leave out the back?"

"After I stepped off the elevator, I realized I still had on my coveralls. I didn't want anyone to see me looking like a house painter. Sonny was in his workshop and didn't hear me come in. When I went into the bedroom, the bed I'd made that morning was messed up, and I could smell Krysta Sanders."

"Her perfume?"

"No." Twila's face grew hard. "The aftermath of her having fucked my husband. That's what I smelled. I went to Sonny to confront him. He didn't even bother to deny it. He told me to get over it, that our marriage was boring. Then he just kept working on his stupid bookcase with his back to me. He was a crappy carpenter, by the way." She looked at me, her eyes leaked tears again, and her voice trembled. "We'd been married twenty-six years and he wouldn't even acknowledge my...my *right* to object. I hardly remember the rest. I took a hammer to him."

"What happened to the hammer?" I asked next, relieved that she seemed willing to give me a detailed account. Kenny's legal exoneration would demand nothing less.

"I wiped my fingerprints off it using a garden glove, then decided I'd better not leave it behind. I took off my bloody coveralls and put them and the hammer in a garbage bag. On my way back to the Tioga I pulled over and threw the bag into the South Slough. It's there somewhere in the mud."

"What about the jewelry, the cash, the wedding ring?"

"At that point I think I was in shock. The only thing I could think of was to make it look like a robbery, so I messed up the bedroom and study, then put everything in a grocery bag and hid it in my apartment at the Tioga. The sheriff never searched my apartment."

"Where are the jewels and ring now?"

"I kept them hidden in a bus locker downtown, and when I bought Seven Devils, I had a wall safe installed. Everything's in the safe but the cash."

I suppressed a smile, thinking how Claire nailed the hiding place. "You came back into the Tioga through the back entrance, right?"

"Of course. Now I was a guilty murderer who didn't want to get caught. In those days, there was a handy little wedge of wood one of the residents had left to keep the door from completely closing. I used it when I left the first time, and it was still there when I returned. I took the wedge, and nobody saw me come back in." Her look turned incredulous. "I never *dreamed* I'd get away with it, Cal."

"Did the detectives ever ask you about the back exit?"

"Yes. I told them I never used it, that it was a self-locking door. They never brought it up again. They thought they had their killer, Cal."

"Okay, you're back in your apartment. What next?"

She sighed and closed her eyes, squeezing out more tears. "I took a shower, cleaned my shoes off, and put on the same clothes I was wearing before. That way I could leave through the front and become the wife who's shocked to discover her husband's body. Before I left, I put some paint on my blouse in the hopes they wouldn't ask me if I wore anything to paint in. It worked. The subject of my coveralls never came up." The wan smile again. "Well, it worked until you figured it out."

The room went silent except for the seconds clicking off on a big circular clock on the wall and the low moaning of a patient next door. Finally, I said, "Is there anything else you want to tell me, Twila?"

"No." She sighed long and deep. "I just used my guilt about Sonny and what I was doing to Kenny to carry me along. I didn't have to act. It was a blackness that looked a lot like grief, you know?"

"Yeah, I can see that now. Look, Twila, if you really want to help Kenny, I'll need you to repeat this story to the District Attorney. Would you be willing to do that?"

She looked at me straight on. Her dark eyes had a light behind them I hadn't seen before. "Yes. I'll do whatever it takes to get that boy out of prison. I'm done with this."

I thanked her and walked out of that hospital room feeling so light I thought I'd float off the tile floor. When I came through the swinging doors into the waiting room, I didn't say a word. I didn't have to. My daughter looked at me, and a smile—the one that always reminded me of her mother—bloomed on her face.

"Oh, Dad. We did it, didn't we?"

My eyes were wet with tears, and I had a golf ball in my throat. I smiled. "I'm going to need a vacation from this vacation."

———

Things moved at warp speed after Twila confessed to me at the hospital. I called Rice that night. "Chet, you're going to be declared a hero for solving a murder, a violent house invasion, an attempted murder by logging truck, and busting up a fentanyl distribution ring, damn near all at once. You want to know how you can repay me?"

"I'm listening."

"Bring District Attorney Gillespie to the Bay Area Hospital tomorrow, first thing. If you can get Sheriff Stoddard, bring him, too. Do whatever you have to do to make this happen, Chet. Twila Jenson's ready to make a *full* confession for the murder of her husband. Kenny Sanders is completely innocent."

A long pause. "You sure? She's not having a breakdown or some damn thing?"

"I'm sure. Have I misled you on *anything*?"

"No. It's just—"

"She told me the entire story just now, damn it. It's rock solid, Chet, and I've got evidence to back it up. I need Gillespie to hear this. There's an innocent kid in prison who needs to get out *now*."

———

Rice came through. The next morning, I ushered him, District Attorney Gillespie, Sheriff Stoddard, and a stenographer into Twila Jenson's hospital room. I was on pins and needles, but she held up well, answering detailed question after detailed question. When they exited an hour and a half later, Gillespie was stone-faced and tight-lipped, and Stoddard's face was the color of wet cement. We drove from there to Seven Devils, because Twila gave them the combination to her wall safe and permission to remove its contents. The jewels and Sonny's ring were recovered, and a week later, divers using a magnetometer found the garbage bag containing the hammer and what was left of the coveralls in the South Slough. They were right where she said they would be.

There was no question regarding the veracity of Twila Jenson's confession.

Gillespie moved fast, securing a date with the trial court to request that Kenny's verdict be vacated. Gillespie and I stood shoulder to shoulder arguing the case. The judge agreed, and three weeks later Kenny Sanders was released from the Oregon State Prison.

Epilogue

The big swells angled in from the north, moving in lockstep on a surface rippled by a brisk, offshore breeze. As the waves encountered the shallowing water a hundred meters out, they humped up before breaking in a muffled rumble, white water feathering off their tops in a veil-like mist. A small group of us had gathered at Bastendorff Beach to celebrate Kenny Sanders' first day of surfing. His doctor had finally, although somewhat reluctantly, given him the go-ahead.

Of course, there had been many celebrations of Kenny's freedom, including one organized by his grandmother that filled the high school gymnasium. But on this day the group consisted of Rori, Anthony the barista, Kathy Harper and her family, and Kenny's four closest surfing buddies, including Stu Foster. Nando and I drove down from Portland the night before. His left arm was in a sling, so I drove his Lexus, although he made it clear he barely trusted me with his beloved car. We carried two passengers in the back seat—my daughter, Claire, and Gabriel Silva. I'd mentioned the gathering to Claire, and they surprised me by showing up at PDX the previous morning. "It was Gabriel's idea," Claire explained, who was mum on how and why they had gotten back together. Nando and I both liked Gabriel and admired his grit for taking on my daughter.

Speaking of Nando, his arm was mending slowly, although there was still a question of whether he would regain the full use of it. He was undaunted, of course. "The physical therapy is torture," he complained to me before showing that sly smile of his. "But my therapist is not only beautiful but an excellent salsa dancer. She is giving me much incentive."

Things had returned to normal for me, well, as normal as they ever get. I'd been moderately successful in repairing the damage my sojourn to Coos Bay did to my private practice in Dundee. My pro bono work in Portland was hit harder, so I was trying to spend two days a week in the city to get things back on track. I was deeply gratified at how things had worked out with Kenny, but at the same time I had a renewed sense of humility. The subversion of justice by people driven by greed, ambition, and private agendas was no surprise to an ex-prosecutor like me. But did my zeal to free Kenny cloud my judgment? After all, I'd nearly convinced myself that Max Sloat killed Sonny Jenson and that Twila Jenson was nothing more than a grieving widow. When I shared my self-doubts with Claire, she said, "Learn from it, Dad." That daughter of mine.

I'd put Rori Dennison on a payment plan to ease the burden on her. Walter Sanders wasn't likely to offer any financial help. He'd just been served with a civil lawsuit for five million dollars by Kathy Harper's lawyer. Rori told me the suit came as quite a shock to Walter, and she quipped that it would be the height of irony if he had to sell his sex shops to pay the bill. Walter had a penchant for sexting to Kathy during their relationship, it turned out, and that didn't bode well for his chances in civil court and begged the question of criminal charges down the road.

Meanwhile, Rori continued to lead the opposition against the proposed LNG facility on Coos Bay, with long distance support from Claire. Rori's group had just received encouraging news—the commissioners in Jackson County had formally requested that the state block the pipeline through southern Oregon, citing significant impacts to water, soil, and people. "No pipeline, no natural gas to process," Rori declared jubilantly. But given the posture of the current federal administration, we both knew pitched battles lay ahead.

Twila Jenson had been charged with the murder of her husband. She secured a lawyer, one of the best in Portland, and was free on a bail bond of half a million dollars while awaiting sentencing. A virtual recluse at Seven Devils, I imagined her listening to opera and painting and hoped her work had gained some light. Rori told me Twila called her out of the blue, and they wound up crying together. "I guess I'm less of a substandard Christian than I thought," she told me.

Robert Barton was apprehended a month ago after taking part in a drunken brawl outside a bar in Seaside. By that time, Chet Rice and his colleagues had the younger brother dead to rights on Howard Coleman's murder, felony assault on Nando, home invasion, and drug trafficking. According to Rice, Robert claimed the murder was solely Darnell's idea, brought about because Coleman was skimming money from the drug operation. Had Max taken kickbacks? Robert claimed he didn't know, and Rice said he'd uncovered no evidence to suggest she had.

Two weeks after Twila Jenson confessed, Max was brought out of the induced coma and was on her way to a full recovery. There might've been lingering doubts about her involvement in the drug operation, but after seeing the urgency in her eyes as she lay bleeding in her office that day, there was no longer any doubt in my mind that she told me the truth—she hadn't ordered the hit on Coleman and the attempt on Claire, Archie, and me. As for the death of her father…well, like the song advises, let it be.

Sissy Anderson was not allowed to plea down by District

Attorney Gillespie, so Mimi Yoshida was preparing to take the case to trial. This meant a return visit to Coos Bay was in my future. When I asked Mimi how she felt about Sissy's chances, she smiled and said, "We're going to kick Gillespie's butt." Sissy was remorseful up to a point, but unlike me, she remained skeptical of Max's innocence in Howard Coleman's murder. The truth, it turns out, can be elusive.

————

A cheer went up from the gathered group on the beach when Kenny finally arrived. He wore a wet suit top and carried his old surfboard, which Rori had kept in storage for just such a day. He was clean-shaven, and his long, blond hair billowed in the breeze. We all watched as he put the board down, scrubbed it with wax, then scored a cross hatch of groves using a wax comb. I was standing next to Rori, who took my hand and squeezed it when Kenny hit the water and started paddling. She looked up at me, her slate-blue eyes blurred with tears. No words were needed from either one of us.

The surf was big that day and Kenny's paddle out was difficult. But he made it outside, and after missing his first three attempts, dropped into a nice green wall and began slashing back and forth like he'd never lost a day of surfing. Whoops and cheers went up from his assembled audience. The wave peaked and shuddered, threatening to close out. Instead of kicking out, Kenny turned hard and crouched as the lip curled over him. He disappeared into the barrel for what seemed an eternity, and we all held a collective breath.

When he emerged at the other end, he stood erect and pumped both arms in triumph, a free man at last.

ACKNOWLEDGMENTS

Writing is a process that is, at least for me, rather inexplicable. However, there is one very plain fact about my effort—I couldn't write this series without the help and support of others. For first readership and "in-house" editing, thanks to Marge Easley. A shout-out to my critique group—LeeAnn McLennan, Janice Maxon, Alison Jakel, Debby Dodds, Lisa Alber, a merry band of gifted Portland writers who never fail to keep me on the straight and narrow. As usual, the talented, responsive crew at Poisoned Pen Press was invaluable, particularly the editing advice and insights provided by Barbara Peters. Cal was saved from making legal blunders thanks to tips from barristers Jay Enloe and former Navy fighter pilot John.

Finally, I would like to acknowledge editors Dave Eggers and Lola Vollen. Their fine book—*Surviving Justice: America's Wrongfully Convicted and Exonerated*—provided inspiration for this work of fiction and insight into the failings of our criminal justice system.

ABOUT THE AUTHOR

Formerly a research scientist and international business executive, Warren C. Easley lives in Oregon where he writes fiction, tutors GED students, fly-fishes, and skis. Easley is the author of the Cal Claxton Oregon Mysteries. He received a Kay Snow National Award for fiction in 2012 and was named the Northwest's Up and Coming Author in 2017, both honors bestowed by Willamette Writers.

For more, visit facebook.com/WarrenCEasley or warreneasley.com

Photo by Corrie Coston Photography